To Caroline &

Very best

Clare

Lament for a SIEGE TOWN

CLARE HAWKINS

This book is a work of fiction. Names, characters, places, and incidents either are products of the author's imagination or are used fictitiously. Any resemblance to actual persons, living or dead, events, or locales is entirely coincidental.

Paperback ISBN –
.epub ISBN –
.mobi ISBN –

In memory of

Sue Barry and Peggy Hawkins

Historical Note

The English Civil Wars, 1642 – 1649, arose out of complex conditions of political rivalry and ideological and religious tensions. Forces loyal to King Charles 1, the Royalists (Cavaliers), went to war against supporters of the Parliamentarian cause (Roundheads) leading to years of brutal battles and sieges, as well as much social and economic disruption. By 1646, Charles 1 had surrendered, but the struggle was not over. Resurgent support for the King, fuelled by dissatisfaction with Parliamentarian rule, brought further conflict. A Royalist army, determined to restore the King to power, was confronted by the forces of the Parliamentarian New Model Army, first in Kent and then in Colchester. Though the town had Parliamentarian sympathies, the population was forced to accommodate the Royalist army on its retreat northwards. Soon, surrounded by the pursuing Parliamentarian army, the Royalists and the townsfolk of Colchester were trapped in a deadly siege.

This is a work of fiction. See 'Author's Notes'

The SIEGE of COLCHESTER
By the Lord Fairfax, As it was with the Line and Outworks
1648
Col. Fothergi
Col. Fothergalls Fort
Horse Guard
Foot Guard
Col. Ewers League
Horse Guard
Horse Guard
The Great Broom Heath
Fort Ingolesby
Col. Ingolesby's quarters of Foot
Scroops quarters of Horse
the Town Waterhouse
Col. Ewers his quarters of Foot at first
Crouched Fryars
Grimsted house burnt
Malden Road
Road into the
bridge Road
London Road
Fort Essex
Lexden head quarters
Foot Guard
Horse Guard
Barksteed Fort
Hundreds
Trane of great Gunns
Col. Cook's Foot quarters
5 Comp. of Col. Barksteads Reg. quarters
4 Comp. of the Lord of Warwick's Regiment
Horse Guard
Hunnwoods quarters
Dragoons Guard and quarters
Col. Harlackendens Horse quarters
The Generalls quarter of Horse
2 Troops of the Lieut. Generalls Horse

A. S. Martins
B. S. Rumbals
C. S. Tenants Chap.
D. S. Nicholas
E. Allhalows
F. S. James
G. S. Botolphs
H. S. Gyles
I. North Gate
K. East Gate
L. Botolphs Gate
M. Shore Gate
N. Head Gate
O. High Street
P. East Street
Q. Botolph Street
& S. Marys
R. Wyer Street
S. Cow Street
T. Middleborow
V. Botchers
W. More-elm Lane
X. Trinity Lane
Y. S. Martins Lane
Z. Tenants Lane
Col. Harvey's quarters
Col. Gourdons Horse quarters
Fort Suffolk
Foot Guard
Horse Guard
Col. Bloyes his quarter
Col. Sir Tho. Barnadistons quarters
Col. Whaley's Horse quarters
Fort Bloyes
Road
Colne River
Horse Guard
Suffolk
Grinsted Church
Fort Whaley
Foot Guard
Water Mill
Black Fryars
East Street
Maudline Chap.
S. Mary Magdalens
Maudline Street
Hithe
Water Mill
Horse Guard
Mersie Road
Fort Needham
Col. Fleetwoods Horse quarters
Mr. Barringtons House

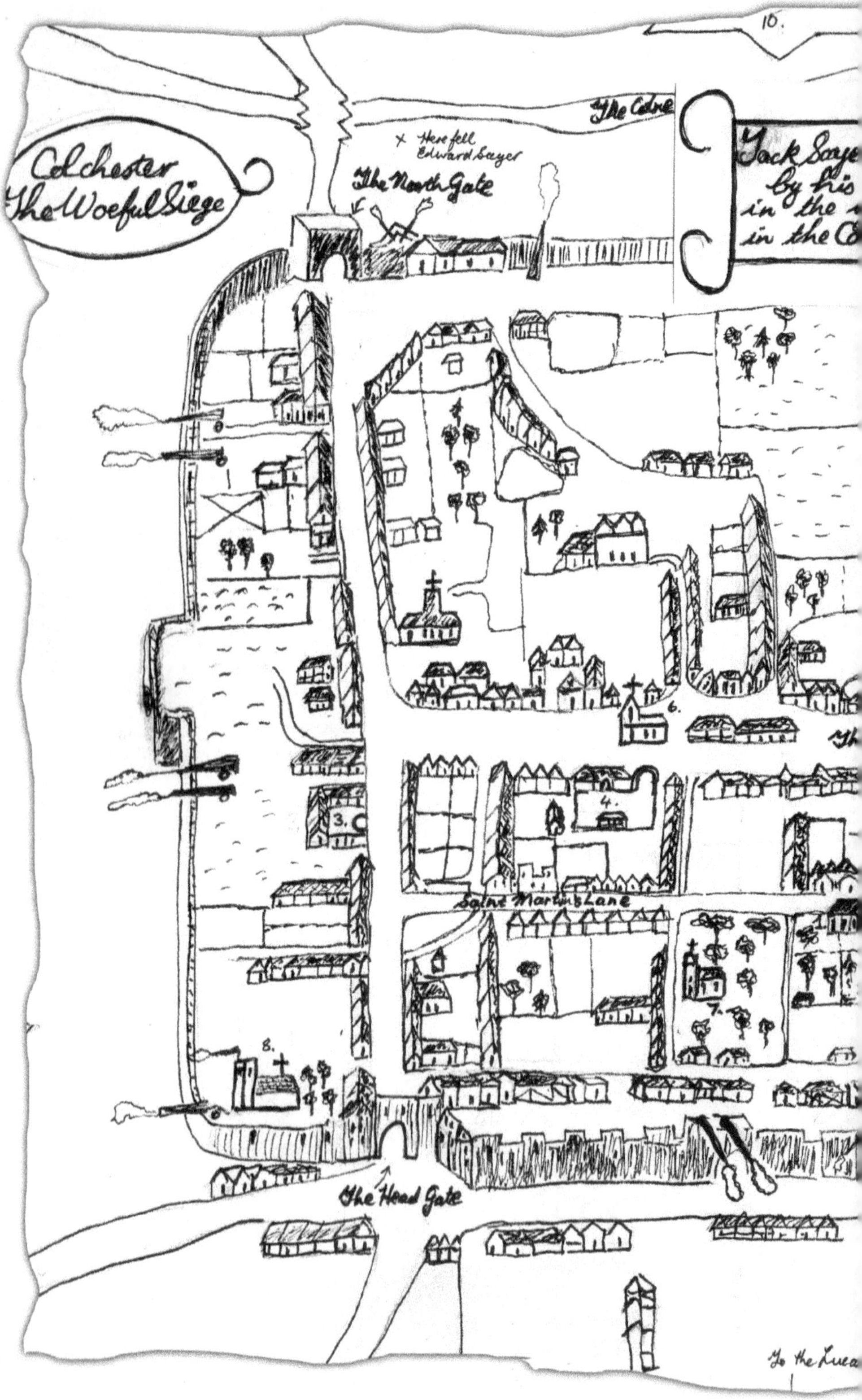
Colchester
The Woeful Siege
10.
The Colne
x Here fell Edward Sayer
The North Gate
Jack Saye
by his
in the
in the Co
3.
4.
6.
Saint Martins Lane
1.
7.
8.
The Head Gate
To the Luca

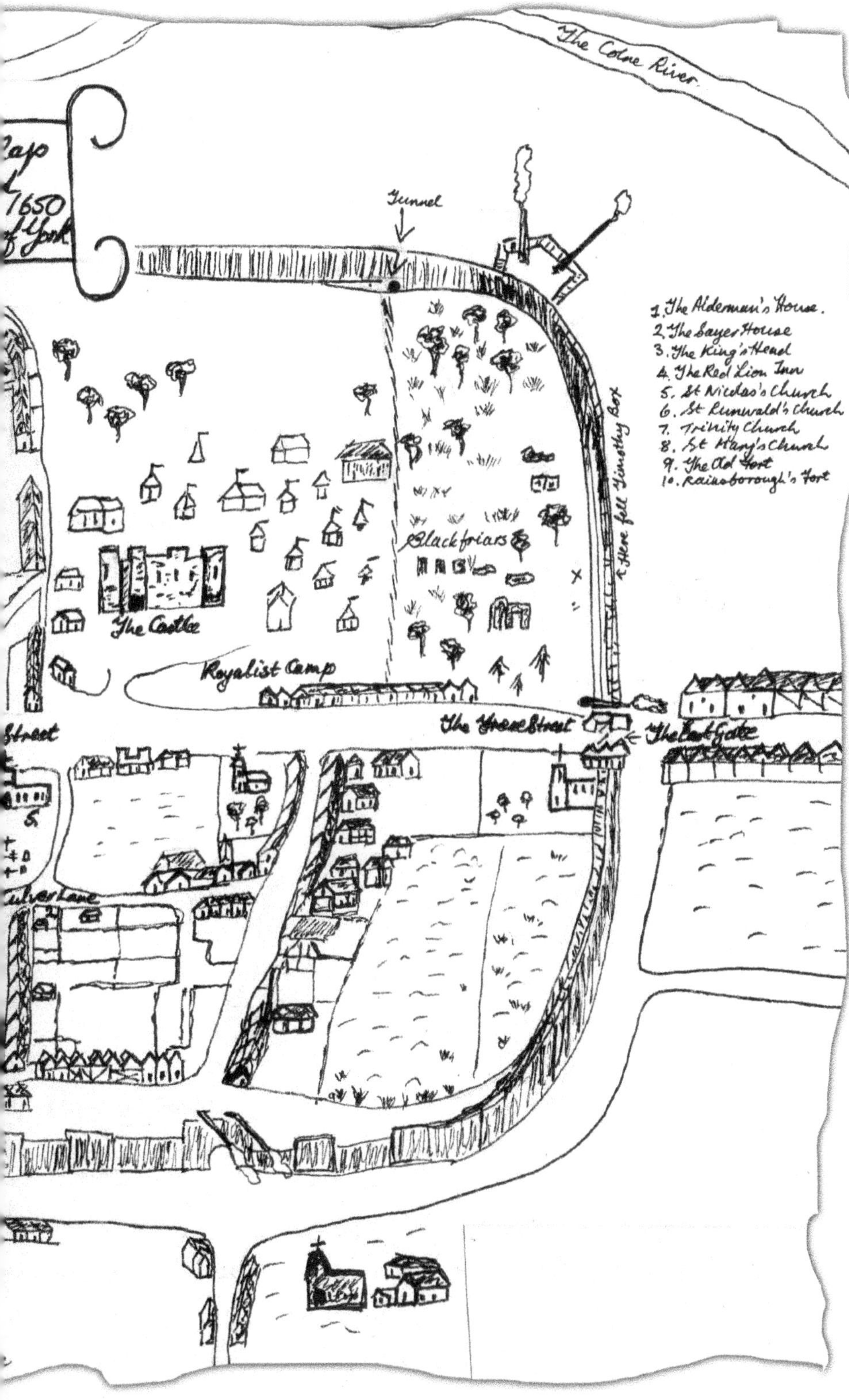

The Colne River
1650
Tunnel
1. The Alderman's House.
2. The Sayer House
3. The King's Head
4. The Red Lion Inn
5. St Nicolas's Church
6. St Runwald's Church
7. Trinity Church
8. St Mary's Church
9. The Old Fort
10. Rainsborough's Fort
Here fell Timothy Box
Blackfriars
The Castle
Royalist Camp
The East Gate
Street
Culver Lane
5

Chapter 1

9th June 1648

'We'll be the first to spy 'em,' says Edward, standing up on the swaying branch.

Jack clings to the trunk of the tree, trying not to think how high they are dangling above the ground. 'But we shouldn't be here,' he says. 'Mother told us, remember, not to go beyond the walls.'

'Shush. Look. Look out there!'

Edward is staring ahead through a frame of leaves.

Jack clutches his brother's arm and pulls himself forward to see. From afar off, maybe half a mile distant, specks of light spark and glint from a moving shape on the roadway. Jack and Edward, wedged together as one on the rolling branch, watch, as gradually a troop of about twenty horsemen, advancing in a body, takes shape before their eyes.

'But that's no army,' Jack says, wondering if all the rumour and fuss in the town might be untrue. A real army has hundreds or even thousands of men, so he's been told, with drums beating, great masses of pikemen and musketeers and cavalry with colours flying.

'No, but they're fighting men,' Edward replies. 'See, that's the sun on their weapons. They're a troop of horse, riding ahead. I reckon the army's right behind.'

They gaze without another word for some moments longer, until Jack is seized by the urgency of their mission.

'We must go back. We've got to warn everyone,' he says, shifting his foot, numb in its toe-hold on the branch, which has started to sway again, as though grasped and shaken by a giant hand.

Then he is falling and bumping, with the branches snatching at his clothes, ripping his breeches, stalling him painfully in his descent. His body jolts to a stop. The arms of the tree have caught him, but his heart is throbbing in panic, his hands grappling for anything that will hold him and not let him drop again. He embraces a bending bough that groans and cracks, then snaps. The air whisks cold past his face, the blow of his landing crunching all the teeth in his head, jarring every bone in his body. Pain tears through his leg. He howls, for there is no preventing the outburst of his hurt. He rolls over on the ground, clutching his ankle, glad to find his foot still attached, his shoe lying forlorn like a dead rabbit some yards from him.

'You noddle-headed numpkin,' shouts Edward from the tree.

Jack tries to curb his cries. He knows he's been screaming like a babe and sticks his fist into his mouth, until he is only moaning quietly. Then Edward is kneeling beside him. Jack's face is hot, his nose streaming, but rolling on the soft earth has calmed him a little, and he rubs his face with his sleeve in angry shame.

'We can't run back now,' Edward says, his brow rumpled with worry, not jesting at Jack's weeping.

Jack is too distraught at the thought of the danger approaching the town to beg his brother's pardon for his failure. He gulps the last of his tears.

'Ed, you run back with the news. You'll be there quick before them. I'm certain you can, if you go now, like the wind.'

Edward hesitates but only for a brief moment.

'All right. I'll go. But can you stand?' he says.

'Just run. Make haste and go!'

Edward leaps up. 'I'll get someone to come for you,' he calls as he turns and bounds off between the trees.

Jack watches his brother springing out of the copse towards the heath, the quickest way back to the town. In the secrecy of the leafy canopy, he weeps again as he tries to rise. His ankle pains him so horribly that he has to lean against the tree to wait for the stabbing to pass. Then he manages to hop forward a few yards, seeing the small speck his brother has become upon the path, wishing he were running with him and not here alone. Jack hobbles on a little further, his eyes scouring the ground for some suitable branch to use as a walking stick or crutch. A few more awkward hops bring him close to a tangle of fallen boughs, amongst which he finds a forked one, gnarled and bent but of a goodly length to fit under his arm and strong enough to hold his weight.

Cheered a little by his cleverness, Jack jerks his way over the rough grassland to the pathway across the heath. Perhaps he might meet a carter from whom he can beg a lift, for his ankle is pulsing with pain. His breeches are badly torn and his doublet too and he has begun to think of his mother's wrath when he returns in this crippled and ragged state. For a sickening moment he wonders if the surgeon will have to cut his leg off. He might manage with one leg, he supposes, like the old soldier in the market place. But then he might not get home at all; the army might catch him and shoot him dead. He sniffs and blinks his eyes a few times to stop these troubling fancies, then limps on.

The next stretch of fifty paces slopes down a slight incline, from which he can see the main roadway, its ruts and hollows newly churned by recent rain. He pauses. There is a sound on the road, muffled hoof beats. Surely this cannot be the distant cavalrymen here so soon. He looks around in alarm for somewhere to duck down out of sight, but there is no hedge nor any piece of scrub nearby. He is out in the open, helpless as a half-dead rabbit in a snare.

From a dip in the road, behind the spikes of a hedge, a feathered hat comes into view, then the buff-coated bodies of mounted men, bandoleers slung across them, swords in belts and pistols fastened on saddles, their horses magnificent beasts, a bay, two blacks and a grey in front, four abreast and six rows behind. They are not hastening, though these are fast horses, Jack reckons. Instead they clop at a leisurely pace, as though returning from a fruitful day of hunting. Jack stares at the marvellous sight, seeing the rippling cloth of the colours flying, held by one of the leading officers, for this is what they must surely be, cavalrymen and gentlemen to boot. Jack wonders for a moment if they will simply ride by, not noticing him, as their eyes are trained ahead and he hears the two at the front exchanging some words. Though they are armed, their weapons are not drawn for fighting and they move along at their ease. But then, of a sudden, the one leading the troop turns his head.

'Hey, hey there,' he calls, reining his horse, slowing the whole troop, then he beckons with a gloved hand to Jack, that he should descend the slope and come towards them.

Jack does not obey, in part because his sound leg is trembling and the end of his gnarled crutch is wedged in a socket of mud upon the ground. He stares back at the officer, noticing with terror that he, after a word to one of his companions, has spurred his horse into a startling leap over the ditch at the side of the roadway on to the heath land. The horse and rider are now cantering up the slope towards him.

'Good day to you, lad,' calls the officer.

Jack's heart twitches in time with the soft thump of the horse's hoofs as they slow on the turf in front of him.

'What's amiss? Have you taken a hurt?' says the horseman, with a smile.

Jack stares back into a dark-eyed face, a neat moustache and pointed beard, with long hair about his lace collar. This is a gentleman, one of the enemy. Folk call them cavaliers, speaking with sour looks and curses, even spitting into the dirt like Jack had seen his neighbour's servant do one time. They fight for the King and are rebels against Parliament. Some of them are even papists and they want to bring idolatry into the land. That's what Father says and so do most people in the town. But Jack has heard other folk say different things: how they wish that the cavaliers would rise up again and bring the King back to his rightful place, for the country has gone to the dogs. Parliament is full of grasping, thieving rogues that God will strike down one day. Jack and Ed cannot fathom at all which is the right side to be on, with all this talk both ways.

'So you'll give me no civil reply?' says the gentleman whose huge horse stamps in the grass and from which Jack finds himself shrinking, as far as his hampered gait will allow. The cavalier rests his hand on his sword hilt, though his face is still smiling.

Jack is on the point of explaining how he has come by his injury when the horse paces sideways, snorts impatiently and the rider has to calm it with a jerk of the reins.

'And where do you live, lad? In the town yonder? In Colchester?'

Something in this gentleman's manner, something dangerous under his smile makes Jack stay silent. It is a good ploy, as he and Ed have often discovered, it being one of their tricks to fool others, to make merry at the expense of those who cannot tell them apart, or simpletons like old William Browne who is thick in one ear and not right in the head. It is good, larking fun and now it seems that playing dumb with this officer might be his wisest course.

Jack nods, staring like an ox and slackening his mouth.

'And is the town for King or for Parliament?' the rider says, his smile shrinking away.

Jack is glad at this point to be playing the mute, for this is a risky question; he has listened to folks' talk about the wars and the horrible, brutish things that cavaliers do to their enemies.

'Are you dumb, boy? Answer me,' says the horseman.

Again Jack nods. The gentleman's response is sudden and, Jack thinks, unreasonably cruel; either that or he has seen the truth behind his pretending. The officer urges his horse forward a step or two until the beast looms over Jack, causing him to tip backwards and hop frantically on his sound foot. Then the officer draws his sword and makes a lunge forward, accompanied by a shout. Jack tumbles backwards and lands on his rump, a sharp pain tearing at his ankle again.

'Captain,' shouts the gentleman, looking back at the other cavalrymen on the road, who have been witnessing the whole of Jack's humiliation. 'Take up this poor dumb wretch of a lad and we'll carry him to the town in fine style. The good people may look kindly upon our act of mercy and tenderness to him.'

Jack tries to slither along the grass on his rear but the next horse, ridden by the captain, has detached itself from the troop and has jumped the ditch. This rider, a sturdy, short man slips off his horse beside the other and approaches Jack.

'Come, wounded soldier,' he says. 'Let's have you up here.'

Jack sits in front of the cavalryman, awkwardly captive in the saddle, being jolted along at this worrying height from the ground, feeling the jabbing hurt in his ankle with each movement of the beast. Fixed on the saddle is a leather holster, which holds the captain's pistol, its butt almost touching Jack's hand. He is riding home, at the head of these strangers and can now see the town in the distance: the towers of the churches and the clusters of roofs rising above the walls. As Jack and the troop of horse pass by a cottage at the side of the road, two figures, a man and a woman are working in a patch of rough garden, their backs humped over as they hoe the soil. They raise their heads and stare, their eyes widening with puzzlement and alarm at the sight. Jack wants to call out to them, though he is not sure exactly what he might say, and cannot risk betraying his falsehood, not yet. His mind runs on what he might do to free himself from the captain's horse, deciding to wait until they are at least in sight of the town gates.

They leave behind the staring cottagers, drawing closer to the town and the Head Gate, whose portal is gaping open, and where Jack can see a cluster of folk gathered. From the houses on either side of the Head Gate, people are leaning out of windows, watching their approach. Other folk are on the parapets of the walls, far along in both directions. The people outside the gate, Jack sees, are important men of the town: the Mayor, Master Cooke, Alderman Barrington and beside him another alderman in a black coat, Master Wade, who lives not far from Jack's family in his grand house in the Wyre Street. One of the town constables, big Master Dodds the blacksmith, is there too, along with his father and Ed, as well as some women. Jack's heart leaps to see that among the women are his mother and his sister Beth.

Jack is filled with the urge to wriggle free from the saddle, fall from the horse, even bear the agony of his foot, just to be in his mother's arms. He sees Ed jumping up and down, tugging at his father's sleeve and pointing. For a brief moment, a terrifying thought grips Jack, that the cavalier might suddenly stick him with his sword and toss his body down in the dirt. He says a prayer to God the Maker of all things and his blessed son Jesus Christ to deliver him safely home this day.

'See, the good burghers of the town have come to welcome us,' the cavalry commander says to the captain.

Jack's rider grunts. 'Well boy, do you think they'll be pleased to let us bide a little in your fine town?' He nudges Jack in the ribs with his fist.

Jack sucks his lips in hard, his face set, determined to utter no sound to this soldier whose voice has a laugh in it.

'A crafty lad or an idiot boy, which are you?' says the captain, poking him in the side, harder this time.

The leader laughs with a short bark as they draw nearer, Jack hearing the steady hoof beats and watching the colour furling and unfurling on its shaft.

'Good day to you all,' the commanding officer calls out to the group at the gate. Three of the townsmen break away from the rest, the Mayor, Master Wade and big Master Dodds the constable. Jack sees that his father and brother are following close behind them.

'Good day to you sir,' says the Mayor, his face white like Mother's best linen on a washday and his eyes flitting about. He does not seem at all like the grand person who stands up on the platform outside the Moot Hall, with his furred robes and his golden chain, addressing the folk of the town on special days. Alderman Wade, taller and thin like a pole, his legs in black hose, his feet in heavy shoes, takes another step forward. His face is old and dark and fearsome, the kind that would send Jack and his brother scuttling away, were they to come upon him in an alley, or worse still when trespassing in his big wild garden as they have done once or twice.

'What is your purpose here?' the Mayor says to the

commander of the troop.

But before he can answer, Jack hears his father's voice and watches him coming forward, pushing past the Mayor, the aldermen and the constable.

'Sir, that is my son. They have my son.'

Jack's father stops a few paces from the horses and stares at the captain, his eyes full of fury, though there is fear in them too.

Jack, unable to stop himself trying to tug free, feels the captain clamp an arm around his middle, in a grip that threatens to crush the breath from him. The commanding officer smiles, glancing at Jack.

'This little lad we rescued along the way. He has ridden here like a true soldier, bearing the pain of his wound like a man. Captain, would you return the boy to his father.'

Jack sees his father and brother advancing and the captain's grip on him loosens.

'Merciful God,' says the captain, staring first at Edward, then back to Jack and then at his father, 'so you've two of these lads, Master, as like as two beans in a pod. I charge you to look to them and thank the Lord for his bounty to you.'

The officer and the other horsemen murmur and laugh. Jack goes to slide from the saddle but finds himself choked, as the captain grasps him tight by the collar and the seat of his breeches and hoists him like a wayward puppy down to his waiting father's arms.

'Thank you, sir,' his father says in a mumbling voice as he slings Jack around upon his back and retreats, with Ed scampering along at his side, to where Beth and his mother are standing.

The Mayor and Alderman Wade stand in their places, facing the commander and his troop. Jack is glad when his father stops just behind them, so that they can hear some of the talk that passes.

'Our business is His Royal Majesty's,' says the commanding officer, his gaze swooping up and beyond the group in front of him. He tosses his head back and continues in a voice that booms over the walls.

'We come on a just mission to bring the realm back from the brink of disaster. Our forces are following behind and we seek only to quarter our army for a night or two, before marching north to join our allies. Already we have swelled our numbers to thousands: the many brave men who see our cause as the only path to peace and freedom. We welcome others in your town, if they have the true minds and stout hearts to join with us too.'

The Mayor coughs and shifts on his feet. 'Sir, we in this town are faithful to the rule of Parliament – .'

'Aye, that I suspected, Master Mayor,' says the officer, 'but we offer no molestation of your town or your people. We have as one of our commanders, Sir Charles Lucas, a gentleman of a family well known to this town, and others too, Colonel Maxey and Colonel Tuke, Essex men and neighbours to you.'

Alderman Wade takes a step closer to the Mayor and whispers some rapid words in his ear. The Mayor shakes his head and murmurs a reply that no one can hear. Then he coughs again, looks at the horseman and speaks in a thin voice, as if someone were choking his throat.

'Sir, we will not suffer you to enter our town, wherever you hail from, whoever you have in command. We ask you to withdraw your troops and take your army elsewhere. We will not debate this further with you, gentlemen.'

The officer says nothing for a moment, exchanging glances with the gentlemen on each side of him. Jack, still clinging to his father's back, feels the muscles tighten as whispering breaks out among the townsfolk gathered there. Jack's mother and sister step closer to his father, their faces drawn and anxious.

'What will happen now?' Beth asks in a small voice, though she receives no reply.

'And you speak for all the good people of Colchester?' calls the officer of the troop.

'Yes sir,' Alderman Wade replies this time. 'We would have you gone. You are not welcome here.'

His voice is full of spite and a few of the townsfolk behind them gasp, as they might at a sudden piece of thievery in the marketplace.

'You will have cause to regret this decision,' says the officer, each word weighted with his anger. 'You will come to see what course wise men would take. Come gentlemen, we have a displeasing message to take to my Lord of Norwich.'

The officer wheels his horse around and leads his troop away at the head. Jack watches, holding tight to his father's shoulders, as they spur their beasts, gather speed and gallop away from the town.

Mother is not gentle with Jack nor with his hurt ankle. She is angry, though at first when Father lowered him on to a stool in the kitchen, she had clutched him tight and whispered a prayer. She orders Ed to bring water and Beth to rip some strips of linen, then binds his ankle very tight. Jack does not dare squeal or complain. Father is angry too, but not with Jack and Edward.

'A Royalist army coming,' he says. 'What more ill can befall us?'

'There's some say that we'd be better off with the King back in his rightful place,' says Mother, 'for things are worse than before, are they not?'

'Woman, you know nothing,' Father says with a sting in his voice.

She looks back at him with her worst frowning face. 'Here's what I know. I know that you've precious little work and we've barely five shillings to our name. And I know there's disorder and disturbance in the town, and that the Corporation have as much idea how to mend it as that old dog over there. What else is to know?'

Father shakes his head and slumps into the chair by the fire.

'There's more trouble on its way, I tell you, if you think we've got it bad now. You heard what the cavalier said. Word is there's a force of 2,000 foot and 1,000 horse and more fools joining them by the day.'

'They're desperate for work and pay,' Mother says with a sigh, her anger suddenly fled. 'And you blame them, do you? At least a soldier's wage will put bread on the table.'

'And when they're slain who'll feed their children then?'

'Will the army try and conquer us?' Edward asks the question that has been hovering on Jack's lips.

Jack shivers as the sweat on his brow turns cold and he waits for Father to reply.

'Let us pray to God they stay clear of this town,' he says at last.

Chapter 2

10th June

When he awakes, Colonel Sir Charles Lucas is weary beyond imagining, not of body, for he is well accustomed to brief nights, long days on the road, the sudden eruption of skirmishes, the fatigue of riding all day and night, the chill of wakefulness after a battle. No, it is deep in his soul where a great weight, like the heaviest shot from a culverin, drags at him, so that at times he can hardly muster the strength to think. He wishes now that he had been absent from England, in some German forest, or flat Hollandish tract, drinking in an obscure inn or hunting afar off, when the commission had come. The Prince of Wales has thrust this command upon him, to fight again for the King, to serve his sovereign and he can no more shed this duty than his skin.

He forces himself to rise from the bed, which last night was comfortable enough, a billet in a farm house near Braintree, where the fellow does not baulk at their talk of the King's cause. But sleep has not eased him. A jug of water and a basin stand on a table by the window, with clean linen, laid out by his servant. He does not know what hour it is, though he suspects it must be just after dawn, for the light shows weak and grey at the window. He hears a clatter from below, servants no doubt. There is no sound of his fellow officers rising, nor any noise outside in the yard. He splashes water into the bowl and plunges his hands, white-skinned, soft cavalryman's hands, swathed and protected by leather gauntlets against the slash of swords; strange womanish hands, he thinks. His body bears the marks of his many battles, as well-healed scars, and he is not blighted by the ills that war has brought to so many, except in his mind, in those covert places where he seldom risks to venture. He washes his face and neck, wonders whether he should ask his man to trim his moustache. Even this trivial thought costs him much effort. Perhaps he is ailing in the body after all, for there is plague about and some of the newly enlisted men have gone down with the flux.

He is putting on his buff coat when he hears the crunch of boots on the stairs outside, the clumsy approach of some fellow or soldier with little respect for the farmer's property. A knock and a voice announces that it is Captain William Hicks, his secretary and one of his captains of horse. He calls for the man to enter.

'Sir, you're summoned for a council of war, downstairs in the parlour,' says the young officer, hatless, though he wears his sword.

'Aye, I'll be with them straight.' He forces a note of vigour into his voice, in spite of the weak state of his brain. 'Is my Lord Norwich risen?'

Captain Hicks smiles. 'Maybe, with help.'

Sir Charles Lucas feels an inclination to share in this mirth at the expense of their elderly commander, though he is, these days, so unfamiliar with lightness of heart that to indulge in such a thing might be an affront to his dignity and that of his lord.

In the parlour of the farmhouse, he finds assembled most of those worthy, and some unworthy, of command, the colonels and the two lords, the Earl of Norwich, Lord Goring, an ancient gentleman with as much knowledge of war as a housemaid. He is feasting happily on a plate of cold meats. On his right sits Lord Capel, groomed as though for an audience with the King, his hooded eyes and proud mouth impassive.

'Eat, eat, gentlemen,' the Earl says, his lip glistening with grease, 'for we must provision ourselves well for what lies ahead.'

The sight of this leisurely repast in place of an urgent council of war causes Charles to groan inwardly. Servants bustle around, bringing more cups of wine, pots of ale, loaves of bread for the table, cheese and meat, his fellow officers pleased to comply with their commander's wish to enjoy a convivial occasion. Charles takes a seat at the end of the table, barely able to contain his irritation at such complacency. While the enemy forces, led by Lord General Thomas Fairfax, are marching across the county in pursuit of them, these colonels are concerned only with filling their bellies. True, they have built up a formidable army, with Lord Capel's horse and foot from Hertfordshire and the London apprentices. They have gathered many from Essex too, along the way, those who have turned against the inglorious rule of Parliament, to the just cause of the King. He is glad that these witless and misguided men have seen their error at last: the freemen of these counties, taxed till they squeal, weavers with no employment, labouring country folk, all suffering for their adherence to a tainted purpose. Above three thousand men now march with them. Even so, it is madness to underestimate Fairfax, who like the devil himself is unremitting in pursuit, lurking ready to pounce when least expected.

'My lords, we should advance north with no further delay,' Charles says, for there is little point in niceties and false politeness at such a time as this.

The Earl glances up from his vigorous chewing.

'Colonel, my dear sir,' he says, waving his knife at him, 'you'll disturb our digestions with such talk. Can you not hold back on these matters, at least until we have finished our breakfasting?'

Lord Capel, on the old Earl's right hand, lets slip a smile to another officer at his side.

'My lords, you should know that Sir Charles Lucas is a gentleman with little time for such trivialities as eating,' says Colonel Bernard Gascoigne, his plump cheeks dimpling like a foolish wench's.

The huge bulk of Colonel Maxey shudders as he crams a piece of pie crust into his mouth and joins in the laughter at Charles's expense.

Charles feels his colour rise.

Gascoigne breaks in with a chuckle. 'Aye, I have served with Colonel Lucas and know him to be a man who loves only soldiering. He's happiest when bedded in the mud with an empty belly, under the stars. Is that not so, my friend?'

Charles grips the plank of his seat to steady his urge for a violent response and takes a gulp of ale from a cup that a servant has poured for him. He says nothing further, for he will not waste his breath, nor risk an outburst of the anger that is thickening in his throat.

Lord Capel leans forward with a conciliatory nod at Charles, as though he at least recognises a little urgency in their position. 'Fairfax is far behind us,' he says. 'We can be well clear of Colchester by the time his Goutship, has managed to trudge his way here. Do you not think this likely, Colonel Lucas?'

'Yes, that is what might be expected,' says Charles, irked by the lord's languid stare, but grateful that the talk has been turned towards strategy. He steadies himself to deliver the essence of his plan. 'What I propose is that we march north from here, circle around on the Cambridge road, through the towns and villages on the Colne. This will steer us clear of Honywood, who has gathered the trained bands from these parts, for our scouts have found them at Coggeshall where they've secured the arsenal. If we take a northerly route, it will likely fool Fairfax and let us make our way untroubled to Colchester.'

'Mighty good piece of mutton, this,' says Maxey, looking round for a servant to bring him more for his plate.

'Aye, this is your home country after all,' George Lisle says to Charles. 'And there are those of your countrymen will join us?'

'I am confident that most fellows will see where their true loyalties lie,' Charles adds, aware that few are listening to his response.

That afternoon, Charles is glad that at last the business has begun in earnest. He is satisfied with his formation of the army into companies of horse and foot and his assignment of officers to command them. His sense of purpose is a little restored too, now that he is riding at the head of his forces, moving towards Colchester.

But, in spite of this, he still cannot throw off the leaden sense of foreboding that hangs around him like a sodden cloak. Where there should be hope and optimism, pride in the fulfilment of his duty again, honour in serving his King, there is only a knot of uncertainty, a dull pain, a suspicion that he, along with this cause, is lost. In part it is his knowledge that in fighting against Parliament, he is violating his parole. He swore an oath to his adversary Fairfax when he suffered the humiliation of being his prisoner, never to take up arms against Parliament again and now his conscience dogs him. As a gentleman, having given his word of honour, he should withdraw from all conflict, just as his brother has done, leaving this fight to others of purer purpose, of unfeigned certainty. But his loyalty is demanded again in this new campaign. He cannot refuse the call, though his conviction about the rightness of the King's judgements and actions is lost, as a proud colour torn down on a battlefield.

As he rides, he scans the familiar undulating landscape of fields, woods, hedgerows and scattered cottages, the places where he rode so many times as a child. Here he used to hunt with his father and brothers, on these lands that his family has owned and prospered in for three generations, before the turmoil in the country, before the outrages committed against them. He is aware that now they are only a matter of five miles from the town of Colchester and, glancing at the sky, he feels a shiver of cold, like a trickle of icy water down his neck, or the cold breath of a soothsayer whispering that he will never ride out of this place again. He shakes his head to clear these foolish thoughts, seeing ahead of him a group of horsemen cantering towards them. These he recognises as the returning advance party led by Colonel Chester, sent out the day before to Colchester, with the task of securing access to the town.

Colonel Chester gallops ahead of his troop towards Charles. He salutes briskly.

'Colonel, we have this morning been scouting for signs of Fairfax, to the south, as far as Tiptree. Fortunately we have seen nothing of his forces. But the news from Colchester is not favourable. The Mayor has refused us entry to the town. We were met with great insolence too.'

'What?' says Charles. 'They have denied us free passage?'

The heat is rising to his face. He has not been prepared for such a rebuff, but as he digests this unwelcome turn, he realises that he should not have been surprised.

'These petty committee men and burghers, men of little minds and great ambitions. They have never known their places. And yet, I had thought there were some amongst them of our inclining.'

With each word Charles's rage grows, stoked by his knowledge that the freemen of Colchester have long resented his family, have shown their upstart lack of respect for gentle status and the power of the Lucases in the county. Now it seems they will defy and insult him again, in this town where he had hopes of raising more troops for the battles ahead. He is sickened to discover this new obstacle, this blight upon the King's cause, the feeling that God again seems to have turned Roundhead.

'Come,' Charles calls, turning his anger to action. 'I can see that the townsfolk need a little persuasion.'

He gestures to four captains of horse to bring detachments of their men, then he digs the spurs into his own mount and leads them all forward at a gallop. The foam is flying from his horse's mouth as they come nearer, seeing the town in the distance, but there also, across the roadway is a body of mounted men, armed and blocking their passage, about sixty of them, Charles reckons. He reins his horse to a halt some hundred paces from them.

'Damn their souls to Hell,' he mutters, hearing Colonel Maxey at his side utter a snort of derision.

'That feeble bunch of townsmen, do they think they can hold us off? Let's test their mettle, eh?'

At that, four of the captains charge forward, before Charles has time to issue an order. He thinks he should shout after them, but it is too late and he is not averse to watching a little sport, particularly at the expense of these fools of the town's militia. Two of his officers have swords drawn, another wields a pistol primed and ready as they hurtle towards the body of horsemen on the road. Charles watches as the townsmen pull back, shrinking from his cavalrymen. A shot cracks out and one of the defenders falls like a stone from his horse. This sets his fellows into a bustling panic, wheeling their horses and scurrying back into the town in cowardly disarray. The gates crash shut behind them. Charles is surprised to see such a weakly attempt at defence; he would be loath to recruit such fellows after all.

Charles turns back, calls to a lieutenant, ordering him to send word back to Lord Goring at the head of the main forces to advance to Colchester at speed. He prepares his own troop to move forward to the gates. They pass a row of suburban houses, where some people stand upon their thresholds, staring and others hang from upper windows. Up on the town walls, behind the parapets, lurk the townsfolk, and he surveys the ancient defences, wondering who will now make the next move. He orders the rash officers to re-join their ranks, without rebuking them for their action, for he is more concerned, as they draw close, to have sight of any guns that may be trained upon them from the battlements. He does not think that this town is a great stronghold, for it has seen no action at all in the earlier wars. This is a place full of weavers, traders, merchants and burghers more intent on lining their pockets, invoking God's help to grow rich rather than to ally themselves to an honourable cause.

Charles halts his troop and turns, seeing the spreading mass of the army advancing behind them, overspilling the roadway: densely packed pikemen, tight ranks of troopers on each side, the beat of drums, the distant thunder of feet. He calls Colonels Maxey and Tuke to his side and in silence they view the walls and the watching townspeople, clustered along the top. Then, from a high window in one of the dwellings abutting the Head Gate, they hear a voice.

'We would parley. Lay down your arms,' a man shouts, waving a white cloth.

Charles peers up at the windows, where many pale faces spy out at them.

'I give my word that no one shall come to harm!' he calls up. 'Send down those that would parley.'

Charles turns to his companions again.

'Order your men to draw back, then come with me, for I'll have need of you.'

Charles dismounts and the two officers, after shouting orders to their captains of horse, do the same. They are Essex men like himself, ready to persuade or, if need be, to force compliance from their countrymen. They watch as the heavy wooden portals of the Head Gate are swung open and a group of men emerges. Charles recognises one, he thinks, a miserable godly looking sort, with a face as white as a wench's shift, the Mayor of the town.

This man once called upon his family at St John's, after their return to that sad ruined and plundered house two years ago. Most of the mayors and their collaborators of the Corporation had quarrelled often and bitterly with his brother, had sourly resisted every attempt by Sir John Lucas to claim his rights to lands lying close to the town. Grasping men of low birth like these now wield their power. It must be that those aldermen who remained loyal to their sovereign have been silenced or deposed. These wrongful times and the wars have dislocated the true ranks from their places, so that such as he must be beholden to creatures like this. Now, however, with this force of arms at his command, he will snatch back this lost power, for himself, his King and his family.

He steps forward, flanked by his fellow colonels Maxey and Tuke, determined to have the first word.

'Sirs, you have refused us the hospitality of your town, but now you must comply with the bidding of our commander my lord of Norwich,' Charles says in an even tone. 'We seek to quarter our troops for one night or two, merely that, for we are set on an expedition to the north. So, I ask you again that you should not offend us by refusing this request and the chance to act with honour to your sovereign lord the King.'

The Mayor opens his mouth as though to speak, though

his fearful look threatens that he might faint away like a feeble maid. His companion, an older, black-coated individual of sour countenance and arrogant bearing, whispers words in the ear of the Mayor, as though the man himself is incapable of speech without prompting.

'You march upon our town,' the Mayor says in a strangled voice, 'with an army in flight, for we know that the Lord General Fairfax is in pursuit of you. You come here full of hatred and desire for revenge against those who adhere to the rule of Parliament. You have killed one of our citizens in cold blood, a man who was doing his duty, defending his town. Now you seek to bring your hordes to wreck and to plunder –.'

Charles's gut writhes with anger at the fellow's words and he can contain his vexation no longer.

'Sir, you dishonour me and my fellow officers as gentlemen well versed in the fair conduct of war. You imply that we have no command over our own men. I give you my word that there will be no plundering, no hurt to any of your people or your property, no violence done against any of your citizens who go peacefully about their business. This I can assure you, in spite of your upstart town's betrayal of your King.'

Charles hears his voice falter close to the edge of fury, but he knows he must keep control of his rage.

The Mayor's face is greenly pale, his companion's scowling, while the others in the group murmur quietly under their breaths to each other.

'Consider carefully,' Charles says, seeing in their hesitation a growing alarm. 'Your position is weak. We have a powerful force of upwards of 4,000 men, well-armed and ready to fight for their just cause.'

The sour-faced alderman's colour rises. He takes a step towards Charles and his fellow officers. 'We'll let no rebels enter this town –.'

The man however, is unable to finish, as two of his fellows have approached and are grasping his arms to usher him away, whispering urgent entreaties to him. The Mayor turns to Charles after a few more moments of desperate talk amongst the party.

'We must call a meeting of the Corporation,' he says, his voice quavering. 'You must wait upon our decision, gentlemen, if it so please you.'

The townsmen turn swiftly, as though fearful that they might be set upon and almost run to the gate, which is again heaved shut behind them.

'Damn their souls,' says Colonel Maxey. 'They'd keep us waiting with their games. Fools. Do they not see that they have no power to bargain? They'd risk their town for their own pride.'

Colonel Tuke turns to Charles. 'Let's to it. They're playing for time, keeping us at bay for their own purposes. Fairfax is in our wake, remember. Let's to the attack.'

'No,' Charles says. 'We will wait. They will capitulate.'

For an hour they wait, the vanguard of the whole army now within one hundred paces of the town walls. Charles and his fellow officers stand together, drinking cups of ale that a servant has brought to them. High up on the rim of the walls, to east and west, they can see the gatherings of townspeople and then, without warning, an object comes hurtling into the air from the dark square of a window, flying up in an arc and landing with a heavy clank at Charles's feet. Before him lie the keys to the town.

Chapter 3

12th June

Beth is awake, although it is not yet dawn. She listens in the darkness. It is so quiet, after the clamour of yesterday. She hears only the gentle breathing of her brothers, asleep in the bed next to hers and the quiet flap-flapping of the cloth, which covers the small window above her head. There is a grey patch of light at the foot of the stairs, just enough to see by, so she rises, restless and troubled by the events that have overtaken the town, knowing that there will be more disturbance to see and hear this day. Many hundreds of soldiers have entered the town, have camped in the castle yard and in other pieces of open land. The officers and their servants have filled all of the inns and folk say there are yet more to come.

Beth gropes for her gown and shoes, carrying them downstairs, to dress below, so as not to disturb her brothers. Dressing hastily, she hears Old Solomon, their ancient dog groaning in his sleep by the fire. She creeps over to the hearth, stirs the fire back into life, puts on another log and pats the smooth flank of the sleeping animal. He lifts his head, then lets it drop slowly again.

'What's to become of us, Solomon?' she whispers to the dog, kneeling beside him. She hates her father's gloomy predictions of war and strife, her mother's fretting and at the same time cannot help but share a little of her brother's frightened wonder at the sight of the Royalist soldiers, the ones that most folk say are their enemies.

Beth rises and opens the back door, which gives on to the yard, stepping out into the grizzled air, with only the blur of the moon visible in the night clouds. She cannot help it, but she is deeply afraid and mouths a prayer for strength to face whatever is to come. She wishes she were not such a timorous creature, not so like her mother, who suffers the pain of all nature of ills and misfortunes simply by conjuring them to mind. Hardship has weakened her, where it has strengthened others. Beth prays for fortitude, even for the boldness of her two little brothers. Or to be rich. What would it be to be wealthy enough to flee away in a carriage to a place of safety and comfort? What need of courage then? She cannot imagine it. She cannot imagine anything but being poor, particularly now, having barely enough food each week to survive, hearing her mother's complaints, her father's misery at his lot, feeling shame at her own threadbare gown.

Back in the kitchen she hears her family stirring above, her brothers mumbling to each other and the sound of her parents' door. She pours water into a pot, sets it over the fire and takes down the small bag of oatmeal to make gruel. As she stirs the pot, she imagines how it might be to find a rich man to marry, one with a grand house and a plot of land, a merchant perhaps, or even a yeoman farmer. How fine it would be to have her own house, to have meat to eat most nights and a new gown for Sundays. It would relieve her mother and father if she had the means to help them, now that her father has no work, but when she conjures thoughts of the prosperous men of the town, she can only bring to mind old ones such as Alderman Wade, who married his wife when she was only Beth's age of sixteen, so Mother has told her. A vision of his ugly face makes her shudder. Marriage is a notion that produces in her more fear than longing.

'Can we go, Father, to see the rest of the soldiers coming?' says Ed at table as Beth pours the gruel into their bowls.

Jack hops on his good leg to his place as her father frowns.

'I suppose we must witness the arrival of these last invaders, now we have given up the town to them,' says her father with his familiar doleful look. 'But we must see to our needs first of all. It would be wise to buy what victuals we can, against the soldiers plundering all from the markets. Wife, you and Beth must go to the shops and stalls as early as you can.

'But Father, I can't walk,' says Jack, his face puckering.

'Then, it seems I must carry you,' says their father.

Ed nudges Jack, his envy unconcealed. 'You'll see mighty well from Father's back.'

Beth's mother sighs, rising from her place. 'I'll not rest easy until these wretched soldiers have quit the town. They'll be all over us like a swarm of wasps. Come let's make haste.'

'Listen, it's a drum,' says Ed as they make their way along the Culver Lane.

Beth, carrying her basket, walks alongside her young brother, behind their mother and father with Jack clamped on his back. Already there are many other folk on the street, roused by the same anxious curiosity and summoned no doubt by the regular beat of the Royalist drums. Beth greets some of their neighbours and sees Mistress Wade coming out of her house with her servant carrying her basket. Mistress Wade looks very fine this morning with a crimson shawl and a dark gown of silk. Beth admires her, but fears her too, for the hard look in her eyes. Her face shows no joy in its beauty. Her husband, Alderman Wade, is not such a one to shed much happiness either, for his face is very unpleasing, even when he tries to smile. At the mention or sight of Mistress Wade, Beth's mother's manner stiffens and she barely replies to any greeting from the lady, remarking that the Wades do not consort with common sorts of folk like themselves and it is best that way.

Her father and mother take the narrow passage that runs by the back of *The Red Lion Inn*, to join the throng upon the High Street. Each side of the street is lined all along with townsfolk, crushed close against market stalls, with shop keepers and customers jostling for a position of vantage, men, women and children pressed back to leave an open channel in the centre. And here comes a tight company of pikemen marching down the street. Beth and Ed slide in behind their parents, Ed peering between the bodies to gain a better view, Jack on his father's back, his eyes alert and excited, gazing at the oncoming body of soldiers.

They are led by a tall officer in half armour and helmet, pike in hand with an ensign marching by him holding the colours aloft, a purple banner flapping in the breeze and two drummer boys, only small lads, fists rising and falling, punching out the rhythm. Beth is struck by this spirited show of power and strength in this body of men. She has seen no such sights in Colchester before, only their own trained band of militia, who are a poor show compared to this: portly innkeepers, pimply apprentices and any man with the mind to handle a musket or pike.

These Royalist soldiers are young men, country boys, Beth thinks, by the look of their fresh faces. Some are Kentish men, so it is said, while others are lads from their own county of Essex. They shoulder their pikes with pride, while others coming behind have long-barrelled muskets, though these are older men, with harder faces. One or two glance aside as they pass, their eyes straying from the straight course of their onward march. One smiles at her, a comely smile, which makes her blush because he is an enemy and she hopes her father does not see.

She wonders as she watches what it is like when armies clash in a battle, when close bodies of soldiers charge upon each other. She has heard that many have been lost in fighting elsewhere in the land. Their town has been preserved, however, as though God Himself is watching over it, whilst other towns have fallen and deeds of great cruelty have been visited on innocent and guilty alike. Her father has read them some of the pamphlets, which come from London, with terrible tales of death and destruction, horrible acts by the cavaliers, who burn houses, kill cattle and ravish women. But Mary, her friend, whose cousin is fighting for the King, has different stories to tell, of the wickedness of the Parliament's men, for all that they claim to be godly. It is all too bewildering to know the truth, to discover the rights and wrongs of these troubles. Parson Roberts of St Nicolas's says it is foul wickedness to rise against God's anointed monarch. But the town preacher, Master Baxter says that the wars are the Almighty's punishment for the sins and corruption of the people. Is this punishment now to fall upon Colchester? As Beth stands on the street, feeling the beat of drums all around, her pulse throbs with the faster rhythm of fear.

At last the soldiers are gone and the folk spill over into the street, to go about their business at the market stalls. There are more people by far than is usual and some strangers too, following the troops, officers' servants, some wives and loose women, her mother says, who travel with the army. While her father talks with some of his acquaintances in the street, Beth and her mother go to the fish market in front of *The Red Lion Inn* where, at a stall selling oysters and whelks, some loud-voiced women are arguing in strange accents with two of the town fishwives, their screeches rising like the very gulls that swooped at the jetty where the fish were landed that morning. And in this crowd, a mood of disturbed excitement swirls about, whispers, huddled conversations, hurried greetings one to another. The stall holders' cries, the rumbling of cartwheels, whinnying of horses, familiar sounds upon a market day, seem sharper, more insistent, pressing and laden with a peculiar menace.

'Two days? Upon my life, they'll bide here more than two days,' barks a stallholder to two customers. 'Have you not seen what they're about? Have you not seen those poxy soldiers down by the Old Fort?'

The customers are a husband and wife, whom Beth recognises as Master and Mistress Janssen, round-faced, respectable Dutch weavers, listening with anxious faces.

'The soldiers? What are the soldiers doing there?' says Master Janssen.

'Digging trenches, throwing up mounds, fortifying the wall, that's what,' the stall keeper tells them.

'Aye, and they're buttressing the wall at Castle Meadow too.

Hardly been here a minute and they're digging in. Last night, I saw a troop of them out with spades and mattocks. Two days, my arse, begging your pardon, Missus.'

By now Beth and her mother have stopped, her mother catching hold of her arm. A group of others has gathered round the source of this stark and loud-voiced opinion.

'The bastards mean to take the town,' says the stallholder, clearly gratified by his growing audience. 'God strike me dead if I speak false. Where there's soldiers digging, it means they're planning to make themselves at home.'

'Oh dear God in his mercy.' Mistress Janssen grasps her husband's arm.

'There's many a town been ruined, so they say,' says another woman in the crowd.

'And that villain Sir Charles Lucas, coming back here, like he's still the great gentleman hereabouts. I reckon he's bent on revenging himself for what happened at St John's,' says another stallholder, drawn into the discussion, abandoning his stall nearby.

'He's sent a whole regiment in there, to take over St John's.'

'Well, I'd see them all in Hell,' mutters one of the gathering.

'Don't much mind where they go, so long as it's out of this town,' says someone else.

'Corporation, the gutless knee-knockers, should've never opened the gates to them. This is a Parliament town,' the cursing man says. 'God mend me, but no good'll come of it. And there's some'll say we're traitors to treat with these cavaliers.'

Beth feels the pressure of her mother's grip upon her arm, urging her away from this ominous talk that compels her to listen.

'Come, let's be done and go home,' her mother says. 'I'm affrighted by such gossip. It'll only stir up more strife in the town.'

'Perhaps the army of Parliament will come and chase away the cavaliers,' says Beth, realising too late that this idea will bring little comfort to her mother.

'Don't speak of it,' says her mother, pulling Beth's arm again and pushing through the listeners, in the direction of the market cross.

But her mother's wish to escape hearing of their present danger is soon thwarted. When they reach the junction of the two main streets, they are forced to halt for two teams of horses drawing a heavy gun on its carriage. The great barrel of the gun is longer than a man lying his length on the ground and the carriage has four iron-rimmed wheels that crunch and groan over the cobbles of the street. Behind them lumbers a cart, high-stacked with a covered load and a gaggle of soldiers - gunners, someone nearby mutters - accompanying this train, then comes another smaller gun mounted on a two-wheeled carriage, hauled by four men with ropes and others at the side to steady it. The trundling vehicles, horses and men fill the roadway, while townsfolk line each side of the street to watch as the slow moving train passes by, to the crest of the hill and down towards the Head Gate, then turning up the lane leading to St Mary's Church.

'May the Lord save us, Beth. I don't like it at all,' says her mother. 'You must quit the town, you and the boys. You must go to Uncle and Aunt Sayer in Brightlingsea.'

'And leave you and father here?' Beth says, shocked by her mother's unexpected suggestion. 'But we can't.'

'No, you're right,' her mother replies, shaking her head. 'It's a foolish thought. We must stay together and in our own town, though to tell you true, I don't know how we'll live, whether we stay or go. Master Thurston's not taking cloth from us, nor from any of the weavers. The merchants aren't buying since the war's started up again. He's not sending any of his wares to London. So what's the good of spinning yarn when there's no cloth to be made?'

Beth sees now that this latest fear, in the shape of a hostile body of soldiers, is a lesser evil than her mother's dread of their poor and worsening state. Beth has heard the complaints for many months now, but has been too witless to see the bitter consequences of her father's lack of work. Taking her mother's arm, she wishes only to make haste back home. They go along the narrower alleys, away from the main thoroughfares, and as they reach their street, Beth is trembling and dangerously close to tears. She is frightened, as one blown out to sea who watches, terrified and helpless, as the safe familiar land shrinks away before her eyes.

But even in the haven of their kitchen, with the pot bubbling over the fire and supper cooking, Beth cannot find her safe, comforting ignorance again. When someone strikes their door with a loud knock, she jumps with shock and her mother goes to open it to their neighbour, Master Jem Symonds standing there, his eyes dark with alarm.

'Have you not heard, neighbour?' says the man, glancing past their mother to where their father is whittling a piece of wood by the fire.

'Come in man,' he says, rising from his place and Master Symonds pulls off his cap and shuffles a few steps inside the door.

'I can't stop. They're here,' he says, 'outside the town.'

'Who?' says their mother.

'Fairfax and his army,' the man says. 'They've chased the Royalists all the way from London. We've all been up at the walls a-watching them.'

'The Parliament's army is here?' Beth's father says, with a deep frown, as though he doubts the truth of the man's statement.

'Come neighbour and see for yourself, the redcoats, a thousand or more outside of the Head Gate and they've sent in a trumpet to the Lord General, Lord Goring at the *The King's Head*. Some say Fairfax means to storm the town, to drive out the Royalist rebels, but others say they'll parley for surrender and it'll all end peaceful. Pray God that this be so.'

Jack, who is sitting by Beth's side, grips her hand but she dares not look at him, for he would read the fear in her face.

'Oh God in Heaven, what's going to happen?' says their mother, going to her husband. 'I told you. I said we should leave.'

'Hold your tongue, woman,' says their father, taking up his hat. 'I'll go out and find what's to be known.'

'Aye, I'll come with you straight,' says Master Symonds. 'And maybe we should call upon the Alderman Wade, for he may know what's afoot.'

As he speaks, they hear the burst of drums striking up, this time inside the town. All in the kitchen are silenced and still, listening.

'What are they drumming for?' Jack and Ed say together.

'Calling the soldiers to order most like, readying them for an attack by Fairfax's army,' says their neighbour.

'Stay in the house,' says their father, looking at them each in turn. 'I'll be back with news when there's some to tell.'

'No,' says their mother, grasping his arm and Beth feels her lip tremble. But what good to shed silly tears, for this childish action would serve only to frighten herself, her mother and brothers the more. She must be strong, though in her belly there is only a sick feeling and a desire to be gone from this place.

'Lock the door,' says their father, his tone softening. 'And calm yourselves. They'll parley now, the commanders of both armies.' His words are certain, though his voice betrays a different state of mind. 'I'll be back anon. Come, neighbour.'

A moment later they are gone. Beth cannot bear the uneasy, troubled silence and takes up her mending, some holed stockings, stabbing too vigorously and piercing her finger with the needle. Her mother's mouth has become a tight line as she moves about the kitchen and bids the boys employ themselves. But her brothers merely fidget by the fire, Edward tickling poor Old Solomon's rump with a piece of kindling, while Jack twirls the knot of his bandage idly. Their mother, distracted, knocks down a platter, which falls with a crack to the floor. Here they are trapped, helpless, ignorant and powerless while outside, unknown men will either bring war or save them from it.

'Stop pestering the old creature,' their mother snaps suddenly to Edward and, in a swift movement, goes to the cupboard and takes out the bowl of beef fat she had boiled and strained the previous day for making candles. Charged with this same unsettling vigour, she assembles some items from the shelf and brings these to the table, where she slaps down pieces of twine, and some small earthen pots, beckoning to Jack and Edward.

'Come now, let's keep ourselves busy with useful chores, all of us. You must prepare wicks for these candles. I'll heat the fat;

you two plait this twine. Go to it, boys.'

Beth watches her brothers take their places at the table, their identical fair heads drooping over the bundles of twine, while their mother scoops the white waxy fat from the top of the bowl.

Much later, a dozen tallow candles stand on the table, the hose are all mended, Jack's torn clothes darned and a pottage is steaming over the fire, but still their father has not returned. It is evening now but Beth's mother does not bid any of her children go to bed. At each noise of feet in the alleyway, or on the street outside, they start. Beth prays only for her father's safe return. She will never complain again of lacking a pretty gown, or of the tedium of hours at the wheel, scrubbing the floor and throwing out the slops, if only her father will come back safe again to them. She asks God to look down upon them with mercy and forgive her sins and her wicked vanities.

Voices sound outside, rousing even Old Solomon from the fireside to sniff the air. Their mother rises quickly to unbolt the door and their father comes in with a slow and deliberate step. He gazes across the kitchen at Beth and her brothers, then reaches out his hand to his wife. Beth's lowers the linen she is stitching, while Edward slips off his stool and comes to stand close by her side.

'We're undone,' her father says. 'The King's army has refused to surrender to the Lord General Fairfax. They will not quit the town. It's war and now we're caught in the midst of it.'

Beth wakes in the black of night to find her brothers crouched at her bedside, their heads dark silhouettes, touching. She sits up, hearing the strange distant sounds outside, which have clearly disturbed them from sleep. She reaches out her hands to catch hold of theirs, listening: a clamour of shouting voices in the distance, faint bursts of fire, the thud of explosions, a howl like a wolf, the scream of a horse.

'There's fighting, out there,' Ed whispers.

'It's quite close by, maybe upon the High Street,' Jack says, squeezing Beth's hand tighter.

Beth pushes back the coverlet of her bed.

'Come,' she says, as they clamber in beside her, one on either side.

'Don't worry, Beth. We'll fight the soldiers if they come,' says Jack.

They lie in the dark, Beth feeling her heart beat as hard and tight as the army drums she has heard all that day.

Chapter 4

13th – 15th June

Already the drums are summoning them to muster under their colour. Tobias picks up his pike and is jostled along in the comradely roughness of the others in his company of foot. He dodges out of the way of some troopers plunging by on their clumsy horses. The bulk of the army, under the command of the Lord General Fairfax, has camped the previous night in a village named Lexden, just a few miles short of the town of Colchester where the rebel Royalist army has taken refuge and barricaded themselves inside. Word has it that they have a force of above 4,000 men and have started strengthening the walls against a storming. Some say too that their own commander, the Lord General Fairfax, is rash and over-bold in thinking their lesser forces can take the fortress of Colchester. But they are going forward now and Tobias has no time nor occasion to doubt that their great general knows better than most what he is doing.

'Come on with you, Tobe,' says his comrade George, hitching up his belt and straightening his battered helmet. 'We're going in. We routed the devils easy and quick at Maidstone, remember.'

Tobias's friend has the look of a vagabond about him, rather than, like himself, a newish recruit to the Lord General Fairfax's New Model Army. They'd all been issued with uniforms, when they enlisted, good thick red woollen coats, brown breeches and shoes like they'd mostly never had in their lives. But already

George's coat is stained with the gravy from a pie they'd had from a generous old dame just outside Chelmsford. They'd camped there in the pouring rain on their march into the north of Essex, chasing after the Royalist army. George's breeches are torn too, on both legs, the result of a tangle with a gorse bush when he'd been relieving himself at the side of the road on the march. But he is a good fellow of even temper and good cheer and Tobias is glad to have him as a companion. They break into a trot along with the others, moving forward to draw up in battle order on the roadway ahead of them.

'I reckon we'll be in the town this very night,' George says. 'Maybe we'll find us a couple of warm wenches, for they'll be glad to see us. It's a Parliament town, so they say.'

Tobias smiles. 'But what of your lady love, Susan, the one you said you'd die for? You'll not be unfaithful, will you?'

George grins at him as they pace along. 'We're far from home, are we not? And who knows, today might be our last on this earth, if God wills it so.'

A drummer boy runs past them, thrumming with his sticks the signal for call to order. Tobias and George stand side by side, as is fitting for friends from the same town, who'd enlisted together and are now on their second campaign, though green enough still, Tobias knows. That day in the market square in Ely, they'd both been moved by the sermon preached about the menace of a wicked monarch who has no truck with the will of his people. Besides this, George had been eager and full of passion for the adventure of it, army life, the regular pay, more than they'd ever earn in the gardens of Barnwell Manor.

Tobias had also been taken by the notion he'd heard, of how a common man might raise himself up with effort, hard work and dedication in the army. That same day a soldier had spoken up too, about how all Englishmen have birthrights, freedoms and liberties and that the New Model Army is fighting for these principles against the forces of tyranny led by the King. Tobias had hesitated only for a moment that day, before signing his name to enlist, knowing that God would determine the moment and manner of his death. At least he has no mother or father to mourn him if he falls in battle, nor wife and children to starve. He stands alone in this world, though each day he gives thanks for what God has gifted him, a healthy strong body, more than a little wit and a determination to make the best of these blessings.

Now, as they prepare to plunge into battle, Tobias sees their company colour, blue on white with three lozenges in the centre, waving up ahead, signalling to them, leading them the way. Captain Cox is at the head talking to the ensign. Tobias and George are in the last of the six forward rows of pikemen, the sergeant on their right, the musketeers drawing up tightly on both sides. There is little talk now, for they can hear ahead the sounds of gun blasts and musket fire, the ringing and clattering of weapons, men's shouts, then they see smoke rising from a burning house. Colonel Barkstead's men had gone in first to the attack, clearing the way for them to advance on the walls of the town. The drum sounds again and the sergeant yells while pikes are straightened and they start the advance in earnest. Tobias grinds his teeth, as he did the other time they marched into battle in Kent. His body is tense and unyielding as iron and he fills his head with muttered prayers, mouthed again and again, admitting nothing else to his mind. He has seen dead men, but he knows he is still untried in battle, by the accident of being at the end of an engagement, arriving after the main slaughter has happened.

They are moving rapidly now and the walls of the town loom up ahead, visible through the bursts of smoke from the muskets. He sees the guns on the wall above them and behind these a church tower and the roofs of the town. The boom of cannon makes the air shudder, the smell of gunpowder drifting towards them like a fog swirling and then there are screams. Shouts and yells of agony from those in front carry back and Tobias feels his stomach turn, his gorge rise.

The drum beats change to 'charge'. Their colour streaks ahead and the captain's pike is raised aloft for all to see.

'Now for it, boys! For God and for Parliament!' shouts the sergeant.

The noise is a hideous mingling of thunder claps from cannon, blasts of firing from the musketeers at his ear, the howls of victims from just ahead and then from among their own. He fixes his eyes on their colour, hears George grunt at his side as their musketeers fire again. Two at Tobias's side fall and he hears the drum again for charge. They are running now, with the walls above them. Their colour quivers as a ball tears through it. In front is the open gate of the town, forced wide by the thrust of the pikemen in front of them, but all along the ground at the foot of the wall men are clashing in hand-to-hand mayhem, swords flying, the chorus of shot, the choking stink of smoke rising. But on they push, closer and closer.

Ahead, Tobias sees Captain Cox raise his pike and lead them on. They are going in. They have won the town already, Tobias thinks with amazement. By now they are running, though still tight in a body, their pikes thrusting forwards.

'Keep tight. Keep together, lads,' he hears the distant call of the sergeant.

Under the archway they go and into a street, a wide paved one, sloping upwards with houses on either side. Their colour is almost at the crest of the hill and the first two rows of pikes well inside and going forward. Tobias feels his heart leap. The street is empty, save for their own company, near a hundred of them, pouring in and George is breathing heavily at his side. They near a junction with another wider street, still tight together and then the fiends of Hell are upon them, musketeers firing on both sides, shot flying, thudding and cracking their targets, as they are hemmed in, crushed in a mass of blood and smoke, screams and curses.

Tobias loses sight of their colour. It is down. Now his body is compacted with others, his ears deafened by burst upon burst of musket fire, howls and bellowing shouts. A musketeer on his left, bleeding from his eyes, stone dead, is stuck to Tobias's side and then a hot fountain spurts from somewhere, spatters his face. George is beside him and moving still, but his throat is blasted out, a red hole, though his body charges on, jammed alongside Tobias. They are swept onward, until ahead there is a clear space where now the dead bodies are dropping; a clear channel is opening up and Tobias is stamping on the fallen, soft and sometimes hard and lumpen as he ploughs forward, for he can do nothing else.

Then his foot strikes the hard surface of the road and, in a momentary gap ahead, he sees horses, cavalry charging at him. He dives to the side of the road, landing upon two corpses, spearing himself with the end of a fallen pike. His helmet is bludgeoned with a sword, which sets his head jangling, dazzles his eyes and he staggers to his knees, only to fall against the wall of a house again and feel the warm soak of blood from a wound in his arm. The horses gallop and crash about him still and he tries to rise again on to all fours, his weapon forgotten, as he becomes a hunted creature, a fox or a hare running from this Hell that is engulfing him and will snuff out his life. He lopes forward, past a looming building, a church, feels a ball hit him in the thigh, then he falls again, his face in the dirt.

His head and shoulders now lie at the end of a narrow lane by the side of the churchyard and, with the last force left in his body, he heaves himself to his feet and scrambles ahead into the darkness, falling heavily in the puddled alley, with the sounds of the horror fading behind him. He stumbles to his feet again, staggering away from the din, from the horses, the swords and pikes, the dead and the dying. His legs plough on somehow, another twenty paces, another ten, to the end of the lane where it meets a wider street and he knows he must not stop, but cross it. In a drunken lurch he falls against a low wooden gate, waist high and doubles over it, unbalancing, falling headlong, his helmet crashing hard upon the ground and his brain exploding.

Tobias opens his eyes and for some time cannot fathom where he is and where he is lying. There is a figure wearing a helmet, a very small soldier, standing by a fire and two women sitting at a table in the centre of a room. This is a kitchen, but not one he has ever seen before. Then, as he tries to move his head, something rips inside it with raw pain. He looks down, along the length of his covered body, which is stretched out upon a bed, a narrow cot bed in the corner of a warm and cluttered kitchen with these strangers in it. The room has a low-beamed ceiling, a trestle table in the centre where the women are seated, and a brick-built hearth.

He breathes but feels something stabbing him in the chest. He is bandaged too, for his one moving hand discovers that beneath this sheet of linen and a woollen blanket he is naked, except for the bindings that he fancies might be holding him together. He wants to speak but cannot trust that his voice will work, for his mouth is dry as ashes. He manages a groan. The midget soldier turns quickly and Tobias sees that it is a young boy wearing his helmet.

'Mother, he's awake,' the boy says, coming across the room towards Tobias.

Both women rise quickly from the table.

'Get your father,' says the older of the two, a handsome woman, plainly dressed and of middle years. The boy runs out of the doorway, still wearing the helmet.

The other woman, Tobias sees now is only a girl, with a pretty round face and fair hair falling from beneath her white cap. She and the mother come to stand over him and he stares back, helplessly, unable to speak, trapped in this prison of his bandaged, wracked body. Two pairs of blue eyes look on and they are joined soon by a man's face, a worn and tired one, then the face of the boy again, only this time without the helmet. Tobias closes his eyes, for he is overwhelmed by the pain, the strangeness and his helpless paralysis of mind.

'Let the poor fellow sleep,' he hears the man say and Tobias wishes above all else that he could. With eyes closed, his splitting head sways, dips and swims on the pillow as the talk continues in snatches, some sharp and close, some whispered far away, beyond him.

'And what would you have us do?'

'Hand him over.'

'He cannot stay here.'

'Mother, no.'
'He may die.'
'He's a danger to us.'

Someone is sitting at his side, holding a cup.

'You'd best drink, if you can,' says a woman's voice.

Tobias's eyes are blurred for a moment and he blinks to clear his sight. It is the fair-haired girl, easing a bolster behind his head. She leans close to him and he smells lavender upon her. Why can he not speak? She takes a spoon next and dips it into the cup, bringing it to his lips. He sucks the sweet liquid that tastes better than anything he has taken in his life and she gives him more, the warmth rolling over his throat. As he sips he looks up into the young woman's face, seeing her quite clearly now, her round smooth cheeks, her dark-lidded eyes trained on the cup and spoon as she dips it again. Her eyes meet his twice, three times, though at each glance she looks quickly away.

'The soldier's awake again, Ed,' he hears a boy say and a small helmeted head appears at the end of the bed.

'Good,' says a matching child who comes to stand at his side, looking at Tobias. 'May I wear your helmet now, sir?'

Tobias looks at the girl again as she brings another spoonful of the sweet cordial to his lips and she smiles at him, her mouth a pretty curve, her eyes bright. He must speak to her. He must find his voice. It comes out as a thin croak but he is relieved to discover that it is not gone forever.

'Thank you,' he says and she nods, bringing the spoon once more, her eyes solemn again, but this time holding his gaze.

Tobias glances at the boys again, who are still standing at the end of the bed watching him expectantly.

'I fear I'm not right in the head,' says Tobias with an effort, 'for I am seeing double.'

The girl smiles at him again and he thanks God a thousand times for his deliverance, for he knows that these people must have saved him. The two boys, on hearing him speak grin at him with identical mouths. Then the girl rises and takes up the cup from the bedside, gesturing to the boys to come with her. Tobias closes his eyes again, the pain of his body duller now. In the kitchen he hears a man's voice and quiet urgent talk, too distant for him to make out the words. A little later, the man is beside the bed, offering a chamber pot, helping Tobias to shift just enough to relieve himself, then calling for one of the boys to take away the pot.

'Sir,' says Tobias, as the boy scampers away with the chamber pot.

The other brother, limping on a bandaged leg joins his father at Tobias's bedside, his face eager and alert, full of the news he wishes to impart.

'We found you in our yard, all covered with blood,' says the child. 'You'd come from the battle on the High Street.'

'We're glad you've come to yourself,' the man says. Tobias watches his haggard, mournful features as he lowers himself on to a stool by the bed. The second twin boy is back again and stands by his brother, letting him lean on his shoulder.

'You were cut up pretty bad,' the man says.

'But Mother and Beth have bound up all your hurts, so you'll be all right again,' says one of the boys.

'Mother says you've used up all her linen,' says the other twin, 'you were bleeding so much.'

'I thank you all,' says Tobias, his voice cracking.

The two women are at the far side of the kitchen, the girl in the corner, spinning, her mother seated at the table cutting an onion. She glances up with a hard and anxious look.

'Are you in the New Model Army?' says one of the boys to Tobias.

Tobias swallows to make a passage for his voice. 'Yes, Colonel Needham's company of foot, in the Lord General's regiment. We charged on the town, to relieve it.' He pauses, remembering. 'Did we succeed? Is the town taken?'

The man shakes his head.

'Your men were all driven back out of the town, or – God bless their departed souls. The gates are closed. We're in the hands of the Royalists now, all of us trapped in the town. It's a siege and you're caught in the midst of it too, my friend.'

The two boys move closer to the bed, one clutching Tobias's helmet as though they mean to offer words of comfort. Tobias feels his eyes filling. He is too weak to prevent himself from weeping and his fragile, fractured thoughts are worse than the hurts to his body. He turns his head away to the wall and tries to banish the sight of George's bloody throat, the moving corpse crushed against him, his own trampling feet upon his fallen comrades. He lets out a sob, realising that but for these people he would be as those who had perished in the streets outside.

He dozes and awakens throughout the day, hearing at a distance the activities of the family, the clatter of pots, the low talk of the women, the whisper of the spinning wheel. It is the fair-haired girl who sits at the wheel for much of the day. Her father has gone to his labours, Tobias assumes. One of the boys brings in firewood and twigs. The other does not move much from the table, for he appears to have an injured foot or ankle and sits making faggots or teasing the old dog, which lies by the fireside as though nailed to the floor. The pain in Tobias's arm is constant, deep and tearing and each breath hurts, though as the day wears on this lessens a little. One arm is unharmed and he can move it with ease and his head is clearing, his sight too. He manages to lift his head when the mother comes to sit by him and feed him some gruel. Her face is hard and she does not smile, but her manner is not untender. She nods but says nothing when he offers his thanks. The boys come to his bedside several times, to tell him that they are Edward and Jack Sayer, that their father is Daniel a weaver by trade, though at present he has no work, Janet is their mother and the fair girl is Beth their sister.

'I am Tobias Waterman,' he says, glad that his voice has returned, 'from the Isle of Ely, one time gardener, but now I bear a pike instead of a hoe.'

The boys relate to him a little of what happened on the day of the battle, how the cavaliers had been waiting and ready on the High Street in force, for the entry of the Parliament men and had fallen on them. The Lord General Fairfax's forces had failed to storm the town, though the two sides had fought for more than eight hours.

'We heard the fighting in the night,' says Edward or maybe Jack.

'Next day there were many dead men in the street, but Mother wouldn't let us go and see,' says his brother.

'So now the Lord General Fairfax's army is outside, nearly all around the town, with the King's cavaliers and soldiers inside, building up the walls and not letting anyone but their own go out.'

Tobias wonders what will become of him, if it is God's will that he should live, a Parliamentarian soldier in the midst of a Royalist garrison, but he supposes that these good people, and most others in the town, are for Parliament and will now have to bear up to the dangers that their unwelcome guests have brought. He is too tender of body and broken in spirit to think of any sort of action, but he thanks God again for His providence in casting him into such merciful hands. He has been saved, he thinks, to do God's work, but for the moment he can do nothing by lie here and listen to those others who must occupy themselves with their daily chores.

That evening Master Sayer comes in with much news of the happenings about the town and Tobias, in less pain now, though a little drowsy with the poppy that the girl has given him, is able to hear most of what he has to tell.

'They're fortifying all round,' says the weaver, supping his ale at the table. 'Setting up more guns along the south wall and building ramparts where the old weaving workshop stood, pulled it down in a matter of hours and used the timbers for bulwarks. Digging for their lives and there's word they're going to make us townsfolk lend a hand. They've shored up the breaches at the bottom of Blackfriars too, though Fairfax has not put any of his forces on the east side of the town. There's still a way out.'

One of the boys, Tobias can't be sure which one, though he thinks it is Edward, the one without the poorly foot, speaks up, unable to conceal his excitement.

'We watched the soldiers filling in a great hole at the Shere

Gate and building up the Old Fort. And we saw outside too. The besiegers are digging ditches and building things. They're building something out by Master Grimstone's house.'

Master Sayer turns a stern face on his sons. 'You keep away from the walls and the guns, do you hear? Stay clear of the soldiers too. Don't dare go a-wandering near them.'

The boys nod solemnly, subdued by their father's warning.

'And may God preserve us all,' sighs Master Sayer.

Mistress Sayer looks up from her stitching. 'Amen to that,' she says. 'And may He preserve us too against punishment.' Her voice is tinged with spite.

'What do you mean, wife?' says Master Sayer.

'I mean, what will happen to us, if the Royalists discover us harbouring one of their enemies?'

'But Master Waterman is not *our* enemy,' says the boy Jack, his eyes wide with outrage. 'He's a Parliament soldier.'

'I know that,' says Mistress Sayer sourly. 'But what if one of our neighbours sees him and lets it be known to the soldiers? What then?'

Beth has left the wheel and is standing now, staring at Tobias.

'Our neighbours are all of our way of thinking, are they not?' she says.

'Aye, they are,' says Master Sayer. 'They'll not inform against him.'

'Well, it's not safe,' the wife says. 'There's some in this town would gladly side with the King, Parson Roberts for one.'

'Parson Roberts? Of course, he's Lucas's man and near enough a papist, to my mind. I'll not listen to the likes of him,' says the weaver, 'though he be our parish priest.'

'I'm not easy about it, whatever you say,' says his wife, 'and this soldier's another mouth to feed too.'

She fixes Tobias with her gaze and Tobias reads the fear in her eyes, knowing it is true, that he has brought more trouble to this house. These people are weary and worn, with strife and worries beyond these new dangers that the armies have visited on their town. He knows little about sieges, but he has heard that

Lord Fairfax is not a commander to give way and the New Model Army has not lost a battle, until this failure to storm the town. If the Royalist commanders are as stubborn and proud, then the townspeople have good reason to dread what may be to come.

'Let us pray and then eat, for we are in God's hands,' Master Sayer says. 'Only He can deliver us from these troubles, if it is His will. And we must pray for Master Waterman's recovery too.'

The eyes of all the family are turned on Tobias and he is glad to be able to give voice to his gratitude.

'I give thanks to God to have brought me here to this house of kindness and mercy,' he says, meeting Beth's eyes again.

He lies silent for the rest of the evening, looking upon a family scene so unfamiliar to him, watching the women, heads bent over their needlework, the master of the house dozing by the fire, while the two boys play with marbles in the corner of the room. Tobias finds his gaze straying frequently to Beth who is stitching some dark cloth, which he recognises as his own breeches, torn no doubt in the fighting. He feels the heat rise to his face to think that she might have seen him stripped, naked and helpless.

The next day, Tobias discovers to his joy that a little of his strength is returning. His legs, though bruised and painful, are strong enough to bear his weight. He hauls himself to sit up, his shoulder and chest still aching and his head throbbing, though more dully now. He is alone for a brief moment, until the door opens and Beth comes in. She smiles at him and comes close to the bed.

'You're mending,' she says.

'Thanks to you,' he replies, finding that he is returning her smile, though he fancies his mouth is crooked and his face still swollen. He must truly be a monster to look upon.

'My mother dug the ball out of your side, which was the worst of your wounds,' she says. 'I bound up your arm and your head.'

Tobias notices a glow on her cheeks. She turns as though she wishes to evade his eyes and takes up his breeches, which are folded on a stool near the table.

'I've stitched these too, for I think you'll have need of your clothes soon.'

He is gripped with the desire to take her hand, overwhelmed by her presence, sensing the quivering of the air between them.

'I'd not for the world have met you in this poor state,' he says, blushing hotly at his confession, 'but then if I'd not been brought low like this, I'd never have met you at all.'

'But it is the mark of a brave man to take hurts for a noble cause,' she says, glancing at him shyly.

He bows his head to hear her talk of his courage, for he knows he has less of this than he'd wish. If she'd seen him throwing his weapon away, scurrying like a rat for its life, she would not think him brave. The door flies open and one boy hurries in, followed by his limping brother.

'Tobias,' they say in unison, 'are you well enough to tell us of all your adventures?'

'You two must not tax Tobias, Master Waterman, with your questions,' Beth says. 'He must rest.'

Her brothers' faces crumple with disappointment.

'But Beth, can he not tell us a little about battles and arms and how he fought so bravely against the cavaliers?'

Tobias cannot endure the persistence of this flattering untruth. He will not fool them with stories, with lies and pretences. He knows, as God does, of his failings and though he longs for the good opinion of these people, in particular one, to whom he owes his life, he cannot accept admiration and praise where none is due.

'I must tell you I am no hero and am raw in the ways of war,' he says, looking at the expectant faces of the two boys. 'I've been a foot soldier for less than a year.'

As he has suspected, the boys' eyes lose a little of their glow of admiration, though they stay by his side, clearly expecting and reconciling themselves to some lesser tale of war.

'But I can tell you,' says Tobias in a moment of inspiration, 'of some of the adventures of the great Lord General Fairfax, our commander-in-chief, one who I am proud to serve, for he is a soldier above all others. I have heard tell, from men who served with him, of his courage and daring, how when his horse was shot from under him at Marston Moor, he fought on the field alongside his men, how he won many great battles and outdid even Prince Rupert's cavalry and many more exploits besides'.

The lads kneel down beside his bed and Beth takes a seat upon a small stool that she has brought quite close. Tobias starts on one of the tales he heard from their sergeant who served under 'Black Tom', the Lord General Thomas Fairfax, from his earliest days, and whom he revered almost as a god. In truth, Tobias has never set eyes on the famous general himself, but feels his ardour grow in the telling of the great man's heroism and with the lovely eyes of Beth Sayer fixed upon him.

The gallant commander of cavalry has just saved his wife and child from capture, in a daring dash through the town of Selby, when Tobias's listeners start with shock at a sharp knock on the door. A loud woman's voice calls from outside.

'Hey there, Janet. I'll have some black linen thread of you, if you've any to spare. Can I come in to you?'

Beth leaps to her feet and runs to catch at the opening door, but too late, for a plump woman has entered and is staring with wide eyes at Tobias and the boys at his bedside.

'Well, what's this? Who's he?' she says.

Chapter 5

18th & 19th June

Though Katherine Wade abhors the presence of the invading army, in one small part of her mind she is pleased that it irks her husband so. When he rages against the Mayor, the feeble Master Cooke and the other members of the Corporation, who gave up the town to the Royalists, she is almost grateful to the proud Sir Charles Lucas for the damage he has done to her husband's nerves. Thomas Wade, the man she is shackled to, she hates with a ferocity that appals her, all the more because when her feelings burst forth, when she gives voice to her loathing, it only brings more pain upon herself.

Returning from the draper's shop, where she has just purchased a piece of silk ribbon, for no good reason beyond keeping the poor shopkeeper in business and escaping the house for a short while, she takes her way past the Holy Trinity Church to see the new fortifications on the south wall. Since the siege has begun, more than a week ago, the Royalist soldiers have been toiling every day to strengthen the town's defences. Some poor cottages and shacks, built into gaps in crumbling parts of the ancient walls during more peaceful times, are being pulled down, their bricks, timbers and rubble now buttressing the walls. Two weeping women stand watching, while an officer turns his face away. Twenty paces further along, six men, straining with ropes are hauling a heavy gun into place on a platform of rubble, its barrel trained on the enemy beyond.

She glances at these soldiers as she passes, these young men, admiring their vigour, their dogged strength, their muscled bodies heaving the earth with spades, hacking the rough ground with mattocks. Fresh-faced young men, like the carpenter she once led into a tangled bushy copse in the castle grounds late one night. She recalls his startled delight, his sudden passion in the darkness and the soft grass beneath them. Another man of the lower sort, she'd invited into their own overgrown garden, where they had sunk together in the long tangle of the grass, even as her husband worked inside in his study. There have been others too, decent and respectful of her, as though she were bestowing some gift upon them, when all she craves is the embrace of a man who is the opposite of her husband, young, kind and full of passion. She hardly fears discovery any more, for she has nothing left to lose and her soiled reputation would strike a pleasingly harmful blow at her husband, should it be made known. He can only contain her and revile her for her sins, while concealing his own fornications with perfected hypocrisy.

One of the soldiers pauses in his digging as she passes, straightening his back, catching sight of her and saluting her with a friendly gesture of the hand. He is handsome enough in a simple, country way, broad shouldered, his shirt sleeves rolled over magnificent arms, a blacksmith's arms maybe. She turns quickly away and hurries on, knowing that she is expected back at the house for supper. It is easier simply to take the meal with her husband, then retire to her room to read or sew. He will not bother her there, as he has his own ways of satisfying his appetites, either in the town or in his chamber. Their maid of all work, who had been in their house for only a month or two had left suddenly, poor wretch. Katherine will not engage another, unless she can find one ill-favoured or old enough to be safe from her husband.

She enters their house, set back a little off the Wyre Street, a handsome, double-gabled, spacious place, built by a wealthy ship's master who had made a fortune in the spice trade. Her husband had purchased it ten years ago as their marital home. Standing inside the door of the large hall, where they lead their public lives, she hears a distant clatter of activity from the kitchen, which is reached by a narrow passage at the far end. She must go and see Mistress Denney the cook about supper and so, she walks the length of the hall, moving swiftly past the door of the small panelled chamber that her husband uses as a study.

In the kitchen, Mistress Denny is jabbing inside a pot hanging over the fire, as though the contents were alive and trying to leap out. Her round face is closed tight in a sulk.

'Master's been in, storming on about when the supper's to be ready,' she says. 'I'm doing my best, but it ain't easy.'

The woman shows little respect for Thomas Wade, in his absence. In his presence, she, like many people, shrinks away as from a rabid dog. She lifts the wooden spoon from the pot and points it at Katherine.

'Waiting above an hour at the butcher's, with all the folks in there pushing and yelling. Then they was buying up everything in his shop. He's got nothing left at all. We're going to be cut off, that's what they're all saying. Ain't no one allowed to go out anywhere now, nor bring us in provisions. We'll starve, I'm telling you.'

'Yes, I've heard such talk as well,' Katherine says with some sympathy for the woman as the butt of her husband's unreasonable anger. 'Perhaps this trouble will not last so long.'

'Well, I don't know. Master ranting on won't get the supper cooked any quicker,' she says, stamping off to the larder.

'Mistress, I thank you for your pains,' Katherine says, wishing to placate the cook, as she and their manservant Walter are the only servants in their household these days.

She returns to the hall and climbs the stairs to her chamber, removes her shawl and sits down at the window, staring out on the tangle of bushes and trees that is their garden. Walter is digging in a small plot of earth that he has cleared near the back door, stabbing rhythmically with his spade. She has neglected her herb garden, though many wild ones grow rampantly in the untamed place: camomile, betony, borage, cowslip and tormentil. Her housekeeping, like her life, is a listless, cheerless business, her engagement with her duties and chores just sufficient to avoid too much censure from her husband. She looks down upon the jungle of the garden, the creepers and straggling brambles clothing the walls, the ivy which clings to the trees and ranges thickly over the small hut, barely visible at the far end. In the centre is a swathe of tall weedy grasses where poppies and foxglove appear in the Spring.

When she had first seen this garden, it had given her a tiny glimmer of light in the darkness of her dread. She had come to this place full of fear, the new bride to Thomas Wade, a senior alderman of the town of Colchester, a prosperous cloth merchant, a man more than twice her age.

'Master Wade is a godly man, a highly respected person in his town,' her father, a grim and distant widower had said. 'You will be well provided for. Be grateful and glad with this arrangement.'

He had patted her hand in an awkward effort to calm her, as she wept on the night before her wedding.

'Come now,' he had said. 'Master Wade will give you a comfortable home, Katherine, and you will have children. Is that not pleasing to you?'

Katherine entered a life devoid of affection, of kindness or even of cold respect. In Thomas Wade's bed she had found no love, no tenderness, just a brutal coupling like the thrust of a knife and his shunning of her when, after some years, she did not give him a child. She saw then that her husband had no more regard for her than for one of the sheep in a far off field, who gave fleece for the making of his cloth. At first she was stricken with guilt for some failure in herself, for not trying to show him warmth or affection, as a good wife should, but soon discovered that these were not things he sought at all, they being alien to him as a velvet cushion to a toad. Like a toad, he would only smear the cold slime of his loathing when she weakly attempted to come close to him. He said that her womb was blighted, a just punishment for her sins, and that he too must suffer her useless presence, her barrenness. One evening, in her misery and loneliness, she threw his curses, redoubled with her hatred, back at him, which set him into a fury that was only relieved by beating her senseless. Later, as she lay on her bed, her head pulsing, her face bruised and bloodied, she realised that if nothing else, she had the power to discompose him.

At supper that evening, it is clear that her husband's temper is precarious, his mood in a state of dangerous imbalance. She derives a perverted pleasure in seeing him thus, feeling a shiver of anticipation, a trembling that she can take advantage of his state, while knowing all the while what will come of it. At least on this occasion there is information to be gleaned from him, which might pass the time until she can quit his company in safety.

'Is there no hope that the commander of the King's forces will surrender?' she says assuming a neutral tone.

Her husband looks up at her, his eyes narrowing as though she seeks to drag some secret from him. His cheeks are hollowed by the tightening of his mouth.

'No, that frivolous cavalier lord amuses himself by insulting the Lord General Fairfax's generous offer of terms,' he says sourly. 'And what's more, these Royalist rebels are settling themselves nicely in our town, provisioning themselves with plunder from round about. A troop of horse went out last evening into the Tendring Hundred, foraging and marauding in the countryside and brought back fifty sheep and as many cattle. They've raided the warehouses at the Hythe too. These Royalists are well practised in thieving other men's goods. They've even filched some millstones for grinding by horsepower.'

'An army must be fed and the Royalists clearly know how it must be done,' Katherine says. 'What provision have you in the Corporation made for us in the town? For if we are to be besieged for long, we might do best to learn from the invaders and be prepared.'

His glare tells her that she has pierced a vulnerable spot.

'You know nothing of the complications of managing the affairs of the town, even in a time of peace. It is a most perplexing responsibility,' he says.

'I can imagine it is,' she replies, revelling in his discomfiture.

'Such things might tax the best of men, demanding a spirit of co-operation, thought and careful consideration. Has the town corporation such qualities as these? I doubt it, so perhaps you should consult our friends the cavaliers about such matters.'

'How dare you. Friends? You dare to use such words to me. They are traitors and rebels.'

Katherine almost laughs at his literal mindedness. She does not think her husband stupid, far from it, though his is a narrow intelligence. He deems his age to be a substitute for wisdom. She sees his knife shaking in his hand and the sense of her triumph goads her on, even as she feels the nausea of mounting danger.

'Some say we shall suffer heavily for treating with the enemy, for opening the gates to the Earl of Norwich and welcoming him in,' she says.

'Do you think I do not know this?' His mouth is quivering with anger now. 'That fool Cooke, he and those other weaklings– I was overruled.'

'An uncomfortable state for you, I'm sure,' she says, hearing the sneering mockery of her tone, 'and one to which you are little accustomed.'

He stares at her with a mixture of disgust and disbelief, she knowing what will occur, but in her madness embracing it.

'Others will stand by me, I'll have you know,' he says, his voice straining in his efforts to control it. 'Barrington, Furley and - others. I am not alone in my loyalty to Parliament.'

'But what if the rebels were to be victorious and the King be in the ascendant? You would surely not wish your loyalty to Parliament to be known. Would you not prefer the side of the victors whatever the cause?' she says, feeling a sickening thrill to expose what is at his core, self-interest.

She has struck home. His face is red, his mouth quivering.

'A wife, even such a one as you, has a duty not to cross her husband,' he says. 'Before God you should ask my pardon for your insolence, your disrespect.'

'And you before God, upon your knees, should beg for His mercy for your cruelty and your hypocrisy.'

A platter crashes on the table, where he has lifted it up and smashed it down upon the surface. The pewter tankards fly to the floor and Katherine feels his hand grip her throat, then the blows upon her ear, the fist striking her cheekbone, before he hurls her to the floor. Her face is sticky with blood where she lies, seeing from the corner of her eye the shuddering of the slammed door behind him as he leaves the room.

She does not move. She has brought this about with her malice, which has swelled like a boil and burst its poison over him. This is her rightful punishment. Hatred brings only pain and grief and yet she can do nothing but hate him, this man who curses her for her barrenness, who exhorts God to punish her weakness and wickedness. Had he, in these ten years, only given her one soft look, one touch of affection, one glance of admiration or approval, she might have borne this life with more patience. Instead, she has devoted what is left of her life to hating him.

'Mistress,' comes a voice above her head, but she cannot move yet. It is Walter, their servant. She feels his hand upon her arm. 'Mistress, come sit up and let me see to your hurts.'

She hears him plunge something into a bowl of water at his side. She feels his arm beneath her, easing her up and sees his pitted, unshaven face, his solemn eyes and hears his voice, soothing as always. He looks at her and dabs gently at her eye, which she knows is swollen. Blood from a cut on her cheek has matted some strands of her hair.

'Mistress, he has overstepped himself. This is monstrous. You must not suffer it,' he says, his eyes narrowing, peering at her as he dips the cloth again.

Katherine feels her familiar gratitude to Walter, who is so much more than a servant to her, a faithful, tender and discreet ally. She has not taken him to her bed, however, for she does not wish to use him this way, nor to risk him losing his place and his livelihood. He is a man of middle years, a distant kinsman of her husband, who some years ago suffered misfortune, the nature of which Katherine does not know, but which left him without home, family or employment. He had told her once that he had owned a farm near Earls Colne, but would say no more of his past and his more prosperous, independent days.

'But I overstepped myself,' she tells him, as he dabs her upper lip, her mouth stiff and painful.

'But why can you not be obedient and wifely to him, to save yourself this hurt? Why provoke his anger?'

'I try, Walter, I try, but I'm too much soured and corrupted. Each word I utter only fills me with more venom until it must come out. I am made only of spite and wickedness. I can only hate.'

'No Mistress, that is not true,' he says.

Dusk is thickening and Katherine has bathed her face again, cooled her hot swollen eye and calmed her sores. This is the aftermath, her misery and loathing outpoured, so that now she dwells in a dull mood of nothingness. She cannot go to bed, for to lie awake will revive more morbid thinking. She will go out, to breathe the night air. The Mayor has advised that all the townspeople should stay safe behind their doors at night, for fear of another attempt to attack the town by the besiegers, under cover of darkness. Katherine has no care for such dangers, though she felt a wrench of horror and pity for the young Parliamentary soldiers who were slaughtered on the streets of the town only days ago. What better for her than to be blasted by shot, blown away to dust for evermore? She wonders if she should say a prayer to prepare her soul, but has little concern for this either, knowing herself to be damned already. There was a time when prayer and reading the scriptures had strengthened her, when she believed that God's hand would help her cling to her faith, might bring her a child, but that conviction has long since departed.

Though her husband has locked her in her chamber as

usual, she removes her hidden key from under a loose floorboard beneath the rug. He has taken to imprisoning her, in the evening, to curb her wandering at night, to contain her erring ways within bounds. But Walter furnished her with another key, some time ago, when she appealed for his help, desperate and outraged by her confinement. Her loyal servant had taken his master's key to the locksmith and had a copy made. This evening, her husband has gone out for a meeting of the Corporation, no doubt keeping his bloodied knuckles below the table, she imagines with grim satisfaction. In leaving the house now she runs little risk of encountering him and can gain entry to the house again by the washhouse door, which Walter always ensures is unlocked for her return. Outside her chamber, on the landing she locks the door again, in case her husband should try it on his return, slips her key inside her bodice and makes her way down the stairs.

She wears her claret cloak, a soft and luxurious garment of velvet with a generous hood which conveniently covers her damaged face. There will be guards, sentries posted all about, who will no doubt challenge her to reveal herself, but seeing a woman, they will most likely consider her no threat. At worst, they will order her home again. She is not going near the walls or the town gates in any case, but instead will make for the churchyard of the Holy Trinity, a quiet, hidden place with many trees.

As she opens the door on to the path leading to the Wyre Street, she has a sudden inspiration never to return here again, wondering if now is the time she should leave the town, with all the disturbance and disruption of the occupying soldiers. Could she escape beyond the walls to the besieging army and beg for mercy and safe passage away from this place? To take this step, however, would reduce her to beggary, for she has no means of her own, beyond the clothes in her cupboard and a few trinkets. Her husband keeps all of his money well hidden and she has no idea of its whereabouts. He gives her only a small allowance each week, some money to Mistress Denney for purchasing food and some to Walter as his meagre wage. Nor has Katherine any kinsfolk to whom she might flee, apart from an aged aunt in Norfolk, who might well be dead now for all she knows. This siege does not steal away her liberty, for she has none, save the secret freedoms she enjoys in deceiving her husband.

The night air is damp, the invisible droplets of moisture drifting around her, the cobblestones of the street glowing, where tiny shreds of light escape from the windows of one or two dwellings. Katherine steps over the slops in the gutter, making her way the short distance to the Holy Trinity Church. The shape of a huge elm tree, heavily cloaked with leaves, overhangs the street and she hears some distant sounds: a few musket shots far away, the shouts of men. She glances up the narrow lane that gives on to the High Street, where a number of figures flit past. She feels no fear however, and would stand firm if a charge of cavalry were to come upon her and trample her body to a pulp.

She turns into the lane at the side of the church and pushes open the gate leading into the churchyard. The rough grass is mounded over old graves with a few small stone slabs, marking the resting places of dead citizens. She picks up her skirts and steps up and over a mound, the wet dampening her feet. On her left the dark wall of the church looms. A yew tree stands only a few paces from the wall, its lower branches knotted and bent, forming a small hollow where a person can be seated in concealment. She moves towards it and gropes her way into this quiet hiding place, blackened by the thick boughs above. She breathes deeply, a miserable calm enveloping her, though preferable by far to the prison of her chamber.

Ahead, a patch of the darkness seems to shiver, a shadow moves, a figure, a man who is following her route along the wall of the church, moving silently as though not of this world, for his feet make no sound. She peers through the darkness and makes out the shape of a broad-brimmed hat, a short cloak, a sword and boots turned down at the top, of the sort worn by gentlemen. He is walking towards her, over the first hummock of earth, head bowed and therefore unlikely to have noticed her. She stays her breathing, shrinking back a little into the branches of the yew, for she does not wish an encounter with anyone, if it can be avoided.

The man advances another step, stops and lifts his head, though she cannot see the features of his face, only its paler shadow beneath his hat.

'Is anyone there?' he says, his voice quiet and low, for he is uncertain, she supposes, of whether he is addressing the empty air. He takes another step forward and she knows that he has seen her, for he is only ten paces away.

'Sir, I am alone. I seek a quiet sanctuary here,' she says, her voice steady.

'I beg your pardon, Mistress,' says the man, or gentleman, for his accent seems to be that of an educated person, refined though reserved. 'I would not disturb you in your contemplation. But is it not dangerous for a lady to be out alone in the town?'

'I have no fear, sir, nor do I have anything at all to lose,' she says, glad of the darkness that provides such welcome anonymity. She does not think she knows this gentleman, at least there is nothing in his voice or bearing that recalls to her anyone of this town.

'Nothing to lose?' he says, his voice distant.

There is a moment's pause before he speaks again. 'Are you a resident of this town, Mistress?'

'Yes sir, I am.'

'Do you not think of the dangers you face?'

As he speaks these words he moves a few steps closer, so that she can see that he is a gentleman of above medium height, of upright bearing, a soldier and an officer she is sure. His lace boot hose proclaim him a gentleman too, as does his short cloak and the ornate hilt of his sword. His collar also is of fine lace. He is one of the Royalist invaders.

'I have told you sir, I fear nothing. There is nothing any person on this earth can do to make me more bereft than I am now. No cavaliers, no rebels with guns, muskets, swords can affright me.' As she speaks she is glad that her voice is devoid of plaintiveness and self pity.

'Mistress, your words are of one in despair.'

'No, you are wrong, sir. I am beyond despair.'

Again there is silence between them for some moments. Katherine feels no tension, no awkwardness, however, no expectation that she should speak nor that he should. The silence hangs in the air like a vapour in the cooling night.

'And how did you travel beyond despair?' he says at last. 'Did you pass through rage?'

'Oh yes, such rage as burned me to the very core,' she says, recognising in this question a sign of one who himself has known a descent into misery.

'But now you have come to this state of mind, this calm acceptance,' he says.

She finds herself astonished at this novel encounter, where a stranger, a gentleman is listening and pondering on what she says and thinks. She knows that she is in the presence of a troubled man.

'It is a sort of calm, I suppose,' she says, 'but more like a death, for I am only half alive. Patient acceptance is something I have tried for, but could never attain.'

'Nor I,' he says, 'and I cannot control the rage. The anger will not be put down.'

She leans forward a little, realising that she is now curious to see the face of this stranger who has revealed something of such intimacy to her. This is a soldier, a usurper of this town's will, a Royalist enemy, who stands before her.

'Perhaps it is necessary for you sir, in your position, to have recourse to anger, for how else could you rouse yourself to fight?' As she speaks she thinks of the power her own rage towards her husband gives her and understands how it is that soldiers must fuel their need to do violence to others.

'Yes, you are right,' he says. 'So you know I am your enemy.'

'That may be,' she says, 'but here in this night world, we can hide, we can deny what we are and what others have made us, can we not?'

'But should we not strive to be always truly ourselves?' His voice betrays the strain of his anguish.

'And how should we know which, from all of our many

parts, makes our true self?' she says, noting a new insistence in her tone.

He says nothing, but steps closer to her, so that she might easily reach out and touch his cloak. She looks up into the shadow of his face, feeling his presence now with more force as though a wind has suddenly blown through the place. He reaches out a hand to her, ungloved, a long, elegant hand with white fingers and she gives him hers and rises to stand before him. She can see by the weak moonlight, dark eyes, a black moustache and dark hair which flows over the lace at his neck. He grasps her hand firmly, looking at her with an intense stare, so that she is glad that the darkness and her hood are shading her damaged face.

'May I know who you are, Mistress?' he says.

She hesitates. 'No, I will not give you my name, for I like this obscurity, this other world where I can be noted for my calm self and where it is safe to speak freely and in anonymity. Tomorrow, I will have to live in the world of the day again and that lights my faults too harshly.'

'I think it is you who judge yourself too harshly, Mistress, not the light. I would speak with you again. I would value it greatly. Will you walk here on another night?'

He still holds her hand in his, but she knows that their encounter must end, though she has little wish for this. She says nothing and his grip tightens.

'May I accompany you back to your house?' he says.

'No, sir. I thank you. I must go.'

'Tomorrow? Will it be tomorrow?'

She steps quickly past him on to the mound of grass towards the path. 'Yes, tomorrow,' she says and goes along by the dark wall of the church with hasty steps.

She runs the last fifty paces to her house, hearing the pounding of her heart, the prickling of the tender skin of her wounded face, longing to fall between her sheets, to lay down her head and escape into sleep. Now she wants to sleep more than anything, lose consciousness and wake again tomorrow. She passes swiftly down the lane at the side of the house, to gain entry by the garden gate. She presses the latch of the gate slowly, steps into the garden, across the damp path to the washhouse door, bolting it behind her, then in the silence of the house, creeps upstairs to her chamber.

Katherine sleeps late the next morning, awakening stiff in her limbs, the skin of her cheek tight and tender, but in spite of these physical discomforts, her mind is strangely more settled, as if there were some new purpose in starting the day. She finds her lace shawl to cover her face and drapes it around the darkest blemishes. From below come the distant sounds of a door banging, voices and footsteps in the hall, as Walter or Mistress Denney go about their morning duties. Hoping that her husband has gone from home on business, she starts down the stairs to break her fast, but to her dismay, comes upon him as he stands in the centre of the hall, hat in hand, in readiness to depart. The surprise of seeing him there causes her shawl to slip and she recoils back one step upon the stairs. He glances at her, his mouth dragged down in the familiar scowl.

'I will be out to a late hour this evening,' he says.

She shrugs her shoulders by way of reply, a gesture she knows provokes him and he strides to the foot of the stairs.

'I am going to meet with others of our trade today. Unless we can petition the Lord General Fairfax to let us take out and sell our wares, we will be ruined. We will be paupers. I thought you had best know this.'

Katherine takes a deep breath, thinking that at least in the poorhouse she would not be forced to look upon his face again. He peers with narrowing eyes, as though to draw some comment from her.

'You may well look unmoved, Mistress,' he says with a pettish snap. 'What? You have no bold answer for me today? Well, you're better silent and you'd best keep indoors today for that face will appal anyone who looks upon it.'

She pulls the edge of the shawl over her cheek again, sickened, in spite of her armour against him. She forces herself to look back at him.

'And to think I once thought you comely,' he says, shaking his head in mock sorrow.

She hardens her stare, seeing in the deep lines of his face the imprints of his cruelty.

'Well I never thought you so,' she says, 'but I thought you honourable and godly and in that I was sorely deceived.'

His face colours as his composure slips, but she moves quickly down the last few steps and flits past him, hastening away along the passageway towards the kitchen, knowing that he will not lay a hand on her in front of others. She bursts in, pleased to find Walter there, calmly stoking the fire.

'Good day, Mistress,' he says with his solemn smile and he sets a jug and cup upon the table for her. 'Take your ease. Would you have some buttermilk? And some bread?'

She nods, grateful and glad of his quiet welcome as she takes a seat.

'Is Mistress Denney not here this morning?' she says.

'She's gone to buy salt and flour and other foodstuffs, for there's panic in the town that we're to be starved out. I doubt she'll find much to buy.'

His brow furrows as he puts a bowl upon the table before her. 'Pray God this terrible business will not last long,' he says, glancing at her.

'Amen to that,' Katherine replies, aware that she should have taken more care and notice of the state of their provisions. 'We have preserves of fruit and of pickles and a cask of salt meat, I believe, and meal and some flour too.'

'Yes, Mistress,' says Walter, standing at her side. 'You're seeming more yourself this morning, Mistress, if I may say. I'm glad you're well rested.'

More myself, Katherine ponders, as she drinks the sour buttermilk greedily, gratefully. She recalls the peculiar encounter of the night before, the exchange of views with the sorrowful gentleman, finding herself more curious this morning to know his identity.

'Will you go, Walter, to seek out any news and information you can glean about our state and that of our enemy guests? Find out what you can, if anybody knows what the commanders propose. I would rather not ask my husband,' she says. 'But take care as you go, for last night I heard the sound of guns from the walls and there are thousands of armed men in our midst. I do not wish to go outdoors myself today.'

'Yes, Mistress, I'll gladly go. They reckon the Lord Fairfax hasn't enough of a force outside to take the town. He lost the best part of a regiment of foot when they tried to storm the Head Gate, poor devils. It was a sorry sight to behold, so many dead, and in our town. But there are reinforcements on their way, so word is they'll try to take the town again. Some of our men have spoken to a captain of the Parliament army, in one of the dugouts at the bottom of the Balkerne Hill. They'll likely bring more intelligence today.'

Katherine is surprised to find her docile servant so well-informed, drawn into some network of intrigue and hearsay by the dangers that have come so suddenly upon the town. She realises how little she knows of the man.

'The Lord Fairfax will starve us like rats, along with the enemy, for that's the nature of sieges if they can't be broken,' he says.

'But we in the town are not to blame,' says Katherine, shocked to hear of such ruthlessness from the general they had hoped would be their saviour. 'What could we do but comply with the Royalists?'

'Defend our town and die in the doing of it,' Walter says with a sigh. 'That's what the Parliament men would have had us do, I suppose.'

Walter departs and is gone for two or three hours to Katherine's surprise, causing her to fret on his behalf. She is on the point of venturing out herself, shielding herself with her shawl again, in spite of the warmth of the day, when she hears a knock upon the door. As Mistress Denney is busy in the kitchen, having returned with only meagre supplies of flour and salt, she goes to the door herself, pulling her shawl over her face before greeting the person who has disturbed her privacy.

On the doorstep stands Beth Sayer, the pretty daughter of her neighbour, the weaver, flustered and with an anxious face.

'Mistress,' she says, 'there's bad trouble. My father and your man Walter are taken, and others too, by the Royalist soldiers. They were all arrested as they gathered in the Marketplace only a short while ago. The soldiers are taking them to the prison.'

'But why? What is their crime?' Katherine says, thinking the honest, dull weaver Master Sayer as unlikely a miscreant as her own well-mannered serving man. 'What madness is this?'

'I don't know,' Beth says and Katherine sees that she is near to tears. 'My mother has charged me to find out, for she will not let my brothers out of her sight. She says I must come to seek out Master Wade, ask him to help, to speak up for the men, for they've done no wrong. Some others have been to the Mayor's house but he's sick and taken to his bed and cannot be roused. The constables of St Nicolas and St James are called for too.'

Katherine hesitates, but only for a moment, for the girl is so fretful and she herself is angered on behalf of Walter. 'My husband is not here,' she says, thinking how like it is of the corporation men to fail the people in time of need. 'But I'll come with you straight. Let's hurry. They are taken to the prison in the castle, you say?'

The girl nods then makes off swiftly ahead with Katherine following, holding her shawl to her bruised cheek. They take the lane by St Nicolas's Church, joining a crowd of other women and some children hastening towards the castle too. Ahead, near the entrance, they catch sight of a bunch of men, upwards of thirty, being driven forward by soldiers armed with pikes, several abreast, with others hemming in the prisoners at the sides. Katherine spies, in advance of the train, two horsemen leading the way into the castle yard.

'How did you hear of this?' Katherine asks the girl, who has wiped dry her eyes and whose face is now set in a look of determination.

'One of my brothers went to find my father. He had gone to the market place to buy bread and meat, anything that could be had. Some men of the town were gathered outside *The Red Lion* when soldiers came along, two colonels of horse and musketeers and rounded them up, saying the men were planning some mischief against the King's army. But there was no trouble or riot. I'm certain my father would not be part of such a thing.'

'No, I am sure he would not,' says Katherine, wondering again about Walter, enraged that free men, meeting together in their own town, should be rounded up like animals.

Katherine and Beth have by now caught up with a crowd of people following the procession of soldiers and prisoners to the castle. The leading horsemen have gone through the gates and the prisoners are herded and hustled inside the castle yard, surrounded by the pikemen. A line of these soldiers turns about face and stands guard across the entrance, then an officer steps forward, raising his sword to the crowd.

'Get you gone, you people,' he shouts.

'What can we do?' Beth Sayer says, her voice trembling.

'They cannot imprison innocent men for no cause,' Katherine says, her indignation transforming itself into action. 'Come let's go ahead. They'll have to knock us down, if they mean to stop us.'

Katherine catches the girl's hand and together they skirt around the edges of the crowd, which is now growing restive.

'Let them free, you bastards,' someone shouts, while a few boys start lobbing stones at the soldiers. 'Let them go!'

The prisoners are now confined within the castle yard by the line of pikemen. The sentries are starting to heave the gates to, but Katherine sees a gap between and, grasping Beth's hand again, she pulls her forward, both of them nimbly slipping through the closing portals. The two sentries, surprised, scramble to catch hold of them, causing the prisoners to shout with delight and the crowd to surge after, forcing open the gates again, knocking over the officer and pushing on into the castle yard.

A raucous chorus has broken out in the crowd. 'We'll not yield! Let them free. That's an alderman's wife. Set our men free!'

Katherine, clutching tightly to her shawl, struggles in the grip of one of the soldiers.

'Where is your commander?' she shouts, powered by her fury. 'Let us be. Tell your commander we demand to speak with him.'

'Yes, bring him. Bring your colonel to face us,' yells a man in the small group that now presses in behind Katherine and Beth. He waves the naked blade of a sword in the air.

The officer, scrambling to his feet, red-faced as he dusts himself down, shouts an order at his men and in a body they force the prisoners back a few paces, then turn once more to form a wall against the crowd. At this moment, the two horsemen who led the prisoners into the castle grounds, come riding back in response to the clamour, steering their horses in front of the pikemen, only ten paces from where Katherine, Beth and the furious officer are standing. These mounted ones are dressed in the buff coats of cavalrymen, with feathered hats and lace collars, armed with pistols and swords. These are not ordinary officers but have the air and the looks of high commanders about them.

Katherine does not wait for them to speak. She is not cowed by the sight of these gentlemen and takes a step closer. She will have the first word and not let these tyrants take charge.

'Why do you take these men, our citizens. Are they arrested? On what charge?' she cries out to the horsemen.

One of the officers speaks up, throwing his voice at the crowd, like fire from a heavy gun.

'These men were assembling to attempt an insurrection against us. They were gathering in the street, planning some mischievous act and refused to disperse on our orders.'

There are shouts from the prisoners, with one spokesman's voice rising louder than the rest. 'It's a lie. We were in search of food from the market. Is it a crime to want food for our bellies?'

Others of the prisoners join in and the protesters behind Katherine add their cries of outrage. The two mounted officers glance at each other, the cacophony increasing, the crowd closing in, then the one who has not previously spoken swiftly draws his sword and raises it aloft in a signal for silence.

'Listen well,' he declares, as the din of voices dies. 'When we, the King's forces, entered this town we gave our word that no one would be harmed, who went peaceably about his business. This promise we give again to those who are obedient to our orders.'

Katherine's chest tightens. Is it with rage at the injustice of the cavaliers' action, or with the knowledge that she knows this colonel, this commander?

'What of these innocent men, these ones you have rounded up for the crime of gathering on the street?' she cries out to him and she sees his eyes fix upon her. 'My servant is one you have taken. You sweep up people on the street, like wolves who ravage all creatures of flesh and blood beyond their hunger. Is this honourable?'

Katherine hears the rumblings of talk swell up behind her, sees the horses of the colonel and his companion stamping their feet and wonders how she can so readily have become the centre of this protest, speaking up so boldly to these armed officers who hold their town by force. She glances at the fair girl beside her, who stares back with wide, blue eyes. Katherine, pulling the shawl over her cheek again, steals another look at the colonel, knowing that he is that same tormented man she met in the churchyard last night, but that this is his other martial self.

'Very well, Mistress,' he says. 'We will take the path of mercy on this occasion. Let these men go free. But know this: we shall search every household for weapons and powder. We shall take all that might be used against us and will punish any who threaten our safety in this town. Those who take arms against us, no matter who they be, will pay with their lives. You have been warned.'

Katherine continues to shield her face with her shawl, for the colonel is looking at her, with a cold and penetrating stare, as the pikemen in front of her part and the captive townsmen move forward with dazed and grateful faces.

Chapter 6

19th – 21st June

Jack has never seen Beth so fevered up. Her face is red with running when she bursts in the door. But where's Father? Then he comes in straight after her and Jack's heart jolts with relief while Ed runs to him.

'Thanks be to God,' says Mother in a loud whisper. 'Did Alderman Wade get you free?'

'No, it was his wife spoke up for us,' says Father, 'but there's no time to tell of it now.'

'The soldiers,' Beth gasps, 'they're coming. They mean to search every house in the town for weapons and powder. They'll come here and – .'

Tobias stands up, gripping the edge of the table to steady himself and Jack wonders if he will fall down again, as he is swaying and his face is a terrible white.

'He must not be found here,' Father says.

'But what can we do?' Mother holds her apron to her face.

'I must go,' says Tobias weakly.

'No,' Jack and Ed say together. 'He can't go.'

Beth runs to the table, where Tobias is struggling to hold himself upright and takes his arm to steady him, then helps him sit again.

'You mustn't go,' says Jack, hearing a tremble in his voice. 'They'll capture you and throw you into prison.'

'The lad's in no state to go anywhere,' says Father shaking his head, coughing and lowering himself to a stool at the table. 'We must think of something.'

'Can we not hide him?' says Beth.

Mother bolts the door with a crack and they all fall silent for some moments. Jack's mind buzzes like a bee trapped in a jar, but he can think of no good way of hiding Tobias.

'There's nowhere. They'll find him,' says Mother and Jack doesn't like the hopeless weakness in her voice.

'Even in the workshop, there's no place safe,' Father says. 'They'll search where folks are likely to hide swords and muskets.'

Jack sees that Tobias's brow is beaded with sweat. 'I'll not have you punished for harbouring me,' he says. His face is grey now. 'I'll surrender myself on the street. Let me go.'

Jack adds his voice to the chorus of 'no' from Ed and Beth.

'We'd not have you languish in some filthy gaol, not with your hurts,' says Father.

Jack sees that Beth's eyes are filling and that she is holding Tobias's hand under the table. Jack thinks he might weep himself. Ed's lip is quivering too, but only for a moment before his eyes light up.

'I know. I know what to do,' Ed says. 'Tobias can pretend to be sick in bed, sick and dying.'

'Yes,' Jack says, hopping up and down on his good leg, quickly possessed with the brilliance of the idea. 'We'll cover him up and say he's dying of something, of –. We can tell the soldiers –.'

Beth touches Tobias's arm. 'Flux. Yes. You could have been struck down with a flux. They'd not wish to come near you.'

Father is shaking his head. 'Well, I don't know. It's an idea but–.'

'It's a good plan,' Beth says, her face brightening. 'We can say he's our kinsman come from the country, from Suffolk or some such place, to find work, but then he fell sick. Mother you have kin in Suffolk, have you not?

Mother lifts her hand to her brow. 'I do, but it's a foolish, dangerous thing.'

'I'd not have you risk –,' says Tobias.

'Hush,' says Beth jumping up. 'Do as we say. Come let's get the bed ready. Mother, may we have another blanket? We'd best get a nightgown to cover him and the binding on his head must come off. Come to the bed and lie down, Tobias.'

Jack is filled with Beth's conviction and energy.

'What shall we do with his soldier's coat?' Ed says.

'You could put it on, Father, under your own, so no one'll see,' Jack says, pulling the red coat from the hook by the fire and handing it to his father, who strips off his own and stands for a moment, staring, in his shirtsleeves.

'Oh dear, what have we come to?' says Mother coming down the stairs with a blanket and Jack wonders why she can't share in the joy and the cleverness of their plan.

'And his helmet?' Jack says. 'It can go in the chamber pot under the bed.'

The kitchen is filled with their busy action. Old Solomon stirs by the fire, disturbed by the breeze of movement around him. Jack and Ed help their father to hide the red coat under his own while Beth unwinds the bandage on Tobias's head.

'Look, there's blood on his head,' Jack says, pointing to the place where Tobias's wound has bled over his hair, which is now matted down one side.

'Wear a nightcap over it,' says Ed. 'Father could lend his.'

Tobias smiles weakly as he is pushed and pummelled by Beth, a nightshirt put upon him to cover his bandages and the nightcap pulled down over his head.

'Now lie down, cousin and say nothing,' she says covering him with the blanket.

'We need another chamber pot by the bed,' says Ed with a grin, 'for his sick to go in.'

'Some terrible coloured piss would do.' Jack laughs and hands the pot to Ed and together they make for the back door.

Outside in the yard, they giggle as they make water into the pot, then add some slivers of mossy growth from the fence and a handful of dirt from the ground, stirring it all with a stick. They hurry back in with the pot and place it by Tobias's bed.

'He's mighty sick, I'd say,' Ed says with a smile, while Beth and their parents peer into the mess in the pot.

'Oh mercy,' says Mother, shaking her head.

'Quiet now, you two,' Beth says, 'for this is a house of sickness,' and she lays her hand on Tobias's unmoving body.

Jack makes Ed go out upon the street three or four times to see if the soldiers are coming, but there is no sign of any search happening at all nearby. Ed returns, scuffing his feet on the floor with disappointment. Tobias has fallen asleep, for which Jack is grateful, as he would have been mightily bored lying there with nothing to do. This is enough to drive a body to desperate acts, all this waiting. Beth sits at the wheel but keeps sighing, rising from her place and going to look at Tobias, as though she really fears he is dying of flux. Mother is in the workshop with Father, who is making repairs to the loom now that it is idle and he needs another pair of hands to help him in the mending of it.

Jack and Ed sit at the fireplace in between the regular forays to look outside the door and Jack inspects his ankle, which is almost sound again, though a little tender if he goes too far on it. Then he picks a scab on his knee so that it bleeds like a real soldier's wound. He and Ed are dull now, after all the excitement of the plotting and the anticipation of the acting out of their plan. Then it comes to Jack, in a rush of fear, that their trick might be discovered and Tobias might be taken, dragged away by the soldiers and chained in a prison. Though the young soldier has been with them for less than two weeks, Jack and Ed cannot imagine his not being there. Beth likes him too, for she is always around him, tending his wounds and bringing him food. Jack and Ed have seen them smiling at each other, touching hands and whispering when their parents are not looking. Beth could marry him. What could be better? Then Tobias would be their brother. In fact, Jack thinks it such a good idea, that he will suggest it to them tomorrow, after the soldiers have searched the house and gone away.

'I'll take Old Solomon outside,' Jack tells his sister and brother, too restless to sit still any more. He rises to urge the old dog from his place. Old Solomon yawns and looks at Jack with filmy eyes, which he knows can see little nowadays. He is almost deaf too and Jack wonders what the world must be like for him, perhaps a little like dreaming, or being in that drowsy state of half sleeping, when Mother is calling for him to rise in the morning. Ed looks up from carding wool, which he has been doing in a weak-handed, lazy fashion.

Old Solomon waddles out the doorway after Jack who, two steps out on to the street, walks straight into the solid bulk of a soldier, with breastplate and helmet, armed with a pistol and sword in his belt. He has two others with him, in battle garb too.

'You live here, boy?' says the soldier who has close-set eyes and a pointed nose. Jack thinks he is probably a captain, or a sergeant as he speaks up for the others.

'I said do you live here, boy?'

'Yes sir,' Jack says in his meekest voice, staying rooted in the gap of the half-open doorway, with Old Solomon leaning against his leg.

'And do you have a father?' says the soldier.

'Yes, sir.'

'And is he at home?'

'He's in the workshop.'

The soldier is shifting on his feet and trying to glance into the kitchen. Jack knows he must keep this questioning going for as long as he can, so that Beth, Ed and Tobias can be ready for the soldiers when they enter and start their searching. Old Solomon is swaying towards the men, lifting his nose to the waft of new scents in the air.

'And where's that?' the soldier says sharply.

'Round the back.'

'Round the back where? We'd speak with your father, you witless little rogue. Where is he?'

'Down the alley, just there,' Jack says, pointing the way,

knowing that he cannot delay the soldiers for much longer.

Old Solomon has ambled past the sergeant and is now blindly sniffing at the leg of one of the other men.

'Get off, you mangy cur,' the man says, kicking out and catching Old Solomon in the ribs. The old dog staggers and grunts, but moves on, as if he has merely bumped against some unseen obstacle in his path.

Jack's pulse races and he would gladly have kicked the soldier himself, if it had not been for his weak ankle and the recklessness of such an action. Instead, he summons his most pious voice. 'Our old dog is one of God's lowly creatures, sir. He is old, near blind and lame. Did not our Lord Jesus Christ bid us –.'

'A pox on you,' says the sergeant, moving to the door and grabbing Jack by the shoulder. 'Let us past, you snivelling little puritan.'

'Sir, we have sickness, terrible sickness in this house. It would be wiser by far to go to my father's workshop, round there by the alley. It's my cousin. He's mighty sick. It might be the plague, and he's lying near dead in the kitchen. We've been on our knees all day in prayer and fasting.'

The soldier hesitates, eyeing him, while Jack notices his comrades edging back a few steps from the door. Up the street, a few of their neighbours stand upon their thresholds, watching the proceedings and at the far end, Jack sees another clutch of armed men approaching on the same mission.

'And my brother's going down with the sickness too, only this morning,' Jack says, aware of the rashness of this claim. 'But my cousin's sorely afflicted.'

'Sergeant, let's go to the workshop,' says one of the soldiers, making to move off towards the alley.

'You'll do as you're ordered, you son of a whore,' the sergeant, replies turning swiftly.

Then he hesitates, staring a moment or two longer at Jack.

'Very well, we'll start in the workshop,' he says and the three stamp off up the alley that leads to the back yard.

Jack hurries into the kitchen, where he notices that Old

Solomon has already retreated and shuts the door firmly behind him. Beth, Ed and Mother stand, shock-faced by the table. Tobias too has awoken, though only his eyes and nose are visible from under the bed coverings.

'They've gone to see Father first, in the workshop,' says Jack in a whisper, a pulsating fear in his head. 'Ed, you've got to be sick too. I told them you were poorly with it.'

'Lord preserve us,' says Mother, shaking her head in dismay as though a cask of gunpowder has just been discovered under her kitchen table.

'Don't fret. I know what to do.' Ed is grinning and Jack is sure in that moment that he can safely trust to his brother's quick wits.

Ed grabs a shawl that hangs on a hook by the door, pours himself a cup of buttermilk from a jug on the table and retreats to the place by the hearth where Old Solomon is lying. He wriggles down on the rug and pulls the shawl around his head, hiding the cup behind a stack of faggots.

From outside in the yard they hear the noise of the soldiers' boots and voices, Father's and the sergeant's, in the tones of an ordinary conversation. Jack at the table, picks up the carding, while Beth takes her place at the wheel again and sets it whirring. Mother stays by the fire, glancing at Ed who is scraping at the soot on the bricks of the hearth, which Jack knows must be some part of his plan. A moment later, Jack hears Father's words clearly outside the door.

'No, we've never had a weapon in this house,' he is saying as the back door swings open. 'But you can search in here, if you wish. I must warn you, however –.'

'Aye, we know of this,' the sergeant says. 'The lad told us. You've sickness here among you.'

His tone is wary now as he looks upon the scene in the kitchen. Jack glances up at him and sees his close-set eyes flit about the room, taking in Beth and resting at last on the moribund body of Tobias under his bedding. The two other soldiers sidle towards the front door on to the street, standing their muskets on the floor.

'That's our young kinsmen, struck down. Only God can

save him now,' says Father.

The sergeant meets Jack's eyes, then nods towards Ed's motionless figure by the hearth.

'And that's your brother, is it? Sick too?'

Jack nods without a word, not wishing to catch Father's eye as he has not been party to this latest twist of the trick. The sergeant scowls again and says nothing, but draws his sword and takes a step towards Tobias. Jack bites his lip and sees Beth's face blanch. With the tip of his sword, the sergeant catches the end of the blanket and raises it up, to reveal Tobias's body covered with the linen night shirt.

'Where did you say he hailed from?' says the sergeant turning round to Father.

'Suffolk.'

'Suffolk? I'm a Suffolk man myself. I'd like a word with him,' says the sergeant.

'He's too sick, sir,' Beth says, looking up from the wheel and fixing her eyes on the soldier. 'He can hardly move his jaws. He's taken nothing but water and even that he can't keep in his stomach.'

Jack is glad to see Beth's bold look and that Mother's frightened face is turned away from the man. Suddenly Ed, lying by the fireplace, groans and turns over, his head still swathed in the shawl. The sergeant lowers his sword and the blanket, glances briefly round at Ed, then turns his attention back again to Tobias. He grimaces as he looks into the chamber pot, but takes a step closer and pokes at the bedclothes with his sword. He jabs at the blanket near Tobias's shoulder and hoists it up again, this time uncovering a small book. Jack's heart thuds desperately, for he knows this book is 'The Soldier's Pocket Bible' which is given, so Tobias tells them, to every man in the New Model Army.

'What's this?' the sergeant says, prodding the book with the end of his sword.

'It's the scriptures of course,' Father says. 'We have been seeking succour in the words of God.'

Jack watches the sergeant jab with the sword point, spear the book then flick it away from the bed, to land on the floor by

Father's feet. Mother gasps aloud. But Ed starts up his groaning again, loudly this time and now he is rising from his place, staggering, making first towards the two soldiers, one of whom scrabbles for the latch and flings opens the door. Then Ed veers around and lurches instead in the direction of the sergeant and with a hideous retching sound, spurts the contents of his mouth in a black fountain on to the soldier's boots. The man yells and dances like a player at a fair and his two comrades dive out of the door on to the street.

'God's wounds, get away from me, boy,' cries the sergeant and crashes out after his men.

'Pardon him, sir,' calls Beth after them, her face red, not with fear or fury but with holding back her laughter. 'He's a poor boy distempered by his sickness. Forgive him.'

For some moments they all stand in silence, Jack feeling the quivering of his limbs, then Father goes to the door, looks outside, closes it and slowly slides the bolt across. Ed jumps in the air, lets out a quiet whoop and grins with the whole of his face, which is smeared with soot around his nose and mouth. Beth runs to embrace first Ed then Jack, then Mother, while Father looks on.

'You two rogues. I don't know how it was we gave birth to such a pair, do you wife?'

He is smiling and even Mother's face looks softer too, at last.

Old Solomon's tail thumps heavily on the floor and Jack feels his heart fill with delight as Tobias sits up, with a bemused expression, pulling off the nightcap.

'I've never seen such play acting,' he says with a smile at Jack and Ed. 'But forgive me for all the trouble I've brought to your house.'

'No trouble but fine entertainment,' Father says, laughing again and Jack cannot remember when last he has seen him in such spirits.

'Well I hope you two little imps will clean up the mess,' says Mother, but Jack knows she is not truly vexed.

'No, I'll happily do it,' Beth says and her eyes are shining, 'for these two have done good work today.'

Jack worries that their trick might have angered God and halted Tobias's recovery. His wounds are healing quite well, all save one. Jack and Ed watch as Beth removes the bandage from his side, where a large scabbed wound has dried to a shiny crust. The hurt to his arm, which was punctured by a ball is red and swollen, however, and Tobias's jaw twitches as Beth takes away the bandage.

'Does it pain you much?' Jack says.

'A little, though I think maybe I've a touch of fever.'

Jack and Ed watch Beth's face as she examines the swollen cut on Tobias's arm.

'Mother,' she says. 'Please come and look. I think the wound's poisoned. We must make a poultice.'

Mother leaves the spinning wheel and comes to the table, leaning over to inspect the wound, her face betraying the same concern that Beth's has shown.

'Edward, fill the pot and put it on to boil, will you?' she says. 'If we could make a green balsam, that might serve well, with adder's tongue, or even burnet. With all the rain we've had, there may be still some about.'

'Perhaps Mistress Wade has some in her garden,' Jack says.

He thinks it very likely that every herb or grass in the world grows in Alderman Wade's huge garden, for it is a wild and wonderful place. He and Ed have climbed over the wall a few times, into the tangle, when there was no one about. Mistress Wade is not quite as fearsome as her husband, though Mother tuts and says she is not respectable. Jack is not sure what is meant by this and thinks Mistress Wade very beautiful, though she always looks sad to him. Beth told them all about her boldness, when she spoke up as brave as any man against the Royalist colonel and made him set Father free and the other men who'd been arrested. Folk all said Mistress Wade was a good sight better than her husband when it came to helping the folks of the town.

'Yes, you might go to Mistress Wade's man Walter, but don't tarry long,' Mother says.

Jack and Ed stay close to Tobias at the table, both struck by their own fears that he might die, for they'd heard of folk dying of poisoned wounds.

'I'll pray for you to be well again,' Jack says.

'Shall I bring your soldier's bible?' says Ed.

Tobias smiles at them. 'You'd have me in my grave, would you?'

He grips first Jack's hand, then Ed's, with his sound one. 'No man could wish for more faithful brothers than you two. I've none of my own, so may I take you two to my bosom?' he says.

Jack wants to say yes and embrace Tobias but thinks this might be wrong or foolish. Ed says nothing but his face is red.

Beth, at the door, hearing their exchange, turns with a smile.

'Tobias, I gift them to you, though you must guide them well and promise not turn them into soldiers.'

It is Tobias's turn to colour in his face as he looks back at her. Beth is impudent in her words to him, bolder and sprightly in her ways since he has been in their house. There is no doubt in Jack's mind at all now. They are sweethearts. Irksome though this is, he'd rather that Tobias should love Beth than some other foolish wench.

'I only wish I had my strength again,' Tobias says to Jack and Ed when Beth has gone, 'for I reckon we could play such tricks on these cavaliers and send more of them scampering on their way.'

'Well, we can menace them, even if we're not big enough to fight them,' Jack says.

Mother looks up from stirring the pot. 'Tobias, these two have enough mischief in their heads without adding more.'

She almost smiles and Jack knows she is not as angry or fearful as she used to be that Tobias is here.

'When you're well again will you go back to your army?' says Ed.

Tobias nods. 'Aye, I must, for it is my duty. As soon as I'm healed I must try and get through their guards somehow and return to my regiment. I'd sooner risk that than be taken as a prisoner.'

Father has come in from the workshop and stands in the doorway listening to their talk. He goes to speak, hesitates, then comes close to the bed before telling what is in his mind. His voice is low and quiet and his eyes are fixed on Tobias.

'You remember the goodwife Symonds, she that came in upon you here that time? Well, Jem her husband, tells me that there are some in the town planning an uprising from within, a rebellion against the Royalists.'

Jack looks at Father, amazed by his new secret manner and his tale of a plot. Ed is staring too, as though he has a marble stuck in his throat.

'Jem says if you've a mind, as soon as you're back on your feet to join them, you'd be most welcome. Would that be duty enough to your general?' says Father. 'There's a band scheming and planning to overthrow the Royalist commanders, so Jem tells me.'

'What's this, husband?' says Mother suddenly and Jack knows she has heard all, in spite of Father's attempt to keep the word from her. 'You're not of this band? You said you'd not take up arms.' Her voice is thin and strained.

Father says nothing for a brief moment, then turns and looks at her. 'No, I'm past fighting. I've hardly the strength of a louse. But I can't sit by and do nothing, while these cavaliers are infesting our town. I must do my part, hide weapons, or men. It's safer now they've searched the house.'

Mother's face is red and angry now. 'Dear God in heaven, surely we must stay safe and do nothing to anger them. You've been taken already. You'd risk our lives for this foolishness?'

'There's danger, for certain,' Father says, but Jack knows that he will not give in to Mother. 'There's no avoiding it now, for any of us.'

Jack and Ed are astonished and excited by the revelation of these happenings and glad too that Father, in his own quiet way, means to fight against those who have conquered their town.

'Master Sayer,' Tobias says, 'I'll gladly join with the men of the town, for these actions may work better than battering at walls in the end. As soon as I'm on my feet again, I'll be gone from your house to other lodgings too, if you wish it.'

'No, you must stay here,' says Ed, looking at Mother with

his most pleading face.

'Another mouth to feed.' Mother turns away and mutters at the fire. 'We've scarce enough for ourselves.'

'You'll be safest here, Tobias,' Father says quietly and Jack cannot hold back a small yelp of glee.

Father turns on them a heavy, solemn look. 'Boys, say nothing of what you have heard today. You may give out that Tobias is our kinsman, living with us, so that he may go freely about, but I want you to swear to say nothing more.'

'I swear,' Jack and Ed say together, Jack feeling proud to bear the weight of this secret knowledge.

Father rises and without further talk, nor a look at Mother, goes back to the workshop.

By the time Beth returns with some limp leaves from Mistress Wade's garden, Jack thinks that Tobias looks sicker than ever, pasty faced and sweating. Beth leads him back to his bed again, takes off his boots for him and lays his swollen arm upon a bolster. He smiles at her and they talk quietly, so quietly that Jack can't hear what they're saying. Tobias seems to rally most times when Beth is with him, like he's almost glad to be weak and in need of tending, but Jack sees that in truth he is fevered and ill and knows he's not a cowardly sort.

Jack follows Ed, trying his best to keep pace, with Old Solomon trailing far behind them both. They are trotting along, past the almshouses by the south wall, near a crumbling and broken part where the Royalist soldiers have been working to shore it up. Their commanders must have reckoned this the most likely place for an attack, though in truth the soldiers are digging and heaving up earth all around the walls of the town. They use earth and flinty stuff and ancient bricks, along with sods of turf to thicken the walls, so that the heavy shot from the guns cannot break through. The Old Fort, a curved bastion near the Schere Gate, has been strengthened too, with timber beams from the demolished houses and a platform built in the middle, with big baskets full of earth to protect the gunners. Ed says these are called gabions. The Royalists have hauled up another gun to mount on top, alongside the town one, and now two barrels poke out over the walls towards their enemy beyond.

Father and Mother would be very angry if they knew that he and Ed were here, so close to the walls and near where the Royalist soldiers are. Jack harbours this guilt at their deceitfulness, along with the fear of meeting the captain on whose horse he rode that day, or the sergeant who fled their house in fear of the plague. But he and Ed are determined to be as brave as soldiers, to do something, like Tobias and Father and the secret band of men in the town, to rid themselves of the Royalist invaders. They might even help the great Lord General Fairfax to win the war.

They move on and see that there are no soldiers, nor anyone in the other bastions further along the wall. Jack sneaks a look at Ed, knowing he's thinking the same. It's wrong, Jack thinks, but just to look over for a quick moment could surely not hurt anyone. They run to the first empty lookout, standing on the stone ledge inside and spying out beyond the town at the besieging soldiers in the distance, like beetles crawling over mounds of earth. They're building something out of great logs of wood, out beyond the priory of St Botolph's.

'That's probably a fort,' Ed says with the air of an expert. 'And they call all these ditches and mounds the leaguer.'

'How do you know the names of all these army things?'

'I heard Master Symonds talking. He used to be a soldier,' says Ed simply.

'Well, I think it's strange to be trapped inside with our foes,' Jack says, wondering if his brother has an explanation for this as well. 'A siege is when folk in a town want to keep their enemies out, but the Lord General Fairfax's army is out there and they've come to rescue us, haven't they?'

If Ed has an answer, he has no time to deliver it, because someone has seen them.

'Hey you little turds, bugger off from there!' They turn to see a Royalist soldier striding towards them, so they jump down and scamper away.

They follow the curving lane further along, leaving behind the excavations and the teams of soldiers. At the side of this small street, lies a piece of open land, where folk graze their sheep or cows, tethered or kept in patches of grass enclosed by rough fences. Some of the Royalists' horses are grazing here now. The grass is well cropped and the ground is muddy. There are trees at the far side and some bushy clumps along the edge of the lane. Old Solomon has sniffed his way after them and lifts his leg against a wooden stump. From here they can also see the backs of a row of houses and yards, a higgledy-piggledy mess of workshops, shacks, and fences.

As Jack and Ed make their way along, they meet a few folk coming in the opposite direction, two skinny dogs trotting along and a woman dragging a child after her. A broken wooden fence with some scrubby bushes between, runs along the edge of the grazing land and ahead two helmeted soldiers are cutting sods of earth with spades. A wheelbarrow stands in the lane half-loaded with a hummock of turfs. This is a quiet enough spot and the two men good targets, for Jack and Ed know that their campaign must start in a small way at first. To attack a large band of soldiers would be too hazardous by far.

Jack follows Ed as he slips behind the fence and creeps along under cover inside it, to a place behind a small bush where they have a good view of the two soldiers, at a distance of about thirty paces. One of the men is a tall, hulking figure who is plunging and lifting his spade with the ease of a practised labourer. His companion is a smaller man, though muscled and strong, chopping at the tough grass as though spearing an enemy. Jack and Ed stop for a moment, peeping out at the men from their hiding place, while Old Solomon snuffles round their feet. Ed has started gathering stones and is filling his pockets with them.

'What are we going to do?' Jack says.

'You stay here and lob stones at them.'

'But there's two of them,' Jack whispers. 'What if they see us and chase us?'

Jack wouldn't welcome a beating from either man, knowing

too that he'd be hard pressed to outrun them, with his ankle still weak and tender. But he quickly scoops some stones into his pocket.

'There's plenty of places to run and hide yonder, if they take after us,' Ed says.

He turns and points to the trees and bushes then to the clutter of shacks and yards at the backs of the houses.

'And I'll make sure they come after me, not you. Remember, there's only one of us today,' Ed says with a grin that fills Jack with fearful glee.

They watch for some moments as the big blockish soldier straightens up, takes off his helmet and wipes his brow. He blows out a breath, then tosses the helmet aside into a clump of grass nearby.

'Want your head blowed off, Timothy?' says his companion, stopping and leaning on the handle of his spade. 'There's bastards down there, ready to fire them guns at us. Ain't you seen them?'

'Eh?' the big man says. 'Don't reckon they could hit us from way down there.'

'Well, I ain't going to risk my head,' says the smaller man. 'They've got the devil of a mortar down there. But you do what you like. Ain't nothing much in your head to lose anyways.'

His companion frowns in puzzlement. 'I don't reckon wearing a helmet would stop your head blowing off your neck, would it?'

The other man looks up at his companion with a sigh, then throws down his spade. 'I've a terrible thirst on me. I'm going for water. There's a well back there.'

'Sergeant won't like it,' says the big soldier.

'Well, I ain't working no more, parched dry like this, so I'll hang for him if he tries to stop me. Give me your bottle and I'll bring you some, you numbskull and put that iron helmet back on your thick head. You should thank me for it, Timothy, for there's many would let you die of thirst or of being a thickwit.'

The big soldier, Timothy, unties a leather bottle that is fastened to his belt and hands it to his companion. 'I'm mighty beholden to you, Henry,' he says, picking up his helmet and replacing it on his head.

Jack and Ed watch as the soldier makes his way back along the lane towards the main body of his fellows. Then they turn their gaze back to Timothy who now stands, bereft and alone, looking around him like an abandoned babe.

Ed whispers his instructions to Jack. 'You stay here. I'll go along there. Start throwing as soon as I give you the signal, then show yourself. When he comes towards you, I'll jump up. He'll not know which way to turn.'

Jack watches as Ed slips nimbly along behind the fence, with the old dog tottering behind. Ed is soon installed at about thirty paces further along, crouching down behind the fence and gives Jack the signal, a wave of the hand.

Jack takes up his first stone. He is a fast and accurate thrower and is pleased when his first stone hits the target, bouncing off the man's helmet with a pleasing musical chime. Jack bobs down out of sight. The soldier stops, looks around and takes off his helmet to inspect it, deeply puzzled. Jack's next stone hits him square on the ear and he yelps, clamping a hand over the side of his head. There are three more, then a hail of smaller pebbles that pepper the soldier's face and shoulders and he ducks and squirms in a useless attempt to avoid them. Then he puts on his helmet, picks up his spade and starts towards the source of these missiles. Jack bobs up quickly in full view and spatters the soldier's chest with another flight of stones.

'You little swine,' says the big soldier with a look of outrage on his wide face. He lumbers forward, but Jack disappears behind the bush.

Jack is crouching low when he hears another yowl of pain from the soldier as he is struck by a shot from Ed. He hears the big man turn and take several bounding steps away from him, along the fence towards Ed's hiding place, then there is another louder howl. Jack sees Ed drop down, then leaps up again himself, aiming a bigger stone at the desperate soldier's head.

'Holy Jesus in Heaven,' says the soldier, whimpering. 'It's an imp, a witch sent by the devil.'

He lurches to his left again, in pursuit of Jack who vanishes at the same time as a triumphant whoop comes from Ed, whose head pokes up once more. The soldier Timothy drops to his knees, raises his face, his hands clasped towards heaven and calls out.

'Lord save me, a poor sinner, from these fiends that plague me,' he sobs and when Jack sneaks a look he is struck with a pang of sorrow for the poor tortured soul. Then a thunderous blast shakes the wall, throwing up a rainstorm of earth and rubble. Timothy jumps to his feet, squeals and takes off at speed along the lane where his comrade had gone only a short time before.

'That's one of their big guns bombarding us,' Jack calls to Ed as they slowly raise themselves up and move closer together. Old Solomon, a few yards away, is completing the voiding of a solid turd.

Ed nudges Jack. 'Pity the soldier's run off. That was my next shot at him.'

Jack joins in with Ed's laughter, until another blast shakes the ground beneath their feet.

'We'd best be gone,' Jack says, but Ed hesitates.

'Come on, just one more job to be done.' He is pulling a handful of grass and leaves from the ground, then picking up Old Solomon's offering and climbing over the fence. Jack doesn't want to go near to the wall, but he can't leave Ed and scampers after him. They run the short distance to the spot where the soldiers had been digging and where a helmet lies abandoned. Ed picks it up and removes the knitted woollen cap inside it and drops Old Solomon's gift into the bottom, covering it again with the cap. Jack giggles but is silenced by another explosion. A thing, like a stone pot, comes hurtling up and over the wall, high in the air and lands in the ragged thatch of one of the houses about fifty paces away on the lane. Jack and Ed watch, knowing that they should run, but are they frozen, fascinated. A moment later, a yellow flame springs up from the roof of the house and someone screams inside. Jack looks at Ed and the last he remembers is another deafening explosion, then seeing his brother's white face, his astonished eyes as he is thrown up and back by a blast of hard, stony air.

Chapter 7

22nd June

The Lord General Fairfax's words to Charles have cut him more viciously than any wound to the body. He strikes the wall with his fist. Fresh pain might replace the rage he has felt, since receiving the reply to his request for an exchange of prisoners.

Sir Charles has forfeited his paroles, his honour and faith, being my prisoner upon parole and therefore not capable of command, or trust in martial affairs.

Now he knows he must calm himself before the council of war; it will serve little purpose to spill out his fury on his fellows. He shouts for his servant to bring him his armour and forces his mind to the urgency of what must be done. He will have to curtail the babbling of his commander the Earl of Norwich, the aged Lord Goring and the showy rhetoric of Lord Capel, for action is needed now. Fairfax is daily closing the net around them on all sides. They must lay in more provisions before it is too late, if they are to hold on until the forces from the north arrive. They must not sit in aimless talk, in lyrical imaginings of the relief that is promised from other uprisings of those loyal to the King. He must make them act and with speed.

His servant hurries in with his half armour and pistol belt and starts fitting the breast plate around him, fumbling a little in his haste. Charles utters a sigh of exasperation, elbowing the doltish fellow out of his way and snatching the belt from his hand. He stamps out of the chamber completing the task with one hand, irked that it is necessary to go armed, but knowing that this is a town full of enemies.

He and the other higher commanders are billeted in *The King's Head,* a sizeable inn, and here it is that they hold their councils of war. In this hostile town, it is the safest billet, for a white flag flies on its rooftop. This signals the presence of Parliamentarian hostages, a number of the County Committee men of Chelmsford, captured on their journey north. These men may prove useful for later bargaining with Fairfax, though at present Charles would prefer to run his great adversary through with a sword than to parley.

Outside the large parlour on the ground floor, Charles finds the commanders assembling, George Lisle and Bernard Gascoigne being joined by others: Tuke, Carter, Chester and Hammond. George Lisle greets Charles with his usual hearty smile.

'Good news, Charles. No, it is glorious news, I must say. A scout has come through early this morning. The Duke of Hamilton and his Scots have crossed the border. They are on their way south. Relief will soon be with us.'

Charles knows that he should feel elation, or at least some sense of optimism but the sour savour of Fairfax's judgement of him lingers still, after many days, and only vigorous action will dispel it. He nods brusquely at Lisle.

'That's welcome news,' he says, hearing the dullness of his voice.

'Do not expect our friend to be fired up by such things,' Gascoigne says to Tuke. 'His duty is to spread gloom and catastrophe all about us.'

Charles ignores the comment, though Tuke grins at it and the four make their way into the chamber. Charles takes a seat at the long table by Tuke and Lisle, determined to steer the talk from the outset to their strategy for managing the siege.

'We must make another sally out to the east, to the Tendring Hundred, while there is still free passage,' he says. 'The enemy will have forts and trenches all around if we do not move at once.'

'Yes, my friend you are right, of course,' Hammond says, as

the door opens to admit the two lords, moving with more speed and purpose than usual. They are followed by two soldiers, haggard-faced and spattered with mud from a recent long ride.

The two high commanders take their seats at the head of the table. The messengers, drooping with exhaustion, stand at the side. Lord Goring with a heavy voice addresses the company.

'These men, I must tell you, have only this hour brought unhappy news of our allies in Cambridgeshire who were marching to join us,' he says. 'Speak up, Sergeant.'

The first of the two scouts clears his throat.

'Sir, we encountered a captain from the Duke of Buckingham's company of horse from St Neot's in Huntingdonshire yesterday. He told us that they were routed sir, by Colonel Scroope's men and a detachment from the New Model Army. Their men and officers were all of them scattered, killed or taken. There are none left to advance to Colchester.'

The Lord of Norwich's face carries no trace of its usual humour as he dismisses the two men, though he draws himself up in his seat to address his officers.

'Gentlemen, this is a setback, but no more, for the Scots are on their way, so we have heard,' he says. 'They are to meet Colonel Langdale within a matter of days. Together, they will make an invincible force and they are on their way to relieve us. So there are happier times ahead.'

The old commander pauses, allowing the hint of a smile to return.

'And I think we know how we should answer this latest offer of terms for our surrender. We can make it amply clear to my Lord Fairfax, His Lameship, where his dishonourable offer should be put.'

There are murmurs and laughs and someone retorts, 'We would not soil a privy with it.'

'My Lord,' Charles says, determined that the session should not descend into purposeless or self-congratulatory nonsense. He sees Lord Capel, self-assured, arrogant-eyed, gazing at some place beyond their immediate surroundings. The man is well capable of brave action as he has proved with feats of personal daring, but he has little interest in strategy.

'The enemy strengthens their positions daily, with detachments from Suffolk and London joining to swell their numbers,' Charles persists.

Lord Goring raises a hand of acknowledgement. 'It is as well we were lucky enough to provision ourselves with the goods at the Hythe,' he says. 'And of course, your good work, Colonel Lucas, in bringing in so much livestock as well. We have water aplenty in wells and springs within the town and I am told even horse drawn mills to grind our grain. It is all most ingenious. No, gentlemen, I think we have little to fear from Fairfax's net, for our friends will be here to cut through it in a matter of weeks.'

The Lord of Norwich's optimism might please some but it only ferments Charles's exasperation. This lord's playful nature and innocence in matters of war is no doubt suitable for entertaining the ignorant and ladies in parlours but is a useless distraction in time of need or a crisis such as this. Charles inwardly bewails his fellow commanders' complacency, though the engineers who are strengthening the woefully weak fortifications are working well to secure the town, in spite of the bombardments on the south wall. What they need now is a sound strategy of sallies against the besiegers, to wreck their works, deplete their numbers and drain the morale of their men. Charles only wishes that his commanders will give him free rein to work with others of his way of thinking.

'My lord,' says Colonel Farre, 'the townspeople are rebellious, as the recent disturbance has shown. But my men have gathered all weapons and powder from every household. And the arrest of that foolhardy gaggle has no doubt shown them the danger of rising against us.'

'Aye, it was a sight to see,' says Colonel Chester, who had ridden with Charles that day when they had rounded up the crowd of men and brought them to the castle.

The woman, whom Charles knows now is an alderman's wife, had appeared at the head of a band of protestors, demanding the release of their menfolk.

Charles shifts in his seat at the mention of this incident and wishes the subject to be quickly passed over.

'Colonel Lucas is tender to his own people, and in truth I think they were little danger to us,' says Chester.

Charles is aware that he has coloured, loathing the attention of all of the company on him. 'We must be on our guard against uprisings,' he manages to state in an even tone.

'I say we press every able-bodied man to serve with the parties buttressing the wall and building barricades,' says Colonel Farre.

'That will be a hard task, with the minds of the Mayor and his Corporation so set against us,' Charles replies.

'The Mayor?' says Lord Capel with a snort, 'that fellow who shambles along like an affrighted old dame. He could no more organise an uprising than my maiden aunt.'

There is a burst of laughter in the company, over which Charles is forced to raise his voice. 'But there are others in the town of a more determined and dangerous character.'

'Yes, that firebrand of a woman, that alderman's wife for one,' says Colonel Chester, still chuckling. 'Her husband may be a sour-faced coward but she –, well, it was she made us free the arrested men, was it not?'

Again Charles feels the heat rush to his face when he thinks of this woman who had transformed herself from a melancholy, contemplative presence in the dark churchyard to a harpy, demanding that an armed garrison bend to her will. He says nothing in reply to this last comment of Chester's, instead drawing the attention of his commander to the need to fortify St John's Abbey more strongly, as he suspects that this could be the next target of the enemy. If they manage to seize it, they will have clear access to the south, where currently they are well contained by crossfire. He proposes his further plans for sallies out of the East Gate, to take the bridge and the dwellings beneath the wall on that side. The lords hand him the command of this operation, for which he rejoices, knowing that he can now gather his strongest cavalry force for the task.

When their business is finished, Charles sets off to see his captains of horse, enquire about the welfare of those injured men of his regiment and check on the state of the horses. He goes on foot with Captain Hicks down the length of the High Street where some townspeople are about their business at market stalls, though these are a poor enough sight, being so meagrely provisioned. Some loiterers turn to stare with venomous looks but Charles trains his eyes straight ahead, viewing the neat dwellings and shops on each side of the cobbled street, from which the debris and destruction of the first failed assault have mostly been cleared away. He thinks about the woman again, in spite of his endeavours to keep his mind on the critical business of planning his attack on Fairfax's positions. A gobbet of spit lands at his feet and he turns to see a group of men retreating quickly, cowards who cannot look him in the face and challenge him like men.

'Sir, shall I accost those fellows?' Captain Hicks says, with a hand on his sword.

'No, for after all they have a right to be disgruntled. We have taken over their town.'

'And it is a goodly town, sir. These are handsome and well-built houses. Pray to God we can have victory before this place suffers more damage.'

'Yes, it is my hope too,' says Charles, finding that he means this most sincerely.

A number of houses near the walls have been burnt out in Fairfax's first assault or destroyed by his forces. The bombardments, which are happening on the west and south side are pounding the ancient walls, though thanks to their own engineers, are making little impact. Fairfax has built numerous forts and strung earthworks in a loop around the town. More threatening still, their own spies have discovered that the siege expert Colonel Thomas Rainsborough has joined Fairfax. The traitorous Suffolk trained bands have chosen to side with the enemy too, to Charles's disgust. There is no choice for him now but to use all the skill at his command in this fight. Through action he can keep alive his conviction, whereas in a state of passive imprisonment, doubts and misgivings creep upon him as rats returning to gnaw at a rotten carcase.

Later, he joins some of his fellow officers in the dining parlour of *The King's Head.* The supper table bears platters of roasted beef and good wine, but Charles eats only to assuage his hunger, tasting little of the cook's efforts to please the palates of the gentlemen gathered there. Talk is of their hopes of relief from the north. There is some conversation too about the recent arrival of the astrologer, Master John Humphrey, in the garrison; he has offered very promising predictions of a happy and glorious outcome for the King's cause. Charles enquires after this man's lodgings, for he is curious to know what this conjuror sees the future holds for the King, and though he does not wish to admit it, for himself.

At supper, Charles is seated beside an officer known only slightly to him, by the name of Sir Hugh Orily. He is a narrow-nosed individual with alert eyes that flit frequently like a bird in search of tasty morsels, pecking pieces of conversation from any place at the table. His hair is curled in an extravagant manner and he has too much silk and lace about him.

'This is a good house and there's a very obliging fellow who will furnish us with women tonight. You wish to partake, Sir Charles?' says Sir Hugh.

Charles cannot conceal his distaste for his companion and his suggestions and shakes his head.

'What, sir?' Sir Hugh smiles. 'There are many willing and attractive ladies. I've had a look at them, unless of course your preferences lie elsewhere.'

Before Charles can respond, Colonel Chester, overhearing this exchange, leans over, mocking in a confidential tone. 'I think Sir Charles has a fancy for that rebellious woman of the town, that alderman's wife.'

'Really?' Sir Hugh Orily proclaims aloud. 'Well, I'm sure something could be arranged with her, for the right price.'

Chester chuckles. 'No, no, sir she's most likely one of these abominable godly women. Remember this cursed town is full of puritans.'

Charles rises, his face burning, knowing that by doing this he is drawing the attention of all the company towards him, a condition that he detests and fears more than any charge into battle. He cannot sit, however, and endure this mischievous speculation at the woman's expense.

'Come, sit down, sir,' Sir Hugh says, putting a hand on Charles's arm.

'I'll not be party to dishonourable talk,' he says, his jaw stiff, throwing off the man's hand.

Sir Hugh's face changes to a look of cunning irritation.

'You're too honourable for this company, Sir Charles, but if you're a man you'd best pray that this siege does not last too long.'

Charles sees the smile in the officer's eyes, hears his impudent chuckle and his own rage erupts. He clutches Sir Hugh by the throat and would in a moment choke the life from him, but he hears the laughing clamour of his fellows, a thundering of boots on the floor and jovial cries that he should desist. With the wretch struggling for breath in his grip, Charles leans close to his face. 'Do not speak to me again, sir, on any matter, unless it be pertaining to our duties here.'

He loosens his grip on the officer's throat, stands up and stalks out of the chamber, hearing the continuing laughter of the others behind him. He bursts out of the door into the dark courtyard of the inn, then on to the main street where sentries stand posted on the Head Gate. Up above on the wall, he sees the dark shapes of others patrolling and steers his steps towards a narrow lane, an obscure route leading east and away from the walls. Dogged now by the knowledge that he has made himself ridiculous, he pounds along, his head throbbing. He knows what they think of him, that he is a humourless boor, an irascible, ill-natured soldier, comfortable only with talk of horses, arms, matters military and he recognises the truth of this judgement. But he can only pursue his goals of honour and duty in a way that is natural to him. He despises the pointless banter of gentlemen, prefers the purposeful talk of lower officers, troopers, infantrymen, gunners, musketeers, men who value their trade, their knowledge and skills honed through practice and effort.

By the time he has walked the length of the narrow lane, his anger has cooled a little and he sees that the moon is full in a clear ink-blue sky. The stillness of the street is punctured only by a dog bark, the shadows of two cats scampering ahead of him and distant muffled voices from behind a lit window in one of the dwellings. In this hushed night, he thinks again of the alderman's wife. He has not returned to the churchyard, though he remembers now how he had entreated her to walk there on the next night after their first encounter. His meeting with her in her different guise, as leader of the band of protestors, has marked out clearly that they are enemies. She must hate him for his action in arresting the men, which in truth he had meant only as a stern warning to those who would foment an uprising. He had meant only to hold them, frighten them with a display of the strength of their forces and then let the hapless fellows return to their homes, on pain of death for further disobedience. He is not brutal and has always adhered to the rules of warfare. Then he stops, checked by this inward lie, the memory of what he had done when he was governor of Berkeley Castle.

He cannot let himself dwell on this or on other troubling images. His mind must not venture there, to revisit the seas of the dead, the torn bodies and faces of the men who had served with him who had given their lives for nothing. He must not think that the cause is lost. This dread, like the thickening cloud on a battlefield, the nauseating stench of powder, death and defeat, threatens to envelop him. He strides on faster, to flee these imaginings into a narrow street that he half recognises then finds himself at the gate of the churchyard of the Holy Trinity. He gasps with relief. Here is a place to quieten his mind, to hide and pray if he can, for God to aid him, strengthen him to fulfil this duty, which he knows will be his last. The huge shadow of the yew tree waits for him as he stumbles in the dark towards it, the place where the woman had sat that night. He falls on his knees in front of it as he would before the King's throne. He knows that he is close to weeping as he prays, mouthing the words, begging forgiveness of his sins and for the restoration of his courage and resolve.

At first he is not sure that the slight pressure on his shoulder is there at all, or whether his hunched posture, which has numbed his body, is betraying his sense. But then he feels the hand lean a little more upon him and the presence of someone beside him. He keeps his head bent and hopes that it is a townsman, an assassin, who with one deft slice of a blade will dispatch him. If so, he is glad that he has prayed and has in some small measure prepared his soul. But the touch is gentle and the hand not one intent on murder.

'Sir, you have been a long time on your knees,' comes a voice which he knows instantly is the woman's, the alderman's wife.

He turns and looks up at the cloaked figure. The moon is shining behind her head so that he can see little of her face. Whether it is the power of prayer or her presence that has calmed him he is unsure, but he rises, taking her hand as he does so, the one that she is resting on his shoulder. He stands beside her now, very close so that their garments touch and he hears her breathing. He is too much surprised to utter a word to her, she who has stood against him as an enemy, a strident woman who forced him to retract his orders in front of others.

'You are very troubled,' she says, her voice soft, her hand warm in his.

'I was praying,' he said, with some difficulty, finding his throat constricting again, 'for forgiveness and for strength. Tonight I have lost it all.'

She says nothing and he wishes that he could see her face, but the dark hood is drawn forward over it. With his free hand he takes the edge of her hood, soft stuff, velvet and pulls it back from her face. In the moonlight it is almost too beautiful for him to bear. This must be his lunacy, another manifestation of the final descent into madness, that she is with him and willingly.

'We have faced each other as enemies,' he says, 'and yet you stand here with me as though the other meeting had never occurred.'

'That was another time and another place, but here we are those different people we might wish to be.'

He does not believe her. It is too foolish, too hopeful and yet she seems to bear no resentment against him, unless it is her intent to stab him with a knife once she has seduced him, bewitched him into trusting her. She might do that easily, for he cannot take his eyes from her face. What does it matter? He has frequently thought about the manner of his death, speared from his horse by an enemy pike or sword, or shot through by a musket ball, some heroic death in the heat of battle, with all the honour of a soldier dying for a just cause. But would it not be more fitting for his private nature, his shy, truculent self to die by the hand of an assassin, a woman, in an obscure churchyard? Perhaps they could talk together for a little while first.

'I am glad that we can speak again,' he says.

'And I too.'

He is stunned by her reply but finds that he is leading her to the twisted tree seat, as he might have done a lady in a parlour, though he is little enough practised in such courtesies. He stands beside her, reluctant to relinquish her hand, but she slips it from his and looks up at him. Her face seems to him most comely, with dark eyes and full lips, black hair which curls around a wide brow. He wishes to tell her how beautiful she is to him but cannot summon the courage for such a confession; even to think it causes him to flush invisibly.

'But what of your troubles?' he says instead. 'Are you easier in your mind now?'

She smiles at him and he can hardly contain his urge to catch her in his arms. There have been women, a mistress when he lived in London and whores of course through all his campaigns in England and in the continental wars, but this woman is like no other he has encountered, though he recognises well enough the lust she provokes in him.

'My mind is a little more at ease,' she says, 'to have found another who knows what it is to be lost. This is a kind of comfort, do you not agree?'

He clutches her hand again and pulls her close. She reaches for his face, touching his cheek with the palm of her hand. Her kiss is deep and sudden and his desire takes charge of him. He wants to devour her, but is aware that he must not be brutish. She is in his arms, locked hard, so when he lowers her to the earth under the yew tree, they move as one and hardly part their mouths. His hands find her open and hotly welcoming, she drawing him into her, such that he cannot contain his delight. They muffle the joy of their coming in the softness of the dark and then lie silent still and bound together.

'That was kind comfort indeed,' he says and she kisses him again, slowly on the lips. His relief is such that he is numbed by it, unable to move, though he feels the dampness of the earth beneath them. She lies with her head upon his shoulder and he smells the faint odour of roses rise from her hair, which he kisses, surprising himself to discover the desire to perform such an action.

'You are tender for a man of war, you see,' she says.

'And you are tough for a delicate woman.'

'So, I am right,' she laughs quietly close to his ear. 'We have made each other anew.'

A distant shout carries from somewhere and he forces himself to sit up, adjusting his clothes. She, holding him still, sits up too. Listening again for a few moments, he satisfies himself that there is no one nearby and kisses her again on the mouth, finding in her response such sweetness that it almost hurts.

'You are wife to an alderman of the town. I know that much,' he says,' but may I not know your Christian name?'

She strokes his cheek and he sees the crease of a frown between her brows. 'If this is all you would know of me, I tell you that I am Katherine and I know that you are Sir Charles Lucas.'

'Yes, for all my sins,' he says, seeing too late the better blessing of anonymity.

'Oh do not talk of sins,' she says, 'for these would take too long in the telling.'

He studies her face for a moment, hesitating, struggling

to express how she has moved him. 'You have gifted me more pleasure, more understanding than any other in my life,' he says.

He knows that this statement is the absolute and astonishing truth, for he has no skills of flattery. She makes no reply for a moment, releasing herself from his arms a little, pushing back some strands of her hair and smoothing the skirt of her gown.

'And you have spoken the kindest truth that I have ever heard,' she says.

He can do nothing but take her in his arms again, kiss her and wish at that moment to die in this state. The thought of rising or parting from her is an agony to him and it seems that she too is content to stay with him here. But a parting has to come; the hour is late.

'Will you come to me again?' he says, rising to his feet and raising her with his arm around her waist. 'Will you consent?'

She nods.

'But I would not have us lie here on the damp ground, or drenched with the rain like two country folk behind a haystack caught in a storm,' he says, realising that he is smiling at her as he talks, a strange and novel sensation.

She laughs. 'I know another place where you may play the rustic, though you be a knight. I am known in the town and could not come to your billet, but we have a small hut, scarce more than a shack, at the end of our garden. It is quite hidden and overgrown with ivy and thorn. If you have no care to share the place with weeds and spiders, we can be secret there.'

'Katherine,' he says, savouring the speaking of her name, wondering if this is all a most monstrous folly, but with little care if it should be. As if she has guessed his thoughts, she takes his hand, fixing her eyes on him.

'Sir, in the real world we are ill-matched in every way, but in this other that we have made, we were born to be together.'

Her words provoke in him an awareness of the place where they are standing, the strangely lit sky, the moon and the smell of damp earth, in a town in peril.

'This town may explode at any moment in victory or defeat.

Tomorrow I must make a sally out beyond the walls and may not return alive. But I must fight this war, for I have no choice.'

'Ssh,' she says, touching his mouth with her fingers. 'Say no more of this. Let us not think about those actions we must perform in the day, nor of our fate. We have found a small precious solace for a moment, a fragile thing that might break at any time. We both know this.'

He walks with her out of the churchyard, she telling him how he can gain access to the back entrance of her garden over the wall and how she will watch for him each night one hour after sunset.

A few moments later, Charles stunned and disbelieving, watches her cloaked figure retreat down the street towards her house. Then he forces his steps through the alleyway on to the High Street. The sky is still lit by the moon, but the night is well-advanced and all honest people lie abed, apart from the guards on the battlements whom he trusts are wakeful and alert about their business. He fancies he hears voices, perhaps from these distant sentries, exchanging words as they patrol the west wall, but he is not sure. Are those footsteps behind him too? His senses are sharpened now as he strides along, his spirit fired with energy, with certainty, like a man felled in battle, thinking his lifeblood to be draining from him, but discovering this a false perception, breathing the air again with a gasp of joy. There are footsteps, however, quickening behind him, not the imaginings of his heated brain and he turns to see a dark figure.

'Who's there? Show yourself,' he calls, unsheathing his sword then stepping towards the shape.

The darkness seems to thicken and the shadow, the figure, the illusion, has sunk away somewhere and though he peers, he can see nothing, no one at all on the empty street.

Chapter 8

2nd – 3rd July

Beth swills the thin broth into the five bowls set upon the table, hoping that it will be enough to fill their bellies, along with the rough breadcake made with the last of their gritty flour. She will have to keep some back for Tobias, who has been gone for all of the day on an unknown mission, about which she does not dare to think. She looks at the fair heads of her brothers, sitting meekly at the table.

'Edward, would you go and call Mother and Father to table?' she says, hearing something of a mother's authority in her voice. In truth, many of the household duties have fallen to her now, since her father's health has been failing badly and her mother spends much of her time in fretful inaction. Beth bears her duties gladly for she must, but to be strong for others as well as herself and to guard her brothers taxes her. She thanks God that Tobias is still with them, though she dreads his going, which she knows will likely be very soon.

Without a word, Edward slips from his chair and runs out through the doorway to the workshop. Jack glances at her with the new uncertain look he has acquired, since the narrow escape he and Edward had by the town walls. The mortar fire had killed several townsfolk, some soldiers too, and had burnt two houses down to the ground. When Jack and Ed had returned, blackened and filthy, with cuts to their faces and hands, their father had beaten them with a stick for their disobedience in going to a place of danger and consorting with enemy soldiers. But Beth knew, that for all his anger, her father gave thanks to God for the saving of his two sons' lives.

At table, Beth half listens as her father gives thanks again for their beggarly meal, with the other half of her mind trained on the sounds outside, longing to hear Tobias's footsteps, yearning for a sight of him, to know that he is safe and well. She cannot deny the truth of her feelings now, for she can think of nothing else but Tobias, when her mind roams free. She had not known it possible to be so afflicted by longing for another person. So in his absence she imagines his brown eyes looking at her, his smooth brow and thick tawny hair which hangs about his cheeks, his chin quite prominent and his mouth, that mouth she longs to feel on hers. She knows too that he has affection for her, though he has not declared it in words. How could there be a life without him, now, though she has known him only a few short weeks? She has tended and touched his wounded body, helped it to heal, with God's great mercy. In her moments of doubt she wonders if perhaps Tobias feels only gratitude for his life, but she sees something else in his eyes when he looks at her. Other men have looked with such eyes and she enjoys with shy pleasure the knowledge that she is blessed and well-favoured in her appearance. She prays to God to make her virtuous too and to repent her sins of envy and discontent at her lot and other feelings that are too wicked to admit, begging Him to give her the gifts of patience and forbearance.

Now that Tobias has nearly recovered, the pain and swelling of his poisoned wound abated, enabling him to venture out, she has become aware of other dangers. He is no longer captive to his infirmity, nor safe within the bosom of their house; he faces the hazards and uncertainties of a soldier again and one in the midst of enemy forces. She weeps to herself sometimes in the privy or in the yard when no one else is about, to think that she and Tobias might never have a life as man and wife. The siege now holds them encircled and imprisoned, with no sign that the besiegers will attempt to take the town, nor the Royalists shift from it. The Sayers have little food and even less money with which to purchase any. Their shelves are miserably empty and the shopkeepers and butchers are charging extravagant prices, far beyond their means. Her father feels this most acutely, he having had no work nor pay for many months. This most of all has reduced him, so shrunken and wretched in his looks.

Now, as has become his habit of late, her father's prayers are longer and Beth listens with difficulty, as hunger grips her belly.

'Almighty and all merciful God, we give our humblest thanks for the food before us. We trust in your bountiful providence to guard and keep us, though we are weak and full of sin. Give us the strength, Lord, to bear our hardships and keep us strong in our faith in your all-knowing and all-seeing wisdom and love. Thank you, Lord God for preserving the lives of our two sons, whose errors they pray to you daily to forgive.'

His prayer is rambling now, in his growing sorrow and desperation at their state and Beth wills him to stop soon. Ed and Jack squirm in their seats. At last they join their father in the Amen and the boys set to with speed. Their mother frowns.

'Go easy now. You'd best make this last,' she says, her voice dulled by her own hunger.

'Master Brown still has some flour. He told me only yesterday,' says Beth.

'Aye, but what will he ask for it, five shillings for a bag of his mouldy meal?' her mother replies.

'It's monstrous,' says her father looking up from his bowl, 'to take advantage of those without means. And we've little that can be turned into money.'

'Father,' Beth says, seeing that now may be the time to voice an idea that has been with her for a few days. 'I could go and call on Mistress Wade, for Walter her man, has told me that she has no laundry maid or maid of all work. I could offer myself in return for pay or even victuals. I like her well and I think she has some regard for me since we went together against the enemy commander.'

Her mother lowers her bowl, which she has lifted to her mouth to drain the last of the pottage.

'No, you will not go to that house,' she says and Beth sees a quick glance exchanged with her father, whose face bears an unreadable expression.

'But why Mother? I'm not above maid's work. I could earn money –.'

'I tell you no. I forbid it,' she says again, her eyes hard.

Ed and Jack peep up from their bowls at their mother's unaccountable anger. Beth, puzzled by this refusal, will not let it rest, this chance of some relief for them. Why can her parents not see this?

'I don't understand,' she says. 'Master and Mistress Wade are well-to-do and Mistress Wade may be able to spare us something from her larder in return for –.'

Her mother slaps her hand upon the table, so that the candle holder leaps up, skids a few inches and sets the empty bowls rattling. 'You will obey me. Tell her, husband, that she must obey.'

'Beth, we'd not have you beholden to Alderman Wade and his wife,' her father says in a heavy tone, but with no anger.

This secretive manner only goads Beth to make another plea.

'But we are beholden to them already, Father, for Mistress Wade it was who made the Royalists release you and the other men. How can there be harm in what I propose?'

'I'll not have you consorting with Mistress Wade,' says her mother in a tone that shocks Beth by its harshness, so that she does not risk speaking again for some moments.

Her mother is unflinching, not from some foolish whim, nor pride, but from covert knowledge that she is not willing to divulge. However, one last idea springs into Beth's mind.

'Perhaps Mistress Wade might need plain sewing or knitted hose. I could bring the work here and do it at home. There would be no need to tarry in their house,' Beth says.

'And we can go with Beth, to protect her,' Ed adds in a small voice.

Their father sighs. 'Wife, there are far greater perils all

around us. The girl has wit and sense enough to do this. Let her go with her brothers.'

Her mother purses her lips in defeat. 'Very well. You can go to Mistress Wade and ask if she has need of any plain sewing or the like, but do not stay long in that house.'

Beth is warmed by this small victory and imagines how the wealthy and kind Mistress Wade might even gift her some food if she tells her of their hardship and want.

'And you two can go to *The Red Lion* again and see if there's any work in the stables in return for a morsel or two,' says their father to Ed and Jack. 'But remember, go nowhere near the walls nor have talk with any soldiers.'

The boys nod, staring down into their empty bowls. They have been much subdued by their punishment. Their parents had reacted with horror and fury when Ed and Jack returned, after the mortar fire by the wall, in their shocked and filthied state, with Old Solomon hanging lifeless in Jack's arms. In weeping bursts, they had confessed to their escapade and told of how heavy shot from a gun had all but burst through the wall. Jack had laid the old dog in front of the fire and they had all rejoiced when they heard a grunt and saw his tail rise and flop weakly against the floor. Tobias had watched all this with a stricken face, asking their father to forgive him for rousing the boys to take action against the enemy. Beth supposed they had deserved their beating, though she pitied them in their earnestness of intent and its painful consequences.

Where is Tobias now? Why does he not come home? Beth sets herself to spinning again, though now she questions the purpose, since she and her mother have many reels ready in the workshop and her father's loom lies silent and still. There is no market for cloth so why weave it? The cloth merchants had been thwarted in their attempt to seek permission from the Lord General Fairfax of the besieging forces to let them ply their trade and take their wares out of the town, to London. He had refused, offering them only the chance to sell their stuffs in a temporary market at the village of Lexden. They had spurned this offer, however, as a fruitless venture. Her father says he may soon lose his skill in his craft if he is forced to stay idle for much longer.

Beth starts the wheel and teases the thin fleece between her fingers, but at that moment hears footsteps outside, the latch clicking and Tobias is there at the door. He is flushed in the face from hurrying and the sight of him makes her heart leap. His eyes seek out hers first of all and in his look of delight at seeing her, there is all she needs to know. He greets her family with good cheer, stepping quickly into the kitchen and closing the door behind him. He is carrying a bulky cloth bundle on his back.

'Pardon me please for my lateness,' he says, dumping the heavy thing upon the table. He wears a woollen cap and an old coat of her father's so that he looks no different from any young weaver or craftsman of the town, though he is by far more comely.

'Look here,' says Tobias, untying the knot in the cloth. Already Ed and Jack are beside him, eyeing the parcel. Her parents rise too from their places by the fire and Beth joins them all at the table.

The bundle contains a fat-covered shoulder of mutton and two large ox tails.

'Flesh for the table,' Tobias says and Beth sees pride glow in his face. He smiles at her.

'But how much did you pay?' says her mother.

'Only two shillings,' Tobias replies. 'It's a fair bargain, do you not think?'

'I do indeed.'

'And you paid from your own pocket, lad?' her father says.

Tobias nods, colouring a little. 'I had two shillings of my pay and this is little enough beside what you've done for me. It's far less than I owe you, for what money can pay for a life?'

Beth watches as her mother, silent in her gratitude touches his arm, while Jack and Ed hug at his legs. Beth, full of envy at those with the liberty to paw at Tobias, manages in the excitement of the moment to squeeze his hand and to receive from him a look that thrills her to her belly. There is nothing else that Tobias can do to endear himself more to her family and for one short, delicious moment Beth thinks about how her greatest wish might come to pass, with God's good grace.

She brings the remains of the watery soup for Tobias and the last crust of bread, as her mother takes away the precious offerings for cooking tomorrow. Beth is glad at last to have the chance to sit by Tobias and listen as he answers the boys' eager questions about the exploits of his day.

'I met with a group of fellows, first at *The Red Lion* then we went to the house of an alderman. There were many there, mostly freemen of the town. There's one who was a gunner in the Bishops' Wars who's got a mighty good plan to take powder and shot from the garrison, muskets and grenadoes too.'

He pauses, his voice having diminished almost to a whisper. He looks at Jack and Ed.

'You boys are hearing of dangerous and secret things that must be told to no other soul. Do you understand?'

Jack's face contorts with outrage and Ed leaps to his feet with a matching expression.

'Of course. We'll die before we speak of these things, Tobias.'

'We're no traitors,' Jack says.

Their father looks up from his chair by the fire. 'Hush,' he says. 'We know you're worthy of our trust and can hold your tongues, but remember well your lesson on obedience.' He looks at Tobias with a frown. 'How will you get into the garrison? The arsenal will be the most heavily guarded of all places.'

Tobias grins. 'Well, this gunner, he's a crafty fellow. He's made an excellent plan. He's found out the names of all the officers of the engineer units working around the walls and those manning the guns on the Old Fort and St Mary's Church and Balkerne Hill. So we'll roll up with a wagon into the arsenal in broad daylight, making out we're from Captain such-and-such's company in need of more powder and shot. We'll load up, then pull the wagon away through the town and hide it well in the workshop of one of the men. Once we have this hoard, we'll have the means to blow up the parlour in *The King's Head*, for that's where the Royalist rebel officers meet. And so, we will dispatch those fine gentlemen as they sit stuffing themselves on the mutton they've plundered from the farms round about. Once most of their commanders are gone, the men will surrender for certain.'

Beth feels something clutch like a cold hand at her innards. Tobias pauses, his eyes alight at first, but losing something of their excitement as he glances around at them all.

'But what of the serving folk in *The King's Head*,' says her mother, 'and the Parliament men who are hostage there?'

An uncomfortable silence creeps into the kitchen. Her father's face is haggard, her mother frowning, while Ed and Jack stare at Tobias, wide-eyed.

'I little thought we'd see such violence and outrage in our town,' her father says quietly.

Beth watches Tobias flush and hears him falter in his reply

'Master Sayer, we are at war. These men, these commanders are enemies who refuse the merciful offers of surrender given by the Lord General Fairfax. They will bring about the ruination of your town. What would you have me do? I am a soldier, sworn before God to do my duty to the army, to Parliament and the people, to take arms against the enemy, these rebels and traitors of the realm.'

Tobias pauses and Beth trembles to hear the distasteful truth of his words. He glances at them all, but does not meet Beth's gaze. His breath comes quickly and he drops his voice.

'In this town I saw my comrades hacked to pieces by the enemy. They do not hesitate in their slaughter; we must have the courage to do likewise.'

Beth's father says nothing and a new silence fills the room. The elation and joy of Tobias's return, the pleasure brought by his generous gift are all fled. Beth swallows the bitter realities: her ignorance of Tobias's other self, his duty, his life as a soldier, and the growing desperation in the town. She feels Tobias's eyes upon her but cannot meet his gaze, rising instead from her place and going to resume her spinning. The light is fading, however and the kitchen is dim. They will light no candles, for everything consumable must be preserved for as long as possible. Beth's mother and father climb the stairs to their chamber. Beth orders the boys to bed and they, after bidding a quiet goodnight, go up to the landing, where Beth's bed also lies.

Beth hears her mother bidding the boys goodnight, then calling down to her.

'Come to bed soon, my girl.'

Beth finishes winding the last of the yarn on to a reel and puts it into a basket at her feet. She sits for some moments waiting, until she hears the click of the latch on her parents' chamber door. Beth glances quickly at Tobias who is sitting at the table peering at his soldier's pocket bible, though she knows that the light is far too faint to read by. She longs to speak to him but doubts his true nature, fears that these feelings for him are foolish and dangerous. Old Solomon twitches in his dream by the fire. Beth bows her head again in a pretence of winding the last length of wool, knowing that she should go upstairs now, yet unable to move. She hears the stool leg scrape on the floor and knows that Tobias is coming towards her. A brief moment later he is kneeling at her side.

'Beth, I beg you not to mislike me for my duty as a soldier,' he says.

She cannot answer him nor look at him, but when he reaches for her hand, she gives it gladly. Though his hand is rough, his grip is gentle and she turns to him at last, thinking that this honest, handsome face, this humble action must surely show the truth of the man he is. He takes her hand to his lips, then leans to kiss her mouth, which draws her to him, so that she shivers with pleasure, craves something more of this. Resting her hand on his shoulder, she slips into his arms.

There is a clatter from above, something dropping upon the floor, which causes them both to start, for Tobias to release his hold on her, as they both know that Beth's father and mother are awake and listening, expecting to hear their daughter climb the stairs to bed.

When Beth rises the next morning, she finds Tobias's bed

empty, he having gone very early, she supposes, to pursue some clandestine business. She has little time to pine or fret, however, for she has her mission to Mistress Wade to undertake this morning. Her mother, with a little of her energy restored, rises soon and sets about cooking the meat that Tobias brought last evening. Beth and her brothers take a mouthful of dry bread and a little ale before going the short distance to Alderman Wade's house. They go up the lane at the side of the house, to enter by the back way, through the garden, Beth remembering the promise that her mother has extracted from her. Walter opens the door, welcoming them with a questioning smile.

'Mistress is not risen yet,' says Walter when he hears Beth's request. 'But if you will step into the kitchen for a little while, I'm sure she will be up soon.'

Beth hesitates and is grateful when Jack speaks up for her.

'We could call back when the mistress is risen,' he says, in a tone of assurance beyond his years.

Walter smiles, the gaunt, unshaven face revealing the trace of a different, prouder youth. 'Cook's most likely got something good to eat. Are you hungry, boys?'

Ed and Jack look at Beth with expressions somewhere between guilt and entreaty.

'Come in. You will disturb no one,' says Walter and Beth can see little harm in accepting his offer, thinking that her mother's concern relates to the tainted company of Mistress Wade and her husband, not to her servants. Beth has always thought Walter a strange sort to be a serving man. He has an air about him of a person of some education. Their mother had heard the tale that he had fallen in the world some time ago, when his wife had died and he had lost ownership of his land.

They follow Walter into the passageway, which leads to the service rooms: the washhouse, the brewhouse, larder and thence to the kitchen. Mrs Denney, the cook is there. She is a short woman with a pleasant round face and a small nose like a cherry placed in the middle of it. She greets them with a friendly but knowing look and Beth is embarrassed that this woman will easily guess the reason for their mission. She does not wish to have her family branded paupers, though in such times as these it is not far from the truth.

'Oh bless the pair of them,' says Mistress Denney, looking at Ed and Jack with a smile on her broad face. 'Made out of the same jelly mould them two, God pardon me. Come on, lovely boys. You'd like a little something to chew on, wouldn't you? And you've brought your sister too. The Almighty spilled his bounties very generous on your family when it came to pretty looks, did He not?'

Beth blushes and sees Ed and Jack eyeing a large seed cake on a platter, sitting in the middle of the table. The woman waves her plump fingers at a narrow bench.

'Well take a seat all of you. Fancy a bit of me cake? Made this out of the last seeds and currants in the larder, so it's to be savoured, I tell you.'

Ed and Jack stare first at the cake then at Beth as though they need her verification that the thing is really there. Beth wishes she could have even one small slice of the cake to take back to her parents, but dare not ask. The woman cuts off five modest portions, including one for Walter too. He finds them all stools so they can take places around the table. There is no further talk for some moments, as this unexpected delight warrants their full attention.

'May as well eat while we can, that's what I say,' Mistress Denney says. 'Only the Almighty in Heaven knows whether we'll live or die in this terrible afflicted time.'

'It's a tasty good cake, thank you Mistress,' says Jack to which Beth and Ed add their agreement.

Walter finishes his piece, and chases some stray crumbs on his coat.

'Yes, it's a good cake, though it'll like be the last for a while, Mistress. If I was a man given to cursing, I'd spend a few oaths on these traitorous rogues that are stopping us having more of your cake,' he says.

Beth hears bitterness beneath his jocular manner.

'Well, there's nothing nobody can do about it now,' Mistress Denney says.

'We should've risen against them,' Walter says, 'not let them come marching in proud as the King himself.'

'Father says the Royalists might surrender, if they don't have any other forces to come and relieve them,' says Ed.

'That would be a fine thing,' Walter says, his voice hardening, 'but these colonels are not the surrendering sort. With the likes of Sir Charles Lucas commanding, there'll be little talk of surrender. He's a hard-headed one, as all his family are. Grand and proud they are and grasping too. It's because of them and his vile brother Sir John that I lost all I had in the world.'

Beth is surprised at Walter's sudden revelation, for they are not well acquainted with him. Perhaps the strife of the times is driving folk to speak what is in their minds more freely, to tell of their lives when peril threatens to end them. Mistress Denney has paused in her scrubbing of a cooking pot, her face alight with the prospect of hearing a good story, the enjoyment of a rich seam of gossip and the chance to share in it.

'And what happened to you at the hands of the Lucases, Walter?' she says boldly.

The man shows no reluctance to relate his story.

'Sir John Lucas, he that's the head of the family, took out a suit against me, claiming that my land was his, north of Colchester, round Aldham way. He paid his lawyers to steal my property, that had been my father's before me. He took away the common land too, so none of us village folk could graze our beasts. So I lost everything. My wife died of the grief of it and I became what you see before you.'

Beth is too struck with sadness and sympathy for the man to make a reply. Her brothers stare at him, wide-eyed. Mistress Denney, however, fills the brief silence which follows.

'Yes, but those gentlefolk the Lucases have had their crosses to bear too,' she says. 'The mother dead, then the daughter too and their fine house at St John's all stripped of rich things, plundered by the Parliament men and some of our own too.'

She leans forward, casts a look around the kitchen as though seeking out any phantom listeners, then whispers across the tabletop at them. 'I know someone in the town what's got two of them Lucases' silver platters taken from off their very dining table back in the time of the riots.'

Walter shrugs his shoulders and sighs, getting slowly to his feet.

'Well, I for one would rejoice to see the Royalists drummed out of the town and quite happy to see someone put a ball through Sir Charles Lucas's head. With luck it may happen some day soon and I'll shake the hand of the man that does it.'

Beth sees Walter's eyes darken, then as he turns to leave the table, he starts, as though caught in the midst of some mischief. She soon sees the reason for his reaction.

'Good morning, Missus,' Mistress Denney says in a squeak of surprise, as she like the rest of them, has not noticed Mistress Wade standing in the doorway of the kitchen.

She is dressed in a fine silk gown, though it looks crumpled in the skirt, and her face is flushed, her hair not yet properly dressed for the morning. She must have risen in a hurry, perhaps. But it is the look in her eyes that surprises Beth most of all, for they are staring as though she has received a truly unpleasant shock.

Chapter 9

5th & 6th July

'What ails you? You have food upon the table and will not eat.'

Thomas Wade has cleaned his plate and is staring at Katherine's meal which, though she has eaten little today, sickens her.

She glances at him quickly, seeing his face set in a sneer, knowing that she must satisfy him with a reply and compliance to his wishes.

'I am distracted to hear of the hardships of people in the town,' she says, before forcing herself to take a small piece of boiled beef into her mouth. This statement is in part the truth; an adequate explanation for the dullness of demeanour and lack of appetite that have provoked her husband's displeasure. She has been half attending to his talk at supper, his customary rant against the wickedness of the Royalist commanders, and exhortations for God to strike them down.

'Pray pardon me,' she says, not meeting his eyes and taking up a small piece of bread.

'I am astonished to find you so meek and mild,' he says in his familiar acid one, 'you who stood against the Royalist tyrants. Running alongside the lower sort in a rabble was reckless on your part, though not unexpected, given your tendencies. Your behaviour demeaned you, but at least the action of the mob led to a good outcome. Now you must work to repair your modesty, I think, as is fitting to your position as my wife.'

He pauses and peers at her again. 'You are not ailing you say? Then I urge you to eat up, for there are many in this town who would pay handsomely for the food on your plate.'

His sniping chafes her anger to life, but it must not be roused. She must forbear and control her tongue. She has need of intelligence from her husband, since the shock of what she overheard in the kitchen only a few days ago: the Sayer children and Mistress Denney listening to Walter's astonishing revelations. Her loyal servant, the kind man who has so often ministered to her and whom she trusts as a friend, was speaking with a different voice, of a former life, of hatred and desire for revenge. This was a strange and different man, a wronged man, whose spite would see Sir Charles Lucas dead. But she recognises too that Walter, like herself and Charles and every mortal man and woman on this earth have secret hidden selves, revealed only by chance or circumstance.

So now she knows of this, she must seek out from her husband anything he might reveal to her of a conspiracy by men of the town.

With an effort, she addresses her husband. 'Is there hope that the siege will be ended soon?'

'There is,' he says, glancing at her. 'There are those loyal townsmen who plan to take action, and when these plans come to fruition, we will have our town again and the gratitude and praise of the Lord General Fairfax, no doubt.'

Katherine is glad that her husband, now that she has distracted him sufficiently with this subject and her obedience to his will, is in a voluble mood. If she can remain cautious and guarded in her questions she might well learn more. She knows that he is vexed by the Lord General Fairfax's refusal of the cloth merchants' request to continue their trade and send their goods through the blockade to London. There is also the disturbing news that the Lord General thinks the townspeople to blame for their own plight, which her husband has taken as a sore affront to himself. As he has told her on countless occasions, he and a number of other allies stood against the Mayor and his associates, the key culprits in this weak and wicked decision to let the Royalist army enter the town.

'It will not be long before the Royalist rebels regret their refusal of terms for surrender. My Lord Fairfax could not have been more generous and merciful. Indeed, these traitors, some of them, may not have breath in their bodies to repent their faults. There are those in the town who may not wait for a settlement of words alone, and I salute them.'

'You mean that there is a plan to rise up against the commanders, to murder them?' says Katherine.

'It is not murder in war.'

'But those who would carry out such an act will surely risk their lives. They may fail in such a venture,' she says.

'Yes, but there are good fellows who will act according to our bidding. The deed will be done at one blow, one strike to send the godless to their master the devil himself,' he says. 'They will pay for the taking of our town.'

Katherine watches her husband's face, animated by an ugly grin. She must not risk angering him, but she cannot endure his self-satisfied spite.

'But does not vengeance belong to God?' she says.

The smile drops from his face. 'Do not speak of things of which you have no understanding. A woman's reason is weak, her passions too overcharged to debate such matters.'

'But I am guided by the scriptures,' she says, knowing that she is stoking his rage, but incapable of desisting.

He looks back at her with a sneering mouth. 'Hah! I see you cannot conquer your perversity for long. The men of this town are only doing their godly duty. You must study the scriptures with more attention. "Be ye come out, as against a thief, with swords and staves." Luke, chapter 22, verse 52. I advise you to humble yourself in prayer and trust to God's providence.'

He does not oblige her with any further information, beyond alluding to the decisive event that is to happen some time soon. So she, in order to maintain his triumphant mood, sinks back into quietness again, counting silently to herself the long seconds until she is able to escape his company. At last he permits her to quit the table and she hurries to her chamber, closing the door and throwing herself on the bed in relief. Lying there, she stares at the small window, seeing only the grey of the sky, knowing that there are still some hours of daylight left before the sunset.

Steady rain has started and she lies there, praying that Charles will come to her again. Will she soon see his shadow in the wet garden as she had only two nights ago? When she had seen his cloaked shape, she had crept down and out of the washhouse door and found him awaiting her in the soft black air. In the velvet darkness of the shack, she had used her other senses in place of sight. She ran her fingers over the features of his face, felt his lips, tasted them, the sharp brush of his moustache, grasped the curling locks of his hair, which fell about her face as he entered her, smelt the scent of his sweat, the salt of him, his breath in her ear and on her neck, his whispered words and his cry of pleasure.

Now as she lies on her bed, gazing at the window, willing him to come to her, she thinks of how she must tell him of the danger he faces. This thought is not comfortable: she is about to play the traitor to her town and act against her conscience. The only common bond between herself and her husband is the cause of Parliament against the King. Though she reviles all else about Thomas Wade, this cause is beyond her feelings for him and against a tyrant, a proud, fickle monarch who would rule according to his whim alone, without recourse to his Parliament. It is true that the regime of Parliament has not brought calm nor prosperity, but she, like many, still harbours some small hope that the men of the Parliament will find a way of ruling the King, or ruling without him.

She rises from the bed, filled with self disgust that she should discover herself a treacherous woman, a creature of no resolve who cannot stand firm to her beliefs, weak-brained, led by passion, all those accusations that her husband has laid upon her. She unlaces the bodice of her gown and loosens her hair. She cannot stop up her desire, no matter the torment of her wavering mind; she must watch for him. She crouches down by the window and waits, gazing out on the darkening garden.

Some hours later, still sitting stiff and numb below the window, she knows that he will not come. She drags herself to the bed, undresses and falls upon it, bereft that she will not feel his touch this night, but released for now at least, from the war between her urge to speak and her duty to stay silent.

Katherine is not rested when she awakens. Her nerves are torn and tender, her need to see Charles like a raw hurt that cannot be salved. She cannot go to the inn, *The King's Head,* where he is billeted, nor to the garrison camp in the castle grounds, unless of course she could devise some cause, some petition to the commander and somehow convey a message for Charles's eyes only. She is appalled again to dwell upon her treachery. She should take the true course of a loyal wife and citizen by harming, hampering or killing the Royalists' most able commander, now that she has his trust and intimate access to him. There have been so many chances. But to commit such an act she would have to cut off the part of her that loves Charles Lucas with all her soul.

She must think, she must think clearly of what else can be done. Even if she were able to take a warning message to him, she knows no details of the plot, how, when and where it is to be perpetrated, though her husband's remark that it will be done in one blast suggests a plan to make an explosion with gunpowder. The commanders, however, are always alert to the chance of uprisings and wary of the citizens, seeing their resentment growing daily alongside their privations. There are spies too amongst the townsfolk, she knows, those who adhere to the King's cause against the Parliament. Is she such a one herself? She no longer understands her allegiance, only that she must save her lover, if it is in her power to do so.

The Sayers may well know something of conspirators in the town, she reckons. There is also a young man living at their house these days, whom she has seen several times. He is striking and comely in his looks and Katherine, convinced he is not a native of the town is curious about his sudden appearance and purpose here. With new suspicions about conspiracies taking hold of her mind, she gets up, washes, dresses and goes down to the kitchen.

She finds Walter there, stacking logs by the hearth. He greets her with his customary mournful smile, telling her that the cook, Mistress Denney has gone out to try and buy some butter.

'She says she must ask you for more money on account of the cost of food,' he says. 'The shopmen are charging four times the old prices for cheese and butter.'

'Yes, I will ask my husband this evening. I will take an inventory of the larder and tell him the situation,' Katherine says, though her mind is working on matters other than butter.

'Walter, would you go to the Sayers' house and ask Beth to come to me, for I have some mending for her and I suppose she might help with washing the linen. But wait until my husband has gone.'

'Yes, Mistress,' Walter says. 'But he has gone from home already, very early. I can go now for Beth Sayer, if you wish.' He pauses at the doorway, 'And Mistress, I wondered if I should dig up some more of the plot and set some kale and cabbage seed for winter harvesting.'

'In the garden?' she says, sharply, shocked at her unguarded response, then lightening her tone. 'Yes, of course, that would be wise, to make provision for the winter, but dig only in the vegetable plot.'

'Yes, Mistress, but you could have a good patch out there for crops, with a bit of tending,' he says. 'There's many a young fellow of the town would dig up the whole plot for you for a shilling, to tame the wildness.'

Katherine shudders to think of the vigorous young man with whom she had coupled in that very place. 'Wildness? I like the wildness,' is all she manages to utter to her servant as he leaves her in the kitchen.

Beth Sayer, poor young woman, keen for any work, arrives very soon with Walter. Her cheeks have hollowed through lack of nourishment, though this renders her more handsome in

Katherine's view. Katherine would gladly have employed her as a housemaid, if it had not been for her husband. The risk is too great. The girl is too pretty, though she is not unprotected, as their last unfortunate maid had been. Katherine is not prepared, however, to risk the girl's virtue for her own comfort and convenience. She may have to take on some of the heavier household work herself. For now she has gathered together all the mending, her husband's linen, her own and some sheets and window draperies that need to be turned and hemmed.

'Good morning, Beth,' says Katherine, greeting her in the hallway. 'Come upstairs with me, will you? I have the work folded for you to take.'

The girl hesitates, but only for a moment as Katherine leads the way upstairs into an empty chamber where the linen is tied in a bundle on the bed. Beth reaches for the bulky parcel.

'It is not too heavy, I hope,' Katherine says.

'No, Mistress, not at all,' says Beth. 'I'm very grateful for the work. Thank you a thousand times.'

Questions hang on Katherine's lips, about what Beth might know of uprisings within the town, but she holds back for a moment, stricken with guilt that she should use this girl for her own traitorous ends.

'Do you have a guest in your house these days?' says Katherine, as casually as she can. 'Is he a Colchester man, a weaver, like your father?'

The girl blushes deeply. 'No Mistress, well yes. He was sick and we took him in. He's my mother's cousin. He is –.'

The girl hugs the bundle of linen to her and looks away, greatly discomfited, which stirs Katherine's curiosity the more.

'You seem troubled, Beth,' she says softly, hoping to draw the girl on to a fuller confession of a truth she has not uttered. She is hiding something. 'You can trust me. I'll say nothing if you have a secret that I have probed.'

Beth looks at her with wide eyes, blue and full of gratitude.

'Mistress, the young man is –, I think I love him. That is my secret.'

Katherine smiles with a pleasant feeling of relief at the sight of the earnest girl and the simplicity of her confession.

'And does he return your love?' she says.

Beth blushes again, a deeper red. 'Yes, I think he does.

Katherine is struck by the hopefulness of the girl's innocence and has the urge to embrace her. She resists such an action, however, as though it might spill the essence of her own corruption upon Beth's purity, as a stain upon clean linen. She is reassured, however, that there is nothing to suspect in this handsome young stranger, except that he might break Beth Sayer's heart.

They descend the stairs and in the hall Katherine grasps the girl's arm.

'Send your brothers to me,' she says, 'for your hands are full and I would give you a few provisions for your family.'

Katherine sees Beth Sayer's eyes fill. 'You are most generous, Mistress. I'll gladly do any task for you as recompense.'

Katherine is moved by her gratitude, but sickened by regret to think how she plans to woo these children with gifts of food and the provision of work, for her own purpose. What better messengers to the garrison than these two harmless boys, she thinks.

The twins, who are impossible to tell apart to Katherine's eyes, are brought to her in the hall by Walter. She bids them follow her into the kitchen where the cook is beating something in a bowl with a quick, vigorous arm.

'Mistress Denney, will you give the boys a slice of pie?' Katherine tells her.

'Gladly, Missus,' the cook replies. She pauses in her action and puts down the bowl, her cherry nose bobbing as she sets about the task, muttering happily to no one in particular, 'little treasures, ain't they.'

'You are Edward and Jack as I believe it,' says Katherine to the boys, 'and which is which?'

'I'm Jack and this is Ed. You can easily tell, for his breeches are dirtier than mine,' says one of the flaxen-haired boys.

'But you can always know him by the holes in his shirt,

Mistress,' says the other.

Katherine looks at the two gazing at her with blue, searching, half-knowing eyes. The sight hurts her like a stab to the breast, that she will never raise a son of her own.

'We'll gladly do chores for you, Mistress,' says one of the boys. 'We can do most things: cutting logs, gathering kindling, digging earth, carding wool, feeding hens –.'

His brother nudges him with his elbow to make him desist. 'Mistress'll tell us what she wants,' he says, with a considered nod.

Katherine smiles. 'Thank you. I have no jobs or errands at present, but will send for you if I have need.'

As she shows the two out bearing their bundles of foodstuffs, she notes that it has stopped raining and the sun has come out in a weak blue sky. She needs air, craves a walk, an escape from her own company. She bids the boys farewell and watches them scamper down the street the short distance to their home. They are pleased with her offerings, though these are little enough. The small parcel of food will hardly last the family more than a day. She returns indoors for her hat and a light shawl, for the day is not cold, in spite of the dampness. The summer has been miserable throughout and crops lie sodden, rotting in the fields beyond the town. Grain of all sorts would have been scant enough, even without the demands of their uninvited visitors and the siege.

She makes her way along the Culver Lane, past St Nicolas Church, then decides to walk some of the way along the main thoroughfare, for there is always news to be heard from an acquaintance or stallholder. She may even pass by the entrance to the castle too, where soldiers are to be seen at all times of the day. As she reaches the narrow lane, she hears a hum of noise. A man appears of a sudden, running, hurtling along so that he nearly collides with her and spills out a garbled stream of talk. 'There's been a fight. Attacking the town – cavalry beaten back. Take care, Mistress. You'd best take care.'

The man does not pause long enough to allow for further questioning and bolts down the lane and out of sight. Katherine hurries on to the High Street to find it alive with people, clustered on each side in groups. A few boys with handcarts have stopped their vehicles and are chattering together, pointing down the length of the street, towards the East Gate. Katherine pushes her way through, looking for someone she recognises, a bearer of news. Ahead she sees a short man, a haberdasher whose shop she frequents, standing with his wife.

'What's happening?' she says hastening towards the couple.

The man's wife clings to her husband's arm as though she thinks Katherine means to pluck him from her.

'Mistress Wade,' he says, 'some say the Royalist cavalry's all slaughtered and the Parliament's army's ready to attack.'

'What riddling rot. That's a lie, for a start,' says another man pushing past, jostling the shopkeeper as he goes. 'Royalists made a breakout at East Gate, that's all, but they were chased back pretty soon. Killed, dozens of them, damn their souls.' The man moves swiftly on towards some happenings that are drawing people further down the street.

'Don't go there, Mistress,' says the haberdasher. 'It's not safe. These cavaliers run wild when they're beaten.'

'But I must see,' Katherine says to the man and his wife. She pushes away into the crowd, past slower folk, keeping to the side of the roadway by the houses and shops, dodging around those who are standing on their thresholds, peering down the road for a sight of something significant, loath to leave the safety of their homes. A little distance ahead of her, Katherine catches sight of a man she knows to be one of the town Corporation. She calls after him and he turns to her, his face changing in recognition as she approaches.

'Can you tell me what's afoot? I've heard talk of an attack,' she says, breathless with hurrying.

The man takes her arm and leads her away from the press of people around them, to an empty spot at the front of a jettied dwelling house. His narrow lips are tight, his voice strained.

'Mistress, it is good and bad news together. The Royalists rode out this morning to attack the leaguer, to wreck the works outside

East Bridge, and to kill as many as they could of the Suffolk bands. But they were surprised. The Parliament men were ready and the New Model bettered them, beat them back and sent them fleeing. See, look, there where some are still coming in.'

The man is pointing along the Frere Street, inside the East Gate where Katherine can see a troop of horse moving slowly towards them.

'But that is good news, surely,' Katherine says, 'that the rebels are beaten, that they did not succeed.'

She forces herself to show the man a triumphant face, though in her mind she pictures the sight of Charles's bloodied body lying in the mud of a trench outside the town.

'Yes,' he says, close and confidential in his manner again, 'but they've taken two of our men, those who feigned loyalty to them and led them into Parliament's guns. They'll hang them as conspirators, though we of the Corporation will plead with the Lord of Norwich for clemency. The Mayor is to gather a party of us to petition the commander. Now you'd best go home, Mistress, for it's dangerous to be abroad.'

'Thank you for your good counsel,' says Katherine. 'I wish you well and pray for the delivery of these men and for our town.'

'Amen, Mistress. May God grant us mercy in our plight,' he says, leaving her side, to make his way across the street.

The rain is starting again, but Katherine does not move from the spot. She has no wish to go home in this uncertain state. She will go as far as the castle gate, fearing no danger now, only longing for some sign that Charles is alive. She starts walking slowly again with those around her forming a sluggishly moving crowd.

This event gives clear proof of conspiracies by the townsfolk, at which she should rejoice, but can find no heart to do so. The betrayal of the Royalist sally forth might be one of many plots by the secret band of townsmen. Another might be that of which her husband spoke, the striking of a decisive blow against the garrison commanders. A body of people is drawing near the castle gates, enticed by their curiosity and the desire to triumph at the sight of the defeated enemy.

Four abreast, the horsemen approach, then wheel into the castle roadway, their beasts at a slow and deliberate pace, their riders helmeted and armed, sashes of red across their chests. Though they hold themselves proudly in their saddles, their faces are downcast. Behind them comes a wagon drawn by two horses, bearing wounded, bloodied men, lying or sitting upon the jolting vehicle. Alongside this wagon, rides an officer, he too wearing the sash of his company, a helmet obscuring his features. His mount walks slowly at the side of the wagon carrying the wounded, and the rider is talking to one, a fallen comrade, as they go. Katherine watches, sees the rider's flick of the reins to urge his horse forward, the turn of his head, the form of his shoulders, his black hair and knows that he is safe. With a lighter heart, she takes the quickest route back to her house.

That afternoon, her husband returns home, bringing with him some of his fellow aldermen. Katherine hears their voices in the hall below from her chamber where she has retreated with a book, content with the solitude, her mind in a much calmer state, now that she has seen that Charles is alive and well. She rises from her chair, thinking it wise to go and greet her husband's associates, spurred now by the need to present a loyal face to everyone she encounters in the town. Walter is taking the men's hats and cloaks at the door as she descends the stairs to them.

'Good day, gentlemen,' she says, smiling graciously to the two senior aldermen, Masters Barrington and Furley.

They bow and Master Furley holds his eyes upon her, lingeringly, after the first brief courtesies. Her husband's face is his expressionless public one and she guesses that he is not displeased on this occasion by her manner and behaviour towards his important guests.

'Will you take refreshments here in the hall?' Katherine asks, glancing quickly at her husband.

'We will withdraw to the study,' he says, without looking at her. 'Walter may bring us a jug of wine.'

Glad to have acquitted herself in a suitably gracious

manner, she follows Walter to the kitchen, to lend a hand with the preparations for supper, aware that her housekeeping has been too slack recently.

'Do you need help with supper for our guests?' Katherine asks Mistress Denney.

'No Missus, they ain't staying for supper, so Walter says,' she replies. 'I can manage.'

Katherine returns upstairs, a little dismayed that others will not join them at their table this evening, a rare circumstance but one that at least compels her husband to adopt a more civil manner towards her. Her thoughts return to Charles and she wishes with all her mental force that he will come to her tonight. He will most likely be too occupied, however, with the aftermath of the fight, even wounded maybe. She must not hope too fervently, even though the disappointment of his absence will gnaw at her. In a sudden inspiration, she decides to prepare herself for him, for she needs to wash her hair and dress it properly. Her grey silk gown would be more becoming, though she smiles to herself at this ridiculous act of vanity for an encounter in a sordid wooden shack. Her gown will surely become stained or torn in that place and yet she wants to please him, to gratify him in any way she can. This is a novel sense of joy, a thrill unprecedented.

She goes down to the kitchen again to warm some water, then in her chamber spends an hour in the unfamiliar actions of enhancing and adorning her person, viewing herself finally in the looking glass and finding the image not unpleasing. Her hair, she rinses in rose petal scented water and as it is drying she binds it up to form smooth curls. Now she will only have to endure supper with her husband before retiring to her chamber. There she will watch by the window for the sun to drop in the sky, see the glow of red, the darkness descend, dreaming and wondering, readying her mind for delight or disappointment. She hears the visitors departing, their voices low and murmuring, the front door closing and her husband's heavy footsteps going along the passageway again.

She descends the staircase to the hall where Walter is laying out platters of meat, of brawn, boiled carrot and mutton pie, plain but palatable food, better than many in the town will enjoy that day. He turns and his face jolts with surprise, his hand knocking over a cup.

'Pardon me, Mistress,' he says and Katherine sees that he is colouring, though he bends his head quickly to the table again.

'Would you call my husband for supper, Walter?' she says, wondering at the cause of her serving man's discomfiture. Has he heard something of her liaison with Charles? It surely could not be. This thought quickens her pulse, unsettles her.

When Thomas Wade enters the hall, some moments later, Katherine manages to greet him with her practised bland expression, seeing a twitch of his mouth as he stares back at her. Under his gaze, she feels a blush heat her face and regrets bitterly her vain practices of the afternoon upon her appearance. He makes no remark, however, and nods that she should take her place at table. Her husband gives thanks to God for His bounties, then helps himself to several pieces of the fare.

'You are going out somewhere?' he says, without looking at her.

'No.'

'Why then do you dress as a whore?'

Katherine's throat tightens as she tries to hold a steady gaze, somewhere beyond her husband's head.

'I ask you why you have prepared yourself for some man's consumption,' he says, this time looking up at her.

She knows by his look that her silence will anger him before too long.

'I simply wish to make myself more presentable, as befits my position as your wife,' she says in a deliberate voice.

'Ah, so you have beautified yourself for me?' She sees the twist of his mouth, the shine of grease from the meat upon his lips.

She cannot look at him again and reaches for a piece of pie, though the thought of eating it turns her stomach.

'Or is it for some other fortunate fellow?'

She must not flinch, not betray with a single flicker of the eye, nor trembling finger her fragile state of mind. She will not look at him but must speak her lie with the certainty of a truth.

'No, it is not,' she says.

His knife clinks against the pewter plate and she reaches her hand for the cup of ale before her. Her wrist looks thin and white as her fingers close around the cup with the deliberation of a blind person who must see with their touch. She sips at the ale and in her husband's continuing silence, breathes again. He suddenly clears his throat and slices into the piece of pie in front of him.

'Well, 'tis glorious news about this humiliation of the cavaliers,' he says in a voice larded with gloating. 'Colonel Lucas and his cavalry routed. What a good piece of work. They must surely see now that their cause is hopeless, though they would have us believe that a great force is marching from Scotland to relieve them. This is all bluster. These are the messages of the desperate.'

'But what of the townsmen who were taken, those who were agents of the Parliament's army?' Katherine says.

'Yes, brave fellows. It is most unfortunate. The Lord of Norwich will hang them, no doubt.'

'But will you not plead on their behalf for clemency?' she says, surprised that he makes no mention of this.

He looks at her and nods. 'Aye, we of the Corporation will endeavour to save them, but we've little power in military matters.' He pauses, narrowing his eyes. '*You* may do better. What if I loose you to the generals to try your powers of persuasion again? You might well beguile the whole troop of them.'

She bites her lip and averts her eyes from him, for she cannot endure the sight of his smile.

'You were much admired today, by my visitors,' he says. 'I was praised for the charm of my wife, her readiness to please. Master Furley congratulated me as a fortunate man to have such a jewel of a wife. What do you think of such opinions?'

Katherine lifts her eyes to him, her fear waning now, heated by her loathing.

'What would you have me say?' Her voice is brittle.

'Ah, a return of your boldness, I see, your true self. I was lacking your spiteful tongue and amazed by this show of elegance before me. You caused me to wonder what kind of a witch I have for a wife, who can transform herself with such ease.'

'I should like to retire now,' she says, feeling the bile rise in her throat. 'I am tired. Will you please permit me?'

'Of course,' he says, staring hard at her. 'Rest well.'

She rises from her seat and bows her head to him, astonished that he should agree so readily, but holding the feeling tight within her until she is well clear of him. She rises, steps soundlessly across the floor to the stairs, which she mounts, breathing slowly and evenly until she reaches her chamber. Safe inside, she falls upon the bed, feeling a laugh rising inside her, her mouth smiling to think of another meeting with Charles. She is filled with the ecstasy of anticipation, fired by the urgency of saving him from the dangers that threaten him. She goes to the window, sits upon a stool and gazes out at the sky, hearing sounds coming faintly from the hall: the clatter of eating irons, the scrape of a chair, a heavy tread upon the stairs.

When the latch of her door clicks, her heart jars in her chest. It is not her husband's practice any more to come to her chamber. They have not lain together for more than two years, she some years before this having relinquished her last hopes of ever bearing a child. When only the law and their mutual loathing bound them together, she was relieved that he sought his body's gratification elsewhere, as she herself had done.

'Yes, you are changed,' he says. 'And I am curious to try this new wife, so full of mettle and so much admired by others.' His eyes are unblinking.

She is seized by a choking panic. 'I told you. I am tired. I cannot–.'

'You are my wife,' he says, closing the door behind him, turning the key and placing it in the pocket of his coat.

'Please,' she says, her courage flooding from her as blood from a cut vein. Where is her anger now when she has need of it?

He comes across the room to where she is standing beside the window, with her head bowed, waiting for what he is about to do to her, thinking that this is the right course, to stop his questioning, to quell his suspicion that she has a lover. Anything, she thinks to make him go away. He is beside her now. She hears his breathing, smells his greasy breath, feels her gorge rise as he clutches her breast, realising that these last years his only touch has been to strike her. This way perhaps, he will leave her face unmarked.

'Come, whore,' he says, snatching her by the back of her neck, pulling her to him then forcing her to the floor upon her knees before him, while he tugs at his breeches with his other hand.

She struggles, filled with disgust, twisting her neck, writhing and pulling away from him, breaking free for a few brief seconds to crawl on hands and knees like a dog, but he is on top of her then, punching the side of her face with his fist, hauling her head up by her hair, ripping the skirt of her gown from her. She clenches her jaw, clamps her eyes shut in an effort to stop off her senses, to gag the scream that threatens to burst from her throat as his force drives into her again and again.

She is not sure how long she has been lying with her cheek pressed against the boards, but slowly becomes aware of the silence of the room, the rawness of the pain and sticky aftermath between her legs. She hauls herself to her feet, then to a chair by her dressing table. There is little blood on her face this time. She dabs her cheek with a cloth, feeling the swelling of a bruise, but at least she is not cut. Her back aches and her gown is badly torn, ruined, though this causes her little anguish, for it was a foolish action on her part, which only drew her husband's attention and thus brought punishment upon herself. She wraps a shawl around her and smooths her hair. With some sense of calm restored, though her face and body smart from the attack, she recalls the urgent action she must take, now that her longed for encounter with Charles will not take place.

She tries the door to her chamber and finds it, to her surprise, unlocked, listens for some moments for any sign of her husband's presence and then risks venturing forth and down the stairs to find Walter. She gains the kitchen safely and discovers her servant there, half-asleep by the fireside. Her hand upon his arm arouses him suddenly and he jumps up, embarrassed, catching sight of her face.

'Mistress, are you hurt? Let me help you,' he says, his expression tense with anguish, reaching a hand towards her.

'No Walter. I am all right.' Her voice is steady, her false story clear in her mind.

'I need you to bring me a quill, ink and paper, for I have to write a letter. I have a notion to write to my aunt in Norfolk.'

His hand drops to his side and he stares at her, a penetrating look that makes her tremble, almost pierces through her feigning.

'You will find these things in my husband's study,' she tells him briskly.

'Of course, Mistress,' Walter says, his voice breaking. 'The master has gone out this evening. I can bring them to you straight.' Katherine sees that his eyes are full. 'Mistress, how can you bear it?'

She turns from him quickly, knowing that in her weakness she could too readily fall into his arms, were he to offer more sympathy and comfort.

'And Walter, will you seek out the Sayer boys and ask them to come to me, as I have an errand for them. Tomorrow morning early, without fail.'

Chapter 10

15th July

In the carpenter's workshop, a rough oblong timber-framed barn of a place, Tobias puts on his helmet. He and three other men are about to become loyal soldiers in Captain Heath's company of engineers, and brave Royalists all.

'Where did you come by these?' says a small wiry man, by the name of John. He is addressing Barty Phillips, the former gunner upon whose knowledge and expertise this venture depends, and in whose workshed they are now assembled.

Barty, with a satisfied intake of breath, hands John a helmet.

'Did some business with some of the Royalist lads. Nice, ain't they? Got the money off one of the aldermen and gave them a tidy price for these, and to keep their mouths shut. Didn't seem much vexed by it.'

Barty Phillips has a well-worn face, pitted with the smallpox, but his eyes are a youthful pale blue and it is difficult to guess his age.

'But Master Waterman here,' Barty continues, nodding at Tobias, still on the topic of infantry helmets, 'he's got his own, from the New Model Army no less, lads. Me, I reckon, I'm more Old Model.'

'What?' says the third man, also named John but of a heavier build and a slower brain. 'You in the New Model? What you doing in the town?'

Tobias feels sheepish as the centre of the men's attention.

'Yes, our company came in with the storming of the town, more than a month ago, it must be,' he says. 'I was cut up badly and the Sayers took me in.'

Barty sighs heavily. 'Brave lads, all them that was cut down by the bastards.'

He pauses for a moment of reverent silence, then resumes in a purposeful tone.

'Well, we're mighty pleased and gratified to have you with us, Tobe. Right, are you ready, men? This is the story. We're collecting two kegs of powder, twenty grenadoes, three muskets and fuses for Captain Heath of Colonel Farre's engineers. Got it, eh?'

They all nod. Tobias sees the same solid confidence in this hardened soldier that he had encountered in his old sergeant, he who had almost certainly met his fate in this town, trampled underfoot by cavalry on the main street, thrown into a ditch somewhere, along with his friend and comrade George and countless others. Thinking of this renews Tobias's resolve and he grips the handle of the cart ready to roll it out. Barty pushes open the doors of his workshop and big John and Tobias rumble the cart over the ground into the alley outside.

'Reckon it looks like an army waggon?' big John asks.

'Aye, near enough. It'll pass muster,' says Barty, stepping forward with a confident limp in front of them, the smaller John behind. Tobias has started sweating already and a pulse beats annoyingly at his temple, he wondering what state of fear and excitement will be provoked in him once they have reached the castle. They have not discussed their strategy for dealing with a disaster, such as their unmasking as frauds, most likely because they expect to be cut down where they stand or shot through, if their counterfeit ploy fails.

The morning sky is misty grey with the threat of more rain, but Tobias sees that Barty has furnished the wagon with a cover of waxed cloth to protect the powder. For a moment, Tobias imagines the best possible outcome of their daring feat: the successful theft of the powder and arms, a skilful and furtive attack upon the Royalist commanders, forcing their surrender, the triumphant freeing of the town by Lord General Fairfax's troops, his own promotion to sergeant with more pay. Then he would be embraced as a hero by the Sayers, as a fit husband for Beth. He would seek a discharge from the army, claiming his arrears of pay, settle here in this fine town of Colchester, taking up his work as a gardener in the gardens of prosperous folk in the suburbs. The sound of the cart wheels grinding over the cobbles of the High Street shakes all such foolish indulgence and vanity from his head, however. His life and his future, he knows, are in the hands of God.

A number of townsfolk are on the street and Tobias and his companions keep their heads down as they proceed, though Barty's occasional nod to an acquaintance shows that he is recognised. They are soon in sight of the entrance to the castle yard and Tobias feels something clutch at his heart. At the gates they pause, encountering another wagon coming out of the place, laden with spades, tools and digging equipment. Barty salutes the driver with a hearty 'Good day' and is greeted with a similar show of camaraderie.

Before the castle is a wide yard, the building itself a great solid hulk, with massy but crumbling walls constructed of ancient bricks, stone, flints and mortar, square towers at each corner and the main entrance, a handsome arch of stone. Around the yard are huts and shacks, some old, some built by the Royalists since their arrival. There are no guns visible above on the crumbling battlements and the place has the air of a ruin; its days as a fortress of defence are long gone. Beyond the yard, the remains of stone outworks protrude from clumps of weeds. The ground itself is well churned by the passage of many vehicles, horses and men. A company of pikemen is exercising in a tight squad, their captain shouting orders, in an area of open space on the east side.

Tobias notices that his legs have started to shake as they enter more deeply into this busy network of military activity. Each shouted command bursts into his ears, threatening to bestir his body to obey the movements of the infantrymen's drill. They trundle on without drawing the unwanted attention of anyone, past the entrance, its oak door lying open, with four guards on duty outside. Two officers are emerging from the entrance, animated in talk and striding out purposefully. One stops for a moment's glance in their direction and then continues on his way.

'God preserve us,' mutters big John on Tobias's right. Barty's head still bobs along in front as they round the east wall of the castle. Then he turns suddenly and, with a nod to the left, indicates the direction of the arsenal store. It is an old timbered building, a carthouse or stable in peacetime, Tobias assumes. Outside its wide doorway is a group of four soldiers, two of whom are arguing loudly with each other, their pikes leaning against the wall of the building. There is no other traffic nearby, though there are noises of scraping and banging within. Tobias hears Barty muttering to himself as they draw nearer still, then he turns to them, his face a determined smile.

'Right boys, keep your heads. Let me speak up for us.'

They push on, until they are a within twenty paces of the two quarrelling soldiers and their comrades.

'You whoreson bastardly dog,' says one, swinging a fist at the other who dodges back out of range, grinning. 'You'd steal the cherries from a rich man's sick, you would.'

'Stop your snivelling,' says the other with a flick of the hand in his antagonist's face. The two onlookers watch the proceedings with amused faces.

The first soldier aims another off-target punch at his opponent, at which point Barty steps forward, beckoning Tobias and the others to pull the cart up behind.

'What's all this?' says Barty cheerily. 'You'd not hurt a brother in arms, surely.'

Tobias thinks this a risky strategy, but it has the effect of stopping the imminent conflict and the incompetent fist fighter's further humiliation.

The four soldiers look at Barty, then take in the rest of them too, along with the cart.

'Brother in arms?' says the belligerent soldier. 'Him? I'd

sooner march alongside the devil himself than that poxy thief.'

'And what's the nature of his crime against you?' Barty says in a tone fit for a magistrate.

'Stole all my poxy ration, dirty blackguard.'

The smiling soldier shrugs his shoulders. 'I swear I never stole any of your pukesome fare,' he says. 'Dogs must have got it.'

The two onlookers shake their heads. 'Stick a boot in your hole and be done,' says one. 'We've none of us got enough grub. Just have to find us a bit of extra somewhere, that's all.'

This more peaceable spectator takes a step towards Barty. 'What company are you?' he says. 'And what's your rations?'

Barty answers with casual confidence. 'We're with Captain Heath's company of foot, Colonel Farre's regiment, and we're on miserable poor rations too. Wouldn't feed a mouse.'

'Aye,' says the soldier, 'but do you get six ounces of rye bread or nine ounces? I've heard tell some gets eight ounces and others gets seven some days, and five on others and some gets oat bread instead.'

Barty considers for a moment. 'Well, it all depends,' he says hedging.

'Captain says all foot gets the same and so it should be six ounces of rye bread, for that'll fill you up better that wheat bread. What did you say you gets?' says the other spectating soldier.

This is not a conversation Tobias and his fellow conspirators have anticipated and the first questioning soldier continues, fired by his search for justice. 'What about salt fish? Do you get any salt fish? I've heard some of the lucky bastards in Lucas's regiment had salt beef last week.'

'Don't know about that,' says Barty, 'all I know is I'd like to quit this miserable town and go home.'

'Amen and amen to that,' says the aggrieved soldier, having lowered his fists, but still glowering at his adversary.

'So we're ordered to pick up two kegs of powder, shot and a dozen fuses for Captain Heath,' says Barty reciting the list in his comfortably casual manner.

The soldier shakes his head with a sharp intake of breath.

'Can't do it, friend. New orders. Just come through today from the Master of Ordnance. Any men wanting arms or powder has to be told to his face direct. We ain't allowed to give out nothing. But he's here, the Master. He's in there.'

The soldier indicates the arsenal store behind him and Tobias feels his heart thudding and his legs starting to shake again. Half of his will would have him run for freedom, but his other dutiful half keeps him locked into this present danger, growing more acute in the light of this new obstacle.

'He's in there doing his inventorying,' says the informative soldier. 'Some say we've enough powder to blow the whole of Fairfax's army to Hell and others reckon we'll run short in a week. Got to keep it safe from the thieving townsfolk too. Wait here, I'll get the Master for you now.'

Barty nods his thanks to the man who turns and disappears inside the storehouse.

'What's it like down there on the south wall?' asks the other waiting soldier. The two enemies having parted now, are leaning against the wall of the building, idly scratching at fleas in their clothing.

Barty has no time to make reply. A man has appeared in the entrance of the building, the said Master of Ordnance. The small John gulps and the big one shifts on his feet. Tobias stares down at his hand, which is still gripping the handle of the cart tightly, his knuckles white.

The officer who appears is a short stocky individual with a square head and small but enquiring eyes. These eyes scan them all for a moment, then he folds his arms and addresses Barty.

'Who's your captain that's ordered powder and shot?' he says, his voice as blunt as his figure.

Barty stands to attention and answers without hesitation.

'Captain Heath of Colonel Farre's regiment, sir,'

The Master of Ordnance stares and his mouth becomes a hard narrow line. He looks first at Barty then at each one of them in turn, as a cattle trader viewing stock for purchase. Then he examines the cart with knowing eyes.

'That's mighty strange,' he says, 'indeed it is, for Captain Heath lies sick of the flux in his billet, all this last week. I know that as certain as the sun will rise tomorrow in the sky. His company's near all gone down with it too. What trickery is this?'

They need no signal from Barty to run and at least have a start on the soldiers. But the alarm is soon noised in every corner, even with the frantic thumping of a drum from a passing drummer boy who sees them bolting away. Tobias turns and pelts after the others, across the open space of yard towards a field full of tents to the north of the castle. He hears shouts behind him, ordering musket fire and sees the hopeless impossibility of escape in this place full of armed, alert and hostile men, but runs as he has never run in his life. The maze of the army camp is ahead of them: huts, shelters, tents and wagons with narrow muddy paths between. They will be brought down in a matter of moments. The two Johns run together and Tobias sees them fall together too, shots blasting their bodies in perfect unison. Barty swerves past a half dressed soldier who's picked up his pike at the sight of the fugitives and the sound of the warning cries. Tobias leaps over a small camp fire at the mouth of one of the tents and miraculously dodges grabbing hands and the swing of a club. There is a yell of triumph from behind and he knows that Barty must have been felled. The sound of shot whistles past his ear, but he has made it as far as the followers' camp and is still on his legs and running.

Taking a crazed zig zag route through the narrow tracks between tents and wagons, he sees ahead a broken hedge marking the boundary into another piece of ground. He scrambles over into an area of scrubby bushes, clumps of trees and the walls of ruined church buildings, with window holes like empty eyes. Glad of some cover, he plunges on, ducking down behind a low ridge of ancient wall, seeing the land sloping down towards a river which he glimpses on the other side of the town wall. The wall has been newly patched and buttressed with earth, and high on its eastern corner is an angled bastion. Tobias can just make out a gun crew of four men on top, occupied with their equipment, arguing among themselves, astonishingly oblivious to the shouts of his pursuers, which he hears behind him. The drumming has ceased however. Tobias's chest heaves painfully as he prepares himself to run again. From here he sees that the wall is only a matter of a hundred paces distant. He can reach it, but how can he scale it without being seen?

Along the whole length of the wall, however, Tobias can see only one soldier on guard, and this man has his back turned, relieving himself against the wall, his pike leaning close by. Tobias, leaps to his feet, propels himself forward, his body driven by the animal urge to preserve his life. He plunges down the slope, hurls himself on to the man's back, pulling him to the ground, wresting the dagger from his belt. The soldier, a strong and lithe fellow, breaks free, and Tobias finds himself sprawling in the mud. The soldier lunges for his pike, grabbing, turning and charging at Tobias in a well-drilled sequence of moves. Tobias feels the spike jab, pull and rip his coat at the shoulder as he ducks to avoid it, charging low with the stolen dagger. He strikes out at his assailant's legs, hearing a howl of pain as the blade meets flesh. The man falls heavily and Tobias, seizing the fallen pike, drives it into the mud at the foot of the wall and launches himself at the wall with shots and yells bursting behind him. His frantic feet, one now shoeless, scramble on the rough surface and he grapples to pull himself over the top, heaving his body and falling headfirst down on to the other side. He lands in a soft cushion of sodden mud at the foot of the wall, winded and stunned by his fall. The soaking sponginess has saved him from broken bones and in a moment he has recovered his sight enough to see the shape of the river ahead, only twenty paces from him.

He drags his limbs from the sucking mire, hauls his body towards the river and staggers to the bank, plunging into the water, sinking down and down, his mouth, nose, eyes filling with the cold green of it. Underneath, in the pressing cloud of the water, his legs flail, slipping on the slimy bottom, until his head breaks the surface again and he sees the other bank, so near, only a reach away. He plunges again, kicking hard with his legs towards a long tuft of grassy stuff on the bank and grasps the rough rope of it in his hand and pulls. His body slides under a forest of tall reeds into a hollow in the riverbank. He gulps, coughs, gasps, mouthing the air.

The fronds of the reeds hang over him and he turns, still submerged to his neck in the water, to look back upon the town. He can see no sign of his pursuers, nor hear any firing of weapons from the walls. The roofs, church towers and chimneys cluster on the rising ridge, looking comfortable and compact in their enclosure, almost proud, he thinks. He stays sunk in the water, for some time, giving thanks to God for preserving his life, then turns back to the bank and, pulling on the reeds, clambers with great difficulty out of the water, to fall on his belly on to the marshy earth. He crawls forward, without the strength to rise to his feet and comes to a tract of open land, of churned brown mud. Ahead, at a distance of only about fifty paces, stands a tall wooden palisade, which juts out sharply towards him and above this fence, the barrels of two guns point towards the town, with the heads of men visible behind parapets. He rises to his feet without any thought for the wisdom of this move and staggers towards the fort. A shout, then a shot explodes in the air and he feels the draught of a ball fly past his head. 'Oh God in Heaven,' he murmurs. 'Let me not meet my end here, in this way.'

He raises his arms and calls out as loudly as his feeble breath will allow.

'Friend. Friend. Hold your fire.'

Colonel Rainsborough's captain of foot does not believe Tobias's story, as he, exhausted and gabbling incoherently can only give a poor account of himself at the gateway to the fort. He falls to his knees and is dragged into a pen within the yard where he is shackled hand and foot. The fenced space contains about twenty prisoners of war, forlorn silent men, slumped against the wall of timber, earth and grassy sods. Tobias rallies himself sufficiently to make a final plea, before the captain leaves him.

'Sir, I'm in Captain Cox's company of foot, Colonel Needham's regiment. We were following up Colonel Barkstead's attack on the town. Got inside, but the cavalry were waiting and muskets and we –. I took some hurts in the fight.'

'You'll wait here upon the Colonel's pleasure,' says the captain walking away.

Tobias lies back against the damp wall of earth among the enemy prisoners, shivering and exhausted. His companions offer him no animosity, however, they seeming as weak and forlorn as he. The enclosure is within a yard surrounded by earth ramparts on all sides, beyond which is a wooden palisade enclosing the fort. There is a range of low timber buildings on one side of the yard and at the main entrance gate, a drawbridge over a trench. He watches a party of soldiers carrying spades and mattocks gathering in the yard, ready to dig more trenches and earth works, Tobias supposes. He listens to the familiar mix of noise of garrisoned troops, hears the gate swing open and sees some officers on horseback enter, followed by a troop of dragoons.

The commander, in the vanguard, on a fine white horse, is clearly a man of importance, flanked by his ensign wielding his blue colours, along with a number of other officers. This general, for such Tobias assumes him to be, is being greeted by another high officer who calls out an order sharply and a soldier comes with a mounting block. The rider is helped to dismount, moving with difficulty as one with a bad leg wound. The two commanders proceed side by side, followed by their lesser officers, towards one of the buildings in the yard.

Tobias slumps down again, wondering miserably what is to become of him now. He is alive, barely, having failed in an ill-fated attempt to fulfil his duty. To die in an heroic mission would at least have given his dead name a place in the hearts of others, but now he is lying a prisoner of his own side, with little possibility of redeeming himself, unless his fortunes change and someone comes to believe his story. Then he thinks of Beth, girlish tears come to his eyes. He had not even bidden her a loving farewell or sworn his devotion to her in life and death and now, most likely, he will never see her again.

It had all started so well, with Barty their assured and capable leader. The guards would have been happy to issue their powder and shot, had it not been for their new orders and the Master of Ordnance. The man had seemed almost to have expected them, to have been on the lookout, to have anticipated the theft of the powder. But what does it matter now? Tobias's sorrow at the terrible end of his co-conspirators floods over him, as the green river water had done over his head.

Someone is kicking Tobias's leg and he jolts awake from an uncomfortable half-doze, to find the captain who had imprisoned him standing above him again.

'Get up. You're called for, on the double,' he says.

'Called for?' Tobias says, rising painfully, struck with the horrible possibility that he might be bound for the hangman's rope.

'Colonel Rainsborough and the Lord General Fairfax, who do you think?' says the captain, unlocking his shackles. 'Dear God, you stink.'

Tobias is stunned, unsure if he has heard aright, that he is to come before the great Lord General Thomas Fairfax himself. Can it be that his story is believed? But why does the commander wish to see a common soldier like himself? He has heard that the Lord General shows great care for his men, ensures their regular pay and pensions for those injured in the call of duty. As he stumbles out of the enclosure and across to the other side of the yard to the wooden building, he is not struck nor pushed by the captain or the soldier on his other hand, though his wrists are still in their shackles. He limps on feet blistered and sore, as his shoes are lost. He is smeared with mud and ashamed that he should be brought to the presence of the Lord General in such a state.

They enter a bare room with only a table and a few chairs as furnishings. About six officers are present in the room, some standing, and others at a table, one writing on a paper in front of him. On one chair sits the Lord General, Tobias supposes, with a heavily bandaged leg resting upon a box. Tobias remembers hearing that he is dogged with ill health, gout and fevers but he endures great pain to command his troops, marching alongside them sometimes and not sparing himself any hardships. At his side sits the other commander, a proud looking gentleman with stern eyes, who might be Colonel Rainsborough. Lord Fairfax is dark of complexion, as legend has it and black haired. His face bears the lines of someone with a pain that tugs at him constantly. His expression is in no way harsh, however, with a sadness about his eyes.

Tobias is unsure whether to bow or kneel to the great general but does the former, hoping that this and his abject state will show courtesy and humility enough.

'Tell me your name and your regiment, man and how you came to enlist,' says the Lord General. His manner and voice are not imperious, but more in the style of a kindly master to his servant.

Tobias gives his details and an account of his military experience up until the attempted storming of the town. The Lord General nods.

'And how did you escape with your life, when most of your company perished in the battle?' he says but with no hint of censure.

'By God's good grace, my Lord, I was taken in and tended by a kind and loyal family. My hurts took some time to heal.'

The Lord General's gaze never leaves Tobias's face as he explains his part in the failed plot by the townsmen against the enemy commanders.

'I see,' says Lord Fairfax, 'it seems that God in his wisdom has spared you to fight another day and you seem to me a clear-headed, loyal and honest fellow. Now tell me of the state of the town from your time there. We have spies and scouts of course, but we must know all of what happens there.'

Tobias, startled by the Lord General's praise, speaks as he is bidden.

'The townsfolk, the poorer sort, are suffering much hardship. They have little flour left, for the supplies are commandeered for the rebel garrison. Prices are high, out of reach for most. It seems that the town authorities did not make good provision before the town was cut off. But the people are hopeful, my Lord, for succour from our forces and mercy from yourself. They are loyal to Parliament.' Tobias hears a note of pleading edge into his voice.

Colonel Rainsborough snorts at Tobias's final comment and scratches his beard.

'The townspeople have brought these ills upon themselves,' he says. 'They must suffer the consequences of their folly and their disloyalty.'

Tobias does not dare to dispute the colonel's statement, though it fills him with dismay.

'I see that you are tender towards these people, Master Waterman,' says Lord General Fairfax, 'but I regret that in times of war, desperate measures must be taken. I pity their plight, but pity will not help us to victory. What I need to know of you, is whether, now that your company is no more, you would go back into the town, as an agent to gather intelligence. You have spent time there and have a refuge with this family, have you not?'

Tobias nods, thinking at once of Beth and the delight of seeing her again.

'You can pass as a townsman and provide us with useful information that may help bring this conflict to a speedier end. This is my earnest wish, as I warrant it is yours. Your actions may hasten the end of the townspeople's suffering and bring the rebels to surrender.'

Tobias is unsure whether this is a request or an order, but hesitates only for a brief moment.

'If you deem me fit for such work, my Lord,' he says, 'I will gladly serve you and the cause.'

'Good,' says Lord Fairfax shifting his foot on its rest. 'May your good fortune continue and God's protection until we meet again.'

Then the Lord General turns to the captain, Tobias's former gaoler.

'See to this man and when he is in the state of a respectable townsman, bring him back here to Colonel Rainsborough for his orders.'

Chapter 11

20th July

Jack can't sleep for thinking about the last mouthful he'd eaten of Mistress Wade's mutton pie. Perhaps if he lies here and imagines it very hard again, its rich smell and its luscious onion savour, this might trick his belly, but he knows that it won't. And when he closes his eyes to see things in his mind, it makes him think about Tobias, which causes his lip to quiver if he does it for too long. So he opens his eyes again in the darkness and kicks Ed, for he hates being awake alone, forlorn and in dread of how things have become. Everyone is woeful and famished, angry and spiteful to each other and full of cursing the Royalists and the Parliament both.

Beth's bed on the landing is empty. She is downstairs still, spinning more and more woollen yarn, though there is no use for it, but she says she can't sleep and might as well spin until she drops down dead. Jack hates to hear her talk so, but he knows it's because she's mourning for Tobias. She has not smiled since he went from them and was killed. It had been a secret, Tobias's mission, but they knew that he and some other men were intent on an act against the Royalist commanders. No one would tell Jack and Ed what exactly had come to pass in the end, when it had all gone awry, beyond saying that some traitorous rogue in the town must have informed against them. The men were all shot down as they fled in the castle yard. Jack feels the tears coming again, though he squeezes his eyelids tight, for he wants Tobias to be alive again, so badly, more than he wants any mutton pie, no matter how delicious. He weeps a little, very quietly, but Ed is still asleep and will not hear.

Then Beth is shaking him awake, so it must be morning. She's saying that they must come with her foraging in Blackfriars.

'Get dressed and be quick,' she says. 'We must go to see if there's anything on the bushes. Though the blackberries are still green, they may boil to make a posset, and there may be some hips too.'

Jack sits up and rubs his eyes, seeing Ed already dressed and standing at the top of the stairs. Beth's face, even in the gloom, looks thin and her eyes are darker, hollow and sad. He wishes he could cheer her, but doesn't know how any more. He slides out of bed and puts on his breeches, stockings and shoes then follows his brother downstairs, hearing Father coughing from his chamber, hoping that today perhaps he might rise from his bed. Mother is in the kitchen, bending over the fire, stirring a pot into which she is sprinkling some oats. She looks up at Jack and Ed as they try not to clatter too loudly down the stairs.

'You'll go with Beth this morning,' she says in a voice, laden and heavy, as though she has hardly the strength to speak. Mother did not weep when she heard about Tobias; she only bewails the fact that they have nothing in the larder to eat. She doesn't chide them any more and spends her time trying to persuade Father to take such food as they can find for him, that they can beg or gather. Father is thin like a stick and grey in the face these days.

'We'll visit Mistress Wade first before we go to seek out berries,' Beth says, as she puts on her shoes and picks up a basket. 'She may have work or messages to run.'

Mother looks at her and nods without saying a word.

Jack hopes that Mistress Wade will have another message for them to deliver and perhaps another two pence to pay them, like last time. He and Ed had taken a message last week, a special secret message, to the rebel garrison camp at the castle. Jack is still puzzled about it and cannot fathom the reason and purpose of what she had them do, but Mother had kissed them when they gave her the money and Jack would gladly carry a message again, if it meant they would have more to eat. That time it had been quite late in the evening when Mistress Wade's servant, Walter, had come to their house telling him and Ed that his mistress wanted to see them for a small job of work the next day.

This time, Walter had taken them into the hall of the Wade's house, grand and spacious like no chamber Jack had ever been in, except the church, with a high beamed ceiling and a huge fireplace at the end. They had gone up the staircase of dark wood, with carved balustrades, which turned a corner and went up again. There were paintings in golden frames on the walls. Walter had knocked on the second door on the right and told them to go in. It was almost dark inside the room and Mistress Wade was sitting on a chair in the corner, so that Jack could hardly see her face at all. He didn't like it in the room and neither did Ed, as he reached for Jack's hand, which he only did when he was very frightened indeed.

'I want you to do something very important for me,' she said. Her voice was soft and quiet, as though she were poorly or weak and Jack stopped being frightened. 'You must take this letter and give it to the soldier, the sentry who is standing by the gate to the castle. Do you understand?'

Jack and Ed nodded together and both said yes, but not very loud.

'You must tell no one of this, not Walter, not your father or mother or Beth or the young man who is living with you. You must swear to me that you will obey my instructions and I will reward you well. And you must run away as soon as it is delivered. You must not dally and be waylaid or questioned about where it has come from. Do you swear on the Bible to carry out my instructions?'

She had the Bible beside her on the table and made them lay their hands upon it, first Jack then Ed and had them swear aloud. Then she handed them a folded paper, all sealed up with wax, but with nothing written upon it. She also gave them two pence and told them to tell their mother this was payment for work they had done in her garden. So Jack and Ed had run as fast as they could to the castle. Jack had lurked at the side of a nearby house, while Ed ran ahead and thrust the paper at the sentry guarding the entrance. There had been a chase of course, but he and his brother had easily fooled the soldiers who came after them.

Jack wishes he could tell Beth about the message, and ask her what she thinks it might have contained, but he had sworn not to, though it doesn't feel right now. Perhaps Mistress Wade was begging the Royalist soldiers for food for the townsfolk, for some say the garrison has plenty of meat and flour in its stores and that the officers feast each night. But if that were the purpose of Mistress Wade's letter, it didn't work, for no food has come their way from the garrison and they're still hungry, except that Mother was able to buy a small bag of meal with the two pence.

So Jack's hopes are high that today, when they go to Mistress Wade's again, he and Ed can run another errand and earn more money. Beth puts their bowls in front of them at the table.

'Take this before you go out,' she says. 'It will fill your bellies for a little while at least.'

Jack and Ed look into the grey water at the bottom of their porringers and swallow the contents in two mouthfuls, Jack feeling a few gritty pieces of oatmeal passing over his tongue.

'Is Father getting up from his bed today?' Jack says, hoping more than anything to see him smoking his pipe at the fireside again.

'Maybe,' Mother says, without looking at them.

Jack nudges Old Solomon and pulls at his neck skin to urge him to rise and come out with them. His smooth brown hide hangs loose on him, his ribs poking through like a willow basket, but he lies as always uncomplaining by the fireside, surviving somehow on the tiny scraps that he is given.

The morning is bright and not raining, as it has been for so many days, so Jack is glad to be out in the air, though it makes him hungry again. He thinks about Mistress Wade's warm kitchen full of food and imagines the smell of cake. Alderman

Wade's house is the grandest by far in the Culver Lane. Jack has always admired it greatly, even more now that he has seen inside. Outside it has two pointed gabled fronts, with carved angel faces on the beams of wood at the doorway, a jettied upper floor and tall brick chimneys rising up to the sky. The garden at the back is enclosed by a brick wall with two gates into it. Jack would like to live in a house like the Wade's, but he would like a big plate of meat and gravy even more.

Today, a handcart is sitting in the lane at the side of the house and the garden gate is open. A man, who they see is Master Cleghorne, a carter who lives in a cottage at the other end of the street and keeps two big grey horses in his yard, is carrying bundles of cut grass and loading them on to his cart outside. When he sees them, he bids them a mournful good day.

Ed and Jack follow Beth in through the open gateway to the back door of the house. She knocks on this and for a while there is no sign of life within, until Walter opens the door to them.

'Good day to you all,' he says 'How are you faring? And your father?'

'He is still abed,' Beth says, 'and we pray each day that he will rally soon. We came wondering if Mistress Wade has any work or errands, for we are ready and willing.'

'Well, you may help Master Cleghorne in the garden,' Walter says. 'He wants the grass for his beasts and the Mistress has told him to take what he needs.'

Walter steps out with them into the garden where Master Cleghorne is carrying a forkful of rough grass out to his cart.

'I'll just take this for the moment,' he says. 'The rest I've cut. Needs to be raked up into stacks and dried, if the rain ever stops. But it'll probably be ate before then anyway, that's if we ain't ate the beasts first.'

Master Cleghorne trundles his loaded cart away down the lane. Jack liked the garden when it had grass waist-high in the centre, thick bushes for hiding in all around the edge, good climbing trees and a secret hut. But now the garden has been mostly cleared, the grass and bushes hacked away to leave yellowed tufts, a square of raw dug earth near the house, with some rows of small green shoots poking through. At the far end of the garden some tangles of ivy, brambles and dog rose remain, though the shack is more visible now.

'Does anyone live there?' Jack says.

'No,' says Walter, 'it was an outhouse or storehouse but it's near collapsing now. Mistress likes it though and won't have it repaired or pulled down.'

Jack, Ed and Beth stare around, Beth's eyes trained on the remaining strip of overgrown weeds and bushes on one side of the garden.

'Down there, amidst all that tangle, there's mint and hyssop and rosemary too,' Walter says. 'And you may find a few leaves of cabbage and kale and some roots of salsify, if you look. Gather anything that can be eaten.'

'But why does not Mistress Wade have a nice big kitchen garden here?' says Ed.

Walter shrugs his shoulders. 'I do my best, but with all the other work–. I've told Mistress she should hire a man, but she's not inclined. Pity, for we could have fed a fair few from this plot, but planting it now isn't going to stop us from starving.'

He sighs and looks at the boys. 'Well, you two get raking up this grass and maybe I can find you each a penny.'

Jack, delighted at the chance to prove his earning power once again, runs to take up the rake and Ed a wooden fork lying close by while Beth plunges into the wild clump with her basket and is soon plucking at stalks and leaves. Jack's spirits lift a little to be thus occupied and soon he and Ed have raked up a good couple of heaps of cut grass, while Beth is still busy in the tangled patch of the garden. Old Solomon who has waddled in after them, sniffs around, surprising a mouse, which shoots out of a clump of grass.

'Will Master Cleghorne really eat his horses?' Jack says to Walter.

'I reckon so, when there's nothing else left.'

'And the cavalry soldiers,' says Ed, 'will they have to kill their horses too?'

'I suppose,' Walter says, straightening up from his digging, 'but they've seen themselves all right, with their stores. There's word the Royalist officers and lords swill themselves each night on plenty of fine fare and wine while the common soldiers feed on their rations. As for us, we're the worst off of all; we've no grain left to be bought at any price.'

His voice is bitter and he suddenly stabs his fork deep into the ground, then sighs again.

'But see, your sister's gathered a basketful. Let's go in now.'

Jack and Ed lay down their tools, as Beth comes up the garden with her basket. Jack, glancing up at the back of the house, is startled to catch sight of someone at the window, the stark-white face of a woman looking out. He tries to draw his gaze away, knowing he should not linger, staring rudely. Ed and Beth have not noticed, as they are examining the contents of the basket and when Jack glances up again, the figure at the window has disappeared.

In the kitchen, Mistress Denney is pleased with Beth's harvest.

'Bit tough some of these, me dear, but they'll most likely boil up soft enough. You take that bunch home and I'll have this. Add a bit of mint to these roots of salsify and you'll have a pottage of sorts.'

As Mistress Denney, Beth and Walter chatter on, Jack wonders about Mistress Wade, curious that she has not come down from her chamber and hoping that she is not as sick as Father is.

'Is Mistress Wade poorly?' he says, for his thoughts sometimes leap out of his head more quickly than he means.

'Not quite herself,' says Walter, 'stopping in her chamber today, that's all.'

'Please give her our kindest good wishes and thanks,' Beth says, while Jack feels disappointed that there will be no more work today.

Walter nods, then goes to a stone jar on the shelf near the door, and tips out some coins.

'Here's a penny each lads, for your work today,' he says.

'Penny won't buy nothing much,' says Mistress Denney, 'and when there's nothing left, money won't do no good at all.'

Walter shakes his head, his face darkening, a look Jack has seen once before, when the man had spoken of the Royalist commander Colonel Lucas.

'The rich will never starve; you can be sure of that. These lords and generals will suffer little hurt by this, whilst others perish around them. So it is and thus it will always be,' he says.

'Could we not go to the Lord General and beg some of the army's provisions?' Beth says.

'The Mayor has already tried it, with his petitioning. But the generals say it is the fault of the town authorities not to look after their own. I'd die rather than fall on my knees before those cavaliers,' Walter says.

'Men,' says Mistress Denney, with a sour look at Walter, 'so full of their own pride. It's always the women have to do the begging. Corporation should rouse themselves more on our account, for they do little except fret about their losses and their profits and whatnot.'

'Maybe,' says Walter with a sullen look.

Jack sees in Ed's glum face a reflection of his own mood. This bitterness and blame brings the familiar gloom upon them again, after only such a brief and pleasant interlude of hope.

'What can we do?' Jack says.

'If we could only get out of the town, we could go to Uncle and Aunt Sayer in Brightlingsea. It's not so very far away,' Ed whispers.

Jack has never been to Brightlingsea but the name conjures for him a happy place of sunshine, a paradise of plenty. Father has spoken about it sometimes, a small town on the edge of the sea, full of boats, where his brother is a fisherman.

'Come boys,' Beth says. 'We've troubled Walter and Mistress Denney too long. Thank you again for your generous gifts.'

'And the pennies,' says Jack.

Outside, they find Old Solomon asleep in a patch of sunlight on the side of the roadway. Ed tugs urgently at Jack's sleeve. By this sudden gesture, Jack knows that his brother has hit upon a notion.

'Beth, we'll go now and look for berries,' Ed says, a keen edge to his voice. 'But first we'll come back home with you, for we'll need a basket.'

'You'll not get up to any mischief, I hope,' Beth says absently, her eyes staring as though she is gazing at something they cannot see.

Jack can tell by Ed's jaunty walk that a moment of inspiration has struck, and he wonders with impatience what scheme has formed in his brother's mind. In the kitchen, they take the empty basket from Beth and, a moment later, are out on the street again. But instead of going in the expected direction, Ed beckons Jack to follow him around into the alley, to their backyard again. Ed opens the gate carefully to avoid making any noise. He gestures that Jack should wait for him outside, steps quickly into Father's workshop and emerges a few moments later, clamping something inside his coat with one arm.

'What have you got? Where are we going?' says Jack, closing the yard gate after Ed.

'Wait and you'll see soon enough,' Ed replies without turning back, heading off down the alley, propelled by his secret purpose.

They run down the lane by St Nicolas Church on to the High Street, near the castle, seeing soldiers standing guard outside, then go east into Blackfriars, which runs down alongside the castle field and is the grounds of an old friary, ruined many years ago. The place is rough land, dotted with bushes and trees and old stone walls and broken pillars. The town preacher once told them that the ghosts of wicked papist monks haunted the place, looking for sinful little boys to eat, but Ed said this would only happen at night, never in the daytime, so they were quite safe to go there now. It's a good place to run and hide, with many narrow paths winding between the trees and the ruins. At the bottom of the slope, towards the river, lies the town wall. There used to be holes in it, where some folk drove cattle and sheep into the town, but now the Royalists have filled it with buttresses of earth and timber struts, so no one can get in or out. On the eastern corner of the wall is a bastion, built some years ago, when Jack and Ed were smaller. It looks like a little fort, its angled points jutting out from the walls. The Royalist rebels have made a high platform of earth on it and mounted their guns and gabions. A group of men is standing upon this platform as Ed and Jack sneak their way down the slope.

Jack wishes they could climb up on the bastion and see what's beyond. Master Symonds says that whichever way you look, the Lord General Fairfax's army has built trenches and forts, lookouts and ramparts all around and guns aiming at the town. Jack thinks it would be very good sport to be out there, to climb on the ramparts and run along the trenches of this thing they call the leaguer, but only when there wasn't a war. Today in Blackfriars, there are no soldiers, only the ones manning the guns on the bastion. Ed dives behind a bush, waving with an urgent hand for Jack to follow. Crouching there, Ed whispers to Jack.

'See where it slopes down there, at the foot of the wall. It's quite deep and there's a sort of ditch. We can go right down into it and no one'll see us.'

'But what are we going to do?' says Jack.

'Dig.'

'Dig underneath, do you mean?'

'Yes, a tunnel.'

'To escape?' Jack says, seeing Ed's face glowing with delight.

'Aye, for this is the only way we can get out of the town.'

'But what about Father and Mother and Beth and Old Solomon?' says Jack, still bemused by the spectacular daring of Ed's idea.

'We'll make a tunnel big enough for everyone, even Father, to get through. Then we can all run away to Brightlingsea. Beth says it's no more than ten miles away so we could walk easily to Uncle Sayer's house.'

'And there'll be fish aplenty in Brightlingsea,' Jack says, thrilling at the simplicity of the plan.

'Aye, sure to be, oysters, cockles, crabs, all sorts. We'll never be hungry again.'

'But what about the soldiers, up there?' says Jack pointing to the bastion and the platform with the gunners upon it.

'They'll not see us when we're down in that gully. They'll be looking at the enemy outside and they have to be ready to fire their guns.'

'But the wall's too thick to dig through,' says Jack, dismayed that Ed has not thought of this new obstacle.

'Ssh,' says his brother, 'just wait till you see.'

They crouch low, running behind each tree and bush to avoid being seen by the soldiers. Ed is right, however, about the direction of the men's attention; their faces are trained all the time out beyond the town, towards the lines of their enemies. They have little regard for the happenings at the foot of the wall, which they know has been shored up solid and strong.

Jack and Ed scramble around the last clump of bramble bushes and reach the top edge of a steep slope, where they slither down to find themselves well hidden at the foot of the wall. Looking up from the bottom of the trench, the wall seems taller to Jack than a house. The place where they have landed has a newly packed section of earth and rubble, strengthened with a hefty timber post.

'See,' says Ed, pulling out of his coat lining the two short iron stakes he has taken from Father's workshop. 'The wall's been filled in with earth and –.' He wields his weapon, stabbing it into the rubble of the wall at the side of the wooden post. 'We can make a hole in it here. You start there at the bottom.'

Jack takes his spike, inspects the place and jabs at the wall. The two brothers set to with their implements, side by side, hacking at the stony earth, which in some places is so soft that it crumbles, but elsewhere is close packed and hard as iron. As Jack hacks out a small hollow, he thinks of another hindrance to their plan.

'Soldiers might come along and see the hole and fill it in again,' he says, pausing for a moment in his digging.

Ed frowns as though irked by his failure to foresee this problem.

'I've a notion,' Jack says, pleased with the solution that has come to him at the sight of a some pieces of stone and flint lying nearby. 'If we put some loose stones back in the hole after we've dug it, then cover it with earth, no one will see.'

Ed grins at Jack and they continue, until they have carved a small hole about six inches square and a finger's depth into the wall.

'Needs to be wider,' Jack says, deflated at the puny result of their efforts.

'Aye of course, numpkin,' says Ed, 'this is just the beginning. We can't do it all in a day. It might take a week or even more. Besides, we've berries to look for now.'

Jack nods and stands up from his crouched position, his legs stiff. He picks up some of the stones, preparing to hide their handiwork, but he stops, hearing a noise from above. From the top of the trench, he is sure he has heard the thump of footsteps, someone coming close and he turns to Ed in a panic.

'Up there, listen,' he whispers, gesturing with a finger and scrambling back to Ed's side. They stand together, both staring upwards, seeing no one for a moment or two until two large feet with lumpen shoes and legs in torn hose appear over the edge of the bank above them. Then some strange noises follow: snuffling, gobbling, someone eating with relish, smacking his lips in eager chomping. Jack's mouth waters with envy as he imagines this lucky man's delicious feast.

They crouch in curious fear, their bodies touching, Jack wishing that he could clutch hold of Ed, but knowing that this would be the act of a fearful baby. The greedy sounds soon die away to be followed by a loud belch, then some muttered words in a deep voice. 'Thangs be to mighty God in Hen.' There is another pop of wind from the eater, then the feet disappear, one at a time, but only a moment later come plunging down again towards Jack and Ed, on legs bearing the body of a huge soldier.

Jack and Ed scuttle along the trench as the soldier descends, seeing that he is about to land only feet away from them. He doesn't see them until his feet are planted, and he straightens up and turns. His eyes widen in terror as he stares at them. In that instant Jack knows him. It is the same soldier they had pelted with stones that day and into whose helmet they had dropped Solomon's turd, just before the wall had exploded. This is the same one they had tormented, big Timothy, who Jack sees, to his astonishment, has now fallen on his knees before them, hands clasped in prayer, just as he had done on that other day.

'Holy God in Heaven, look down upon your poor servant Timothy. Save me from these sprites of the Devil,' he says in a whimpering voice.

Jack exchanges a look of puzzlement with his brother, wondering if, while the soldier is so distracted, they might abandon their hole, run along the trench and make good their escape. However, Ed makes no move and Jack finds himself more fascinated than affrighted, realising that this hefty man is too baffled for the moment to take any action. Jack catches a change in Ed's expression, that familiar mischievous glint, a sign of his conjuring some new trick. But now is not a time for more japes.

'Sir, we're no Devil's sprites,' Jack says quickly. 'We're God-fearing boys and mean you no harm, as God is our witness.'

The big soldier opens his eyes and looks at Jack then at Ed, lowering his praying hands and peering again.

'We're twins. That's all,' says Ed. 'I'm Edward and he's Jack.'

The soldier's square face cracks into a smile, the furrow in his brow slackening.

'So there's two of you? Holy God be praised,' he says. 'Here's me thinking you was one little witch's imp sent to punish me for my sins, tempt me to the Devil's ways. I han't never seen such a thing on this earth. So when you was up there, running faster than the wind, you was just –.'

Jack realises now that his true confession might prove a foolish strategy, for this soldier, Timothy, is built like a bull and if he wanted to wreak a terrible revenge upon them for their trickery, he could likely snuff their lives out with one blow of his fist. However, nothing in his manner, as he slowly rises to his feet, gives any sign of anger towards them. Jack reckons it might be a while before he becomes vexed enough to think at all of vengeance. His broad face smiles again and he looks at them in turn.

'You two's little villains, amn't you? I never seen such a clever trick as that,' he says.

Ed is grinning too by now and Jack cannot help joining in this exchange.

'Pray pardon our mischief, sir,' Jack says meekly, glancing at Ed who clearly approves of his words. 'And we're mighty sorry for putting our dog's doings in your helmet.'

The soldier bursts out in a loud guffaw, noisy enough, Jack thinks, to attract the attention of more soldiers and some awful consequences.

'Don't fret none about that. That was Henry's helmet, not mine,' he says. 'It sent him wild, that did, with the smell off of him. But it was good sport, for he's a mean, miserable villain, is Henry.'

The soldier pauses and looks at the hollowed earth in the wall, noticing it for the first time, frowning in puzzlement.

'What you about?' he says pointing to the raw earth. 'Digging?'

Ed answers with the words Jack would have used a moment later.

'We're digging a tunnel. We don't mean to do any harm. We just want to escape,' he says.

'To Brightlingsea,' Jack says helpfully.

'You mean, you're planning on running away?' says the soldier, looking doubtfully at the wall again.

'Aye, we are, for we're starving hungry and Father's poorly and our friend who was helping us - he's dead,' Jack says, aware that his tongue is too loose for speaking to a stranger, but he cannot hold back. 'This is the only way, for they won't let us out, the army in here or the army out there. We're stuck here and if we don't get out we'll die.'

The big soldier considers this for a moment, as Jack feels his lip trembling at the horrible picture he has created with his own words.

'Aye, there's some of our lads escaped already, over the wall at night,' the soldier says, then with a brightening of his eye. 'I've a mind to lend you a hand, for you're two brave lads and it'd be mighty fine to get out there with you.'

Jack exchanges a puzzled glance with his brother.

'But sir –,' says Ed.

'I amn't no sir,' says the soldier. 'I'm Master Timothy Box, at your service.'

'But sir, Master Box,' Jack says. 'You're a soldier. Are you not meant to be keeping folk in and your enemies out? You're not allowed to run off and be a deserter. Wouldn't you be punished if you were caught?'

Timothy Box nods. 'Reckon so,' he says.

'So will we,' Ed says, eyeing this strange, simple man who is supposed to be their enemy.

'Might get hung or get above thirty lashes,' he says, his brows furrowing, 'but me and some of the lads are in trouble anyway. We thieved a horse and ate it. We was dying of hunger, so we did it. It was mighty tasty, I can tell you.'

Jack and Ed gape at Timothy Box, watching him wipe his mouth with his sleeve, as though enjoying the savour of the flesh again.

'It was one of the cavalry horses from them prideful cavalrymen that thinks they're above us common men. It was dark, so we sneaks into the shelter where they're stabled and me, I calm the beast. I talks to it nice and we leads it out, through a gap in the wall into an alley, where I slits its throat quick and neat. Then we takes it off to the Shambles and sells it to a butcher. He gives us a good price and we gets some big joints off it and roasts them on a fire out on the south wall. I kept a bit for today.'

'So if somebody finds out that you stole the horse, you'll be in trouble?' Jack says.

'Aye,' says Timothy. 'Could get hung for that too. But they can't hang me twice, can they?'

Jack's stomach flutters to hear the soldier talk so lightly about his own death.

'Sometimes, you gets transportated to a plantation,' he continues, in the same matter-of-fact tone, 'chained up like a slave, so I reckon I'd be better digging your hole and getting away from here. I didn't want to be no soldier anyway and I want to go home.'

His voice has turned plaintive.

'Where is your home, Master Box?' says Ed.

'You can call me Timothy or Tim if you've a liking to, for that's my Christian name what my ma calls me,' he says, looking a little more cheerful. 'I lives in Slampton, just on the corner where the road bends round by Brice's pond, with my ma and my brother.'

He is gazing ahead of him as though the place lies just beyond the wall. 'It's far away from hereabouts, in the country of Hertfordshire,' he says.

'So how did you come to be in the army?' Jack asks.

Timothy's eyes fill. 'My ma said we'd be throwed out of our house if I didn't join up to the Lord Capel's foot and fight for the King, so I did and we was marching for miles and miles. Then we came here.'

Jack thinks it best not to ask Timothy how he intends to find his way back home again, and be content for the moment with his generous but risky offer of help to dig the tunnel. Ed seems anxious to go, however, as he keeps glancing up the bank as though he expects a troop of horse to charge down upon them at any moment.

'We must hide the hole for now,' Ed says, starting to haul one of the heavy stones into the hollow.

Timothy, seeing him struggling, bends forward and embraces the boulder, lifting it with ease and planting it down into the raw earth hollow.

'That where you want it?' he says with a grin.

Jack scoops up some handfuls of mud from the pile they have removed and splatters it over the boulder, Ed and Timothy join in the camouflaging of their works, kicking the excess soil over the bottom of the trench and stamping it down with their feet.

'Thank you, Timothy,' says Jack and the big soldier smiles. He grabs hold of Jack's wrist then Ed's and charges up the steep side of the bank to the top in a few powerful strides, then releases them, laughing.

'Anyone sees us, I've taken you prisoner,' he says in his bellowing voice, making Ed flinch and put his fingers to his lips in an effort to silence the big man.

Jack spies up at the bastion where they can just see the backs of the gunners, behind the gabions.

'We must keep this a secret, Timothy,' says Ed. 'You must not tell a soul. Swear upon your honour.'

'I swear before God,' says Timothy Box solemnly, his face downcast as though in shame at his earlier imprudence. 'I swear before God and before you two brave boys, Ed and Jack or is it Jack and Ed?'

The boys run back as fast as they can, dodging through the old ruins and bushes of Blackfriars, to avoid being sighted by the soldiers on the bastion. They both know they are late and that their basket is empty. They have been too long away and are now to return with nothing. Jack's gladness at their meeting with Timothy and his promise of help is soon replaced by dread at the thought of Mother's anger. But more than this is the fear that Father will not be sitting at the fire smoking his pipe and that he still lies mighty sick in bed. Jack and Ed creep into the kitchen, Jack realising that their hands and clothes are thickly daubed with mud from their excavations, and that they should have stopped by a water trough to wash off the worst of it before returning home. They have been too charged up with the events of the day, the meeting with their new ally and their ravenous hunger.

'How dare you,' Mother says and Jack cringes back from her, for she is making towards them as they stand by the door. He readies himself for the blow.

'You've been out all of the day on some mischief or other and now – . Look at the disgusting sight of you both. You're filthy, wicked and sinful boys, with your father lying desperate in his bed, asking for you both all day long.'

The blows to Jack's ear are hard and stinging and Ed staggers over when she strikes him, but the pain is nothing to Mother's tears and the terrible knowledge that Father is dying.

Chapter 12

25th July

Doctor John Humphrey, renowned astrologer, is sipping daintily at a glass of wine when Charles enters the room. Before him on the long table in this upper chamber of *The King's Head* lie his charts and other papers, documents densely covered with ink scribblings and diagrams.

'Ah, my dear Sir Charles,' says Dr Humphrey, placing his wine glass down, his cheeks plumping into a smile.

The man is a simpering fool, Charles thinks. His dimpled hands finger the charts, then he lifts a round eye glass to his face and leans over the table, with his nose nearly touching the parchment.

'Come sir. See, the charts show quite clearly the advance of Saturn towards the Sun, the puissant forces from the planet drawing nearer together each day to the source of power, your goodself. It is clear as any crystal that these movements represent the advance of the army of Sir Marmaduke Langdale, who as we speak, is marching with his forces for your relief and for the glory of the King's cause.'

Dr Humphrey smiles again, his fingertip still planted upon one of the orb shapes on the chart in front of him. Charles takes a step closer but his mind has no inclination to grapple with the explanations, the calculations, nor endure this man's fulsome flattery, his predictions, his dripping obsequiousness.

'My Lord Goring has been informed of my prognostications and my Lord Capel too. They are both most profoundly gratified,' he says and Charles notices his smooth skin, glistening with perspiration as he glows in the heat of self-satisfaction.

'And what of the failures, the uprisings that have been crushed, the defeat of our allies in Cambridgeshire, in Kent, in Surrey? Do you see the influence of the stars in such events too?' says Charles hearing the sourness in his voice.

Dr Humphrey's cheeks deflate and he nods with a deep frown to denote the profundity of his thought.

'Of course, my good sir. If one considers the precise dates and times of these occurrences, the routing of the troops, the capture of a commander, one can see the conflicts between their zodiacal emplacement in relation to the position of Jupiter and of course the planet Uranus. Disastrous events are always the result of inauspicious configurations of the planets, though the lay person cannot possibly divine these factors. These events are the unfortunate falling together of unfavourable celestial conditions, which sadly influence our terrestrial realities. Only those of superior wisdom and scientific expertise are able to fathom these depths.'

'Those like yourself?' Charles says, his bitterness a little blunted now by the distraction of some noise outside the window. He has heard a hubbub of voices, some raised and urgent. It is most likely another collection of townspeople, wishing to press on the commanders their demands. There have been a number of petitions from desperate people, demanding relief from their wants, requesting food from the garrison stores, women howling that their children are starving, some even begging to be let to go out of the town.

'Maybe,' says Charles, 'we should announce to these people outside and our men on their meagre rations that the stars are moving in their favour. Will that fill their bellies, sir?'

The astrologer coughs and starts to roll up one of the charts, his smile now vanished.

'It would give them hope, my good sir,' he says, 'and hope

is a precious jewel, whose lustre fills the heart and mind with pleasure and delight.'

'That may be true,' says Charles, 'but such hope is unlikely to appease the hungry for long.'

Charles wishes that he could have a little faith in the man's powers, in place of the disbelieving depression that afflicts him. But he has to admit to some truth in what the astrologer says. Even some little hope of relief would lend courage and spirit to those cast down and restore the patience of doubters; these predictions might serve well to encourage his men. He will let Dr Humphrey's assurances of success and victory be spread abroad, to strengthen the waverers. There have been some new desertions from the ranks of men, twenty escaping through a sally port the previous night and five the night before.

'Thank you, sir,' Charles says, forcing himself to adopt a more courteous tone with the fellow.

Dr Humphrey bows and his smile returns. 'I am your most humble servant, Sir Charles,' he says, pausing for a moment. 'But my good sir, I wonder if you would wish me to cast you a horoscope, as I am something of a specialist in nativities. If you are able to furnish me with the day, month and year of your birth, in a matter of moments, I can predict the significant events to come in your life.'

Charles hesitates. He has no wish to spend any more time in the company of this tiresome individual, but he cannot feign indifference to what he is offering. Curiosity assails him, convinced as he is of his ultimate fate, lurking nearby, closely, like a stalking enemy in a thick fog. So he gives the man the details of his birth and watches him unfurl another of his charts of the heavens and lean over it. His finger traces a pathway from one figure to another, then he peers closer, scribbles some calculations in the notebook, pausing to consider what he has observed or concluded. Some minutes pass and now the astrologer is pressing a thumb to his forehead as though trying to prise a hidden answer directly from his brain.

'May I ask, Sir Charles, are you a married gentleman?'

'No sir, I am not.' Charles, irritated, wonders whether this delay is some ridiculous ruse, part of the trickery to lend authenticity to his deliberations.

'Sir, I need more time,' he says, turning his reddening face to Charles. 'I have more calculations to do. Your case is more complex than I could have imagined. The forces that have shaped your life are powerful indeed and exert a–, well –er –. Sir, if you will return tomorrow, I will have completed my analysis.'

Charles takes a step nearer to the man, seeing him shrink as though he fears he is about to be struck. 'I have no time for such fripperies,' he says, trying to constrict the anger that is swelling inside him. 'All I would know, sir, is whether I will die an honourable death.'

Dr Humphrey turns back to the chart, consults his notebook again and does not look up. 'Sir, you will die a death that will not be forgotten.'

Charles will stay no longer and listen to more of this charlatan's ramblings. He nods curtly and leaves the room, quickly descending the stairs to find William Hicks awaiting him, ready to accompany him to a stronghold in the castle for a council of war. Captain Hicks stands in front of the door as Charles approaches. The young officer's face betrays his agitation.

'Sir, there is a mob of townspeople outside, calling for you and for my Lord Norwich to take action to relieve their sad condition. They grow more desperate. I think we should make our exit by the back door, if you will, to escape their abuse of your person.'

Charles is grateful for his secretary's solicitude, but without a word, gestures that he should step aside to allow him free passage out on to the street. He wonders whether his fate is to be mauled and trampled underfoot by a starving crowd of townspeople, a death not fitting to a gentleman. Did the astrologer perhaps see such a thing in his chart of the heavenly bodies? If it is to be, he will not sneak coward-like from what he must face. Captain Hicks follows him out and stays close by his side, with one hand on his pistol butt. Charles wishes these starving wretches would quit the town, for they are a daily scourge to the garrison with their unrest, their complaints, their pleas for surrender becoming more strident and unsettling to the ears of the soldiers.

'Sir Charles Lucas,' someone shouts from the crowd, which comprises around thirty people, mostly poor looking women, some with children and a few men of the lower sort too. The one who has called out in a belligerent tone, however, is an older, serious-faced man in a brown coat and woollen cap, a weaver or servant perhaps, though his voice is bold and his manner forthright. He speaks again and those in the crowd curb their noise to let him be heard.

'You are a gentleman of this town and we appeal to you, to your good conscience and your honour,' says the man. 'These people are starving and in great need, because of the burden of your forces. Their children go hungry each night. They have no bread, nor any scrap of meat. We ask you to order the release of food from the army's store, else these children will perish on the street by your agency, as surely as if you had strangled them with your own hand.'

Charles winces at the man's impudence and sees some in the crowd of low women look with surprise and shock at the foolhardiness of his words. The women start their clamour again. He despises them in their beggarly, wretched state, their fickle allegiance to whoever will fill their bellies, but he would not be vengeful against them on account of this rude, outspoken fellow who has insulted him openly.

'I hear your request,' he says, 'and will convey it to my Lord Goring this morning.'

He strides towards the centre of the crowd and the women part to make a path for him. The outspoken man, who looks somehow familiar, stands aside and fixes him with a stare of pure loathing. Charles keeps his gaze trained ahead of him, however, hearing the continuing pleas and calls from the women behind him, as he and William Hicks make their way speedily along the street. Leaving the gaggle behind, they head on past the church of St Runwald towards the castle, where the council of war is to be held. After some conspirators had been captured attempting to steal powder and arms, the commanders have deemed it wiser to hold their war council within the castle itself. There is at least one fortified hall, as well as the gaol where prisoners of war, enemy agents, insurgents and criminals are held.

The foiling of the recent plot has shown that the Royalists have some allies within the town, in spite of the increasing discontent among the meaner sort of the populace. A boy had delivered a message warning about a conspiracy against the lives of the commanders. This note had mentioned a plan to set an explosion at a gathering of their higher officers. It was written in a hand, disguised by a shaking irregularity, but which looked to Charles like that of a woman. He had thought immediately of Katherine, as the note had been addressed to him by name, inside its anonymous outer wrapping. It was possible also that Katherine would know of those in the town who intended to rise up against them, because of her husband's anti-Royalist sympathies. But he knows that this is all conjecture, influenced by his too frequent thoughts of Katherine, when his mind should be fixed instead on the urgent business of war.

Charles knows too that the true extent of conspiracy in the town is unlikely to be discovered, as the messenger boy had run off, evading capture in spite of a rapid pursuit by a number of men. The child had covered the ground like a witch's cat, apparently appearing and disappearing in front of his pursuers' eyes. And the one conspirator captured alive had not yielded any intelligence of use, even under torture, before his corpse joined those of his two comrades in the pit in the castle yard. A fourth man had escaped over the wall to the leaguer. However, the boy's message had almost certainly saved them all from being blown apart, as it had led Charles to command the Master of Ordnance to increase surveillance of the powder stores and issue new orders about the authorised dispersal of arms.

'Sir,' says William Hicks interrupting Charles's silent speculations. 'Twenty men were captured yesterday trying to cross over, deserting their posts. There's mutinous talk amongst our men. They complain of their rations and now with Fairfax's dishonourable offer to them, that all common soldiers will be given quarter and leave to return to their homes, it's likely to lead to more unrest.'

'I know this well,' says Charles. 'It is Fairfax's and Rainsborough's strategy to win over those of weaker minds and hearts, because their bombardments cannot break the walls of the town. But I believe that our men, save for a few raw country lads, are loyal and true and ready to die in the service of the King.'

'They are sir,' says Captain Hicks. 'I believe they are sound behind us.'

This assurance from the reliable officer, Charles finds more solid than any of the pompous assertions of the astrologer, but it gives little relief to his troubled spirits. His only hope of this is to be found in Katherine's arms but now, with their situation becoming daily more critical, he doubts whether he will ever have the opportunity to seek her out again. He has gone twice, fruitlessly, to her garden, climbing the ivy-clad, crumbling back wall as he had done before. He had waited both times upwards of an hour but she had not been at her window, nor had there been any sign of life, no light, no sound from the house.

Her wild garden has also been roughly shorn of its foliage, he supposes as fodder for beasts. Some have even started feeding their horses with the thatch from their roofs. Even trees are losing their leaves to hungry animals. The hut in Katherine's garden, however, still offers good shelter and dark cover and he harbours a longing, like an acute pain, that they might some time soon be together again. He has to see her before, before what? Before the town has been burned and blasted to ruin, before he is struck dead as he rides in his last battle against Fairfax? He is certain of one thing only, that he must see her. Her absence makes his hold upon his temper more fragile, the foulness of his mood more poisonous, liable to rise unchecked in the company of his fellows, so that even Tuke and Maxey, his main allies and friends, offended by his cold words, by his discourtesies, have shunned his company.

Charles and the young officer have just reached the castle gates when from behind comes the sound of rapid footsteps, a soldier running at full speed towards them, hallooing to the sentries at the gate.

'Sir, sir,' calls the soldier, gasping for breath, drawing himself up before Charles. 'The enemy's attacking the fortress at St John's Abbey. They're marching on it now from the east, and from the west as well.'

Charles spends no time deliberating this news, but sends William Hicks to report at once to the commanders assembled at the council of war, orders a sentry to bring his horse and his lieutenants to muster five hundred troopers at the Head Gate for a charge on the enemy. His horse is brought within a short space of time, and he gallops to the south wall, to find Colonel Bowman's gunners firing out on the field beyond the walls. The enemy lines have been moving gradually, day by day, nearer to St John's, his family home, half a mile distant, where he stationed more than a hundred musketeers in the gatehouse at the start of the siege. The place has been strongly fortified since and is a vital line of attack for their forces outside the wall, cutting off Fairfax's troops with fire whenever they attempt to move closer to the walls of the town. St John's Abbey has been in his family for more than a hundred years. It had been violated, plundered and denuded in the earlier years of the war and now Fairfax means to destroy it.

Charles moves as close as he can, his horse a reliable and fearless creature, which can endure such blastings without flinching. An officer waves to Charles, however, to dismount, for fear of firing from below the walls, but he will not, for he has to see the progress of the troops upon his home with his own eyes. From the east side, successive blasts of cannon pound again and again, smoke clouding the sky. Will the walls of his home hold against this onslaught? He cannot see clearly the state of the damage and is tortured by his impotence, trapped as he is in the town. Colonel Bowman hurries to him.

'I'll take my troopers down there,' Charles shouts over the

sound of their own guns from the walls.

'No, it's madness, Colonel. They'll cut you down from both sides. See there are four companies advancing from the west too. 'We can do nothing but trust to the defences in the gatehouse.'

These last words are partly obliterated by a deafening explosion from the direction of St John's. The air shivers and ahead Charles sees a huge, hideous billow of black smoke and yellow flames leaping up high in the air. A great blot of thickening sky hangs where the gatehouse has been. He hears Colonel Bowman shout to his men to cover those who are fleeing away from the place, back towards the town, and orders the Head Gate to be opened to admit them. Charles cannot wait to watch more of this hellish sight and sends an order to his troopers to return to the camp.

It is late in the evening when the commanding officers assemble again. Charles sits at the right of a gloomy, respectful Lord Goring, as they listen to the report of a captain of musketeers, one of the surviving defenders of St John's, which is now in the hands of the enemy.

'They brought their demi-cannons, four of them and battered at us in the Gate house until one side was broken down to rubble. But it was grenadoes in the end, thrown in, caught the powder magazine. It's all but gone, my Lord,' says the man, still in his filthy clothes, his face blackened. 'There are terrible tales too of what the barbarians did, in the vault, the sacred resting place –.'

Charles sees the officer hesitate, knowing that his reluctance arises from knowledge of some atrocity carried out upon his family's remains, but which the man cannot bring himself to state in this company.

'I will hear more of your testimony tomorrow,' Charles says, finding himself badly afflicted by a shaking in his limbs, an alarming tightness in his chest. He must quit this place or collapse like a fainting old dame. 'My lords, gentlemen, I beg you will pardon me.'

Lord Goring nods. 'Sir Charles, I see you are moved by this

terrible, dishonourable act against your family. Please withdraw and rest tonight. We will seek your good counsel tomorrow. We will not submit to the indignities of savages, for such the enemy has proved himself to be this day. They will feel the full force of our justice upon them. Good night, sir.'

Charles hears the murmurs of his fellow commanders as he leaves the room, grateful for this release, finding his mastery of himself slipping into an unaccustomed trembling, not fear, but a terrible uncertainty, as though the earth upon which he walks is caving in with each step. He returns to the chamber in *The King's Head*, dismisses his servant sharply as the man starts to disrobe him of his sword and coat. He tears off his boots and falls down on the bed, his head throbbing. He shuts his eyes, hoping that his brain will cease its workings, lie still as his body does, perhaps halt all thinking, all imagining of the destruction of his family home, the desecration of his mother's grave.

He awakes in the darkness of night, having slept he thinks, for an hour or so. His head pulses dully now, but immediately his mind is flooded again with the anguish of the events and accounts of what had passed in the day. He rises and opening the door, looks for his servant who is slumped dozing on a chair outside on the landing. Charles bids the man bring him ale and something to eat, he thinking that this might in a little way restore his strength, rid him of this sickening dolour. The servant gets to his feet, shaking himself awake and makes his way down the stairs.

Charles returns to the room, pours water into a basin and washes his face, knowing that his only solace, his only hope of saving his sanity is with the woman, Katherine. He will go to her, no matter what the hour, what happenings are abroad upon the street, whether Fairfax himself stands armed outside the inn, sword drawn ready to cut him down. This is madness, he knows, but he cannot control it. He throws on his coat and boots, gulps a few mouthfuls of the bread, cheese and ale that the servant has brought and leaves the room, muttering that he is intent on taking the air. The man's eyes flicker with alarm.

'Sir, shall I go and rouse Captain Hicks to accompany you?' he says. 'It's not safe out upon the streets. The folk grow desperate and there's much ill will against us.'

Charles looks at the man and shakes his head. 'No matter. Do not rouse anyone. What hour is it?'

'It's gone midnight, sir.'

'Get you to bed then,' Charles says. 'I have no more need of you.'

He goes swiftly down the stairs, crosses the flagged hallway and out into the cobbled courtyard of the inn, revealing himself to the two sentries at the door, who leap from their slumped postures against the wall to attention. No one else is abroad upon the street, as he moves quickly along, driven now as though pursued by a beast, tormented by his desire for her. He will go to her front door, if necessary, force his way in on some pretext of security in the town, though her husband the alderman, aroused, will be a difficult obstacle. He could seize her, take her away, flee with her from this town. His pace quickens, each step pounding upon his sickly, mad hopes of finding her there, waiting for him. He turns the corner around the side of the house, the tall trees leaning over and leaps upon the broken wall, dropping down silently inside, close to the shack.

He peers through the darkness towards the rear of the house, sees the small square of her window, glowing faintly yellow and rejoices. His heart beats less wildly now as he moves closer, over the cut clumps of the massacred garden. When he is close to the window, he listens, hearing no sound from any part of the house. He stoops down to grasp a handful of gritty earth from beside his feet, tossing it up at the window, hearing it spatter on the glass, waiting in agony, but for only one brief moment. She is there. Her face is at the window and she raises her hand to him. He hesitates when he sees her face disappear again, wondering whether he should retreat to the shelter at the bottom of the garden to await her there, or stand here to catch her in his arms as she comes out of the servants' door into the garden. He stands, unable to move, hears the door creak faintly, sees the shadow of her, feels her presence and hears her whisper his name.

He takes only one step towards her, finds her arms embracing his body, her head upon his chest, the soft hair against his face, then he searches for her mouth, which she gives up to him. Her kiss is as a sweet salve, a balm to soothe the smarting wound of his mind, the misery of his soul. Her hands touch his face, lightly, gently caressing him, as though she seeks to draw out the pain from him with all her tenderness. He wraps his cloak around her and they move slowly, as mourners in a train, to the end of the garden to their secret closet, edging their way inside this place that is not of this world, and there lie down together.

They do not speak. He needs touch, not words. He needs to feel her skin against his, her soft mouth open to him, her gentle curing hands undoing him, her body a soft pool that he enters in a drowning of delight. Afterwards, he feels her breath upon his neck, where she has loosened his shirt, where her hand lies inside upon his flesh. He kisses her again and she murmurs, her mouth answering with such delicacy that he feels himself in danger of weeping in gratitude to her.

At last she speaks, in a whisper, as though she does not wish to break into the calm that they have created.

'I have sorely lacked you,' she says. 'I feared for your safety.'

He grasps her hand and tightens his hold around her. 'As I did for you. I came in search of you, but you were not here.'

'Forgive me,' she says. 'I was not–'

'You were not ill?' he says, raising himself a little, longing to see her face.

'No, not ill.' There is uneasiness in her tone.

He sits up, drawing her with him, seeing that the sky is beginning to lighten to grey. They have been here for the darkest hours of the night.

'You have restored me from madness this night, Katherine,' he says.

'I am glad of that, but are we not both a little mad?'

'Yes, but this is lunacy I would gladly embrace for the rest of my days,' he says, remembering what else he must declare to her. 'You saved me too from those who conspired against us. I believe it was your message that prevented us from being blown to pieces.'

Her body tenses in his hold and he is struck by the rashness of his statement. He has blundered. He should have kept his suspicions secret and not have spoken of this. Now she is about to reject him.

'In doing that, I have made myself a traitor,' she says quietly.

'Forgive me, please, I beg you.' There is pleading in his voice, unfamiliar and shocking to him for its weakness. 'I would die rather than cause you pain. Others would think your act truly heroic, brave and loyal, if you were for the King.'

He feels her shudder and dreads that this parting, which he has known would have to come, should be now when he is so consumed with love for her. How foolish and wishful they have been in their place of sanctuary, to think that the real world would not enter it.

'You have acted against your conscience,' he says, 'and I am heartily sorry to have been the cause of this. But, you must realise how this makes me love you more.'

She reaches her mouth to his again, kisses him and then replies. 'You are truly honourable in all you do, though I cannot adhere to your principles, nor to your cause. But I confess that I return your love an hundredfold. And, though our hearts are joined, we each must follow our separate ways.'

Though the dawn is arriving and the sky lightens around them, they make love again and cannot move from each other's arms until the sun sparks through the net of ivy and dazzles their eyes.

'You think me honourable,' he says, taking her hand and kissing it. 'This is what I have always striven to be, though I have failed in this twice in my life.'

'Does it not prove your honour beyond a doubt, that you should confess this to me?'

He sees in the light of the morning that she is smiling. Her eyes are clear and beautiful, but there are marks upon her face, shadows of bruising about her temples and on her chin. He reaches to touch her face.

'No, do not examine me too closely,' she says. 'Go now, quickly, before Walter my servant comes into the garden.'

'Katherine,' he says, 'Please –'.

'Go, we have been too long. I would not have you discovered here.'

He knows that the morning has broken into their other world. Cartwheels rumble in the street nearby and a child cries. Peering between the rotted timbers of the hut, Charles puts on his coat, seeing to his alarm the back door open and a servant, a man, that same one who from amidst the riotous people had shouted his rude rebukes. He is coming out into the garden and staring up at the sky.

Chapter 13

7th August

Beth sees a man appearing from under the arch between two houses on St Helen's Street and he, noticing her, swiftly turns and hurries away. Two limp animal corpses hang from each of his hands, swinging as he hastens along. Rabbits, Beth thinks for a moment before realising her mistake, for they are larger, hairier, one with patches of black on white, the other brindled; they are dogs. She feels a shiver of surprise at first, though it is known that many poor folk have been killing and eating any living thing they can lay their hands upon, cats, dogs and rats. Word has it too that Royalist soldiers loiter in alleyways, awaiting dogs to club down and sell or consume themselves. She tries to dismiss such thoughts, pressing on to the apothecary's shop, for her mission is urgent. Master Van der Welde is her only hope, since Master Wickham's shop was burned to the ground last week, fired by a mortar shell that had caught the thatch. Mercifully, the family had escaped and fled to safety but all of his apothecary's wares are gone.

Beth prays that the Dutch apothecary will take pity on her and be generous, though he is known to charge high prices for his powders and potions. She has brought two shillings with her, the last of all the money they have in the world, one shilling of this borrowed from the kind Mistress Wade. She would have given more, but Beth's mother has bidden her not to fall into debt to the Wades, nor succumb to the woman's spell. Beth wonders if her mother's wits have turned to say such a thing, but she has been brought low by their father's illness, as though his ailing is drawing her down with him into a pit. They are all weak for lack of nourishment, her mother haggard, her father like skin over bone. Even her young brothers, so lithe and vigorous in their bodies are subdued, fatigued she reckons by their time spent foraging, or maybe begging. Beth and the boys pray every night upon their knees for their father and mother, hoping that God in His mercy sees their suffering, their painful fasting and will soon take pity on them.

As she nears Master Van der Welde's small shop, which lies on the lower end of Angel Lane, a hilly street, she wonders whether she has ever felt contentment or happiness in her life, for their present woes blot out all remembrance of times past. Even her memory of Tobias, whom she had loved so completely, so fervently, is as a shadow that she can hardly discern in the darkened room that her mind has become. Beth is glad of this errand as a small distraction from her troubled thoughts.

Two women emerge from a front door on to the street before her and at the foot of the hill, she spies a band of Royalist soldiers on the loose, not officers but ordinary men, not commanded or marching in any order, more like a rabble, shouting as they come in a disorderly gabble. The sight fills her with dread. There have been incidents where bands of soldiers have rampaged in the streets at night, stealing anything they can from passersby, even entering some people's homes for plunder. Fortunately, she is now only a few steps from the shop and runs quickly to the door, seeking a sanctuary away from the street. She pulls at the handle, finding the door locked and tugs again, her panic rising in her throat. He must be there, the apothecary, surely, unless he and his family have fled. But where? He has more likely bolted his door against those who would invade his house and threaten his business. Beth bangs with her fist, her knuckles stinging, and calls aloud, begging that she has urgent need of medicine.

She glances down the narrow sloping street, sees the two women scurrying back to the house that they have just quitted and disappearing inside it again. The soldiers have stopped, however, and Beth sees one of them, his arm outstretched behind him, poised in a throwing motion, take aim, then hears the smash of window glass, a shout then another crash. Beth turns to the apothecary's door and strikes it again. She should turn and run, tell her mother that the apothecary would not let her in, but the vision of her father's shrunken body holds her there outside the door.

'Please, please,' she calls again. 'My father, Master Sayer, is very ill. I need medicine.'

The shape of a face appears for a brief moment at the window, then Beth hears the crunch of a bolt inside the door, which opens just enough to admit her. She slips in quickly and finds herself inside the small room, with Master Van der Welde hastily bolting the door behind her. He is a small plump man, his face a white mask of fear. Behind him stands his wife, who is clutching a bible in one hand, her other holding a small child, a girl of about two years of age with an older one clinging to the skirt of her gown.

'Pardon me please,' Beth says. 'I need medicine for my father. He is very sick.'

Beth sees now what she has entered, an inescapable trap with this terrified family, like a nest of cornered rabbits, facing a pack of dogs.

Master Van der Welde shakes his head. 'We try to save our shop from them. But if they want, they will break in. They have weapons.'

'Let us pray, Hendrik,' says the woman, the edge of her neat linen cap trembling as she speaks.

One of the children starts to cry. The small space of the shop is a pocket of concentrated terror into which Beth knows she has added her own fear. What little courage she owns seems to her as frail as a cobweb in a storm. This sensation, of feeble infirmity she has felt many times before, and conquered only once or twice. With Mistress Wade, bold and affirmative, when they had stood that time against the Royalist commander Sir Charles

Lucas, Beth's alarm had been transformed into bravery. She had exulted to see him bow to the woman's demands, seeming astonished, unmanned almost by Mistress Wade's power, though she risked being struck down, gagged and ridiculed as a foolish hysteric, a screeching scold not worthy of the attention of men. Now, suddenly, a spark of this woman's courage fires Beth again.

'Let these men dare to come charging in upon us when we are going about our business. Master Van der Welde, let's to our affairs. Open your shop.' Beth is glad and surprised at her steady tone, the damping of her agitation as she speaks. 'Mistress, I am sure you have chores, the floor to sweep maybe, the steps to wash and the fire to make up.'

'But, Mistress Sayer,' says the man, 'we make them angry, if we are too bold. They have frighted our neighbour Janssen. His wife died of the shock of it. They demanded money of him, not to fire his house and so he gave it.'

'Then we must show them more strength,' Beth says, uttering the words of some person stronger than herself.

The apothecary stares at her for a moment, then swiftly removes his coat, taking a large black apron from the hook behind the counter and tying it around him, before turning to open one of the cupboards.

'Unbolt the door, Gerda,' he says to his wife, who hesitates for a moment then scurries across the floor of the shop and pulls back the bolt. She then picks up her broom and starts sweeping vigorously at the floor, her two daughters still holding tight to her skirts.

'Now, tell me about your father's ailment,' says Master Van der Welde.

'He has terrible pains in the stomach. He is thin, as though something devours him from the inside. We have offered him a little gruel but he cannot take it. Nor can he move from his bed.'

'I see. Does he vomit?'

Beth is glad to see the shopkeeper's new attentive and purposeful manner. The older of the two girls is now holding a wooden shovel as her mother sweeps a little dust from the floor.

They are speaking to each other in small voices in their own tongue. From outside comes the clatter of boots upon the street and the guttural shouts of the approaching men.

'I'll make a powder of galangal. Your father must take some each morning,' says the apothecary. 'Have you any walnuts at home to make oil?'

'No, sir,' Beth says, holding her attention on the movements of the apothecary behind the counter, but seeing the shadows of the men outside the window. 'You must furnish me with all of the things I need. I have money.'

A barking voice sounds outside the window. 'What's this? An apothecary?'

One of the soldiers starts beating at the door with a weapon.

'Hey, Master Apothecary. We need some of your good medicines, for Henry here's got a dose of the pox!'

Beth glances at the apothecary whose fingers are quivering as they work, weighing out scoops of a brown powder on to the pan of his scales. The door bursts open wide with a bang and two soldiers crash in.

'Damn you, man. Are you deaf? I said, have you anything for the scabby pox?' cries the soldier.

Beth prepares her hard face, digs her nails into the palms of her hands and turns around, fixing the intruders with an indignant stare. The speaker is a square-faced, fair-haired country man, by the look of him, with a coarse wool doublet and tattered breeches. In his hand he holds a drawn sword.

'Gentlemen,' says the Dutchman, 'I will attend to you presently, as soon as I have served this lady.' His voice is remarkably steady and clear.

Beth forces herself to turn around again, her back to the soldiers, her face to the apothecary. She hears the swishing of the broom in the corner of the shop. There is a moment of silence, broken only by the sweeping sounds and the clink of the apothecary's balance as he pours the contents of the weighing pan into a small fold of cloth.

'Master Quack, you foreign devil,' says the second soldier,

tramping into the middle of the floor, so that Beth can see him from the corner of her eye. She hears a clamour from the others outside the shop. 'We'll have a guinea from you, else we'll pull down your shop. What do you say? Now leave this pretty maid for a moment, though she's a happy sight for any man's eye, and get us the money.'

Beth feels the prickling of heat on her brow, a clutching in her stomach but she spins round and faces the two soldiers.

'What wickedness is this? Here is a good man who seeks only to cure the sick and afflicted,' she says, her voice steady, seeing the surprise in the men's eyes. 'My father is lying ill in bed, starved close to death because of your army in our town. I wish to ease his pain and you burst in here with your vile threats. The town authorities will know of this. I am neighbour to Alderman Wade, a powerful man on the town Corporation. He will have constables come and arrest you for your roguery. And your commander, Sir Charles Lucas, will not stand for such villainous acts against his own townspeople. He shall know of your crimes, unless you are gone this instant.'

Beth's voice has thinned sharp as an arrow. Her body is shaking now and her face burning. Catching sight of the broom handle, the implement that the apothecary's wife has just propped against the counter, she grabs hold of it and thrusts its end into the soldier's chest, jabbing him hard, seeing him flinch and take a step back, his companion looking on astonished.

'Aye,' says Beth, her rage harnessed and strong, her voice restored to a calm threat, 'Sir Charles Lucas shall know how you, brave soldiers, have menaced honest folks about their business. He shall hear how you cut down one weak woman armed with a wooden besom. He shall know what fine men of war you are!'

Beth is startled by the effect of the commander's name upon the men, cheered to see her desperate strategy strike home. The two soldiers edge backwards to the threshold and Beth continues her advance, still wielding the broom handle. Behind them on the street, the others have broken into a squabbling argument, with two ready to come to blows, while most of the group are dispersing. Turning their heads, the two soldiers glance out and step back to join their fellows outside. None acknowledges their return, for they are now not a body of men, but a scattering of aimless individuals wandering upon the street.

Beth lowers the broom and closes the door. The latch clicks and with that sound, the wall of her strength collapses in a gasp of relief. Mistress Van der Welde is beside her, embracing her tightly, murmuring something in her own language. Beth gulps and shudders, slowly recovering her composure.

'So brave against those men,' says Master Van der Welde quietly. 'We must thank you, Mistress, for what I should have done myself.'

'Sometimes,' Beth says, still trembling, looking at the apothecary and his wife, 'it is better to be a woman, for only true cowards knock women down. Whatever those soldiers are, I do not think they are cowards.'

They pause in the quiet of the shop, hearing no voices outside now, only a dull thudding of guns, the bombardment of the walls again, as on every day recently, but louder in this part of the town. The apothecary picks up a jar and dispenses some seeds into another piece of linen, which he folds carefully and fastens with a pin.

'You must go to your father now,' he says. 'Take some grains of mastel too, for this may calm his pain and aid sleep. Give him a little broth, if he will take it, and wine. Do you have any?'

Beth shakes her head and the man looks at his wife, says something to her in the Dutch tongue, at which she withdraws followed by the two children.

'And how is your mother?' the man says.

'Not well, sir,' she replies, returning to the familiar gnawing state of worry, thinking of how her mother will not leave her father's bedside. At this moment she will no doubt be pining, fretting about what has kept Beth away so long.

'It is hard for you, so young, to have this burden upon you,' he says.

His wife returns with a bulging cloth bag. She hands it to

Beth. 'Here, to eat,' she says.

Beth takes the parcel in both hands for it is quite heavy.

'Mistress, can you spare this? What about your children?' says Beth.

'Take it.' The woman presses Beth's hand, closing it upon the purse she is trying to open to offer up her coins.

'Here are the medicines,' the apothecary says. 'Go with God's blessings and our thanks most humbly.'

Beth, moved by their generosity, nods and returns her thanks and blessings too, leaving them in the shop as two other customers approach and enter. She hurries up the street, clutching the bundle to her chest, the small parcels of medicine in her pocket, exulting at the thought of bringing back some solid food and the means to relieve her father.

The sound of cannon fire continues, one dull thump, then another, then a roar of triumph, followed by the rumbling of falling masonry, the crash of another house tumbling down. She can hardly bear to look upon more wreckage and destruction. Colchester was so fine a town, with good houses, solid and sturdy, wide paved thoroughfares, pleasant to walk through, a place of pride and elegance. Now it is a torn, damaged place, with all of its suburbs in ruins. Even the abbey and the church of St Botolph are burned and wrecked, blackened skeletons, some say the work of the besiegers, others that the besieged gunners, grown desperate, turned their cannon upon this house of God. So many fine dwellings within the walls are reduced to hummocks of rubble too. All around lies the debris of broken lives, as a daily witness to their suffering.

She hastens on, meeting a man, running along the street with a wheelbarrow, laden with pots and pans, turning his head frequently in the direction of the thudding guns. Two women, neighbours of the Sayers, arm in arm, come the other way, their faces blanched with fear. 'They're coming,' one calls to Beth. 'They're going to break through. God aid them and preserve us, too.' Beth shares her neighbours' apprehension, though rumours of the fall of the town are daily occurrences, whipped up by folk desperate for something to break them free from the prison their town has become. Another thick boom sounds out from the south wall, where the besieging army continues its battering, since the Royalist stronghold, the Lucas family home was captured. This surely must signify the end.

As Beth passes by the front of the house of Alderman Wade, the door opens and the Master himself comes out. He sees her and nods with a grim face. She, not wishing to pause, makes a quick curtsey on her way without stopping. But the man is coming after her.

'Mistress, young mistress, I'd have some words with you,' he cries, his features shifting into an ugly smile. 'You and your brothers have been visiting my house, I hear.'

Beth has no wish to tarry, nor to speak to him, now that she is so near home and her father in such need, but she does not dare to ignore the Alderman, for the sake of his wife's kindness.

'Mistress Wade has been most generous to us. We have been of service to her in some small ways, I believe. Forgive me, sir. I must go quickly, for my father is very ill and I have medicines for him.'

The man's face changes to a grimace, perhaps meant as a sign of concern. 'May God speed his recovery and bring us happier times soon. And if you have need of work, come to me, young Mistress, for I have a good occupation for you,' he says, standing on the spot, allowing Beth to turn away from him and run gratefully to her door.

The kitchen is empty, the fire burnt low with Old Solomon lying motionless in front of it. Ed and Jack are abroad, Beth assumes, as they have been every day on some errand or mischief, she does not know which, and has little leisure to investigate further. They sometimes bring back food offerings, once a few scraps of salt meat and another time a small piece of rye bread. When Beth had asked how they had come by these, Ed had replied that a kindly old man had given them when they helped him carry in some firewood to his kitchen. Another time, when Beth had found mud from their clothes on the floor, their reply to her questioning was a story about helping a poor man forced by the soldiers to dig fortifications on the Moor Lane. It is true that many able-bodied men of the town have been pressed to such labour, though some refuse on grounds of conscience. Beth's mother now seems to care little of the whereabouts of the boys each day, so she must take upon herself this weight of worry too.

Beth opens the bundle on the table, discovering to her joy a stoppered stone bottle of wine. She pours some into a small pan, stokes the fire with the little fuel they have left and sets it on a stone to warm. Old Solomon lifts his head and beats his tail once upon the floor. The sight of him, poor old creature, starving and helpless, prompts Beth to return to the table, tear a small piece of the hard bread from the loaf that Mistress Van der Welde has gifted her, put this in a porringer and pour on a little of the wine.

'Here, old dog,' she says, placing her hand on his thin flank. 'While we have food, you will eat.'

It is foolish, she knows, but she is stirred by the knowledge that she alone in the household is now responsible for the survival of all. She will need to summon up all of her strength and courage each day, as she has just done in the apothecary's shop, even when fear threatens to cripple her. This thought for one weak moment plunges her into a pool of misery, but she will not allow herself to indulge in such helplessness, for then they will all be truly lost. She takes another bowl, pours in the warmed wine and drops in half of the powders the apothecary has given her, then climbs the stairs to her parents' bedchamber.

It is dark with no candle lit and the air smells sour, of sweat and sickness. Her mother, a shadowy shape at the bedside, sits motionless, turns a white face to look at Beth as she approaches.

'Mother, I have some wine and medicine.'

'That is good,' says her mother not moving.

Beth kneels down at her father's bedside. 'Help me, Mother.'

She can hear his breathing, hoarse and rasping. His eyes are like clouded glass but he looks at her with a sign of grateful recognition.

'Father, here is a restorative drink,' she says.

Her mother rouses herself sufficiently to bring a bolster to prop behind the sick man's head and together they raise him so that Beth can spoon the liquid into his mouth. She rejoices to see that he takes it, sucks it down and finishes it all.

He draws his hand from beneath the covers and grasps Beth's wrist, squeezing it weakly and she smiles at him, hardly daring to hope that this might signal recovery.

'You must take some wine too, Mother,' she says looking up. 'I have food as well and will make an onion gruel for tonight's supper.'

Her mother rises at last and comes around to Beth, embracing her, though her body is a hard, unyielding cage of bone.

'Let us say some psalms together as father is not fit to read the Scriptures,' says Beth.

'Bring me the Bible.' Beth is surprised to hear her father's voice a little stronger already and she is more pleased to comply with this request than any other duty she has ever performed for him.

She lights one of their remaining precious tallow candles at his bedside and she and her mother hold the book for him as he reads in a clear whisper,

... The Lord is my rock and my fortress, and my deliverer; the God of my rock; in him will I trust: he is my shield, and the horn of my salvation, my high tower, and my refuge, my saviour....

In the kitchen, Beth chops the onion, enjoying the false tingling tears that stream down her face, cleansing tears that revive her as she gives thanks for the generosity of others. In the bundle, Mistress Van der Welde has also put a small pot of pickled beet and a bunch of cabbage leaves. It will be a feast this day, Beth thinks with satisfaction, glad to be able to offer something to the boys, hoping too that their foraging might also have been fruitful. The troubling thought strikes her that her brothers might be thieving from others, for all she knows, but yet she cannot find it in her heart to condemn them, whose only motives are the survival of their family and whose nature is always to share. Old Solomon has eaten the offering she gave him and is now hauling himself to his feet and plodding to the door. Beth tastes the gruel then takes two bowls upstairs to her father and mother.

'She is a blessed daughter, is she not?' says her father as she holds the bowl for him.

'Aye, she has proved her worth in this terrible time,' her mother says. 'But Beth, I did so long to see you married to some good man.'

Beth feels her cheeks flush, though in the dim chamber she knows that this will not be observed.

'And I too,' her father says.

'Well, I'm hardly too old,' says Beth, 'though I'll have to find a good man first.'

She has meant to lighten the mood, but her mother looks at her sadly. 'The pity of it,' is all she says, as Beth's courage wavers when she thinks of Tobias.

'The soldiers in the garrison are hungry too,' Beth says, briskly, to change to subject. 'We can only hope now that their commanders will see sense, that so many cannot survive for much longer. They will have to surrender. So we in the town must hold on. All of us.'

Neither of her parents give any reply, but after a moment or two of silence, her father speaks. 'Look after your brothers, my girl.'

Beth is heartily glad when Ed and Jack return, both, in spite of their hunger, looking bright about their eyes, as though they have discovered some marvel or the promise of relief amidst this want and deprivation. Their lively spirits relieve the mournful monotony that hangs about her parents. The boys' joy at the watery onion gruel and their chatter pleases Beth and cheers her a little. Ed brings from his pocket a dusty piece of oatcake.

'And where, may I ask, did you get that?' says Beth, as they sit at table, having licked their bowls clean.

'From a man labouring on the wall,' Ed says, trying with great care to break the small hard biscuit into three portions.

Beth looks at Jack who is watching this operation with great interest.

'Make sure you divide it equal,' he says.

'So this generous soul has food to spare,' says Beth. 'Who is this man?'

'Just a man,' Jack says, stuffing his piece of oakcake into his mouth, 'helping the soldiers.'

'You've not been consorting with the soldiers again, have you?' Beth says.

'No Mother –, I mean Beth,' says Ed and she sees a little colour rise to his cheeks.

'Ed, Jack, tell me, you're not thieving this food,' she says, putting on her most serious face.

Jack leaps up from his seat. 'As God is our witness, we've never stolen a crumb. I speak the truth, do I not Ed?'

Beth lets slip a small smile at the look of outrage on her young brothers' faces.

'Well, we have eaten heartily enough tonight, so let's give thanks to God,' she says.

Beth speaks the words of the prayer as they sit, heads bowed around the table, though she is distracted by a sound she fancies she has heard outside their door. She hurries through the last phrases of the prayer and turns to the door, listening, hearing footsteps and seeing that Jack and Ed have heard it too. There is someone outside their door. A soft knock. Then silence. Beth's heart thuds in her chest. She rises, her memory of the encounter with the menacing soldiers still fresh, and reaches for the nearest weapon, a heavy wooden spoon. Ed and Jack have risen too and are following close behind. As they approach the door, their shared relief at seeing the bolt secured, is palpable and Beth casts a glance at her two young brothers, their faces taut.

She moves slowly and leans close to the door. 'Who's there?' she says.

The knock comes again and a man's voice answers, quiet and carrying no hint of danger or threat. 'Mistress Sayer? I am a friend.'

Beth freezes for she knows the voice, but also that this knowledge can only be a horrible delusion.

'And how do we know you're a friend?' she says.

'If you'll open the door, you may judge with your own eyes.'

Chapter 14

7th & 8th August

She is so thin, hardly any weight at all in Tobias's arms. For a moment he thinks she might faint, for her eyelids flutter and her body loosens, but only for one brief snatch of time before she recovers herself, her blue eyes fixed on him, her mouth open with the shock of seeing him, laughing in disbelief. He laughs too and clasps her to him, though he is anxious of her fragility.

'Are you Tobias's brother?' says one of the boys, standing close, staring in wonderment. The other touches his arm, stroking the sleeve of his coat, as though to prove that Tobias is made of solid flesh.

'We thought you were dead,' he says. 'They said all the men were dead and only one captured, which wasn't you. We heard it, afterwards.'

'Are you wounded? We can tend to you again,' says his brother.

Tobias laughs again, full of joy to see their earnest faces and to have Beth in his arms. They all join in more clumsy embraces and then more laughter. This is a homecoming the like of which Tobias has never known, his orphan life spent in the house of a solitary uncle now dead.

'But how did you do it, Tobias?' says the boy he thinks is Ed.

Tobias relates to them briefly the tale of his desperate flight over the wall to the leaguer and Rainsborough's Fort. He pauses, suddenly aware of the absence of the parents.

'Your father and mother?' Tobias says, dreading as he asks what the answer might be.

'Father is very sick,' Beth says, still holding on to his arm, as though she will never loose her grip. 'Mother sits all day by his bedside in the chamber. She is much cast down. But it will cheer them so, to know that you are alive and are come back to us.'

'Shall I run up and tell them?' says the twin, who Tobias sees now is Jack.

He has no time to move, however, for a voice calls from above. 'Who's there?' and a moment later Mistress Sayer appears on the stairs.

'God be praised,' she says as she looks down at them. Tobias finds it hard to conceal his shock at the sight of the hollow-eyed woman, her cheeks sunken, wrists skinny as thread. Her gown hangs limply about her shoulders, her hair ragged and her apron soiled.

'Tobias Waterman, God has preserved you,' she says, whispering, her mouth twitching, her eyes sharpening in recognition.

He greets her with a smile and a brief bow of the head, worried now that his 'resurrection' might cause her more distress than pleasure, for he had not known that the family thought him dead.

'He was not captured, Mother,' Beth says, her face alight.

'He escaped and jumped over the wall,' the boys say together.

Tobias himself is overcome at the effect of his return upon the family and finds himself choked for a moment, such that he can utter no more words.

'Will you come to my husband, for it will gladden him to see you again,' says the woman, her voice weak, her mouth attempting a smile.

Tobias goes upstairs with Mistress Sayer, Beth and the boys into the foetid chamber, dark and full of the smell of death. Now is no time to tell the family that he is still a soldier, bound to his duty, in Colchester only on a short mission and obliged to return to his company and to the war. Master Sayer has the glazed eyes and the waxy skin of a dying man. Tobias has seen this before in his own father and then his uncle, both taken by a sickness that had shrunk the flesh on their bones.

'It's good to see you here, lad,' says the weaver. 'It lifts my heart and my hopes. You'll care for them, will you?'

Tobias kneels down by the bed. 'Master Sayer, it was you gave me my life again when I lay wounded and bleeding. This I owe to you and your family. I will do everything in my power to help them.' He hears his voice break and feels Beth's hand upon his shoulder.

In the kitchen, Tobias unloads the small bundle of food he has brought, thinking how meagre it looks spread out on the table. But Beth and her mother are full of gratitude to him and the boys ogle the pieces of salt pork and sausage, as though they are delicacies laid before the king. As they sit at supper, Tobias is touched by their care of him, serving his food first upon a platter, carefully cut and giving him a larger portion.

'Here, lads,' he says, handing a piece from his plate to the boys, 'I've had more than a few days with a full belly. Have this, for you are growing into men.'

'I pray God that they will,' Mistress Sayer says. 'Will you give thanks, Tobias?'

He says the prayer with a sinking heart in spite of the warmth of his welcome. He will not tell them tonight of another parting.

'You will sleep in the corner, here, where you did before,' Jack and Ed say together.

'Aye and I hope you'll be comfortable,' says Mistress Sayer, rising to her feet. 'Come boys, to bed, for it is late.'

'I'll see to the fire, Mother,' says Beth.

Tobias bids them all goodnight, hoping at last for some precious moments alone with Beth. She rises and goes to the fire, pats the old dog and places some pieces of sea coal upon the glowing cinders. He watches the curve of her back, her white neck and the pretty cheek, which has lost its plumpness, but which he has dreamed of kissing many times. She turns to him then, with eyes at once shy and beckoning. He comes to her quickly, taking her in his arms. He loosens her cap from her head and her fair hair falls around her shoulders. He kisses it, smelling the faint rose scent of it, pulling her close, thrilling to discover her body melting into his, knowing he should go no further. Her mouth is tender, luscious as she answers his kiss, arousing him fiercely. But he cannot take her here, on the floor of the kitchen with her parents upstairs, in an act of sin in a house where he has been nurtured and treated like a son. She cleaves to him, her body pressing against him.

'I have nothing else to give you, Tobias,' she says in a whisper.

'Tis a precious thing that you offer,' he says, 'not something to be thrown away lightly upon some passing soldier.'

She pulls away from him, suddenly and he is cut as with a knife, knowing that he has offended her.

'You will leave us again,' she says turning her back on him.

'I must,' he says, dismayed at his foolish words, 'though in my heart I would stay with you forever. I love you, Beth.'

'Why should I trust the word of some passing soldier?' she says quietly, still looking away.

'Beth, my dearest love –.' He is panic-stricken, stung by her words, until she turns to him again and he sees that she is smiling.

'Say it again, Tobias,' she says and they cling to each other, muffling their laughter in kisses.

Tobias wakes early, before dawn, but lies in the small cot bed in the corner of the familiar kitchen, warmed by the knowledge that Beth returns his love, frustrated though glad of their restraint of the previous night, but fearful too. He gets up and steals out into the yard to the privy and then, returning to the still silent house, pokes the tiny embers of the fire back into life, throws on the last piece of fuel to feed it. The ancient dog grunts in his dream world, and Tobias feels the creeping uncertainty of this new day. He washes his face and neck, dresses quickly and sits down at the table.

Is there really hope of a life with Beth in this world of hazards and war? He might be killed, she dragged further down by want and starvation. It is simple foolishness to imagine marrying her now, though as a soldier's wife she might have a better chance of survival than in her present state. But what of her family? She will never leave them, nor would he think of taking her from them. They are as good as his family too and he is bound to them all while he lives and breathes. If they were to marry now, he could enjoy her, he thinks in an agony of guilty desire, but to be wed in such haste in these desperate circumstances, and leave her a widow would be too cruel. He sits, head in hands, sunk in the mire of his dilemma. There is his duty too, which he cannot deny. He is bound by his oath to Lord Fairfax. And if, as the Lord General has said, the siege will soon be broken, there is the chance of victory for Parliament and the town being set free again. Then he and Beth might be married at the beginning of a new peace. These hopes are surely not all in vain.

A noise on the stairs brings a sudden end to his deliberations. Beth appears, coming slowly down the stairs, her face pale and without expression. Tobias jumps to his feet, thinking for a moment that her father must have died in the night. Her look, however, is not of grief but is a hard, unmoving mask that shuts him out. Where are the smiles she had bestowed upon him the previous day? He cannot believe it, nor bear it and comes towards her.

'Beth, are you ailing?' he says.

She brushes past him quickly, swerving to avoid his touch, turning her face to the yard door, opening it quickly and is gone. Next comes the clattering descent of the two boys on the stairs, assailing him with greetings and questions and so the morning in the Sayer household has begun. The twins' cheerful chatter is a good distraction to Tobias's mind, as they go about their duties, emptying the chamber pots, bringing some sticks of wood for the fire, setting a pot of water on to heat and putting the porringers on the table. Beth comes in from the yard amidst the activity, but still does not meet his eye. Mistress Sayer, looking a little more like herself, her hair tidied under a linen cap and wearing a clean apron, comes down into the kitchen saying that her husband has passed quite a peaceful night and wishes to take a little gruel this morning. Still Beth does not look at Tobias. She takes only a few mouthfuls of gruel, a cup of ale then sets about clearing ash from the hearth and sweeping the kitchen floor.

'What will you do today, Tobias?' Jack says as they sit at table.

'I am sworn by my duty still,' he says, glancing up to see if Beth is listening, hoping to meet her eye, to see some sign that she still has some regard for him. But she has gone into the corner of the kitchen to her wheel, where she sits, head down, sorting the reels of yarn she has spun, so he continues with the boys and the mother as his audience.

'I have been sent by the Lord General Fairfax,' he says.

'You have met the Lord General Fairfax himself?' says Ed, his eyes wide with admiration. 'Is he very grand and fearsome?'

'I found him not so at all, but respectful and courteous to me, though I stood before him like a pig muddied in a sty. He and Colonel Rainsborough have ordered me to gather information from the town about the state of things here. I must go about town and glean what I can of the condition of the people and –.'

'Well, you may tell your fine Lord General Fairfax,' says Beth, her voice ringing out from the corner of the room, 'that we are suffering and dying, that his army has imprisoned us, for no fault of ours. Will it please him to know that he will win a glorious victory over us? Will he rejoice to march into a town full of corpses?'

Tobias cannot answer, nor say a word, for he is cut by the sharpness of her despair. Although he wants to defend the strategy of the Lord General, the arguments stick in his throat.

'But Tobias is going to help rid the town of the invaders,' Ed says.

'We want them to quit the town and leave us be,' Jack adds, looking with a bewildered expression at Beth, who has turned away from them again.

'Beth, do not be harsh with Tobias,' Mistress Sayer says,

frowning towards her daughter. '*He* did not bring this ill upon us.'

Tobias, deeply miserable now, tries to reassert his conviction by explaining what his duties and actions are to be. 'I must find out how much powder and shot remain to the Royalists, for this will show how long they can hold out. I'm to speak to the soldiers too and let them know that their cause is lost, but if they surrender they will be guaranteed their safety and freedom to return to their homes.'

'But the Royalists might capture you or shoot you,' Jack says.

'Well, I must be careful to avoid that,' Tobias replies, bowing his head.

Tobias leaves them, with his thanks and his promise to return that evening, as he has been charged to stay for a number of days in the town, before re-joining his company in the leaguer and reporting his findings to the generals. Beth's coldness to him, after such a loving welcome on the previous day, wounds him sorely and he hopes that it only arises from the cruelty of their circumstances, rather than a sudden loss of affection for him through some wrongdoing on his part. Perhaps he has been dishonourable to her, too forward, too full of lust. But he cannot dwell on this now, with urgent work to be done.

Forcing his mind to focus upon the tasks before him, he sets off from the Sayers' yard, having borrowed a spade from Master Sayer's workshop. He has decided to seek out a work party of townsmen and join them in their digging and fortifying of the walls and battlements. This way he may gain access to enemy soldiers without arousing suspicion. He has seen some of these men, pressed by the Royalist officers into the business of strengthening the defences of the town.

Tobias had re-entered the town in secret the day before, by a narrow tunnel below the south wall, where the Parliamentary army is now in full control, since the taking of the fortress of St John's Abbey. The trenches and earthworks are extensive, drawing ever nearer to their targets: the heavy guns upon the town walls and bastions. It is a dangerous patch, however, with gunners or even an opportunist bowman from the top of the walls taking shots at anyone reckless enough to move unprotected below. At least their own guns had blasted the tower of St Mary's Church within the walls, where a crafty lone gunner with his saker had, for many weeks, enjoyed picking off their men below in the earthworks.

Shouldering his spade, Tobias turns into the lane that runs close to the southern wall, to discover two more charred and smouldering houses and seeing a troop of foot soldiers and engineers assembled by the Old Fort. Nearby, he sees a number of holes and hollows where mortar shells have blasted the wall and caused it to crumble. A group of glum-faced townsmen stand nearby and Tobias heads over to join them, drawing the notice of only one of the party.

'Who are you?' says a man of middle years in a ragged woollen cap and a coat in a similar state, with the look of a carter or labouring man about him.

'Cousin of Mistress Sayer on the Wyre Street,' Tobias says. 'Been sick of the flux for a while, but I'm up and about now.'

His new acquaintance nods. 'Aye, no man able in the body can escape this toil. Miserable business, but there's nothing else to do, except dig ourselves out.'

'You men, over here,' shouts a soldier, a captain by the way he bears himself. 'Here, come and shore this up.' He is pointing to a number of ragged holes in the wall.

Tobias moves with the other men to a heap of rubble and is soon driving his spade into the pile alongside them and throwing earth into the first hole. There is little talk among the men who labour on this task and little chance therefore to glean any useful intelligence. He sees the engineers examining a place further along the wall, ordering some men to drag a charred timber from a broken house nearby. Now he is here, to engage in espionage, Tobias realises that he has little idea about how to proceed, without drawing attention to himself. He knows that to continue as a dumb workhorse may yield very little, so taking a deep breath, resolves upon a bolder approach. In his present guise he is no soldier, but a townsman and therefore entitled to speak up as he wishes.

'Hey soldier,' he calls to the nearest one digging near to them. 'I hear you've so little powder left, you'll hardly keep the enemy off more than a few days.'

On hearing this, a number of the soldiers stop their digging, lift their heads and stare at Tobias. The captain too has overheard and strides up to him.

'Shut your mouth, fellow,' he says with his hand on his sword hilt.

Tobias meets his gaze, hoping that the shaking of his legs is not visible to any about him.

'I simply ask, for the purpose of knowing how much longer we'll be expected to toil for you. How many days can you hold the enemy off?'

Two of the townsmen at his side mumble a half-hearted affirmation of this question, though without looking at the officer. The captain draws his sword and stepping up to Tobias aims the hilt in a swipe at his head, but he, anticipating this action, ducks neatly below the flight of the intended blow, side-steps and finds himself safely a few paces from the officer, whose face has reddened in anger.

'Well done, neighbour,' says one of the townsmen.

The captain, furious, thrusts his sword point and jabs Tobias in the chest. He feels the point nick his skin as it pierces through his shirt.

'What? You'd kill me rather than answer a simple question?' he says.

'Leave him,' shouts one of the townsmen who moves up to stand beside Tobias. 'Touch him and you'll have to kill us all.'

The captain lowers his sword with a scowl, just as a missile comes flying, hits him with a clunking but harmless blow on the helmet and glances off on to the ground at his feet. At first Tobias thinks it must be a stick or some such, thrown by one of the townsfolk, but when a few more come flying he sees that they are arrows, fired up from the besiegers below the wall. Some of the townsmen and soldiers jump aside or crouch down, fearing an attack.

'God's body, what's this? Arrows? See who's run out of powder now, you impudent bastard,' says one of the soldiers to Tobias.

'Pox on it. There's messages on them. Look,' says another man.

These arrows are no weapons of war, but bear upon their shafts pieces of paper. One arrow drops upon the heaps of rubble; two become lodged in the roof of a hut and another falls on the ground by the men's feet. The captain takes up one of the arrows, snaps the shaft over his knee and unfolds the small piece of paper. He reads for a few moments before screwing it up into a ball, turning round and tossing it high over the wall.

'Take your filth again, you sons of whores,' he shouts. 'Gather these up, men and throw the trash away. Destroy them all.'

'I'd read it first, Captain,' says one of his men, a small wiry one of an unsoldierly appearance.

'Read? You can read, can you?' says the captain, unable to conceal a sneer in his voice.

The soldier's eyes narrow and he returns a sour look to match that of the officer's.

'I'm schooled in letters as good as you, I don't doubt, Captain.'

'Read it,' shouts one of his comrades, handing him another of the pieces of paper. 'Let's hear what it says.'

The townsmen too are silent while the soldier scans the paper and reads in a slow, deliberate voice.

Brave Soldiers of the rebel army,

The Lord General Fairfax extends to you the hand of mercy. He knows of your courage and of your sufferings for this cause that is lost. If you will lay down your arms, leave the town, surrender yourselves to us, we give our assurance that you will have fair quarter, pardon for your actions and liberty to go to your homes again. You will have free passes, will not suffer plundering, prejudice or injury by us. Think well on this to preserve your lives and liberty.

By order of the Lord General Fairfax

'Aye, let's do it. Let's give ourselves up,' shouts a hefty soldier at the edge of the group, which has now gathered around the reader.

'You whoreson dog, Timothy,' says a comrade at his side. 'You snivelling wretch. We'll not surrender to the bastards.'

The captain's face reddens in outrage at the guileless Timothy and, drawing his sword, makes a swipe of the blade within inches of his face, then turns and waves his weapon aloft, shouting over the wall. 'May you rot in Hell, Fairfax!'

This action rouses the soldiers to a burst of energy.

'Let's send him a reply, for is that not courtesy?' says the reader of the letter.

'Aye, let's send one, Captain.'

The big soldier, Timothy, has slunk away back to his digging, driving his spade into a pile of rubble. The captain looks at Tobias.

'There's your answer, traitor,' he says. 'We'll fight with honour to our deaths, powder or no.'

The officer turns to the reader who is still holding the paper.

'Right man, will you pen a reply? Do it in mud or blood, for I'd not waste good ink on those sons of whores. And someone, you fellow,' he says to another soldier, 'seek out a longbow from one of these houses.'

Tobias thinks it wise now to keep his head down and continue with the digging until such time as he can spy an opportunity to retreat unseen from this fruitless activity. He can tell, in spite of the blustering show of heroics in spurning the offer of surrender from Lord Fairfax, that there are some among the soldiers of a like mind to the poor, outspoken Timothy. These are the ones who have resumed their toil with surly expressions and no show of joining in the joking at the expense of Fairfax and his army. Tobias suspects too that the Royalists' powder and shot is running very low, else the captain, boastful and swaggering, would have proclaimed the abundance of their remaining supplies. Tobias determines to go to the encampment in the castle grounds to find others willing to talk and perhaps gain sight of the arsenal, though this thought brings back unwanted memories to mind.

He also wishes to buy some food for the Sayers, if there is any to be had, and imagines wistfully, how by these means he might perhaps win Beth's affections again.

He is looking around for the best escape route when the soldier returns from his mission, carrying an ancient long bow and joins the group that has gathered around the writer. The man is struggling to make marks upon the paper, with a piece of charred stick then looks up, as though suddenly inspired. The captain has moved away and is now in conversation with one of the engineers further along the wall. Most of the other soldiers and some of the townsmen have broken off from their labours, to await the results of the writer's composition.

'Any of you boys want to empty yourselves?' says the soldier-writer with a grin.

One of them answers. 'Aye, I reckon I could drop a load.'

'Well, go to it,' says the writer.

The obliging soldier climbs over behind a pile of rubble and crouches down, while the writer starts scratching with deliberation on the paper. Some moments later, he holds the paper up and waves it in the air.

'Finished your job yet, eh?' he calls to the crouching man. 'Soon as you're done, wrap it in this and we'll send it back to the bastards.'

'What does it say?' says another of the soldiers.

'*An answer from Colchester, August 9th 1648, as you may smell.*' reads the man proudly.

The man wielding the bow chuckles and twangs the string of his instrument in happy anticipation.

'Hurry up then,' cries someone.

There is much laughter and capering as the missile is loaded, followed by a rejoicing roar as the bowman flights the arrow high into the air and over the wall. This gives Tobias the chance that he needs to slip away, towards the Church of the Holy Trinity, through the churchyard, joining the Culver Lane, glad to have made his escape unnoticed. His freedom is short lived, however, as he is waylaid by a troop of Royalist engineers with another bunch of conscripted townsmen. He has no choice but to comply with the armed officer's orders and thus spends above three hours shovelling rubble for the engineers re-building a bastion by the North Gate.

He is freed at last from the toil and, dismayed by his wasted day, sets out on his next quest, which he hopes will bear more fruit than his attempts to gather information. He has five shillings in his pocket, his part wages given to him at the fort before his departure, with a bonus payment from the Lord General for undertaking this mission. He will find some meat for the Sayers, though he has to part with all of his money.

In the centre of the High Street is a row of houses, shops and stalls, where most of the butchers do business. However, it is not a promising sight; two of the shops lie empty, the door of one, hanging ragged on its hinges, revealing a counter scoured of all but some dried blood stains. A smell of rotting flesh and the metallic stench of guts pervade the place, though further down the row is one small stall, where it seems some transaction is taking place. Two housewives are arguing with a man, a butcher, who is standing defending his property, which seems to consist of a plank of wood with a few lumps of grey stuff and the corpse of a small dog.

'Six shillings? That's robbery,' says one of the women.

Her companion, a younger one, bursts into tears. 'Can't we have half for a shilling? Have pity.'

'No chance. Market price, Missus,' says the man, planting his feet more firmly where he stands.

'You wicked rogue,' says the older woman. 'God curse you. May you never rest easy in your bed.'

Tobias approaches the stall and the women turn to him.

'Good day to you,' he says, hoping to calm the ill tempers by a show of good humour, though the sour looks of the trio soon give him little hope of this. 'What flesh have you for sale?'

'Mangy little dog,' says one of the women bitterly. 'Six shilling for that.'

'Go get yourself some vermin then, Missus,' the butcher says, jabbing a finger at her, 'that's if you don't scare the rats away with one look at your face.'

'You villain,' says the woman, her face reddening, taking a step forward and raising her fist.

The man meets this threat with a guffaw of laughter.

'What's that?' says Tobias, partly to distract the two, but also because, as the butcher moves a step to the side, Tobias has glimpsed something half concealed in a wooden box behind the man's legs.

The butcher skips back in front of the box, to hide its contents again, but Tobias has seen a bloodied cloth bundle, which the man is for some reason concealing.

'That's spoken for,' he says, his eyes looking around as if expecting the customer for whom it is intended.

'Well, we're here ready to buy, so your other customer will have to be disappointed,' says Tobias.

'Aye that's right, you scoundrel. This young man's right,' says the older woman.

'Get away with you,' says the butcher, shifting on his feet, his eyes flicking nervously.

'I'd say that's a piece of fresh horse flesh,' says Tobias, seeing the butcher's face flush, knowing that his lucky speculation is almost certainly true.

'No friend,' he says, 'you're mistaken. It's just a piece of old mutton.'

'That's rot, that is,' says the older woman. 'There's been no mutton in the town for a month and more, you scoundrel. Let's have a look at it.'

Tobias feels the promise of an approaching victory. 'I reckon that's one of Sir Charles Lucas's finest cavalry horses, thieved from its stable.'

'No it ain't,' says the butcher, guilt twitching all over his face.

'Sir Charles Lucas would deal soundly with any person of the town receiving stolen horse flesh, especially one of his fine beasts,' says Tobias.

'What do you want? Who are you anyway?' The butcher's voice now betrays a note of panic.

'We'll take a look at the piece of flesh, shall we not, ladies?' Tobias says and sees that the sobbing young woman has stopped and is now gazing at him, her eyes wide.

The butcher bends down to the box, pulls out the wrapped bundle and lays it on the counter before them. He slowly unfolds a piece of cloth to reveal a horse's lower leg bone, streaked with sinew and slivers of flesh.

'How much?' says Tobias.

'Ten shillings.'

The angry woman spits out an oath of disgust.

Tobias sighs in dismay. 'Well, I see I must go straight to the garrison for a word with Colonel Lucas.'

'Nine shillings,' says the butcher.

'Six,' says Tobias, seeing the man's eyes flitting as with a passing pain in the head.

'All right.'

'Cut it in half, would you?' Tobias says, 'for I will share this with the ladies, if they can give a shilling.'

With their separate pieces of bony horseflesh, Tobias and the women part, but not before the angry one, calm and smiling now, has thanked him and blessed him profusely.

'Sir, you are so kind. You're not from round here, are you? May we know your name? My daughter is so gratified to have met you. She would most gladly know the name of such a noble, generous and honourable a person as your goodself.'

Tobias has not expected such fulsome praise, nor this request and, blushing, gives the name of John Smith and hurries away up the street.

Beth's pottage is tasty, for she has flavoured the tough horse flesh and bone with herbs from her neighbour's garden and has made some small dumplings of oatmeal and water. Master Sayer has left his bed and sits at table too, sipping the stew, having delivered first a long prayer of thanks to God for his bounties and for the kindness of His blessed servant Tobias. The boys eat greedily, in spite of their mother's command to savour each mouthful. Beth still does not look at Tobias, though he gazes at her often, in the hope of some sign of affection or even the acknowledgement of his presence. He compliments her on the supper and thanks her, to which she simply nods with head bowed. Mistress Sayer glances at her once or twice too and Jack tries to draw her into their talk, but she answers briefly in a scarcely audible voice. Tobias's spirits sink.

After supper, as the women clear away, Master Sayer beckons to Tobias. 'Will you come with me to the workshop?' he says. 'There's something I'd have you do for me.' Then he beckons Jack to him, whispering into the lad's ear. Tobias in puzzled misery wonders why Master Sayer should wish to go to his weaving shed at all, for he has not worked there for many months and the loom lies silent and dusty in its neglected space. Neither is the man in any state to labour, even if there were work to be had. However, he helps Master Sayer to the workshop and to a stool near the loom, as he is barely capable of standing upon his legs.

The weaver clears his throat. 'Master Waterman, Tobias,' he says, his voice thin but steady. 'Will you marry my daughter? It would please me and much relieve my mind.'

Tobias feels the heat rush to his face. 'Master Sayer, I'd –. I'd be glad, but I think she doesn't care for me. She has changed – she has–. I think I am not pleasing to her.'

His stammering foolishness shames him, but he can no more make a steady answer than he can fly through the window, so great is his surprise and consternation.

'Tobias,' says Master Sayer, in a lighter tone. 'You are surely not so cowardly that you'll not speak to her. You'll not be affrighted by a woman's looks?'

There are sounds in the yard, footsteps and Jack's chattering voice, then the door of the workshop creaks open and the boy comes in first, with Beth following behind. Master Sayer rises with some difficulty to his feet and Jack runs to him, offering his shoulder as a support and the two make their way out of the workshop and into the yard, the door swinging shut behind them. Beth stands with her head bowed and Tobias, afflicted and delighted in equal measure, steps towards her and reaches for her hand. She looks up at him with eyes soft again, full of tenderness and his doubts flee away.

'Why were you so cold to me, Beth?' he says.

'I am not brave, Tobias,' she says in a quiet voice. 'I have to make my heart hard to find courage. I have tried to harden my heart against you, for to love you hurts too much.'

He leans to kiss her and her lips soften to him.

'I lost you once and I could not bear it again,' she says, tightening her grip upon his hand. 'I have to make myself strong to care for them all. I cannot bear the pain of your absence, the fear of your death as well, while I carry this burden.'

He enfolds her in his arms and holds her, knowing that there is no other comfort that he can offer her than this.

'And will it work, do you think, this hardening of your heart against me?'

'No, never,' she says.

Chapter 15

12th August

Katherine pulls her old grey gown from the bottom of the oak chest in her chamber and shakes it out. She puts on the skirt and laces the bodice, noticing how it hangs loose about her, so thin has she become. The skirt is crumpled and suitably drab and she can easily tear off the lace trim from the sleeves. She will also put on one of Mistress Denney's coarse brown aprons, which the woman leaves in the kitchen, so with her hair hidden under a linen hood, she will most certainly pass as a maid servant. She laughs to think of Charles's plan, for it excites her in a way she scarcely dares to admit. She is to go out and meet his servant in the lane at the side of their house after dark and venture with him, in the guise of his wife to *The Bear Inn* on North Hill, where Charles has taken a chamber for the night. Her main fear is of encountering her husband as she creeps from the house, but he has retired early, telling Walter not to disturb him, no doubt satisfied that she is securely locked in her chamber for the night.

The sky darkens as she sits at the window, first to a pink glow, then to grey-blue, hiding the scrubby garden, the hut where she and Charles had been so nearly discovered by Walter that morning some weeks ago. It was this which has prompted Charles to propose their new meeting place. She hears faint sounds from her husband in his chamber, the creak of floorboards as he walks about. He is much distracted at the moment by the difficult business of the removal of the Mayor, Master Cooke, this and the fact that he wishes beyond all else to step back into that place of power that he once occupied. He judges himself the only one capable of such a position. She knows, however, that he is fearful of the mood of the people, their distrust of the Corporation for letting them starve, while the Royalist garrison has provided somewhat better for their soldiers and officers.

Katherine herself is much perturbed by this, having witnessed at first hand the desperate state of many of the townsfolk, some of whom are her neighbours in the streets round about. She wonders if she might woo Charles into an act of mercy on their behalf. She sees that his proud nature, his reserve and discomfort, when confronted with the vulgar feelings of the lower sort of people, make him seem cold, almost brutal. But she has discovered true tenderness and compassion in him, which moves her more than in a man of a softer disposition. He is a gentleman and cannot help his heritage, his upbringing, his superior sense of himself, no more than a toothless beggar can be blamed for lack of fine manners.

It is dark now, the garden turned black by the night. She fancies that she hears footsteps in the lane, though the wall of the garden prevents viewing it from her chamber window. She readies herself to go down, soundlessly turning her own secret key in the lock, opening the door, locking it again then gliding down stairs. There is no sign of Walter, though he would never question her going out. She dismisses a momentary rush of shame, imagining what her loyal servant would think of her liaison. This ranks low against the strength of her desire for Charles, however. She goes out by the washhouse door, into the garden and pushes open the gate, which squeals thinly on its hinges. A dark figure leans on the wall half way down the lane.

The man says nothing to her by way of greeting. His features are obscured under his cap but he offers his arm, which she takes and they move together, he with a lurching limp, along the alley on to the High Street, crossing it quickly. Only a few people are abroad on the streets and none shows any interest or suspicion at their passing. Past St Runwald's Church, they descend the steep lane to its lower reaches. *The Bear Inn* stands on the corner of the curving roadway, an ancient three storey, leaning building, its windows small glowing patches of light. Groups of soldiers have spilled on to the lane, talking in drink-laden voices.

'Mistress,' says the servant as they approach the place, 'we must take a cup of ale inside first, so as to look the part of man and wife. Then I will take you to my master.'

Katherine nods, feeling awkward in the company of this man, but thanking him. She is anxious for a moment that she might be recognised, if there are men of the town in the inn, but on entering the dim, low-beamed, smoky place, she finds it full of common Royalist soldiers only, realising that the place has been commandeered by them. Katherine has never been inside an establishment like this before. There are no women, beyond the landlady, a sturdy barging person who shoves her body through her customers with a look of contempt and a skinny girl who is tapping ale from a cask. Charles's serving man pushes through the press of drinkers and Katherine follows, with her eyes deflected to the floor, her face masked with the shawl.

Relieved by the anonymity of the place and the protection of the servant, who finds her a stool in a corner of the room out of the notice of the main body of the customers, she looks around. There is no one she recognises at all at first, except perhaps for a handsome, dark-haired young man in the garb of a weaver or craftsman of the town. She peers at him, convinced now that he is the cousin of the Sayers, struck down with sickness while staying in their house. She has seen him only a few times, at a distance upon the street, but she is sure that this is the same one, the young man who has stolen Beth Sayer's affections. She wonders at his presence here, drinking with Royalist soldiers, as she knows the Sayers to be staunchly for Parliament. Her curiosity provokes an uncomfortable awareness of her own subterfuge, a supporter of the Parliamentarian cause, consorting willingly with the enemy. Charles's servant returns with two cups of ale.

The place is filled with noise, rowdy talk, bursts of laughter punching the air, snatches of singing and for some moments, one voice hushes the company to near silence with his vigorous song.

Here's a health to all fellows who fight for the King.
It's death to all roundheads we gladly will bring.
Oh, we'll blow up old Fairfax and Whalley and all
Stick our pikes in, fire our muskets, we'll fight till we fall.
Twanky dillo, twanky dillo, twanky dillo, dillo, dillo
And he that loves strong beer is a hearty good fellow.

Katherine looks at the servant, a man of around thirty years with a plain but open face, and thick curly hair and is grateful for his discreet manner and his loyalty to his master. She takes a sip of the ale and notices his hands, red-skinned and maimed by burning, as he drinks from his cup.

'How long have you served your master?' she says, her voice low, realising that she does not know the man's name.

'Six years,' he says, glancing at her. She is reassured that their bowed heads and mumbling talk will likely be seen, if at all, as the dull, sporadic exchanges of husband and wife.

'And he is a good master?' she says, though doubting that this man will offer a candid opinion to her, a strange woman, his master's whore, possibly even a spy against their cause.

His gaze meets hers then and she sees no sign upon his face of falsehood or pretence.

'There's many say he's hard and rough with folk, but he's been fair with me and I owe my life to him. Dragged me out of a billet fired by the enemy when I'd been left for dead. He has no time for fancy talk and pleasing folks, like most gentlemen, but I'd serve no other.'

The man then downs the rest of his ale. 'Best go upstairs now,' he says.

The moment is well-chosen, for a cluster of men has gathered around one individual who is reading from a paper. Some of the other soldiers are holding copies of this pamphlet too, which Katherine sees are being handed out by the young man, the Sayers' cousin. It is clear that Beth's young lover is not in this place for a convivial evening of drinking and that in this action he is hazarding his life. There are cries of 'Read! Read!' from some, while the reader at the centre, a small wiry soldier is still scanning the paper he holds in his hands. Katherine and the servant are able to slip easily behind the tight-packed bodies to reach a narrow staircase at the back of the room. She follows the man up the curving stairs for two flights, to a small landing with two doors. He knocks upon one and Charles is there in a moment, his eyes giving only a flicker of welcome to her. He nods to the man.

'Before dawn tomorrow. Be here,' he says.

The servant bows his head to Charles then to Katherine, before descending the stairs. Katherine steps inside the chamber, which is a simple, barely furnished room with a single candle burning, but clean-looking, with a bed in the centre, a table, water jug and basin and on a chest in the corner, a tray spread with cheese and bread, an earthen pot and a bottle of wine. There is no fire, but the room is not cold.

Charles is half-dressed, his shirt loose, his hair uncombed. His face is heavy with worry and fatigue. This is the same troubled man she had first encountered in the churchyard those weeks ago. She will console him, soothe him, take her to him.

'Forgive me for my careless and ragged state,' he says, taking her hand.

She smiles. 'It matters not at all, for you are entertaining no fine lady tonight.'

She takes off her shawl and the cap, loosens her hair and moves close, passing her arms around his body, feeling the warmth of him, though he seems forlorn, almost lifeless in her embrace. She reaches to stroke his cheek and kisses him, seeing his eyes lose a little of their anguish. 'Forget Charles, forget the trials which torment you, even for this little while,' she whispers to him as she kisses him.

Slowly their passions are awakened, gently at first as she caresses him, beneath his shirt, undoing his breeches to pleasure him and he unlacing her bodice, to kiss her breasts until he lifts her, swiftly in his arms to the bed where they fall, laughing in this foretaste of the ecstasy, which is about to sweep them away, swallow them wholly.

Later, she sits up, gripped by a terrible hunger. 'May we eat now?' she says, kissing him.

'Of course,' he says, catching her in his arms, calm and loving now, a different man.

They sit close together, dishevelled, half dressed in their shifts at the small table and eat hungrily.

She sees him watching her for a moment, such that she is embarrassed by her over-eager devouring of the food.

'Are you in want?' he says. 'Do you still have victuals in your larder?'

She smiles to see his face, concerned as a dutiful husband might be for his wife's welfare.

She reaches for his hand. 'We have more than many people. I gorge now, because you have given me my appetite again.'

He returns her smile and catches her hand, kissing it. 'Your husband will not notice you are gone?' he says.

'He thinks I am securely locked in my room and he is a heavy sleeper. He would not wake even for a cannon blast. This is the only quality in him that I admire.'

She hears the spite in her voice, the irony that she reserves only for her husband himself. She had not wished to reveal this poisonous side of her nature to Charles.

'He is not kind to you, I think,' he says, rising from the table and taking the candle from the mantelshelf nearby.

She wonders what he intends, then finds him kneeling at her side, lifting the candle close to her face. She flushes and turns away from him.

'I am much better in the shadow. Do not examine me closely, for what you find may repel you.'

'Never,' he says, putting down the candlestick upon the table and leaning to kiss her face, her temples where she knows she still bears some faint bruising.

'Katherine,' he says. 'How can I protect you? I'd gladly put him to the sword for hurting you.'

'That is the solution of a soldier, is it not?' she says, touched by his concern and half-amused at the image of her husband cringing before this gentleman's sword drawn on her behalf.

'Come, let's not spoil our time with talk of him,' she says. 'Let's eat and drink our fill, for I am happy in these moments here with you. There is no more than this, nor can there ever be. We'll drink to one more meeting, or two, or–'

But he has stood up, then drinks a mouthful of wine and wipes his moustache on his sleeve, looking down at her with a sad and penetrating gaze.

'You long for an end to the siege and measure each day and minute until your liberation, as all others do,' he says.

She flushes, seeing that her words have disturbed him. 'But surely you do too, to end this intolerable suffering.'

'Aye, it will end my suffering for ever,' he says.

The truth strikes her like a blow to the chest and she rises to stand close to him, to embrace him. 'Forgive me, forgive me. I should not have voiced such thoughts. I cannot bear to think of you defeated, but no more can I wish for your victory. Can you not escape, if all is lost?'

'Escape?' he says, easing her a little from him so that he is looking into her face. 'Yes, I have a fine horse, though it has lost a little speed, I do not doubt, through lack of fodder. Yes, I could break out with those of my horse who still have mounts and take my chance, run away from Fairfax. The way of a coward tempts me greatly.'

'You are no coward, Charles,' she says. 'You are a man of honour, brave in every part of you. Forgive me.'

'Honour?' he says, and she sees a tightening of his face. 'I could bear all this and more, if I knew with certitude that I had kept my honour.'

He is sinking fast, losing his carefree self again, she fears.

'Tell me,' she says, hoping that she can relieve his tormented state and that they will not part in anguish. She takes his hand and leads him to the bed, where they lie down together, she leaning her head against his shoulder, he staring at the ceiling.

'Tell me,' she says again.

He clutches her hand. 'It was in Gloucestershire, two years, no three years past,' he says, his voice sinking low. 'I was sent to take command of Berkeley Castle, a mean and lowly position, not fitting to my rank and experience, insulting to my status as Lieutenant General of the King's Horse. It was a petty post, out of the way of the field campaigns. I was devoured by envy and ire to be so ill-treated. No appeals to the King who I had served loyally and without question, nor to His Highness Prince Rupert yielded any relief from this tedious appointment. I well know that I am sour of temper and choleric in my humour and so these horrible qualities festered in me all the more. Thus it was that I took a troop of 300 horse and foot in pursuit of a Parliamentary force, when there was no purpose or gain but to satisfy my pride and my urge for combat, but we were cut down in a narrow pass. I took a hurt and lost sixteen good men and countless prisoners. Then came the dire news that the Scots, fighting for Parliament, had slaughtered nearly all at our garrison at Stinchcombe. My mind was filled only with revenge, as though the devil himself stood at my side. We rode out against the enemy, attacked and overwhelmed them, took many prisoners. I gave no quarter to them. With my own hand I cut two of them down and had the rest put to the sword. This haunts me still, for I had until that time, conducted myself according to the rules of war. Tell me, where was my honour then?'

She says nothing but tightens her grip upon his hand, looking at his face as he lies, staring up. She sees his jaw tighten, his teeth clench.

'Only God can forgive your sins,' she says after some moments. 'But He also sees your worth and your virtues. You have been loyal and true to your lord and master, the King. In that you have never wavered, where others have seen fit only to save themselves. You have the terrible burden of a commander of men in time of war. Such trials and strife would test all mortal men and lead the most virtuous to falter. I too know what it is to sink to dishonourable behaviour, to bear a foul stain upon my soul.'

She says no more, but he draws her to him and they lie embracing for some time in silence. She is glad to see that soon he is asleep.

The servant's knock upon the door drags Katherine out of her half-slumber. She leaves the bed, dressing quickly in her maid's gown and apron, twisting her loose hair under the linen hood. Charles lies watching her.

'Send for me again,' she says. 'I will wait. I will long for that time.'

He leaps from the bed and takes her in his arms, kissing her fiercely this time, clasping her close. Then, slowly, he releases her and opens the door to find the servant standing there.

She has scarcely managed to strip herself of her old garments when she hears her husband's footsteps in the hallway and his voice raised in an exchange with Walter. Their talk is distant, so that she cannot fully hear the matter they are discussing, though their tone is low and urgent, her husband's full of angry questioning. She hastens to make herself presentable and descends to the kitchen where both men have gone, taking their conversation with them.

'You must go after the thieving woman and bring back what you can,' her husband is saying.

'Well sir –,' says Walter.

'What's amiss?' Katherine says, coming in to find in her husband's face the familiar scowl of displeasure.

'That woman, Denney, has stolen the contents of our larder,' he says.

Katherine looks at Walter, finding his expression blank, his shoulders shrugging.

'Why did you not see that she was plundering us, you fool?' says her husband. 'You were not in league with her, I hope?'

'No sir.' Walter flushes with anger at this affront. 'Her family were hard-pressed, her daughter poorly. The woman was driven to it, like so many in the town who are near dying.'

'You excuse thievery, you villain,' Thomas Wade says, the spit flying from his mouth. 'You must go and raise the constable to arrest the woman. Go now, I tell you. I'll have my property returned.'

'That may be impossible, sir, if it's all been eaten.' Walter's voice is sour.

'Is there nothing left at all, Walter?' Katherine says, looking around. The parcel of cheese that lay on the table is gone. No jars of pickled onions or preserves of fruit remain upon the kitchen shelves. Katherine crosses the kitchen towards the door of the cold larder. Though their stock of food has been much diminished, the larder is now completely empty, as though a great flood has washed it clean away.

'You must go to Mistress Furley or Mistress Barrington,' says her husband, looking at Katherine. 'You must request some relief for us from their supplies.'

For the first time, Katherine notices a flicker of uncertainty in her husband's eyes. She sees then that he has thought himself above the privations afflicting the poorer folk of the town. He has imagined their complaints and pleas as the grumbling ingratitude of the idle, made needy by their own profligacy and stupidity.

'I will give you money, and you Walter go and seek out any shopkeeper with flesh or bread or flour, whatever you can find,' he says.

'Sir,' says Walter, his surprise displacing his earlier ill-humour. 'There's no shop with any food. People are starving. Do you not know?'

Thomas Wade's answer is to turn and leave the kitchen, retreating to the parlour where he keeps his money.

'Will you pardon me, Mistress,' Walter says. 'I should have stored some of our food out of view. I did not think the siege could last so long.'

'No more did I, nor anyone.'

Her husband stalks back into the kitchen, holding a leather purse from which he empties several gold guineas on to the table.

'Food can always be found where there is money,' he says,

staring at Katherine and Walter, challenging them to disagree. 'Go even to Buxton or Leming, if need be, for they are ones who favour the rebels and may have access to their bounties.'

Katherine takes up two of the gold coins from the table, with a shiver of satisfaction to find her husband so discomfited as to seek succour from his enemies.

'Well, I think it is clear what you and the Corporation must do now,' she says, sensing that, on this occasion, she may make her point with impunity. 'You must go now to the garrison commander and demand that they lend us, the townspeople, some relief. You must delay no longer. You must act now, or watch more people perish around you.'

Unusually, his response is no more than a sneering glance and he leaves the room without another word. Katherine wishes Walter good fortune in his search for food and goes to prepare herself for her own task. She is not keen to go begging at the houses of other aldermen, though she guesses that some will be generous enough to help where they have the means. Alderman Furley lives in a street next to St Runwald's and Katherine decides to appeal first to his wife who is a kindly and pleasant person. However, she proceeds no further than a few steps from her front door, before catching sight of Beth Sayer and her two young brothers hurrying towards her.

'Mistress Wade, if you please,' says Beth, her eyes hollow and pleading. 'Will you come with us? We are going to the quarters of the Lord General to beg for relief. If we gather more women and children, he will surely see our plight.'

Katherine, taken aback by this request but struck by the strength of the girl's supplication, hesitates. Here is a young woman, no more than a girl taking bold and desperate action while men such as her husband vacillate in impotence or cowardice.

'Mistress, he will listen to you, more than to lower folk like us,' Beth says. 'You made Sir Charles Lucas change his mind. Will you help us again? Please, I beg you.'

The girl's twin brothers are at her side, their matching stares fixed upon Katherine.

'I'll come,' she says and sets off with them along the Culver Lane.

Many women and children upon the street join them as they go, Beth knocking on the doors of neighbours, telling them briefly of their mission. The girl is fired by determination, her shyness gone, fearless and heedless it seems of what these actions might lead to, or of the possibility of their failure, as with other complaints by the starving people. The band grows to around forty women, some with babes in arms and others with their skinny offspring hanging at their sides as they go. They straggle along in a noisy bunch, pushing on under the archway and into the yard of *The King's Head,* surprising half a dozen soldiers on guard at the door, who swing their pikes forward, as though in battle readiness, their backs to the building, staring with suspicious eyes.

Katherine and Beth, at the head of the throng of women, stand firm, though the spikes of the weapons are only inches from them. Katherine hears the infectious urgings of some behind her, along with the wails and cries of others. The soldiers bar the entrance to the inn and one, with a sword, hammers hard with the butt upon the door.

'What's this, you women?' he calls stepping towards them, sword pointing at Katherine's breast. The blade wavers however, and she sees the soldier's eyes flitting uncertainly. 'Get you gone, else you'll see your own guts.'

Some women shrink back, crying out in response to this threat, but Katherine knows that the generals will not order a crowd of women to be cut down in cold blood. She is determined, if it has to be, to confront Charles himself, though in her heart she hopes he is gone from his billet. But she will make their demands boldly, will pit her strident self against Charles, the soldier hardened by the necessities of his trade in this war, his contract of honour. Here in the stark daylight, in public view, in the midst of this conflict, their other tender selves would never survive, would perish as fragile flowers blasted by foul weather. To oppose him will pain her, but she has no choice. She and Beth are flanked by a thin woman with a small bundle containing a baby and another woman of middle years with a small girl beside her. Beth's young brothers are standing close behind them, where Beth has ordered them to stay out of sight.

Katherine speaks up, her voice firm and strong, while those around her hush their clamour.

'We have come to petition the Lord General Goring.'

The soldier with the sword scowls at her, his comrades looking on.

'Go back to your homes,' he says. 'I warn you. You will get nothing here.'

Katherine draws in a deep breath. 'I say again, we demand to see the Lord General. He must hear our pleas. You must send word to him.'

'Damn you all to Hell,' the soldier says, his eyes hardening.

A few of the women set up a chorus of wailing, a ragged, desperate cacophony. 'Have pity. My children are starving. Have mercy. We've nothing to eat. We're dying.'

'We will not move from here, until Lord Goring hears us,' Katherine says, staring back at the soldier, though a pulse throbs in her head as her fear grows that all of this is in vain. The soldiers will charge on them with their pikes and chase them from the yard, scatter them back to their pathetic homes, crush their pitiful endeavour.

'Get you gone, I tell you again,' growls the soldier, signalling with his hand to the pikemen. 'Advance!'

Katherine and Beth are forced to recoil, shuffling back a few steps into the crowd of wailing women. Then in a move that startles Katherine, Beth leaps forward, trying to dodge past the man and plunge towards the inn door. She is not quick enough, however, and the soldier lunges, grabbing her arm, throwing her back with such force that she falls upon the ground at Katherine's feet, hitting her head upon the cobbles, drawing blood. There is a shriek of outrage from the crowd, then Katherine, as she kneels to help the girl to her feet, sees a small figure dart out from behind, one of the twin brothers, who lands a fast kick on the stockinged shin of the soldier. He yowls in surprise and pain, flails with his blade, but the child, too nimble, dives sideways, then back into the crowd. Katherine feels the boy lurking close behind her, and clamps him with her arm, holding him securely at her back. She stands her ground as the soldier advances.

'You'll kill me before you touch him,' Katherine says in a low voice, hearing gasps and cheers from some of the women. A baby squeals loudly, as, from behind the soldier, another small body hurtles, kicking wildly at his other leg.

The man turns, unbalanced, staggers, almost losing his sword, while the second twin flies back into the crowd, amidst the laughter of the hapless soldier's comrades. The women too, set up shrieks of derision.

'Serves you right, you godless bastard,' shouts one from the crowd.

Katherine cringes inwardly but gleefully, preparing herself for the soldier's violent response, but he has no chance to utter, as behind him the door of the inn is opened and an officer stands in the threshold.

The officer eyes the women at the front of the crowd.

'You wish to see my Lord Goring? Two of you women only, the leaders,' he says, pointing to Katherine and Beth. 'The rest, withdraw, get back and hush that terrible din, or else we'll beat you back to your houses.'

The officer leads the way into the flagged open hall of the inn, cluttered with tables and joint stools and a wide fireplace at the end. From the opposite side of the hall, a maid, broom in hand, looks up at their entry and scuttles away along a passage. The officer and another soldier flank Katherine and Beth, as though they fancy that these wild women might need restraining from laying their mad hands upon the gentlemen within.

Katherine and Beth are steered along the passage where the maid has scampered, into a large chamber with a long table and dark heavy oak chairs all around. At the end of the table sits an elderly gentleman, whom Katherine takes to be the Lord

General Goring, the Earl of Norwich himself. His face sags with age, though beneath the lines and folds of skin is the trace of a mischievous, youthful former self. He, relaxed with his hands resting on the carved arms of his chair, his mouth quivering in the beginnings of a smile, watches as Katherine and Beth are directed to the far end of the table. Katherine feels Beth's shoulder brush her own, the girl's apprehension at finding herself in an audience with such gentlemen almost palpable. At the Lord General's side sit two officers, of lesser rank, one with a plump face and extravagantly curled hair, the other a hard-faced, narrow-eyed individual. It is clear that they consider this interruption an irksome inconvenience.

'Good women,' the Lord General says, smiling now. 'You wish to make a petition?'

'My lord,' says Katherine curtseying and seeing Beth do the same at her side.

'I would know who you are, first of all, Mistress,' he says.

'I am wife to Alderman Thomas Wade.'

'And your husband knows of your leading this rabble here, does he?'

Katherine's rage rises inside her belly, not least because she imagines how as a man, she would be considered as her own person, how she might draw a sword against such impudence from another, even a gentleman. She swallows hard.

'He does not, sir. I come to speak for the women of this town and their children. They do not think that you hear their pleas for relief.'

'Oh we have heard them plain enough, like the screeching of cats,' Lord General says, smirking at one of the officers at his side who laughs in response.

Katherine clutches the stuff of her gown and holds her voice steady.

'My lord, the people are starving. They have no bread, no grain, nor any meat. The poor are forced to eat vermin. We beg you to look with pity upon them and give some relief from your own stores of food.'

The Lord General's face changes, his smile dropping and eyes narrowing. He leans forward in his seat towards them.

'You ask me to give up victuals meant for the mouths of my own men to your people? One may well ask why your own town Corporation does not see to the needs of its own citizens. Your distress is none of our doing.'

'My Lord,' Katherine says, unable to harness her tongue, knowing that she risks all by crossing this commander. 'It is very much your doing. Your army has rendered us prisoners in our own town. We cannot go freely about, trade our goods, earn our living, quit the place of our own volition, nor seek food from outside. You have stripped us of our power to do anything for ourselves about our sad state.'

The plump-faced officer at the Lord General's side goes to rise from his seat, casting a dangerous look at Katherine.

'My Lord, shall I remove these impudent women?' he says.

Sweat prickles Katherine's brow. Beth is clutching her arm.

'My Lord, Sir Charles Lucas would listen to our pleas,' says Katherine quickly, before the officer can act on his suggestion. 'He is a Colchester gentleman and would not dismiss our requests with so little compassion. His family have lived in this town for many years and have an affinity with the county.'

She knows that her face has coloured, but continues, hoping that the ageing commander will judge this a consequence of her passion for her cause and no other.

'Well,' he says, eyeing her closely. 'You are acquainted with Colonel Lucas?'

'I am, my Lord,' says Katherine, staring back at the commander, with all the power of her will keeping her voice steady.

There is an empty pause and Katherine does not dare to breathe.

'If that is the case,' says the Lord General sitting back in his chair, the smirk upon his lips again, 'there is nothing to do but to summon Colonel Lucas here.'

At this, Katherine and Beth are ushered back out into the

hall, to a dark corner seat, while a soldier opens the front door, departing on his commission to summon Charles to the place. From outside in the yard Katherine hears, through the opened door, the women set up a questioning shout, a collective howl of appeal. This then subsides when Katherine and Beth do not appear, the women's submissive behaviour perhaps due to fear for the safety of their leaders.

'Mistress,' Beth says in a small voice at her side. 'Do you think Sir Charles Lucas will truly lend us aid?'

Chapter 16

13th & 14th August

Jack and Ed rejoice when Beth comes back with a small sack of grain. Mother doesn't seem much cheered by it, however, saying it's little enough and will last them only a day or two and they'll have to grind it with stones.

'But it'll make bread for Father, will it not?' Jack says.

'It'll help him be strong again.' Ed's voice fades away in his failed effort to be hopeful.

Jack knows that nothing they can say or do will make things any better.

'Aye,' Mother says.

'Come boys,' says Beth, 'let's find us a quernstone in the yard to grind some flour.'

They do their best to crush the grain between two flat pieces of stone, the dust gritting the flour, making a small heap of rough dirty powder. It's enough, however, for Beth to make small, flat, tasteless cakes on a griddle, which fills them for a while. She says she'll boil the rest of the grain for the next day. Father will take none of it and Mother gives his griddle cake to the boys to share.

'Sir Charles Lucas ordered the grain to be given from the army stores,' Beth tells them after they have eaten. 'Mistress Wade turned his mind again and he bowed to her will. I wonder how it is that she knows him.'

Jack sees Mother make a strange face with her mouth

twisting, but she says nothing.

'What is he like, Sir Charles Lucas?' says Jack, recalling Mistress Wade's servant Walter and his hard and angry words against that gentleman and his family.

'Very soldierly and proud,' says Beth. 'He did not speak to us at all, not even to Mistress Wade. He only told the officer who was with him, to give out a bag of grain for each household, then went quickly away. I think maybe he is troubled in his conscience about the grief and suffering he has brought to his own town.'

Jack hopes that the hateful Sir Charles Lucas will have more similar afflictions in the days to come.

'Boys, go and draw some water,' Mother says in her same dull voice. 'I must make a drink for your father.'

'Then you must go and search for more fuel for the fire,' Beth orders.

Jack and Ed take a bucket each and go to the pump at the end of the lane, Jack looking up at Mistress Wade's house as they pass, wondering how much food she has left and whether Sir Charles Lucas gave her more because she is known to him. Perhaps they could call on her and ask if they can dig for roots in her garden again and hope she will offer them something to eat as well. Jack tries to remember what it was like not to be hungry. He wonders if he'll even have the strength to go looking for something to burn in the fire. They have to wait for a neighbour to fill a cask of water first, so it is a little while before they bring their buckets back into the kitchen.

Neither Beth nor Mother is there. Jack looks at Ed in a silence they both wish will soon be filled by some comforting, familiar sound, but they hear only the creak of floor timbers as someone shifts or walks in the bedchamber above. They glance up at the low ceiling, hearing the noise of sobbing travelling down to them. Jack takes Ed's hand as they go upstairs together.

Father looks peaceful in his face when they go to him. The lines of worry and pain are all smoothed away. They kneel around his bed, Mother holding his hand and Beth saying a prayer for his departed soul while Jack and Ed weep as quietly as they can.

They stay there for a long time, praying on their knees until Jack can no longer feel his legs and thinks he might soon fall over. Mother looks up at last.

'Jack, Ed, bring the water up here, will you, please,' she says. 'Beth would you go to St Nicolas's for Parson Roberts and see if he will come to us.'

Two days later, they watch the coffin being lowered into the earth in the churchyard where so many others in the town lie new buried too, their souls at rest, like Father's. There are many folk and neighbours there, weavers who had known Father well and even Master and Mistress Wade. Most of those gathered there look miserable and tattered to Jack's eyes and he wishes that Tobias was there, for Father liked him well and blessed his betrothal to Beth. Perhaps, thinks Jack, they might never see Tobias again, like Father, never again in this world and will have to pray to meet him in the next. He has gone back to his army and might even now be dead and buried in the earth himself, killed by a musket ball or blown apart by a huge shot from a gun. Jack is filled with a sense of his own feeble helplessness. He and Ed will never be apprenticed, now that Father is gone and they have no money. Mother is old and tired all the time. Beth is their one hope. She has never failed them, but she is only a woman. They, Ed and Jack, are the men of the family now and are meant to provide, but Jack doesn't know how.

The minister's prayers go on and on, but Jack would endure ten hundred more of them to ensure that Father's soul is at peace in heaven. Does God look down on them and see their hunger, he wonders. Is it really wickedness and evil in the town that made the Royalist army come here? That's what most folk say. Would God make the Royalists ride away again if all the folk in the town were to repent of their sins? Jack is sure that everyone has most certainly tried this, probably many times over. But even were this marvellous and wonderful thing to happen, it will never be the same again. It is all gone, the time when there was food to eat every day, when Mother would scold them one minute, then embrace them the next, when he and Ed would play at fighting in the yard and Father would grumble at them for not doing their chores. If Father were alive again, Jack would never make him grumble, ever.

Mother and Beth lead them away through the churchyard along with the other folk and Jack is glad to find Mistress Wade at their side. He thinks her such a brave and beautiful lady and admires her very much, for going against the Royalists and because she is always tender to them. She touches Jack and Ed on their shoulders, and looks sorrowful in her eyes, then goes to talk to Beth and Mother. She is carrying a small parcel wrapped in oiled cloth and hands it to Beth. Beth is weeping a little again and Mistress Wade puts her arm around her.

'What's that in the parcel?' asks Jack when they have returned to the kitchen.

Beth unwraps the covering and reveals half of a bony carcase with some flesh on it, like a rabbit but bigger, maybe a hare.

'We must give thanks to God for such a generous neighbour,' says Beth, going to the shelf by the door for a jug.

'Aye, a bountiful sinner,' says Mother in a low voice, which Beth doesn't hear and Jack wonders what Mother could mean by this. He'll ask Ed about it later.

Beth boils up the hare with some rosemary and shares it out between them into the four porringers. Jack gulps it down, unable to control his ravenous craving. Ed drains his bowl and sucks it all round the edges, then they all bow their heads and say a prayer of thanks to God for his bounties.

Later, they all sit in the miserable dullness of the kitchen, Jack and Ed rolling a clay marble to each other along a hollow between the flagstones, while Old Solomon lies, watching them with one eye. Mother doesn't move but sits staring at Father's empty chair, while Beth mends something with her needle by the window in the better light.

Ed suddenly catches up the marble and looks at Jack with the glint in his eye, the sign that he's had an idea.

'Mother, may we go out, to look for food?' Ed says, though

Jack knows that this hopeless quest is not the true purpose behind his seeking permission.

Mother's eyes seem not to see them properly when she nods her head without a word but Beth looks up from her sewing.

'Don't tarry too long out of doors,' she says.

They can't take Old Solomon now because he no longer has the strength to stand on his legs and they have to carry him into the yard each day, though little enough comes out of him now. Jack follows Ed outside on to the street where they see at once something amiss further up, at Master Symond's. His door is wide open and his daughter is there, arguing with some soldiers. There are six of them, armed with swords and one has a pistol. Another soldier is pulling a cart upon which lie some sacks half full and a number of stone pots and jars. Some of their other neighbours have come out on the street too and a commotion is building up, with angry voices. Jack sees Master Symonds, who is quite an old man, swinging his arm to strike a blow at one of the soldiers, but he hits back with the butt of his pistol and their neighbour falls down in the street. His daughter screams.

'What are they doing?' Jack says, feeling ill in his stomach again.

'Taking things,' says Ed. 'Let's go closer and see.'

'But the soldiers have weapons.'

Ed's face has gone white.

'We've got to be brave now. We've got to be like men,' he says, though his voice quivers as he speaks.

They edge a little further along the street towards the group of folk gathered around Master Symonds who has got to his feet again, but there is blood coming out of his head.

'Stinking cowardly thieves,' says a woman with a crying child on her hip. 'We've got nothing, you bastards.'

One of the soldiers turns an ugly face to her. 'Stop your scolding mouth, wife. That plump child you've got in your arms would make a goodly dish.'

The woman shrieks then turns and runs back into her house.

Ed grabs Jack by the arm and pulls him away, back along the road. They burst into the kitchen.

'There's soldiers coming,' Ed says. 'They're looking for food. They're taking things from folks' houses.'

Beth throws her sewing aside and rises quickly. 'What, on our street?'

Mother looks up, her eyes glazed and unseeing and with a peculiar twisted smile on her face.

'Well, they'll be sorely aggrieved if they come here. Bid them not to waste their time stepping inside our empty place,' she says, casting her eyes around the kitchen.

But Jack and Ed, following Mother's gaze have both seen Old Solomon. Jack feels his gut twist in a knot and cannot move for a moment. Ed runs to pull a shawl from the hook by the door, then throws it over the old dog, covering him completely, gesturing for Jack to come to him. Beth has risen from her stool and watches as Ed makes a bundle of Solomon so that he looks like a bed bolster or parcel of clothes. But Jack imagines the soldiers tramping in, poking with their swords, just as they had when the family had saved Tobias from capture. Jack and Ed know that they must use this trick again, or something like it.

'Lie down,' says Jack to Ed, placing his head on Solomon's flank and groaning as though in pain. Ed obeys and throws himself down at Jack's side.

The soldiers do not knock but two burst in upon them, pushing their way into the kitchen, unarmed but with hungry eyes that rove around the room, pausing for a moment on Jack and Ed lying lifeless by the dead fire.

'Bring us any victuals you've got, Missus,' says one of the soldiers. 'Orders of the Lord General. We're to take all stores of food. Hurry.'

Mother stands up and takes a step towards the soldier, laughing a horrible laugh, which turns into a sob. Beth goes to her side, putting her arm around her waist to steady her.

'You have come for plunder, have you?' Beth says, with a different, hard voice. 'We have nothing. We've just this day buried my father who wasted away. See, my two brothers lie there, too weak to move.'

The men say nothing, but the one who is standing near the shelf by the door sweeps away a few cups and platters stored there and grabs their remaining four tallow candles, holding them in his hand and challenging Beth with his stare. Jack, watching from the corner of his eye, dreading and praying as Beth moves towards him, wonders what he and Ed will do if the man strikes her down. But she goes to him with no fear, grasps his wrist with the candles still in his grip, while the other soldier looks on.

'As you are a Christian, I beg you,' she says and her voice is small but steady, her eyes fixed on the soldier's face. She takes the candles from his hand one by one and puts them into the pocket of her apron.

'You fool,' says the soldier's comrade.

'Let's be gone,' says the first, now empty-handed.

They hesitate for only a moment longer, glancing around swiftly before turning and clattering out through the doorway. Beth sinks down on to a stool at the table and covers her face with her hands. Mother is sitting now too, in Father's chair, and no words are spoken. Ed gasps as he breathes again and Jack, feeling the warm body of Old Solomon beneath him, sits up. He draws back the shawl from the old dog whose eyes are closed in a peaceful sleep, from which Jack sees he will never awake. He says nothing, but picks up the clay marble and rolls it along the floor to Ed, who pushes it back to him again, without looking up.

The night fills the kitchen with blackness. They have no fire even to lend any light. Beth comes and kneels down beside Jack and Ed, laying her hand on Old Solomon's body.

'It was better like this,' she says. 'The soldiers did not take him.'

Jack and Ed say nothing, now that they are both full of the horror of what has to be done. Jack wants to howl and bawl like a babe, because he knows he is supposed to be a man and do what Father would have done. But they will have to wait for the morning, for there is no light to see by. Jack rises, legs stiff with sitting as he and Ed grope their way in the darkness towards the stairs and up to bed.

The sheets are cold and Jack is too full of misery to sleep. Ed is fidgeting and snuffling too, but he hears Beth breathing steadily.

'Ed, when should we go?' Jack whispers.

'Through the tunnel? Soon.'

'Shall we tell Beth?'

'No, not yet. When we're ready to escape, we'll go there in the night, so that the soldiers won't see. Just in case,' says Ed.

'But they might attack in the night. Sometimes armies do that, to catch the enemy asleep. They creep up on them and stab them with their swords.'

Jack's skin prickles with horror at the imagined scene and a sudden soft banging from downstairs starts his body trembling. He clutches Ed, whose cold, bony embrace strengthens him enough to strain his hearing and listen again.

'It's in the yard,' says Jack.

'It's just the wind.'

'It might be one of those soldiers come back.'

'Ssh.'

It is a tapping, a soft, regular tapping, which stops after an interval, then starts again.

'Shall we wake Beth?' says Jack.

'No.' Ed slips from the bed. 'Come, we must see to this ourselves. Let's get our spikes for swords.'

Jack can see nothing through the thick blackness around them, but he gropes beneath the bed and finds the piece of cloth in which they hide their digging tools, the two iron stakes. Handing one to Ed, he follows him down the stairs. He knows well the familiar hollows and ridges of the wooden boards under his bare feet, the worn handrail at the side of the staircase and the undulating plaster walls, which he touches with his fingers, until his feet reach the cold flags of the kitchen floor. A blind man would be in a world like this, Jack thinks. The man, if indeed there is someone outside in the yard, will be no better able to see than they are, so if it is someone bent on evil, Jack and Ed can surprise him and hit him. Jack is glad too that the darkness hides Old Solomon's body from his eyes.

'We'll stand behind the door then open it quickly so we'll be ready to strike him,' Ed says and, holding on to each other, their free hands wielding their weapons, they creep over to the door.

'Jack, Ed, are you there?' comes a voice.

They both throw down their weapons and scramble for the bolt, their hands fumbling and fighting in their excitement, then shoot it back and open the door. Jack tries hard not to weep with relief and happiness, his eyeballs aching as though they will burst from his head. Tobias has his arms around them both and Jack wishes that he will never leave hold.

'Father's dead,' Jack says, with a painful lump in his throat, hearing Ed sob in the darkness, but knowing that Tobias will not mind their tears.

'Lord bless his departed soul,' Tobias says quietly, still clutching them tightly to him.

'Old Solomon's dead too,' Ed says.

'Dear God in Heaven.'

They stand together with Tobias's arms around them, so that Jack hears his breathing, smells the cold earthy night air on his coat. It is some time before Tobias speaks.

'Go back to bed now, boys. Go to sleep. I'll rest here a while too. In the light of the morning, we'll see better what to do.'

Jack lies in bed watching the light arrive slowly, hearing Beth shift in her bed and knows that he must tell her at once of the marvel that has happened in the night. But a terrible thought strikes him, a panic low in his stomach that he has only imagined or dreamed Tobias's return. Should he run downstairs to see for himself before he shakes Beth awake? He does not dare, in case he discovers the kitchen empty and himself devastated by the truth of his delusion. Instead, he nudges Ed.

'Is it true? Is Tobias really here?' he says.

Ed's eyes flick open. 'Did you dream it too?'

Jack slides out of bed and Ed thuds out after him.

'Almighty God, I pray you make it true,' Jack murmurs all the way down the stairs until he spies Tobias's sleeping form on the bed in the corner. Then with strength from heaven Jack runs up the stairs almost knocking Ed down in his haste to wake Beth and Mother. He babbles in his excitement and makes Beth think that his wits are gone, by the look on her face, though when she hears Tobias's name her eyes shine.

Only a short time later, Tobias is holding Mother's hand in both of his and Jack thinks he is weeping when he speaks of his sorrow about Father. He embraces Beth and kisses her for quite a long time on the mouth, like lovers are supposed to do. They are betrothed, which Jack knows means promised to each other for ever, though they can't be as glad yet as folk on their wedding day. Jack rejoices in his mind, however, to think that one day Tobias will truly be their brother. Now that it is daytime and the light has come back into the kitchen, they can see Old Solomon lying in front of the hearth. Tobias goes to him, laying a hand upon his head.

Ed looks at Jack and they exchange the awful unstated thing that can't be escaped any longer. They crouch down together beside Tobias, sliding their arms underneath the stiff body of the dog.

'We'll do it outside in the yard,' says Ed.

'No, let me,' Tobias says, taking Old Solomon's body in his arms and rising to his feet.

As they watch him go out of the back door, Beth lifts up one of their small, three-legged stools.

'We must break this up for the fire,' she says. 'Ed, Jack, bring water for the pot.'

Hunger, and trying not to think, has driven Jack to gulp and guzzle the stuff in his bowl, though now he fears he might throw up his stomach. To distract his troubling thoughts he imagines how they might all run away now to Brightlingsea, Tobias too where he could be wed to Beth. There is nothing but starvation and death here in Colchester. He and Ed must take action very soon, even this very day. They must get Timothy to help them finish their tunnel.

'I'll not return,' Tobias says suddenly as they sit at the table after their hasty meal. 'I'll stay here with you.'

'Not go back to the army?' says Beth.

'I have half my pay,' he says, but his face is solemn and sad.

Mother gets up from the table, knocking over her stool and fixes her eyes on him. They are staring hard at Tobias and Jack doesn't know why she's so angry with him.

'You mean to desert?' she says.

Tobias reddens in his face and looks first at Mother then at Beth.

'They will kill you for it,' Mother says, looking as though she might attack him herself.

Jack's heart pounds, for he's heard folk in the town talk of deserters, cowardly men who run from their duty. But this is not Tobias.

'They'll hang you. Fairfax will hang you.' Mother's hand is clutching at her apron.

'Is this true, Tobias, if they caught you?' Beth says.

'I'd best not be caught then.'

Tobias is holding Beth's hand in both of his and his voice is heavy. 'I've had my fill of fighting and wars, causes that bring only misery. I used to be proud of my duty. I used to believe that what I did would make life better in the end. But what good can arise from all this grief, only more hatred and hunger for revenge? It is God's punishment for the wickedness of man, of Royalists and Roundheads, innocent and guilty. All must suffer for it. To fight each other is our worst and most hateful sin.'

'God's punishment is enough, Tobias,' says Mother. 'You must not suffer man's as well.'

Beth gets to her feet and lays her hand on his shoulder.

'Mother is right. You must go back and serve your time, do your duty as you swore, while we stay strong in our hopes and prayers.'

Jack wonders about the usefulness of praying to God, who only seems to answer prayers very rarely and then when it is least expected of all. Tobias bows his head and says nothing, though he holds Beth's hand. Mother has gone quiet again too. Jack feels the uneasy stillness in the air. Prayers will not keep Tobias safe in the war. Escaping seems altogether a much better idea and their tunnel is nearly finished. If they tell Tobias about their tunnel, once it is broken right through the wall, he might consider coming along with them after all. The army would surely not find him so far away in Brightlingsea.

There are many hazards and obstacles, however, not least the chance of Tobias meeting Timothy, if he does come with them through the tunnel. They have not been there for some days, but the hole is good and strong now, since Timothy, following Ed's suggestion, put in some strong pieces of timber to shore it up at the top and sides, to stop the earth tumbling down and filling it in again. Timothy is good at digging it with his pike too and there's only a little way to go, for Jack can crawl right inside the hole now. So Jack and Ed must go back to the tunnel and see if they can find Timothy too. And they must stop Tobias from meeting him, for they might try and kill each other, being enemy soldiers. Timothy is the bigger and stronger of the two, though Tobias is quicker of mind and of body. Jack blinks his eyes to stop thinking about the terrible possibility of a fight.

'We know a place where there might be some roots to dig up,' Ed says quickly. 'Can we go?'

Jack is pleased that his brother has given a reason for them to quit the house.

Beth frowns. 'Where? I'd have thought all the ground would be scoured bare by now. Go then, but be back soon and go carefully.'

Jack and Ed bid them all a swift farewell, leaving Tobias and Beth sitting close, talking in whispers. The brothers exchange no words, dodging along on their familiar route through Blackfriars. This is more difficult now, as most of the leaves and soft boughs have been eaten by horses or other beasts, so the trees are skeletons, with bare bones for branches. About fifty paces on their right, near the east part of the town walls, a party of soldiers is digging up earth and heaping it into a pile. One of these soldiers, Jack sees, is Timothy. Jack would recognise his bulky form from any distance and he nudges Ed as they sneak past. The gunners are up on the bastion looking over the wall as always, spying out at the enemy, so Ed and Jack slip by unnoticed, down to the trench at the foot of the wall and their hidden excavations. Jack wishes they could have brought Timothy, for they will need his help to hack out the last hard earth in the tunnel. It will take so long with only their small implements, but they did not dare to call to him at work with the other men.

Rain has soaked the earth at the foot of the trench, so that it is ankle deep in mud when Jack and Ed slide down to the place. For a moment Jack wonders if all of their work has been in vain, if the mud has flowed into the hole and filled it up again. They start to scrape at the mud camouflage, finding the boulders still in place and the hole of the tunnel holding up quite well with the timber supports. Ed and Jack heave one of the stones aside to allow Jack to crawl in and start hacking at the remaining part of the wall. In the dark earthy hole Jack's feet sink in the sludge underfoot and his iron spike is a useless thing against the hard bulk of the wall. After some time, Jack backs out and lets Ed take a turn, but he too crawls out again soon. Their clothes are smeared with wet dirt, their feet soaked and cold.

'We can't do it without him,' Ed says, in a flat-sounding voice.

Jack, crouching in the mud, feels his hopes slip away again.

'Can I help?' says a voice from above them, at the top of the slope.

Tobias is standing there, with a questioning smile on his face and Jack and Ed are struck dumb for a moment.

'Come down, quick,' Jack says, realising that Tobias at the top of the ditch might be seen by a soldier on the bastion.

'How did you find us?' says Ed.

'Beth asked me to follow you. She's long wished to know what mischief has been taking you so often from home,' Tobias says, sliding down nimbly, his feet sinking into the mud in the bottom of the trench.

He sees the opening to their tunnel, his eyes astonished.

'Boys, what are you doing, destroying the enemy's fortifications? Right under their noses. This is devilish dangerous.'

'Aye,' Ed says with a look of pride, 'it's a good trick, is it not?'

Tobias shakes his head, half smiling and half in dismay. 'And what is it to be, a tunnel out?'

'Yes' says Jack, 'we're going to escape to Brightlingsea, a goodly town with plenty of fish and our uncle and aunt too. You'll come with us. Please say you'll come with us and not go away again, Tobias.'

'God's body,' he says scratching his head, 'would you have us all hanged together?'

Jack is struck with alarm, for Tobias is not wholly jesting. He looks up suddenly, to the top of the slope again, for a spattering sound of water has started above them. Ed puts his finger to his lips, but they are already frozen in silence. It is a man, just out of their view, making his water in a powerful spurt. They hear the water decrease to a trickle, then a heavy sigh, followed by the sudden descent of the large body of Timothy sliding down into the ditch. He is wearing his helmet and carrying a sawn-off pike in his grip. Tobias starts back, with his hand moving swiftly to the knife at his belt, though he does not bare its blade.

'God be praised but it's good to see you lads,' Timothy says, a grin on his square face and a nod at Tobias, as though they are acquaintances happily met on a market day, 'and this is your cousin, I reckon.'

'Aye,' Ed says quickly, 'he had the flux and was lying sick in our house for a long while. But he's better now so he's come to help us with the digging.'

Tobias nods, though Jack sees suspicion still lurking in his eye.

'Honoured to meet you, sir,' Timothy says, 'I'm Timothy Box at your service.' He plants the end of his pike in the mud and bows politely.

It is clear that Tobias is too startled to make any reply, even to state his name but Timothy does not seem to notice nor care.

'I'm ready for finishing the job today,' Timothy says, holding up his weapon and looking at Ed. 'This'll do it nice, I reckon. And I'm ready to go whenever you says the word. Are you a-coming with us, sir?'

Tobias seems to gather his wits at last. 'Master Box, this is a mighty fine plan for escaping the town, but do you not risk your neck by leaving your post?'

Timothy sighs and bows his head like a boy caught thieving an apple from a market stall. 'I've no care of that, sir. I just want to go home. I don't care about no army and I've no wish for more fighting.'

Jack wishes he could comfort Timothy with words of encouragement but Tobias is keen to engage him in more talk.

'Are there many others of your comrades of a like mind?' he says.

Timothy nods. 'Aye sir, plenty. Most of them would be away from here tomorrow. That's if they weren't afeared of getting shot when they're a-running, or hung from a tree for deserting. But then there's others say they'll fight and die for the King. Them's the foolish ones and the officers mainly.'

'That's true,' says Tobias, 'And what if your officers make a break for safety, leaving all of you, all the common men here at the mercy of the Lord General Fairfax's army? You know that the Lord General has offered many times to give quarter to all men who lay down their arms and come out of the town. You'd be safe and free to go. But if your commanders keep refusing, there'll be no mercy for any.'

Jack is shocked to hear Tobias's grim warning and watches Timothy's face crumple with fear and confusion.

'But what can us poor men do?' Timothy says in a small voice.

'Well, you can escape, through your tunnel when it's done, if you can, though there's no knowing what might happen to you on the other side. Or you could rise up against your commanders. For they are nothing without you common soldiers, are they? Make them surrender now, if you wish to be saved.'

Timothy's face is crumpled with doubt and Jack does not like to hear Tobias put more fear into him. Tobias is different now. His voice is hard and he's turned into a soldier.

'But they're our betters. They're gentlemen,' Timothy says.

Tobias gropes in his pocket and takes out a folded paper.

'Here, take this to one of your comrades who can read it. It will show you the way to rise up against your officers and set yourselves free.'

Timothy's frown deepens as he takes the paper from Tobias, turning it over in his hand.

'I'd not do you wrong, my friend,' Tobias says. 'Are we not all sick to our souls of war and fighting? You wish for an end to it as I do. I'd not have more innocent folk die, nor more honest soldiers.'

Jack sees Timothy's terror turn to a look of agreement, his eyes glistening as he glances back at Tobias. 'I'll tell them, sir,' he says, 'thanking you, sir.'

Timothy turns over the paper again, though it is clear he can't read. 'May you come here tomorrow?' he says, turning to clamber up the slope again.

Jack and Ed reply together that they will, as they watch the soldier heave himself up the bank to the top, then disappear.

'We'd best get this hidden again,' Jack says, looking back at the black hole of their tunnel.

'There's not far to go,' Tobias says, picking up a discarded iron stake and reaching with it into the hole.

Jack wants badly to be gone, though he can't say exactly why. Around him and inside him is a shaking uneasiness, as though the air is quivering with danger.

'Let's cover the opening and go,' says Ed, leaning on the boulder to roll it back into the hole.

Tobias gives his strength to the job and they quickly throw back enough earth to cover the workings. Then he turns to them with his new, stern face that Jack does not fully recognise, though when he smiles and claps them on their backs, he looks a little more like their same dear friend, soon to be their brother. He suggests that they should run a little way along the trench to avoid being seen by any soldiers. Neither Jack nor Ed tell him of how often they have visited the place with Timothy and have worked untroubled on their tunnel. Jack supposes that Tobias, being a spy, is used to creeping around and escaping from enemies, so they follow him along for a little way and then head up the slope of Blackfriars, hiding behind the old walls and ruins as they go. They pause about fifty paces from where the men of

Timothy's party are still occupied in shoring up the wall. Some soldiers are shovelling earth into wheelbarrows, while others are levering up one of the ancient stones from the ground. Jack peers at the scene, searching for Timothy amongst the activity.

He is there, close to the wall, holding the paper that Tobias has given him, showing it to another soldier. The next moment is filled with a thunderous roaring sound and Jack feels Tobias tug him back by the shoulder painfully, hears him gasp, then the ground where the soldiers are standing explodes and bodies fly up into the air. As the smell of smoke swirls around Jack's head, Tobias is pulling him and Ed back, away from the place.

They cannot see for a while, until the stuff that flew into the air drops and settles. On the ground lie a number of soldiers, one writhing and screaming in pain, others, unhurt or bloodied jumping up or crawling away from the wall. Jack feels his stomach rise up and his throat drily retching, for there is nothing to come out. But he has to go forward and see. He has to know and Ed grabs hold of him, urging him forward, both resisting Tobias's hold.

'Don't go near,' Tobias says, struggling to keep his grip on them both, as a white thing, a paper, drifts up into the air close to where the bodies are lying. 'It's mortar fire. They may send another. It's not safe. Stay back!'

But Ed is pulling Jack and they break free from Tobias, though he leaps forward too, ahead of them, for he is much quicker and turns on them, to block their way, holding his arms out wide. Soldiers are yelling for Tobias to move away and he catches Ed and Jack in his arms, hugging them tightly, but Jack has seen a part of Timothy's body, his head and his chest laid out flat with a great slab of blood in the middle.

Chapter 17

21st & 22nd August

'Are you in accordance with us, Sir Charles?' a voice says from somewhere distant, somewhere in a place where he is not.

When the question is asked again, amidst shuffling feet and the murmurs of others around him, Charles becomes aware of his surroundings, the identity of the questioner and flushes deeply, mumbling an apology, grappling for a hold on the proceedings.

'Are you ailing, Colonel Lucas?' Lord Capel is speaking, his face towards Charles, an amused face, with full lips, the mouth turned up at each side in a permanent but mild-mannered smile.

'I beg your pardon,' Charles says, noting the circle of faces around him, his fellow commanders, in a council of war. Maxey shifts in his seat, while Tuke sighs aloud without an effort to conceal it. 'I am distracted,' Charles adds, 'troubled by our circumstances.'

'Indeed we are all brought a little low by concerns about our relief,' the Lord General says in his familiar affable tone, which helps to restore Charles's grip on the present.

'Our supplies of powder are not plentiful,' he manages to say, which seems to have relevance to the talk, as some of the commanders nod solemnly in agreement.

'I regret that we have little choice, gentlemen,' says the Lord General, 'but to send to the enemy again, seek out the concessions that Fairfax will afford us. Do you all agree?'

There are murmurs all around, a blur of noise to Charles, whose fuddled brain and throbbing head are the result of the flagons of Rhenish wine he had downed with George Lisle the night before, when he had longed for oblivion. He has no recollection of how he had returned to his chamber. He must have been carried there by servants, he supposes, for he found himself stretched on the bed, with sour breath and visions tormenting his head in the blackness of night.

Then he had thought of Katherine as he lay there, of her beautiful, proud face, her strong bearing as she stood in that chamber in front of Lord Goring, demanding that the people of the town be relieved with rations of corn. She and another woman, a small, pretty, fair-haired girl, leaders of a crowd, had somehow gained an audience with the Lord General and she, Katherine, had asked for him by name. Does she not know how tongues will wag, how gossip will grow of their liaison? She is prepared to sacrifice her good name for her cause, to help the poor wretches of this miserable town, people who will most likely crush her, condemn her when they know of her secret self, of her sins with an enemy soldier. He had stood during that audience, only ten paces from her, longing to take her in his arms and run from the place, but instead had stared, holding every sinew of his body tight, so as to betray nothing of the raging of his heart. After hearing her appeal, he had taken it upon himself to send Captain Hicks to release from the garrison stores one bag of corn per household. His fellow commanders will no doubt condemn such purloining of their army's supplies and his weakness in giving in to the townsfolk, but he will endure their censure.

This act of mercy has given him little ease, however, for he wonders now what kind of a man he has become, a weak and lily-livered creature who is ruled by his passion for a woman. It is not wise to be such a man. It has led to many distrusting the King himself, for his submission to his papist queen. And yet, he cannot deny Katherine, nor his love for her, which at times seems to him more powerful than any bond, any oath, any desire he has held in his life. But it must not override his duty. Duty only must drive him now and there is no place for love next to duty. So, with an effort, he turns his mind to the business around him, looks at his fellows, is appalled by them but bound to them, with no escape.

'We will meet tomorrow for another council of war, gentlemen,' the Lord General says. 'Be ready to receive Fairfax's answer. You will be called. In the meantime, I exhort you to see to your men. There must be no talk of mutiny. Go to them. Encourage them. Tell them that there is still hope of relief, for the Duke of Hamilton and his Scots forces have joined our own Sir Marmaduke Langdale. They are marching south. We still have cause to hope.'

Charles rises, along with the other commanders, preparing to depart. He has only one wish, which is to return to his chamber and rest, avoid company, sleep if he can. In the passage, he hears a voice behind him, a false whisper intended to be heard.

'In the name of God, keep Lucas away from the men. One look at him will set them all a-running for the other side.'

Charles does not turn, has no wish to see which one of his fellows has defamed him in this manner. He must direct all his venom, all anger at himself, and expend none on any other man on this earth, even Thomas Fairfax. He goes back to his billet, refusing the offers from his fellows to dine with them or take a glass of wine as they wait for a reply from the enemy. He returns to his room, shouts for his man. If he could only be with Katherine, she who is not revolted by him, who takes him body and soul and sees something in him that is worthy of love. But when the servant enters, he cannot make the demand that is on his lips, instead asking for a cup of ale and then to be roused only when the Lord General calls for him. He lies on the bed and wishes that he might never have to rise again.

He has no idea what hour it is when he awakes, though it is not yet dawn. His head is at least a little clearer than the day before and he drinks the ale that his manservant has left him, then washes in the cold water in a basin and sits in the gloom, wondering whether he has any power remaining to him to fulfil his duty. The siege is lost, the King's cause also. There is only one course left to retain honour and frustrate the enemy. Victory is impossible now, he knows, but a glorious defeat, a show of courage and the ultimate sacrifice might have stronger consequences than surrender. It would trouble Fairfax's army and stir more dissent in a warring Parliament. By these means, they might keep alive the hopes of the King. Charles determines to make his proposal to Lord General Goring and his fellow commanders this morning, and is sure that there are others of his persuasion, the weathered soldiers among them, those who know war and its outcomes, often unexpected, and the advantages to be gained even in defeat. He will think no more of Katherine, for she has made him weak, distracted, doubting of his purpose. She has uncovered his softer self, made him consider other matters: conscience, pleasure, the delight of being loved and of giving joy to another. But all this simply tangles and confuses the simplicity of his fight for the King. He must obliterate these complications. His mind and soul must be filled with one duty alone.

He makes ready to face what he must and is dressed by the time his servant comes to rouse him. He steps out in full control of himself, strong and resilient again. He hopes there will be time for him to go and see his officers and men in their quarters, in spite of the earlier admonition of his fellow commander. He will lend his men the strength and courage that he now possesses, praise them for their bravery and worthiness, exhort them to taste and share in the honour of the battles to come. But William Hicks is waiting downstairs to accompany him to the council of war. The young officer is solicitous, anxious to assure himself of Charles's well being, so much so that Charles becomes irked by his questioning, by the implication that he is in some way in need of protection like a feeble girl. He is curt with Captain Hicks, leaves him at the door of the meeting chamber and enters briskly to find the two lords and their staff already seated, with papers in front of them and most of the other commanders around the table. The Lord General's mouth is downcast, his eyes hooded with weariness, all humour sucked from him as he addresses the assembly.

'Gentlemen, I have to tell you that Fairfax will give no concessions. His conditions of surrender are the same: free quarter to all common soldiers and lower officers, surrender to mercy for all higher officers and commanders. It is dishonourable and an insult to us,' he says, but his voice is watery thin.

Lord Capel speaks up, clearing his throat, betraying some disturbance in his languid demeanour. 'These conditions are not acceptable. We cannot submit to them. I declare that we should refuse to comply.'

'Yes, my Lord,' Charles says, for he has waited impatiently for this moment and is ready to state his strategy without hesitation. He has the attention of all at last.

'There is only one course open to us now. We must make an attack upon them. It must be our strongest break, and if need be our final action, the only honourable way left to us. All must march out against the enemy, horse and foot with all the ammunition remaining at our disposal. It shall be in the deadest time of the night, when we are least expected. We will set open two of the gates and storm their line. I will lead the forlorn out to break the enemy line at Fothergall's Fort. Meanwhile, Colonel Farre's horse should skirt round Rainsborough's Fort and draw his men after them to the east. The foot should follow through the breach. There are some townsmen loyal to us who will man the guns upon North Gate, to fire upon Ingoldsby's Fort with the last shot until the powder is gone.'

The commanders listen, silent with concentration as Charles details the preparations and the timing of their last and greatest fight. The Lord General exchanges some words with Lord Capel and Colonel Lisle at his side.

'Colonel Lucas's strategy is the boldest and most courageous course for us. It is the only way to gain honour from this sad venture,' the old commander says, his back hunched, his voice quavering with exhaustion. 'We must prepare the men for this and be wary of the townspeople, for they grow more desperate by the hour. They would have us lay down our arms and give way. They must be kept at bay.'

The Lord General's suppositions are well-founded, for during their proceedings, Charles has been aware of a tumult of voices, the familiar sound of a rabble outside the building. As Charles and his fellow colonels make to leave the inn by the door into the yard, they are met with a hideous chorus of shouting, wild people pressing in upon the door.

'Curse them, this rabble,' Charles says, seeing the ravaged features, the ugly mouths, a pack of hungry dogs who will be trampled rather than submit.

'Surrender, you villains!' shouts one of the mob, whipping up a chorus of the same plea.

'Set us free, in the name of pity,' a woman shrieks above the churning of bodies and voices. 'God will strike you all dead!'

'Let us out of the town,' shouts another. 'Surrender or let us go. We'll not lie down and die here. Open the gates.'

Charles stands his ground on the threshold, with Maxey and Tuke at his side.

'What are they asking, the wretches?' says Maxey. 'There will be no succour, nor mercy from Fairfax.'

A moment later, the Lord General himself is behind them, whispering to Charles.

'Dear God, what a sight,' he says. 'Let us open the gates for them, if they prefer to seek mercy from the enemy. Let them see what awaits them. Give the order to open the North Gate.'

Colonel Maxey steps forward and raises his arm, bellowing at the crowd.

'The Lord General Goring has heard your pleas. Those who wish to leave the town may do so, at your own peril. The North Gate will be opened. On your own heads be it!'

The mass of people swells and heaves, turning around and surging back under the archway to the street beyond. Charles sees that they are desperate women and children, a sight he has seen before, when storming the town of Breda to discover a starving, depraved people who had been reduced, some had said, to eating human flesh. His horror at their state grips him ferociously now; that people of this town, the place of his origins and his family lands, should have suffered such ruination, strikes him as never before. His certain death in the sally forth will be a fitting retribution. He finds himself following the clamouring crowd, no longer howling their deprecations at him and his fellow officers, driven only by their desire to run from this place. They are now heading down the hill towards the North Gate. Children and babes scream in their mothers' arms and to his dismay and shock he sees among them, near the head of the crowd, a woman whose figure and bearing is imprinted on his mind. It is Katherine. He starts running after them, unnoticed in the chaos, knowing it is irresponsible lunacy to go, when he should be planning the strategy for his action against the enemy.

Amidst a tight group of women, moving now towards the vanguard of the train, Katherine is pushing forward, with the same young fair girl at her side, the one who had been with her that day when he had released corn to the starving. Other women are clinging close to her, as though she were carrying their colours into battle. Katherine wears a white cap over her bunched curls, her slender figure in a plain dark gown with a white neckerchief. He follows, keeping to the side of the road. Down the slope of North Hill they go, some slower ones and small children straggling behind. What can Katherine and this ravenous, desperate band of women and their children achieve, Charles thinks, horrified that she should demean herself so, to lead such a rabble. But is she not bold, courageous to risk her safety for the sake of her neighbours? These foolish ignorant women, for all that they show themselves as brave as men, know nothing of the ruthlessness of war, the necessary cruelty. They do not know how the enemy will view their plight. Charles knows and dreads witnessing it. They are running towards Rainsborough's fort. These women imagine that they will appeal to that general's pity, that he out of compassion will offer them aid, food and safety. God preserve them.

The North Gate is heavily guarded by pikemen, with musketeers ready at loopholes in the wall and a bastion armed with two demi-cannon. A troop of cavalrymen, on their wretched underfed horses has been ordered to the place too. By now, the crowd, with Katherine leading, is milling around the gates and Charles sees two soldiers heave out the iron bar that secures them and swing them open. He glimpses the muddy pathways outside and the burnt out ruins of the houses, where only last month he had fought a pitched battle with the enemy in one of his sallies.

The first are going through, with Katherine and the fair girl at the head. He must not let her go. She must not go. But what can he do, run after her and pluck her from the middle of the mob? He hastens down closer to the gates, then mounts the earth rampart, which leads up to the bastion above, from which position he will be able to view the events beyond, dreading it but knowing he must. The gunners and their teams are in position; more musketeers are taking up positions on the ramparts on top of the wall. The horses of the cavalrymen swerve to let the flood of people through the gates. He sees some terrified women draw back, weeping pitifully, staying within the walls, watching as the last stragglers, children and some older folk go out through the open gates. A shout from a captain orders the gates shut and secured again.

Charles stands on the bastion, behind the gun crew, who are working busily to prepare their cannon.

'Sir, you've come to see the madness of the townsfolk?' the gun commander says to him, in a tone that does not hide his scorn.

Looking behind him, Charles sees that Captain Hicks, his faithful secretary, has followed him here and is now making his way up to join him at this vantage point. Without a word to each other, they watch the stream of the fleeing people trailing over the tracks tramped by the feet of the besiegers, over what was once rich meadowland. In the distance, lie the ramparts of earth and the wooden palisade of Rainsborough's Fort. There is barren ground between, over which Fairfax has for weeks hurled his futile bombardments at the town walls. Charles can see the gun barrels on the fort and along the line of earthworks, trained upon the town. He marvels now at how their own determination and doggedness in strengthening the walls and fortifications, their painstaking renewal has held off the enemy for so long. Fairfax, however, knows his business too well; he has them truly caged in and at his mercy.

The crowd of women is drawing closer to the fort, where the gate in the stockade has opened and a company of around sixty dragoons, their horses tight-packed together, is moving out in battle order. They are advancing slowly on the crowd, muskets poised and ready. There are screams and shouts from the women, high pitched and piercing as the squad moves closer.

'They'll never shoot them down,' Captain Hicks murmurs at Charles's side. 'Though it might serve us well to be rid of them.'

The dragoons halt and Charles's heart stops when he sees they are preparing to fire. A burst of shots rings out, but through the smoke and the screams, he knows that they have fired over the heads of the crowd, meaning to terrify the women into a retreat. Relief floods his brain, as with blood from a hot wound in the head. After the cloud of smoke has sunk down, the dragoons advance again, but those people at the head stand firm. From this distance he cannot discern whether one of them is Katherine, though he is certain she is there.

'Desperation has driven them to madness,' says Hicks. 'A mad sort of bravery, and women too.'

Charles thinks grimly that the suicidal breakout he has planned will need just such lunatic courage. He hears wild cries and exchanges between the women and the officer at the head of the dragoons. Another volley of shots rings out and some of the crowd start back in retreat, along the pathway towards the town gates.

'They think to enter again. What folly is this?' Hicks says. 'The orders of the Lord General are to keep the gates closed.'

'It must not be,' says Charles, turning to him. 'What will become of them?'

'That is little concern of ours. They have chosen their course and must bear the consequences.'

Charles swallows hard and sees a party of six dragoons dismounting and running to the women at the front. The soldiers are grappling with four of the women now, tugging and pulling at their garments, tearing them off, while the mass of others scream and turn, running in straggling bunches back towards the walls of the town. The white, naked bodies of the women are writhing and struggling as they try to reclaim their garments, tossed away by the soldiers. The melee around the dragoons thickens; more shots are fired. An officer of the dragoons is struck down from his horse, it appears by one of his own men, but Charles cannot be sure at this distance, though what he sees fills him with a sickening weakness of the stomach.

'Holy God,' Hicks says, 'they've stripped the women naked.'

Charles watches, appalled, as the gunners stop. The soldiers on the parapet are staring too, some shouting oaths and lewdness, though one, noticing two officers nearby, curbs his swearing tongue and nudges his fellows to do likewise. Below on the street, just inside the gates, a few townspeople are clamouring to know what is happening outside.

Over the muddy open ground, the weeping women and children come hurrying back, followed now by the four wretched creatures who have been stripped, who clutch the remains of their garments to their bodies to cover themselves. Katherine is one, her shoulders bared, her white, naked legs showing as she runs. The fair girl, in little but her torn shift, stumbles alongside her, with two young boys in her wake.

'That'll learn them, the strumpets! They think to tempt puritans by bearing their breasts?' shouts a laughing soldier nearby.

Charles finds himself trembling with impotent fury. A cannon blasts from Rainsborough's fort towards the town, over the fleeing crowd, who run faster still, now in terror for their lives. Some have reached the gate and are pounding it with their fists, shrieking to be let in again, but the captains, stone-faced make no move to order their opening, just as Hicks has predicted. Behind the fugitive crowd, the enemy troopers have advanced and are firing again, this time at the guns on the town walls. From high on the wall comes a deafening blast of a cannon and the ball flies over the heads of the fleeing people. It plunges into the middle of the troopers, sending horses screaming and bucking, men blown off them like pieces of rag into the air. The gunners firing from the town bastion, set to work in a fury again, loading the ball into the barrel and igniting the charge, deafening those around and sending a shudder through the structure of the wall itself. Charles coughs as the smoke blinds him for some moments, along with the familiar stench of powder.

Through the thinning smoke Charles sees the fugitives again, caught below, outside in a field of battle. They wail and cry for pity whilst, over their heads, explosions erupt from both sides at once. Charles scrambles and slides down from the bastion, jumping on to street level, shouting to the foot soldiers standing guard at the gates.

'Open, in the name of God!'

'But, sir, the Lord General –.'

'Do as I say or you'll hang,' he shouts louder, charging at the soldier. 'Unbar the gates.'

From the first opening crack, the gate is thrust wide by the force of the pitiful, mud-spattered women, falling and stumbling their way back into town, to the jeers of the soldiers. Charles draws back and watches for Katherine, knowing that now she will be one of the last to enter, praying that he will see her return safe and not maimed by her ordeal. He longs to run to her, take her in his arms, comfort her, as she has him, but to acknowledge her here in this crowd, amongst his own men and her neighbours would be an act of impossible rashness and folly. He must be gone, as soon as he sees she is safe. He moves back against the wall of a house and starts making his way up the street, catching only a glimpse, but enough, of Katherine, her garments rent, holding the young woman as she weeps and cries out hysterically, with a sobbing boy at her side. Here Katherine is giving succour to others, who howl as though their limbs have been severed from their bodies.

He turns, hurries back up the hill, hearing behind him the muffled shot of a cannon and the continuing cries of the stricken people. At the upper reaches of the hill, another knot of townspeople has gathered. They are staring up, transfixed, at the sky, which is remarkably cloudless and blue and where, hanging, wafting gently backwards and forwards, a strange white kite is flying.

Chapter 18

'My brother! He's out there. Let me bring him back. Please, please, I beg of you.'

Beth is screaming, clawing at the breast of a soldier against whom she has been thrown by the surge of bodies pushing her forward. The soldier thrusts her off roughly so that, with Jack clinging to her, they both tumble down upon the road, Beth cracking her forehead on the cobbles. The gates crash shut behind them and all around is the noise and press of people. Jack clings to her arm, his eyes staring, mute and whey-faced, while she is still fired by the horror of seeing Edward fall in the mud with a red hole in his back as they fled.

The howling and laughter of men batter her too as she and Jack are hauled away from the gates by their arms, like corpses to be cast on a mound of the dead.

'Get away, you stupid whore,' cries a soldier, kicking at Beth's legs as she struggles to gain her footing. 'You're lucky you're not blasted to a pulp out there. Get you gone from here.'

'Leave her, leave her,' a woman's voice is calling, Mistress Wade's, close to her. Beth's mind will not work, nor her eyes see clearly, but someone's arms are around her and she thinks Jack is still holding on. But Edward? He's not here. He's outside in the mud under the horses' hoofs and still there is terrible noise, the thudding of gunfire, the shouts of men, but she is being dragged away up the road. Mistress Wade is holding her, with a tight arm around her waist.

Two soldiers come stamping up beside them as they go.

'Mercy? A fine kind of mercy you found out there,' laughs one, his leering, ugly face muttering foul words at them, while his companion grins at Mistress Wade, making to pluck at her gown.

'Here's a lusty whore, this one. Hey, Mistress, I warrant you didn't find such mercy in the arms of Black Tom Fairfax as you've had in Colonel Charlie Lucas's bed, eh.'

Beth stumbles and falls again, her face in a soft patch of mud and once again she is lifted up. Jack is whimpering, catching at her shift. 'Beth, Jack, come. It's not far now.' It is Mistress Wade's voice still.

Beth sees the white skin of the woman's bare shoulders, the shreds of her gown loose about her and then feels her own half-nakedness. The skirt of her gown is gone, her shift sticking to her legs with mud or blood. She tightens her grip on Jack's hand and tries to steady herself as the gabble of folk dies down a little and she can see to the top of the Head Street. Something else has captured the attention of those at the top of the hill. A small crowd is gathered there, looking up at the sky, at a white thing that appears to be floating there, a strange kite swaying high up in the breeze.

'What it is?' people are asking. 'A message?' 'A witch's curse?' 'What is it?' 'Is it surrender?' It's a sign.' 'Is it over?'

Beth, Jack and Mistress Wade stumble on, to the crest of the hill, Beth weeping half with relief that at last they have slid out of view, in favour of this new curiosity.

When Beth closes the door of the kitchen, she wishes never to go out again. She only wants to lie down by the fire, as Old Solomon had done, close her eyes and never open them upon the world. Her mother comes to them and clutches Beth and Jack to her breast, murmuring, 'Edward? Where is Edward?' Neither can reply and they stay in this embrace for some time. At last, her mother breaks away and draws Beth to sit upon the chair by the fire, Jack refusing to leave hold of Beth's hand. Her mother brings a bowl of water then and places it on the table, taking up a linen cloth from her work basket, peering at Beth's cut brow and bruised face.

'Edward? Is he coming behind?' Beth's mother says, as though she expects that he has simply been waylaid by a stone in his shoe and will in the next moment be with them in the kitchen.

'Mother, we should never have gone.' Beth is weeping. Her voice is shredded, rasping. Her mother continues to dab at the cut upon her forehead. 'They fired above us and upon us, the soldiers, the Parliamentary soldiers. They drove us back to the town and fired and Ed –.'

Beth's mouth dries to a harsh sob, while her mother drops the cloth on the floor and covers her face with her apron. Jack, his face blank, his eyes unblinking says nothing, nor does he weep.

After some time, her mother's noise subsides a little and Beth sits numbly watching her body shuddering.

'I'll go to Mistress Wade,' Beth says. 'She knows people. She might persuade them– might let us go outside the walls again and look for him, bring him back.' As she speaks she does not dare to think of the sight she had seen outside.

Jack will not move, nor speak and Beth tries to ease his fingers open, free her hand from his, but he starts whimpering and grasps the stuff of her sleeve instead and will not be parted from it. She puts her arm around him and, overwhelmed with the exhaustion of grief and shock, leads her young brother to the cot bed in the corner where Tobias had spent those weeks of his recovery. She lies down, pulling Jack down at her side. There they stay, she embracing him, until the light has gone and night has crept into the silent kitchen.

Beth sees their mother moving, quiet as a shadow, lighting a small fire, made with the splinters of their last wooden stool, which lends a feeble glow to the room. She watches her figure pour water into a pot and drop in a few leaves. A cupful of warm water with leaves of mint will at least fill their bellies for a little while. Beth, feeling Jack's body against her, watches the small flames and the red glow of the fire. Her mother reaches for the last tallow candles, those which Beth saved from the plundering soldiers, and places them on the table, then she pours the water into the three cups.

'Come,' she says, her voice low, her face blank of expression, beckoning to them as she stands by the table.

'Jack, get up with me now,' Beth says, gently touching his arm, his hand still in hers and pulling him from the bed.

Beth and Jack crouch by the chair where their mother sits in front of the fire.

'Dear Lord in Heaven,' Beth says, 'take our dear child Edward to your loving breast–'

As she speaks the words of the prayer, her head fills with thoughts of her brother, a knowing, curious child, delighting in all he found around him and sharing this joy with others. His living image sits still and silent at her side.

Their mother has the tallow candles in her lap and hands them one each. Beth bites into hers first, the hard fat turning to rancid slime in her mouth, before she swallows it. She watches her mother do the same. Jack sits staring, with his candle in his palm, however, and Beth is fearful that her young brother's wits are so maimed by the horror and the loss of Ed that he will never find himself again.

'Jack,' she says. 'Eat. Edward would want you to. He would want you to eat his share, for he was always a good and generous boy.'

Jack hesitates and looks at her, blinking once, then breaks the candle in half, gulping one down and placing the other piece in his pocket. Their mother holds out the last spare candle to Jack, who rises to his feet, takes it and lights the wick from a glowing stick in the fire.

Beth sees her mother's face, grey and waxy as a corpse. They watch Jack, who is standing with the candle in his hand, staring at the small yellow flame.

The house is so still and quiet that Beth fancies she can hear the feet of beetles skittering in the cracks between the timbers, moths' wings brushing the plaster walls, or the last breath of a starving mouse dying between the laths. The faint sound of a distant voice then another answering are the only signs of life outside. No horses, no beasts of any sort go by, no cart wheels, nor barrows either. Silence fills Jack's being too, for he still says nothing. There is no comforting chatter, no scuffling play, no vital purpose in the air of the morning. What point is there in rising from their beds, Beth wonders, thinking of her mother, broken with grief, reduced to a wreck of skin and bone, her stricken brother, dumb and blighted in his child's mind, with half of his life cut from him. And for herself, her hopes have perished too, the joy that she had discovered in the love of a man, only a weak trace in her memory now. Tobias has been gone for some time, leaving his promises with her. She believes in his sincerity and his love, but these are weak and flimsy defences against the ball of a cannon or the slash of a sword, useless against starvation. Where is he now? She does not dare to think. Even if the Parliamentary army were to storm the town, how many would die in the fight? Tobias might be killed, even if their forces were victorious. And if he were saved to march in triumph into the town, she might not live to see it.

Beth thinks that lying in bed, motionless, might curb hunger and preserve what little strength she has to last another day, but to what end? She wonders about Mistress Wade and how she is faring. The woman had been so strong and resolute throughout their ordeal, even as the clothes were ripped from her body. Beth's mind shrinks in shame to remember their nakedness, their humiliation in the eyes of all who witnessed it. Mistress Wade had held Beth up and brought her back with Jack into the town again; she had brought them home. Beth hopes that the lady's husband, that stern and unkindly man, has not punished his wife for taking part in their foolhardy bid to seek relief. Master Wade, if he were a true advocate of the people, should have been with them, leading the townspeople to plead on their behalf. Instead, he and his fellows left such things to powerless, starving women and children. Where are the men, their leaders and masters at this terrible time?

Beth is perplexed too by a muddled memory, the half-heard mocking words of the two soldiers who had taunted them as they had stumbled back up the hill. One had spoken of Sir Charles Lucas's bed, that Mistress Wade had found some comfort there. Was this a terrible affront to her, a piece of foul gossip or the reason for Mistress Wade's power to sway the Royalist commander? Perhaps this woman is truly a whore? Her mother's unease about Mistress Wade is no mystery now. Dismayed, Beth wonders how many have known of the sinful behaviour of the alderman's wife. But worse by far, more puzzling and dreadful than the sin of an adulterous woman, is the mystery of how men can wage war against their countrymen and neighbours in the name of God.

In spite of the weight of her misery, Beth forces herself to rise from her bed, thinking of Jack and her mother and how, without her, they will not survive. While this is so and they have breath in their bodies, she must carry on, for she cannot simply lie down and wait for death to come upon her, nor has she the right to will it upon others. She has to rise and join the day, glean whatever scrap of hope might lie waiting to be found by the persistent spirit, the small mercies or bounties God might gift to them in their sin and ignorance. She kneels by the bed to pray, that God will forgive her weakness and her woe and promises to place her faith in His wisdom, which is so far beyond what her feeble mind can fathom. Feeling a little stronger, she washes her face and dresses, tying her apron on, as though ready to prepare a hearty breakfast, knowing that cold water is all she has to offer. Jack, fitfully asleep, tosses and writhes in his bed, mumbling, tormented still. She will not wake him yet. She hears her mother stir, then goes downstairs.

No sooner has her foot touched the floor than there comes a knocking on the door and her heart leaps. Tobias, please may it be he, she prays, rushing to unbolt the door but finding instead Mistress Wade's servant Walter standing there. She gasps, surprised, struck with the folly of her anticipation. Walter is holding a small packet in his hand.

'Good day to you, Beth. Mistress sends you this,' he says. 'The Master and Mistress have had some small provisions from others. It's not much, but might fill a hole for a while.'

She thanks him but he does not move from the threshold and Beth sees that his eyes are full.

'My heart aches for the lad, Beth, your beloved boy –.'

Beth's eyes smart to see the man so moved and she bows her head, looking down at the hard round thing in her hand, perhaps a baked biscuit. With this she might be able to tempt Jack to speak.

'How is your mistress faring?' Beth says, with an effort, looking up at the man. 'I hope she's well recovered. Please give to her my thanks and good wishes.'

Walter nods. 'She is well enough, though she has kept to her chamber since those cruel happenings.'

He hesitates then and glances to the right and left up the street, as though he were wary of spies and listeners. He lowers his voice and leans closer to Beth.

'I think there may soon be an end to the siege and our suffering,' he says. 'There's trouble among the common soldiers, word of mutiny. Their hunger afflicts them badly but there's fear too of defeat and what will happen afterwards. It's all the talk of the taverns, so I've heard. And your young cousin, Master Waterman, has done his duty well in turning the soldiers.'

'You've heard word of him?' Beth says, unable to contain her delight at the mention of his name. 'Where is he now?'

'I know nothing of him, beyond what he did in going among the soldiers, more than a week ago, telling them of the hopeless state of their cause, of Fairfax's certain victory and his promise of quarter for those who would lay down their arms. It was a risky business, him going among those men, for many have stayed stout and loyal to their commanders, indeed they'd lay down their lives for them and for the King. Your cousin was chased for his life by some who knew he spoke with the voice of their enemy. But he's a brave lad and I reckon he may have got back safe, somehow, to the leaguer, though the route on the south wall's all blocked up now.'

Beth shudders with anxiety for Tobias, but with a small hope trembling to life again, like a sick animal discovering suddenly that it can stand upon its legs.

'So you think the soldiers will mutiny and surrender themselves?' she says.

'I do believe it, for there is no hope left of relief for the Royalists. There was a message, sent on a kite by Fairfax. Those forces that were coming are well beaten, routed by General Cromwell and Colonel Lambert, up north. The King's cause is lost. Have courage now, Beth Sayer. There will be an end to this.'

Beth looks into the face of the man, animated as she had seen it once before, when he spoke of his hatred of the Lucases.

'I pray it may come soon,' she says, grateful to Walter for this scrap of hope, 'but there has been so much hurt, so much is ruined. These troubles have killed my father and my brother. My mother too is so weak that she can hardly stand and Jack will not speak. These are griefs that can never be mended.'

'I know this,' Walter says, 'you've had much to endure, but you are strong and brave and the boy is young. Tyrants will be overthrown through our suffering. We'll see them fall, Goring, Capel, Lucas, all and may they soon taste the misery they have inflicted upon us.'

Beth sees the man's face darken at the mention of Sir Charles Lucas and wonders that he has not heard of his mistress's bond with his despised enemy. Walter would surely not know of this and continue in her service. Beth finds herself torn by her loyalty to the woman who has shown such kindness to them and her abhorrence at the thought of her liaison with an enemy commander. Mistress Wade had stood against the Royalist invaders, had fought for succour for the people of the town. There is no sense nor reason to it, but then it was most likely not sense nor reason that drove Mistress Wade to Sir Charles Lucas's bed. Beth knows well what it is to ache with love and longing for a man. She bids Walter farewell with thanks for the gift of food and his information and finds Jack lying on the rug before the fire.

'Jack, please go and draw some water,' she says, but he does not move, lying motionless as Old Solomon had done on his long slow journey towards death.

Beth is seized with fear for him and crouches by him, opening the small bundle before his face. It contains a round, hard-cooked griddle cake.

'Jack come. Rouse yourself. I need you to help me. I need you to get water. If you bring water, we will eat and drink.'

He raises his head and looks at her, though she cannot see behind his eyes, their stare dead and glazed like a veil permitting no light to enter, shading what is within. But he stirs himself slowly, without a word and takes up the pail, going out of the back door into the yard, his skinny arm pulled tight by the weight of the wooden vessel. Beth is glad that at least he has moved from that spot. Next, she goes to rouse her mother who opens her eyes when Beth shakes her and seems for a moment bemused, unsure of who it is that is forcing her back from her comfortable oblivion.

'Mother, I have something for us to eat.'

In the kitchen again, Beth helps her mother to the chair by the fire, breaks the hard biscuit into three pieces with some difficulty and hands her mother a piece which she puts to her mouth and sucks, for it is too hard to bite. Beth blows the embers to life and puts on another stick, for the morning is chill. It is another dreary dark day, wet like so many that summer and she tries to recover the hope that Walter has given her, telling her mother of the chance of a surrender of the Royalists soon. Her mother's face betrays little understanding or interest in this news and Beth feels the burden descend upon her again, too great, too weighty, threatening to crush the life from her.

'Where's the boy?' her mother says a moment later, in a shrivelled voice.

At first Beth is unsure whether her mother's mind is still searching for Edward, but her eyes are fixed on the door. Jack has not returned.

'I'll go after him, Mother. The water may be too heavy for

him to carry.'

Beth goes out of the back door and finds there, in the middle of the yard, the abandoned bucket. The gate hangs open and Beth, driven by a growing fear, goes out into the alleyway and along to the end where the pump stands. By the pump, in the process of filling a large pot jug, is a woman, a neighbour, to whom Beth appeals.

'Have you seen Jack?'

The woman's hand pauses upon the handle of the pump and she frowns at Beth.

'No my dear. I ain't set eyes upon him, poor child. How does he fare without his brother?'

Beth cannot bear to answer the woman's question and indeed is keen to quit her company as quickly as she can, to avoid further painful talk.

'I used to see them, often,' the woman says, in the toneless voice of a person drained of energy, 'the two of them running along here each day, along the Culver Lane and turning at the end like they was heading for, well, I don't know where exactly, but up there anyway.'

Beth thanks the woman and hurries along the street. She will go to Blackfriars, remembering that it was in this place that Tobias had discovered her brothers, on that terrible day when they had witnessed the soldiers being blown apart by mortar fire. It is also the place where plentiful blackberry bushes grow in tangles, but where she has not been since the beginning of the siege. She is weak and her head pounds with a dizzy throbbing, but she must go on. As she crosses the Frere Street, she sees two men coming along, one of whom is Alderman Wade, heading towards the High Street.

'Sir,' Beth says approaching the alderman, careless now of meeting his dangerous staring eyes. 'Have you seen my brother? He has gone from home.'

Master Wade and his companion stop, the alderman frowning at her. 'No, we have not, young Mistress. And I would advise that you keep to your house, for there is trouble on the streets again. No one will be safe from the soldiers,' he says. 'You above all should know what befalls those who try to meddle. Have you not learned your lesson? Get you home.'

He and the other man hurry on and Beth continues on her own way, expending only a little of her strength in anger at the man's callous advice. This latest alarm must be the trouble that Walter spoke of, mutiny among the soldiers. But whatever the danger, she cannot turn back; she must find her brother. She is nearing the edge of Blackfriars when she hears a shout, then sees a group of about ten soldiers, dragging a man along in their midst, his feet trailing on the ground, his arms held by two others. The captive in the centre is bellowing and struggling, though he is powerless against their hold.

'Let me go, you villains. You'll hang for this!'

The unfortunate man must be the men's officer. Though Beth recoils at the sight of this violent act, it shows that the soldiers' minds and hearts at this perilous time are set on things other than doing mischief to townsfolk. The men continue to drag their shouting victim away towards the East Gate.

Beth finds Blackfriars transformed into a ravaged patch of land of skeleton trees and grassless earth, the ruins of the ancient monastery, protruding from the ground like the ugly ribs of some huge dead creature. As she walks, her eyes scan the network of tracks leading down an incline to the town walls, which have been patched at various weak and crumbling places. At the corner of the walls is a platform for defence, with cannon upon it. Beth can see no soldiers manning the guns, but on the ground just below, is a group of around six men, some armed with swords, arguing and gesturing towards the wall. Their attention is fixed on a point only twenty paces from them where Beth sees, to her astonishment and shock, the small figure of Jack. He is waving at them, beckoning them to follow him and then he disappears, down into a hollow that seems to fall away to the foot of the wall beyond. The soldiers stop their quarrel and run towards the place where Jack has gone. Beth cannot think what is afoot, why Jack is here and what the soldiers are intending. She tries to run towards the wall, though her legs are weak and her body incapable of swift movement.

'Jack,' she calls, knowing that he cannot hear her, glad and appalled at once to find him in this place.

'Jack,' she cries again, but her breath is too feeble, her steps slowing, as though she were labouring through thick mire. The men are now descending after Jack, though one hears her shout, turns to look back at her, but then follows the rest and disappears into the trench.

At last, Beth, gasping for breath, reaches the top of the slope and looks down upon an extraordinary sight. Jack is standing at the foot of the wall beside a dark hole, about two feet square, edged with timbers, even a crude lintel to hold up the weight of the earth above it. The six men are standing in the ditch, one crouching down to examine the place where Jack is pointing, the opening of the hole.

'God's blood,' the crouching soldier calls out, 'it's a tunnel. Someone's been through here already.'

He thrusts his sword arm into the hole and turns to his comrades.

'Lord bless us. We can get out here, see,' he says, his eyes bright with disbelief.

Beth sees Jack's small figure pressed against the wall, watching the men. He has not seen her, or chooses not to look and she does not dare to call to him again. The men edge closer to the tunnel opening. The first soldier withdraws his weapon and stands up, seeing Beth and all eyes turn to her.

'Don't say a word, Mistress,' calls the soldier, with a look more of pleading than menace. 'We'll be gone from here and won't cause you harm, I swear it.'

'Make haste, in the name of God,' says another, pushing past his comrades. 'I'll go first.'

'Aye, go on with you Joseph,' say the others, crowding round the hole. 'We'll follow.'

The man, Joseph, stoops down, falls on his hands and knees, thrusts his head in, then squeezes his shoulders after, his body and legs disappearing in a few moments. The first soldier with the sword, waiting behind, looks along at Jack who stands staring, mutely.

'Thanks to you lad, for showing us this way. God bless and keep you in your life to come.'

Chapter 19

27th August

Even the shifting clouds seem to be fleeing the noise, racing across the sky as though pursued by the booming volleys that are sounding all around, some close at hand, others answering from a distance. Trumpets blast the air, again and again in repeated fanfares over the sputtering sound of musket fire. It is no attack, however; it is a celebration. Tobias lifts his head from the mud wall against which he is lying, moving one of his shackled legs to shake away the numbness.

'What's afoot?' he calls to a guard outside the enclosure where he is confined along with two other prisoners of war. 'Is it surrender?'

The guard, whose face appears over the top of the fence, shouts in a tone of triumph.

'Near enough. They're done for now. Cromwell's beaten the Scots. There's no relief for the devils in the town. They're making terms for surrender. It's over and it's victory for us. Praise God.'

The two other prisoners shift and grumble where they sit, one of them spitting into the dirt.

'Well,' says he, a thick-legged infantryman, with a strange accent. 'We shouldn't never have trusted the Scotch, murdering savages they are. Best keep foreigners out of it, I always say, nothing but trouble.'

'Aye,' Tobias says, 'we Englishmen can make enough trouble

among ourselves without the aid of foreigners.'

'Yes, you're right, friend, though you be our enemy,' says the other, an older man with a cast in one eye, which makes the direction of his gaze hard to fathom. 'I'm sick to the belly of the whole business of war.'

'Well, I'm game to fight for the roundheads if there's regular pay in it,' the first man says. 'Comes to a choice of transporting as a slave or swearing for Parliament, I knows which way I'll take.'

'Need to stop calling them roundheads for a start,' suggests his cross-eyed companion helpfully, nodding in Tobias's direction. 'And are you sure you want to join the Parliament's army? Look what they done to one of their own.'

The thick-legged soldier eyes Tobias. 'What you done then, soldier? You didn't try to come over to our side, did you? You'd be the biggest fool in Christendom if you had.'

Tobias raises his head and looks at the man. 'No, I'm no turncoat, though I'd not blame a man who's forced to it,' he says, thinking it wise not to antagonise his wavering fellow prisoners.

'Well, tell us then. What crime was it you done, brought you to this?' the first man persists.

'Striking an officer,' Tobias says, hoping that this will satisfy the questioner sufficiently to stop his curiosity, but instead it serves to enliven him the more.

'Dangerous business, hitting an officer. I've known men hanged for that,' says the man, drawing in his breath noisily, in readiness for imparting his tale. 'Just after a battle up near Nottingham way, a few years back, there was a bunch of us told to run against two roundhead sakers and us with no powder. So one of our lads says the officer could go hang, for he wasn't going to charge against guns for nobody, and the officer says, no you'll hang, you saucy fellow. So our lad smacks this officer in the face. Officer lost his pride and our lad lost his life on the end of a rope. God save your soul, if you done such a thing.' The man shakes his head solemnly.

Tobias will say no more, no matter how much his fellow prisoners pester for an account of his crime. He cannot bear to tell these men of what drove him to it, of the sight that torments his mind still, most of all because he had been powerless to stop it. He and his company had been forming in battle readiness, in Rainsborough's Fort, behind the dragoons, to advance on the town, to storm it, or so he'd thought. Word was that the Royalists had no powder left to resist an assault, but this was not to be a storming of the town, he soon realised and it was not enemy soldiers they would be facing.

A crowd of people had been let out of the town and were coming in a straggling bunch along the track towards the fort, women and children, no doubt driven by their desperate starving state. The dragoons were ordered to advance on them, the foot to draw up behind. He could not believe the order to fire and saw the musketeers make ready and let loose a volley, though mercifully over the heads of the folk, to affright them and send them back. Some women screamed and turned, but others held their ground and that was when he saw Beth with her two brothers, standing at the side of a tall woman at the front of the crowd. His heart nearly stopped when the dragoons fired again and their captain ordered them to advance. Why did the women not turn and run? Would they stand there and be trampled or shot? He could not endure it, his stomach sickening, wanting only to run to Beth and sweep her away out of danger. Then, on the order of the captain, eight of the dragoons dismounted, ran at the women at the head of the group and began tearing their garments from them, stripping them naked. At that, Tobias had broken from his rank, charging at the dragooners' captain, swinging his pike and felling the officer, who tumbled heavily to the ground. Another officer close by, wheeled his horse and struck Tobias with his pistol butt and he was dragged back, beaten and locked in irons, a prisoner again.

Tobias knows that he had not hurt the officer seriously, if at all, as his attack had been clumsy and he had been easily felled and disarmed. He also knows, however, that harsh punishment awaits him, if not the same fate as that described by his fellow prosioner. But whatever his suffering, it is nothing to Beth's.

He never saw nor heard what happened after the foul act was committed on the women. When he prays, it is for Beth's safety and that of her family and he realises that he would happily give his life just to know that she is alive and well. There is no bargaining with God or with army generals, however, and in this state of wretchedness he cannot imagine that he will ever see his betrothed again.

Two guards come for him and drag him out of the prisoners' enclosure into the yard of the fort, where his company has been assembled to watch his punishment. He does not know these men well, having only joined their numbers under Captain Grimes on his last return to the leaguer from the town a week ago. Better that he should have died then, pursued by a bunch of Royalist soldiers who had discovered his true intent in the inn. He had nearly met his death at their hands, on discovering the secret exit below the south wall blocked and guarded. He had dashed through the town, knowing that his only hope of escape was the tunnel in Blackfriars, dug by the Sayer boys and the unfortunate Royalist soldier they had befriended. Concealed inside the tunnel and hacking with his knife, he had finally broken through the remaining earth section of the wall and forced his body out to the other side. Now he thinks bitterly about this fruitless flight.

He sees the place of punishment but no gibbet or noose stands there, so at least he is not to pay with his life. The men of his company stand to attention, awaiting a stark lesson about the consequences of the crime of insubordination and assault upon an officer. The whipping posts are at a distance from the wooden building at the centre, where Tobias sees a number of officers enter and a horseman ride up with speed, leaning down from his saddle to deliver a message to a soldier stationed at the door. For the officers, Tobias thinks, this is a time of action and anticipation of their victory, in which the punishment of a common miscreant foot soldier is a time-wasting necessity.

The officer whom Tobias had unhorsed, a captain of Colonel Rainsborough's dragoons, is present, his face wearing a grim look of satisfaction at the sight of Tobias in chains. The captain of his own infantry company stands by his men, his face expressionless. Two other officers are positioned opposite at a distance of about twenty paces, one making ready to issue the order for the punishment. The soldier with the whip unleashes his instrument.

'Tobias Waterman, of Captain Grimes's foot, for attacking a superior officer and breaking rank, the punishment is twenty lashes.'

Tobias feels his legs trembling but hopes that he can bear the pain to come without screaming out or losing control of his water as he has seen happen to some. He tightens his jaw and tries to think of Beth's face and how she had promised herself to him that night. If he can manage to transport his mind elsewhere, perhaps he might lessen the agony to come, of the lash on his back and of the miserable conviction that his hopes were folly. The soldiers unlock the shackles from his wrists and strip the shirt from him. His body is tied around the post, to hold him upright and he hears the crack of the whip behind him in the air. Then it cuts into his back like a knife. He closes his eyes, presses his head against the post and prays for strength. The pain rips through him, as though his skin were being torn strip by strip from his body and he longs only to die and be free of it.

He does not know how many times the flail has struck him, but it stops suddenly and he hears shouting, his head swooning with the agony and the strain of suppressing the howl that has been rising in his throat. He hears orders being called by someone in command from somewhere far away from him. There are many voices, the sound of pounding feet, men marching away. Then someone cuts his bonds and he falls to the ground, feeling arms grab him on either side and pull him to his feet.

'Bring him to the Lord General,' an officer says, from somewhere outside Tobias's vision. His head is heavy and lolls on his neck as he is dragged along. He must try to control his body, he thinks, stand on his own feet, not be hauled like some dead beast. But his back stings and burns, bubbling with pain as though a handful of grit has been stamped into his raw flesh.

'What?' says one of the soldiers who is holding him. 'We're

to take him before the Lord General like this?'

Tobias's feet hit the ground and he regains some control of them, taking his weight, pulling back, so that the men who have him by the arms relax their hold and let him walk between them. They stop and one draws his shirt over his head and pulls it down to cover his nakedness. He is taken into the hut, where once before he has been and now, he can hardly believe it, he is being brought before the Lord General Fairfax again. The general is sitting in the centre of the room on a chair with arms. Two other officers sit at a table nearby with a clerk scribbling busily beside them. The two guards still hold him by his arms and steer him to stand in front of the Lord General. Tobias does not think that he can bow without falling over so he lowers his eyes, his humiliation and disgrace before the great man, smarting as much as his pain. When he looks up at the Lord General, he sees again the expression of remarkable mildness, a slight frown, almost of concern.

'Master Waterman, I took you for a loyal and upright soldier when last we met and I commissioned you with some service in this cause.' Thomas Fairfax speaks in a quiet, serious manner, more expressive of hurt than of censure. 'But here I find you guilty of attacking a superior. I would know your reason for such an action and the state of your mind.'

'My lord,' Tobias says, astonished to be so addressed, wondering about the purpose of this inquisition. He has committed a serious but simple crime. Does the Lord General intend to punish him further? He swallows hard, trusting that truth is the best and only course, even though he knows that what he is about to say might sorely offend the general. But he has nothing left in the world to lose. 'My lord, I did not join the army to wage war against women and children. I cannot punish or demean those defenceless in the face of muskets and swords. I could not stand by and see such things done to those innocent people, to the women and children of this town.'

Lord Thomas Fairfax says nothing for a moment, his eyes heavy and mournful. He sighs deeply.

'War is brutal and those with a tenderness of heart, such as yourself, suffer most to look upon it. But when politicking and discussion flounder, when lies and deceit keep a tyrant in power, men of good conscience have no choice but to take up arms. Violence is repugnant but it moves, where words do nothing. You think I want it thus, a tedious waiting game, men forced to toil up to their knees in mud all day, futile bombardments against impenetrable walls, a fine town and its suburbs in ruins, its people dying of starvation?'

Lord Fairfax shifts in his seat, a twitch of anguish or is it pain, passing over his face. Tobias notices that again his foot is heavily bandaged. He rubs his brow then continues.

'All this could have been avoided, if our offers of peace had been accepted by the enemy. Yes, we have been cruel, but against such an enemy as would fire poisoned bullets, threaten to hang our trumpets bearing messages, fire the suburbs and houses around the town. These Royalist commanders, too full of their own pride and importance would not see reason where it lay, would not take the hand of peace and compromise. There are some among them too who are no more than soldiers of fortune, dishonourable men, not fit to bear the name of gentlemen and commanders. These have held too much sway, have led their men to destruction.'

Tobias straightens his back, though it is stabbing with pain and his head throbs at the temples. He remains still in a state of astonishment that this great general seems to be justifying himself to a lowly foot soldier, an insubordinate wretch who could have been dangling on the end of a rope.

'The war had to be won, you see that, do you not?' the Lord General says. 'We knew it and these poor starving people were our best weapon by far. Our actions against them were cruel but necessary, to break this siege and punish them for admitting the enemy to their town. The people too must bear some blame for the misfortunes they brought upon themselves, through their own ill-judgement and disloyalty.'

The Lord General's voice is low, his face solemn and Tobias is struck by the sincerity of the regret that he expresses, though he himself winces to hear his last statement. He swallows, wishing to speak, willing himself to counter this charge against powerless folk, like Beth and her family, but the Lord General continues.

'There are rules in war,' he says, clearly not expecting, nor inviting any response from Tobias, 'codes of honour and conduct too, which we commanders demand of our men, as you know. But we are human, weak, sinful creatures, wanting in many things, all of us, we commanders and you men. We can only put our trust in God to guide us, with His strong hand, back to the ways of truth, honour and mercy.'

The words of the Lord General strike Tobias with an ugly truth. His own conduct and covert strategies of turning the Royalist soldiers against their commanders, to mutiny, of using the simple soldier Timothy Box for his warlike ends, are little different from the ruthless tactics employed by the besiegers. This thought weighs on him heavily as he watches Lord General Fairfax grimace.

'You have taken the punishment that was your due. Now you will put on your uniform and ready yourself to march into the town, for the rebels are at last ready to surrender to us. The siege is broken.'

Tobias knows that he has been treated with fairness and respect beyond anything he could have expected or hoped for.

'Thank you, my Lord,' he says bowing his head, looking down at the red welts on his wrists where the shackles have left their mark.

The Lord General sighs again and Tobias looks up at him.

'You are a young man of courage and principles. You must hold hard to that courage and loyalty, for these are paramount in this army; but your principles you must sometimes put aside. Do not lose sight of them, however, Master Waterman, for you must take them up again when you lay down your arms. This, I pray to God, for you and for myself also, and for all in the realm, will come very soon.'

Chapter 20

27th & 28th August

'Mistress, are you awake? There is news.' It is Walter's voice at her chamber door.

Katherine rouses herself and draws back the cover from the bed, where she has fallen into another half doze, though she knows it must be morning. She is beaten now, completely and utterly, by her failure, by the merciless response of the forces of Parliament and the derision of the Royalists. She has no will to rise, shift from her bed, risk another encounter with her husband. He has ordered her incarceration, since she returned from the attempted break out from the town. Accusing her of being deranged, he has commanded Walter that for her safety she must be locked up night and day. This new order for her confinement does not concern her greatly, however, for Walter's assistance and her own secret key will enable escape as before, if she has the need or inclination to go out. What affects her most profoundly is her lack of will to do so, tied as it is to her conviction that she will never see Charles Lucas again.

'Mistress,' comes her servant's voice once more.

She sits up, pulls her silk shawl from where it lies on the bedclothes and wraps it around her shoulders, lowering her legs to the floor, as though she fears they will not bear her weight. She stands close to the door, hearing Walter's urgent breathing outside.

'Mistress, the Royalist commanders have agreed to the terms of surrender. They are to send back word to the Lord General Fairfax that they accept his conditions. It is over. I have heard it from a man who works in the kitchen of *The King's Head*. Your husband has gone this morning to a meeting of the Corporation. He thinks that by tomorrow the town will be back in their hands, though most likely it will be Fairfax's army in charge.'

Katherine retrieves the door key, which hangs around her neck upon a ribbon and opens the door to Walter. The man's eyes are alert, fired by this news, betraying his relish for the events to come. Katherine's confused relief stalls her response for some moments. She watches Walter's expression change to a look of concern.

'You should eat, Mistress. We have only some oaten cakes and a little honey,' he says. 'But it will not be long now until you will have something more nourishing. The Royalist rebels are defeated, thanks be to God.'

As she stands there, a small spark of energy impels her at last to know more.

'I will dress now and come down to the hall, if you would be as good as to take the food there. I would beg a favour of you too, Walter.'

She has to know more of what is to happen now, what is to become of Charles. The thought of not being able to take her leave of him fills her with sorrow and yet to do so would surely be a greater misery. The Royalists, officers and men, will all be made prisoners soon, that she knows, but if only she might see him, be with him for one last time.

'Yes Mistress,' Walter says. 'How can I serve you?'

'Find out what is to happen to the rebels,' she says. 'It would satisfy me to know the fate of their commanders, those who have been responsible for this terrible siege.'

'Aye Mistress, I'd know that too and will go straightway and speak to the one I know at *The King's Head*. But I know that noblemen and gentlemen are able to purchase their freedom, even as their men are bound in chains and sent into slavery. The powerful are seldom the ones who suffer in the end.'

She closes the door on her servant with no further talk and starts to make herself ready, putting on a black silk gown, spending some time combing and curling her hair. She has fortunately not suffered too much physical hurt in their vain and terrible foray out of the town. This time she will not creep along like a thief in servant's garb to a secret, sordid place. It is too late now for subterfuge. The impudent soldiers have named her as Charles Lucas's whore, so what point in hiding it? She knows that her husband must have had word and she wonders how long it will be before he confronts her. Nothing matters now, however. She will think only of the moment, no further beyond.

As she looks into the glass, her face pale and bloodless, her eyes darkened hollows and her cheeks sunken, this image is only what she expects to see. However, she will adorn those vestiges of the beauty she once had, colouring her lips with a little wax of carmine and putting on her pearl necklace and earrings. She does not hurry, waiting and hoping for Walter's return and the information she now craves. She needs Walter's loyalty for this one last duty; after that she will be loathed by him. Only this she regrets and that the girl Beth Sayer too will discover her to be a duplicitous scheming traitor. For she betrayed the conspirators in the town by warning Charles, which had led to the deaths of a number of townsmen. She cannot escape the accusations and blame that will ensue. She is also an adulteress and as such deserving of the strongest censure. What people think of her, however, arouses little dread, for this captive life will not last much longer. Sitting at the table in the hall, she takes a mouthful or two of the dry oatcake and drinks a cup of watery ale, waiting for Walter to return and hoping fervently that her husband will not.

She waits an hour or more before her servant comes back, the smell of drink on his breath, his face flushed with more news.

'I have been at *The Red Lion* and thence to *The Angel*, talking with soldiers and others. There's no fire at all between the two sides now, as though the surrender's already been made. The Royalists have only to put their traitorous names to the articles and then it's over. Once Fairfax has received the signed papers, he will march his army into the town and we shall be liberated.'

'And the higher officers and commanders? Are they to remain in their quarters until this is done?' Katherine says, affecting a casual tone.

Walter frowns. 'I suppose they will be, until they are sent to prison, the Tower or some other stronghold. This is of particular interest to you, Mistress?' he says.

'No, I ask merely because – '

She falters, seeing Walter's eyes, full of doubt and suspicion, following her as she rises from her seat and pulls her silk shawl over her head. 'Have you heard ill talk about me?'

He must surely know, he who has contact with spies from the town, who has consorted with the Royalist soldiers to discover their commanders' intentions.

'Mistress,' he says, bowing his head, turning from her as he speaks.

'When you do, Walter,' she says, her voice trembling, catching his hand in hers, at which he, startled, flinches at this action, his face flushing. Though he has touched her tenderly when he has ministered to her hurts, has soothed her, this has been a servant's intimacy and she knows that her gesture now is of a different character altogether, a manifestation of friendship and gratitude.

'When you hear ill spoken of me, it will be true,' she says. 'I cannot excuse myself for my sins, but I am grateful to you for your loyalty and your tenderness. With all my heart I wish you well.'

His eyes are bright with alarm. 'Mistress, you speak as though you mean to depart somewhere. Do you mean to quit your husband's house? May I lend you aid to escape from him? Tell me what I can do for you. I would serve you in any way –.'

Katherine, much moved by the man's perplexity and his desire to assist her, starts to ease her hand from his. His hold is tight and urgent, however, and she sees in his eyes the truth behind his fidelity, finding herself flattered and astonished in equal measure. But she cannot be deflected from her course.

'I am going out now but will likely be back for supper, if any can be found,' she says, drawing her shawl around her and leaving him standing in the hall.

She has no other thought in her head now than to see Charles and will fight with all the wiles and tricks she can muster to bring this to pass. Strangely, the yard of *The King's Head* is deserted; there are no guards at the door, nor servants about their business. Perhaps the officers have been forced to quit their billets already and Walter's informant has been mistaken. Perhaps they are already incarcerated somewhere, a place where she will never gain entry. She should have questioned Walter more closely. There must be someone who can tell her of Charles's whereabouts. The door is locked, however and so she lifts the knocker and pounds it hard several times. As she waits, wondering about gaining entry by a back way, two Royalist officers come through the archway into the yard. They look at her with suspicious interest, making their way towards her across the cobbles.

'I am seeking Sir Charles Lucas,' she says.

The two exchange glances, then eye her.

'And why might that be, Mistress?' says one, the older of the two. 'The Colonel is in no mood for dalliance now. There are more important matters afoot.'

His companion snorts bitterly. 'Mayhap he's in need of some distraction, for there's little enough to cheer the spirit now. Are you willing to serve other gentlemen as readily as the colonel? We too would welcome a little of what you offer.'

The officer reaches out to catch Katherine by the arm, but she steps back, swerving from his clutch.

'I will treat only with Sir Charles Lucas,' she says, her voice sharp. 'I have an urgent message for him. Will you let me go in and enquire of his whereabouts.'

In a swift movement, she grasps the knocker again and strikes the door three more times. But the officer has caught hold of her this time in a strong grip and is pulling her back. She, violent in her resolve, turns on him, flailing her other arm at his face and catching his cheek with her ring, hearing his curse as he recoils from her.

'You devil's whore,' he mutters while his comrade makes a lunge for her. But at the same moment someone inside unbolts the door and swings it open. She leaps forward at the opening, nearly colliding with the one who has unlocked the door, a man in the plain garb of a servant, Charles's manservant.

Katherine, relieved to find herself in the presence of a more likely ally, steps inside, her assailants forced to halt on the threshold by the presence of the serving man.

'Mistress?' says the servant in a startled voice, glancing first at her and then the two officers. 'Sirs, this lady is –.'

'A vicious strumpet, if ever there was one,' says the officer she has wounded in the face, his cheekbone now streaked with blood.

'This lady,' continues the servant, standing his ground, facing the two soldiers, 'is a kinswoman of Sir Charles Lucas. She must not be harmed.'

Katherine manages to conceal her astonishment at this declaration, adjusting her shawl, which has been pulled from her shoulders in the struggle.

'Kinswoman?' the wounded officer says with a sneer, touching his cheek.

'Sir Charles is a Colchester gentleman,' says the servant. 'There's many of his kin in the parishes hereabouts and some in the town as well, are there not, Mistress?'

'Yes that's true,' Katherine says, feigning confidence. 'And as I say, I have an important message for him, a family matter.'

The two officers glance at each other.

'Well, fellow,' says the uninjured one to Charles's servant. 'Be it known that we did not give this woman leave to enter these quarters. If she is a spy, or bent on some mischief then be it on your miserable head.'

The servant says nothing, bows and then closes the door on the two officers.

'I am much beholden to you,' Katherine says to the man. 'You know that I mean no harm to your master.'

He nods. 'But he's not here, Mistress. He's with the generals at the Moot Hall, for the enemy forces are coming into the town tomorrow morning and we'll all be prisoners then.'

'You too?' says Katherine.

'Aye.'

'You will suffer for your loyalty.'

'And so will Sir Charles,' says the man, his tone calm and unprotesting, 'for his loyalty to the King. He and I are alike in that, in giving our service and maybe our lives.'

'I only hope the King is worthy of such gifts,' Katherine says, almost to herself.

'Come Mistress. You can wait in his chamber. He will return anon. Be hasty, if you please, for others may see you and question your presence.'

The manservant starts towards the staircase. She follows him up the first flight of stairs to a landing and into a room on the right hand side, a large bedchamber, comfortably furnished with a curtained bed, a table, two chairs and an upholstered couch.

'Take your ease, Mistress,' the servant says. 'I will wait outside to keep guard.'

'God bless you,' she says, going to the window and looking out on to the empty inn yard.

On her own in the chamber, Katherine moves to the bed, lays her face upon the bolster where he has rested his head, smells the traces of him on the sheets, longing to feel his arms around her, to touch his skin, kiss his lips and his body again. She will not think of the agony of parting from him. He will be racked by his own troubles, greater by far than the matter of causing distress to a mistress. The failure of his cause, the humiliation of his defeat by an enemy who has triumphed over him before, will be a torment to him. Now he faces imprisonment and a trial, maybe for his life. But he had always known that he faced such an end. She had found him that first time in this pit of depression, had shared his misery and lifted him free of it, if only for some brief fugitive times of bliss and forgetfulness. In doing this she had found a reward that had warmed her own cold and bitter soul, reminded her of the woman she once had been. Now there will be no more relief, except in taking the final course open to her.

She will happily do this, if she can only once more be with him.

There is now little anxiety in her wait for him, her longing a calmer yearning now, rich with moments of recollection and imagining. When he comes, it will mean that their time together is finite but while she waits, she can indulge the delight of anticipation. She hears his steps outside the door, then his servant's words, his own stern, hard voice. He enters, standing in the doorway for a moment, then stepping in and closing the door behind him. His eyes are expressionless, his face taut and he breathes deeply, staring at her.

'I cannot have this. I cannot have you here, not now,' he says in a brittle voice. 'My situation is –.'

She is struck with his coldness, but knows it is his armour, as surely as the iron breast plate he wears into battle, to guard him strongly, fortify him against weakness. She rises and drops the shawl from her shoulders. Coming close to him, she reaches for his hand, which she grasps, though it is clenched and resists her touch.

'I know of the surrender,' she says.

'And you have come to offer me comfort.' His tone is as sour and cruel as ever her husband has used against her.

She flinches to hear this, but searches his face for something of his softer self.

'I know there is no comfort I can offer, Charles, only to share in your sorrow, and to bless you for our times together. You have given me pleasure and joy in the midst of unfathomable misery and in doing so, have let me discover that better part of myself again. I thank you with all my heart.'

He bows his head and she slides her arms around his waist, leans her head against his chest and holds him gently and patiently, feeling his hand on her hair, a sob strangled in his throat. She unbuttons his coat and takes it from him, his sword belt too, loosing the weapon to the ground, then leads him to the bed, pushes him gently back upon it and tugs off his boots. Next she lies down beside him and they are together, as they were that first time in the dark churchyard, silent but bound forever.

'There are nine articles in the surrender that we have signed,' he says, his voice dulled by his desolation. 'And tomorrow by eight of the clock all guards must be withdrawn from the line, all horses, saddles and bridles taken to St Mary's churchyard, all arms colours and drums to St James's church, all ammunition and heavy guns left in place. Private soldiers and lower officers must go to Fayer's Yard. Lords, captains and we, the superior officers are to assemble here at this inn, to submit ourselves to the mercy of Lord General Fairfax.'

'What punishment will you suffer?' she says.

He is silent, though she hears him sigh and she sits up, looking into his face, whose features have softened now.

'They will not take your life?' she says, her chest heavy, as though a stone has lodged itself there.

'That may be,' he says, 'but I along with my lords Capel and Norwich will most likely be sent to the Tower and face trial by Parliament. Fairfax, though he is my bitter enemy, has no taint on him of dishonour. He has accused me of breaking my parole, of being unfit for military command, of defying my oath never to take up arms against Parliament. But I can refute his accusations. I can argue my case, for I paid my dues and my penalty. I have fought in a new commission for the King, who is my master, the anointed monarch of this realm. The King called me to his service. What else could I do but obey?'

He looks into her face at last, reaches for her and draws her to him, touching his lips gently to hers.

'You must plead for your life, Charles,' she says.

'Yes I suppose I must, though if I am granted this privilege, whether by God or by Fairfax, it will be intolerable to me.'

The starkness of his admission shocks her, such that she clings to him.

'But you must live. If it shall be, you must embrace your life again, lift yourself as you have done before from despair.'

'And how may I do this without you?' he says.

'I will be with you, if that is your wish,' she says, desperation adding force to her desire for him. 'I give myself freely and gladly to you, at this moment and forever, if that is what you choose.'

He grasps her close, kissing her deeply. She is glad to have aroused him and he takes her strongly and passionately while they are still fully clad. She weeps at their coupling, knowing that this is the last night of the blissful, heedless life they have made together.

'We have travelled together in our fall,' she says, 'and have found a little joy in all this strife.'

'It is a different pain, to part from you,' he says. 'I have borne many, many others, but wonder if I have the courage to endure this.'

'No man could equal your courage, to fight with loyalty in spite of your doubts, to lose everything for a cause that you could never win. I praise and love you for it.'

The dawn arrives as they doze after a night spent in tender words and promises of what might come to pass if they find themselves free, joining their bodies, pleasuring each other many times. This night has been more than she could have wished for and she is filled with the joy of it.

Soon she hears the servant's tread on the landing outside the chamber door and sees that weak grey light is entering the window.

'Sir, you must rise now,' comes the servant's whisper. 'I'll bring you water.'

She lies watching from behind the half-drawn curtains of the bed as the dark figure of the servant enters, carrying a jug and basin, a cloth and accoutrements for Charles's toilet and lays these on the table in the corner of the chamber.

'Sir, do you wish that I should –?'

'No,' says Charles from the bed. 'I shall tend to myself. I thank you. You may go.'

Charles rises quickly from the bed and in the corner washes his body all over, with a cloth and the basin of water. She watches the taut muscles of his back, his arms scarred in places, his white hands moving rapidly as he with careless haste dries himself on a linen cloth. She leaves the bed and comes close to him, just as he picks up the razor, with its naked blade.

'Let me,' she says, taking it from him and he looks at her

with a doubtful smile. 'I have a delicate touch.'

'I know that well,' he says, as she pushes him gently down on to the chair.

She dips her hand into the water in the basin and wets the skin of his cheeks and chin. With feather-light brushes of the fine blade she smoothes away the coarse growth, delicately trimming the wayward hairs at the edge of his moustache, then with the damp linen cloth wipes his brow, his neck, his mouth. Next she takes up the comb from the table and combs through his long, dark hair wetting the tangles. Lastly, she kisses him on the lips, a reverent, farewell kiss. He touches her cheek, then with a changed look, briskly stands up. He moves from her, to pick up his clothes, put on his breeches, shirt, coat and boots. They speak no further words to each other, as both fear the consequences, wishing to keep their bond strong and intact.

She moves swiftly, like an efficient servant, to smooth his coat, fasten his sword belt, his red sash and hand him his hat where he stands, magnificent before her. She, her hair dishevelled, still in her crumpled shift, curtseys to him and he bows low to her with his hat in one hand. A moment later, he is gone from the room and she stands there alone.

She climbs back into the bed, between the crumpled empty remnants of their passion, burying her head in the hollow where he had lain. She pulls the sheet over her head and holding her breath wills herself to die. She thinks of the razor too, which lies innocently waiting upon the table.

Some time later, maybe a matter of hours, from a state of half-awareness she hears the servant on the landing again, his knock upon the door.

'Mistress, you must go now,' he says from outside the door. 'All the gentlemen and officers have left. They have all been taken from here to places of imprisonment. Sir Charles and two others are now at the castle. The Lord General Fairfax's forces have taken possession of the whole town. I must go too.'

She rises, and takes up the cloth that Charles had used to wash himself and applies it to her skin, dips the linen again and cools her hot face. Then in imitation of his purposeful haste, puts on her gown, coils her hair quickly to tame it and covers her head with her shawl. She opens the door to find the servant on the landing, waiting to conduct her down the stairs. In the hallway they stop, hearing from outside the sound of drums, a trumpet, the thunderous tramp of many feet. In the inn yard, they stand, glimpsing through the archway the dense body of red coats as they pass by on the main thoroughfare. Turning to Charles's servant, Katherine bids him farewell and gives him her thanks and her blessing again.

The thought of returning to her house, seeing her husband, fills her with a nausea that she can barely contain, as though she has been struck with a flux. With this sickness of her mind and body, comes her resolve to run from him. Why fear destitution when by embracing this course, she would be free of him? She will go to one of the Parliamentary colonels and beg safe passage out of the town, on the pretext of visiting a sick relative. She will need money however and determines that night to search the house for anything she can find of value, even the place where her husband has hidden his gold and silver. She will look all night by candle light, if need be and with Walter's help. This plan fires her to bolder leaps of fancy, of hope and triumph; she will go to London, for that is where Charles will to be taken, as a prisoner. While he is there and alive, there is the hope of him gaining his freedom again, by purchase, pleas, by bargaining. When he is free she can be with him again, as his loyal and loving mistress. It is feverish madness, ridiculous imagining, but she will hold fast to this folly until it is wrested from her.

She finds her way home along the narrow alleys that run close to the High Street, to avoid the clamour and triumph of the victorious army in the street. She meets a few other folk, skulking or dying in the gloom, unaware or uncaring of the liberation of the town, too close to death or despair to notice.

The house is empty and silent with a chill in the air. There is no sound of Walter in the kitchen or elsewhere. The door to her husband's study is closed and she listens for a moment outside to detect any sound of his presence but there is none. Might she, in his absence, start a search of the parlour for money or any valuable items? No, there is the risk that he will return at any time and so she decides instead to gather her own belongings together in preparation for her departure. In her chamber, she folds her best items of linen and changes the silk gown she is wearing, putting on a plain dark one. The pearl necklace and earrings and a few other trinkets will provide a means of survival for a time at least, but she needs more.

As she bundles her clothes and jewellery into a tapestry bag, she hears from below the sound of a door opening and closing, footsteps far away, in the passageway. It must be Walter. Then, only a little later, comes her husband's unmistakable heavy tread across the hall. There might be supper of sorts this evening, she supposes, but if it is only the usual gruel or pottage, their meal-taking will be a short affair, as has been their practice since the shortages have gripped their household. She fastens her bag and readies herself to go down, on the pretext of finding out what Walter has for them to eat, though her most urgent, desperate quest is to know about the fate of the Royalist commanders.

Her husband's study door swings open, just as she is descending the stairs. He has been lurking in wait for her.

'Come here. I would speak with you,' he says, moving swiftly and grasping her by the arm.

He knows. News of her infamy and treachery is noised about the town and has come to his ears at last. This time, however, she has little fear of him. Her only need is to escape serious injury by his hand. She must not find herself beaten and incapable of carrying out her plan of escape. She struggles in his grip.

'Walter,' she cries aloud, turning her head in the direction of the kitchen. 'I have need of you in the hall. Come at once.'

'Be quiet,' her husband says in a hoarse whisper. 'We don't want that fellow here.'

His hold is painful, pressing hard on the bone and flesh of her upper arm, though she pulls hard against him.

'Why? Do you want no witness for what you would do to

me?' she says, writhing in his hold. 'What do you intend? To kill me this time? Walter, help me!'

Her husband raises his hand to strike her, but Walter is there and has leapt forward and seized his arm, wrenching him away from her.

'Sir, I'll not let you strike her,' he says and she sees that he is trembling with anger.

Thomas Wade throws off Walter's hand and pushes him away, the servant making no further attempt to restrain his master, but standing close at Katherine's side. Her husband steps back, adjusting his coat, which has been pulled awry in the struggle. His eyes are dark, his mouth already contorting with the malice forming upon his lips. He nods his head, looking first at Katherine then at their servant.

'So, you have had him in your bed too,' he says to her.

'No sir,' Walter says, taking a step towards his master and Katherine wills him to strike out, though she knows he will not.

Thomas Wade snorts. 'Forgive me, I wrong you, man. She prefers gentlemen, for she is a whore of the better sort. You are too lowly for her tastes. She has her sights set higher these days.'

Katherine shudders as she stands, knowing what he is about to announce and dreading what Walter will think of her treachery. She does not care for the sullying of her name but to have deceived this faithful servant makes her sick with shame. If she has a chance she will try to explain to him, after her husband has revealed the scandal, which hangs upon his lips like the last tasty morsel of a rich dish.

'She is the whore of the rebel Colonel Sir Charles Lucas, no less,' says her husband. 'Has she not excelled herself this time, and with an enemy? She has added traitor to her name of harlot.'

Walter says nothing, betrays no shock nor outrage and, turning to Katherine with mournful eyes, touches her arm lightly. She is choked by the sudden realisation of the depth of this man's fidelity.

'You poor fool,' says her husband, 'to admire your mistress as though she were in some way respectable. You are more foolish than a lovesick boy. But now that the proud rebels have been forced to their knees in surrender, it is all at an end.'

He is triumphant, almost laughing with pleasure to have so cowed them both, to have another revelation, which threatens to burst from him in his elation.

'She weeps no doubt for the defeat of her lover, do you not wife?' he says, lowering his voice. 'And now you may weep more tears, for he has been shot, executed as a traitor by a firing squad at the castle, only an hour ago.'

Katherine is still running, though more slowly now, for her chest is tight with pain and her legs weak, threatening to buckle beneath her. The Head Gate lies open, the thoroughfare streaming with soldiers, horsemen, carts, waggons and guards on each side of the portal letting no townsfolk by them. There are too many people here and noise everywhere. She stops, spins around amidst this ghastly hubbub, gasping and sobbing. A women stares at her, no doubt wondering about her frantic, lunatic state. Two small children totter to her, their hands outstretched, their filthy faces turned up towards her in listless hope.

She pushes through the people, crosses the road, running again, along the lane towards St Mary's Church. The churchyard is strewn with rubble, crumbling pieces of mortar and stone from the smashed tower. The door hangs open and she creeps inside its dusty sordid interior, stumbling over debris to reach the altar, where a cross still hangs against the wall. She falls on her knees and prays for Charles's soul, weeping freely now for his cruel and sudden end. He knew that he was doomed but that he should have had no trial, no chance to speak of his cause, of his loyalty to the King, appals her. The thought of this act, decisive and brutal, is the only force that drives her now. She prays to God, begging forgiveness of her sins and weakness, commending her soul to Him, though in this broken place she feels nothing of His presence.

She presses on to the Balkerne Hill, for there must be an exit, a way to escape. One of the gates must surely be open for the people, to let them break free from the town, this prison. A group of soldiers of the Parliamentary army stand talking and laughing, while a team of their comrades lower the barrel of a gun with ropes from the bastion on to a cart. Two of the soldiers look up at her as she approaches and she turns from them, running away, colliding with a gaggle of townsfolk, stumbling between their bodies, hearing their curses. Her throat is raw, her eyes smarting, dry of tears. For a moment she pauses, leaning against the wall of a house on the hill leading down towards the North Gate, but she can see that it too is heavily guarded with soldiers. Katherine has no more strength to run and wanders instead along the High Street, numb in mind and body, shrinking aside as a pack of men, heads bowed in wretchedness, Royalist prisoners, are herded past her. A little later, she finds herself near to the castle. Is Charles's body lying there, bloodied and shunned or have his enemies treated him with the honour due to a noble soldier?

The East Gate too is guarded, against those enemies who might try to flee amidst the disturbance and disruption of the town. There will be no quick return to daily business, no passage out. She must find instead a quiet place to hide and rest, until such time as she can make her escape. The grounds of Blackfriars nearby might afford her such a sanctuary and there are fewer people and soldiers about the entry to the place. She takes a pathway into the barren space, hearing the voices of men as she proceeds, seeing the bastion on the far corner of the wall, a cart and horse below on the ground and above on the platform a group of soldiers. The men, distant and intent upon their task of dismantling and shifting the guns, take no note of her as she stumbles her way down in the direction of the town wall. She pauses a while, sits upon a stone of the ruined monastery, seeing the way ahead, down a slope. Perhaps there, at the foot of the wall, she might find a place to lie. She drags herself to her feet again and at last comes upon the edge of a ditch and, losing her footing, slips down the side, falling into soft mud at the bottom. Lifting her head slowly, she discovers, to her surprise, a hole framed with crude timbers. It is a tunnel through the wall to the other side.

The ground is sticky where the feet of escapees have

trodden and then squeezed their way through the aperture. She crawls through the mud to the opening, spying a small patch of blue beyond, then upon her belly she wriggles her body into the hole, her hands scraping the earth as she burrows her way forward. Hauling herself out on the other side, she sees a gradient stretching down to the river beyond, at about fifty paces distant. On her feet again, her garments weighted with mire, she stands and gazes ahead at the swell of the river, which is brimming full.

She lurches forward, away from the town walls into open ground, where she can be seen. The men working on the battery will spy her and if they have orders to shoot at those who are fleeing, then she might fall with a musket ball in her back. Others have no doubt died here, so it is fitting. Charles himself only some hours before, has ended his life less than a mile from this place. His body might not yet be cold. If only she could lie with him, warm him with the last of her own breath. She starts trudging towards the swelling level of the river. A wooden fort stands upon her left and she is not sure whether this is the same one where she and the women and children had fled and been repulsed that day. She must reach that smooth silver water and as she draws nearer she is glad to think that soon she will be able to stop and lie down, for she is so weary with walking.

There are only twenty paces to the river bank and she, stumbling forward, trips and falls over a hard object in the muddy grass. Her fall is not painful, for the ground is spongy and soft. She sits up to steady the dizzying in her head, and finds the cause of her fall: a heavy stone shot from a gun, now half embedded in the turf. It had fallen short of its target and now lies harmless and innocent in the earth. She touches its cold, rough surface, then with both hands around it, hauls it into her embrace, as though it were a monstrous weighty child. It presses upon her belly and, lifting the skirt of her gown to wrap it round, she struggles to her feet with the burden hanging before her. She staggers forward, four, five steps, one pace at a time until she is there, with her feet on the edge of the riverbank. Staring down into the black, welcoming water, Katherine slides with her burden into the silk of its surface without a splash.

Chapter 21

20th September

Jack wants to tell Tobias and Beth of his gladness, of the strange feeling that has visited him, as it used to long ago, when he was happy. But he can't make his voice sound out aloud. It isn't there anymore, except when he's talking to Ed. Jack walks beside Tobias, who is the handsomest man he's ever seen, even though he has a scar on his face now and is still a soldier. He wears a red coat and his breeches are new, his shoes and hose too. His old ones were ruined, he says, when he was escaping out of the town, through their tunnel. Beth walks on his other side, looking comely in a white dress that used to be Mother's, but she has no need of it now. Jack misses her, though she looked peaceful when she was dead, just like Father and now they are together, with no trouble and hardship, Beth says, with God and his holy son Jesus Christ. Jack and Beth are orphans, Edward too, but they are all going to have a new life, for Tobias and Beth are on their way to the church to be made man and wife in the sight of God.

Everyone's praying in church. Jack begs God, in a special prayer that they will never be hungry again, then he listens to the minister blessing the union of this man and this woman, Tobias and Beth and he feels happy again. Jack prays every day for the souls of Mother and Father and Ed and Old Solomon and Mistress Wade and Timothy Box too, even though he was an enemy. Praying is like speaking in your head. You don't need any voice to do it. Jack doesn't know if God hears him, nor any of the others he loves who are with Him in heavenly bliss. But Ed hears him, because he always answers and tells Jack things he needs to know, when he is doubtful or lonely.

'There's going to be food aplenty,' Ed tells Jack on their way along the road, back to the house.

'Yes, a feast,' Jack says, 'bread and meat and cheese and cake.'

'A yellow cake with nuts and sugar on top.'

Jack can almost taste the sweetness on his tongue as he thinks of it.

There's food for everyone, even the other folks that come into their kitchen. Jack's belly feels tight, he's had so much cake. Their neighbours come and say things to him, then shake their heads and look sorrowful when he can't make reply, though he wants to.

Later, when all the people have gone, Tobias kisses Beth and she kisses him many many times, until Jack wonders how often you can kiss someone until your mouth dries up. His mouth has dried up, but not through kissing. Beth kisses him too, but only on the cheek and tells him that she loves him dearly. Tobias shakes his hand and then hugs him, which makes Jack feel safe for a moment.

'We're going with Tobias when the army leaves, which will be very soon,' Beth says.

Jack wants to tell Beth that he'd rather stay here, but she seems to know and tells him to have no fear, that she and Tobias will care for him now. Jack takes another piece of cake and goes to sit in the place in front of the fire by himself.

'I don't want to go away,' he says to Ed.

'Why not?'

'Mother and Father are here in the churchyard.'

'Yes, but they can look down on you from Heaven.'

'But where will we live when we're travelling with the army?'

'It will most likely be in a big wagon,' Ed tells him. 'One like those we saw in the soldiers' camp. Do you remember? It'll be like a moving house.'

Jack is pleased to think of living in a house on wheels and watches Beth folding up a shawl and putting it on a pile of other clothes and things. Tobias is mending the broken hinge of an old wooden box to put them in.

'We'll be travelling with one of the Colonel's wives, along with their servants, so we will have company and safety with them,' Beth tells Jack as she folds up his spare shirt to put on the pile. 'And Tobias will come and be with us as often as he can.'

'It may not be for long, Jack,' Tobias says, 'for I've a mind to quit the army as soon as I am able. But I must find work and will have to go where it is. The Lord General Fairfax has told me he has need of a gardener, which is my true craft, so we may go into the county of Yorkshire. That's where he has his estates. What do you think of such a plan?'

In bed at night Jack can't sleep. He doesn't like the bed anymore, so he goes downstairs in the dark, though the moon makes a little slit of light under the door. He lies in the place where Old Solomon used to be and tries not to weep, for only little babes do that.

'I don't want to go away,' he tells Ed. 'I don't know what Yorkshire is, except it's very far away. I want to stay here.'

'You noddle head,' says Ed, 'it will be venturesome to travel to a distant place, to ride in a wagon and maybe even on a horse again. Think of that.'

'Yes, I might even see the Lord Fairfax himself,' says Jack feeling a small shiver of excitement.

'That would be a very great honour indeed,' Ed says.

Author's Notes

This is a work of fiction, although it is closely based on recorded historical events and the actions of real people. It makes no claim, however, to add to the interpretation of these events or the period. As with many historical novels, the imaginative re-creation of the past has led to omissions and some manipulation of known facts and chronologies, to suit the purposes of the narrative. My hope is that readers, particularly those well informed about the period and the siege, will not be offended by the liberties taken and will enjoy the story, as well as its 'authentic' elements. Perhaps it might even encourage readers to explore more fully the history of the siege and also this shocking period of British history, or excite further interest in the rich and varied history of Colchester, still present and visible today.

For a bibliography of sources and further information about the writing of this novel, please refer to **www.clarehawkins.co.uk**

Historical personages appearing in the story

Royalists

Lord Goring, The Earl of Norwich, Commander of the Royalist forces
Lord Arthur Capel
Sir Charles Lucas
Colonel William Maxey
Colonel Samuel Tuke
Captain William Hicks
Sir George Lisle
Sir Bernard Gascoigne
Colonel Chester
Colonel Farre
Dr John Humphrey, Astrologer

Parliamentarians

Sir Thomas Fairfax, Lord General of the New Model Army
Sir Thomas Rainsborough, Colonel and siege expert

Citizens of Colchester

Mayor Thomas Cooke
Alderman Thomas Wade
(There is no evidence that TW was the villain portrayed in the novel)
Alderman Henry Barrington

All other characters are fictitious, though most are named with reference to contemporary records.

The Aftermath

Heavy fines were levied by Parliament on the people of Colchester after the siege, as reparations for their capitulation. Sir Charles Lucas and Sir George Lisle, executed on the orders of Lord General Fairfax, soon became lauded as martyrs to the Royalist cause. Thomas Wade became Mayor of Colchester again after the siege. In 1648 King Charles I was beheaded and twelve years later, Lord Thomas Fairfax was among those supporting the return of his son, as King Charles II.

Acknowledgements

My thanks are due to many people who have helped and supported me during the writing of this novel. Andrew Phillips's guidance, advice and corrections on a draft of the novel were vital and much appreciated. My writing group, Sue Dawes, Philippa Hawley, Pauline Rendal and Eleanor Young, have also given me much encouragement and feedback on early drafts. I am also hugely grateful to others who read and commented on versions of the novel: Sue Barry, Carol Ellis, Vivienne Goldsmith, Brian Harmer, Graham Heddle, Pam Job, Heather Marks and Caroline Phillips. I owe sincere thanks also to my family, Roger, Norah, Liz, Laura and John, for their moral and practical support

Thanks and appreciation are also due to the helpful staff in the Local Studies section of Colchester Library, as well as the local historians whose meticulous work made researching this book achievable.